Titles by
Jill Marie Landis...

Just Once

". . . a superb reading experience, rich in poignancy and humor."
—*Romantic Times*

"Characters that come alive and make you cry—Jill Marie Landis is a winner!!!"
—*Kat Martin*

Day Dreamer

When Celine Winters exchanged cloaks—and futures—with a stranger, she hoped to find a destiny greater than any daydream.

"Not since *Jade* has Jill Marie Landis delved into romantic suspense with as much verve and skillful storytelling as she has done in *Day Dreamer*."
—*Romantic Times*

Last Chance

Rachel McKenna shocked everyone when she danced with legendary gunfighter Lane Cassidy. But she knew he could be her last chance for happiness...

"Readers who loved *After All* . . . will be overjoyed with this first-rate spinoff."
—*Publishers Weekly*

After All

The passionate and moving story of a dance hall girl trying to change her life in the town of Last Chance, Montana...

"Historical romance at its very best."
—*Publishers Weekly*

Until Tomorrow

A soldier returning from war shows a backwoods beauty that every dream is possible—even the dream of love...

"Landis does what she does best by creating characters of great dimension, compassion, and strength."

—*Publishers Weekly*

Past Promises

She was a brilliant paleontologist who went west in search of dinosaurs. But a rugged cowboy poet was determined to unearth the beauty and passion behind her bookish spectacles...

"Warmth, charm, and appeal...*Past Promises* is guaranteed to satisfy romance readers everywhere." —*Amanda Quick*

"An incredible, poignant, and humorous story...*Past Promises* shimmers with vitality...a love story of grand proportions!"

—*Romantic Times*

Come Spring

WINNER OF THE "BEST ROMANCE NOVEL OF THE YEAR" AWARD

Snowbound in a mountain man's cabin, beautiful Annika tried to resist his hungry glances—but learned that unexpected love can grow as surely as the seasons change...

"A beautiful love story." —*Julie Garwood*

"A world-class novel...It's fabulous!" —*Linda Lael Miller*

"A winner." —*Dorothy Garlock*

Jade

Her exotic beauty captured the heart of a rugged rancher. But could he forget the past—and love again?

"Guaranteed to enthrall...an unusual, fast-paced love story."
—*Romantic Times*

Rose

Across the golden frontier, her passionate heart dared to dream...

"A gentle romance that will warm your soul."
—*Heartland Critiques*

Wildflower

Amidst the untamed beauty of the Rocky Mountains, two daring hearts forged a perilous passion...

"A delight from start to finish!"
—*Rendezvous*

Sunflower

**WINNER OF THE ROMANCE WRITERS OF AMERICA'S
"GOLDEN MEDALLION FOR BEST HISTORICAL ROMANCE"**

A spirited woman of the prairie. A handsome half-breed who stole her heart. A love as wild as the wind...

Jill Marie Landis's stunning debut novel, this sweeping love story astonished critics, earning glowing reviews including a FIVE STAR rating from *Affaire de Coeur*...

"A truly fabulous read! The story comes vibrantly alive, making you laugh and cry..."
—*Affaire de Coeur*

Titles by Jill Marie Landis

JUST ONCE

DAY DREAMER

LAST CHANCE

AFTER ALL

UNTIL TOMORROW

PAST PROMISES

COME SPRING

JADE

ROSE

WILDFLOWER

SUNFLOWER

UNTIL TOMORROW

JILL MARIE LANDIS

J

JOVE BOOKS, NEW YORK

UNTIL TOMORROW

A Jove Book / published by arrangement with
the author

PRINTING HISTORY
Jove edition / July 1994

The Putnam Berkley World Wide Web site address is
http://www.berkley.com

ISBN: 0-515-11403-0

A JOVE BOOK®
Jove Books are published by The Berkley Publishing Group,
200 Madison Avenue, New York, New York 10016.
JOVE and the "J" design are trademarks
belonging to Jove Publications, Inc.

PRINTED IN THE UNITED STATES OF AMERICA

15   14   13   12   11   10

To Harry and Phyllis Landis;
To Robin Holly Davis;
To Ellen Marie Landis;

To Melinda Dunn, Curator, Old State Bank,
Decatur, Alabama, for graciously answering so many questions.
To Jonathan Baggs, of the *Decatur Daily*, for his help.

And to Nanny Ruby—again—
for her wisdom and outlook on life.

"Oh God! That one might read the book of fate!"
Shakespeare, *King Henry IV,* Pt. II, III.

Prologue

September 1867

The lone horseman rode beside the Neosho River, following twists and turns through the slough grass that bordered its banks. To his mind it seemed he had been riding across Kansas for weeks. In reality, it had only been days. As he dogged the river's edge he crossed flat, low plains and broad valleys, thankful for occasional stands of red cedar, linden, oak, and black walnut that offered shelter on nights when he was far from a settlement. Pressing southeastward, he left behind Fort Dodge and the open prairie, a windy, boundless universe of yellowed grasses he hoped never to lay eyes on again.

His clothes were new. Unfamiliar. Foreign after seven years in Union blue. Headed for Alabama, Dake Reed certainly had no use for his old uniform. The sutler at the fort had assured him Levi Strauss denims would be far more suitable to the trail.

Not only was he outfitted in the new pants and shirt, but he was the proud owner of a fringed buckskin jacket. He had admired the butter-colored piece enough to buy it for an outrageous amount from a Kiowa scout. The jacket was finely tanned to a velvet softness and fit the width of his shoulders as if it had been tailored expressly for him.

In a matter of days Dake had grown curiously attached to the buckskin. Perhaps, he decided, because it not only offered

1

more comfort than the heavy navy wool he had worn so long, but because it was neither blue nor gray, colors associated with the war. Slipping on the buckskin had been like fitting himself with a new identity symbolic of his last stint of service on the frontier. The war and the military were finally behind him. Now he journeyed along a trail toward not only his past, but an uncertain future.

He shifted in the saddle and adjusted the brim of his black hat, pulling it low over his brow, and focused on a curious dark spot on a rise far ahead of him. From this distance he could not make out exactly what that object might be. Dake spurred his horse and rode on, knowing sooner rather than later he would be passing by it.

As far as he could tell, he was nearing Oswego, a settlement on the west bank of the Neosho, little more than a trading post with a well and a ferry that operated on the river—but since the war a traveler couldn't be too sure about finding anything where it used to be. The closer he came to the Missouri border, the harder it was to stem his growing anxiety. When he had left home, he thought he would never return to Alabama. Indeed, both the war and his military career had kept him away for years. Then, a month ago, about the time he was faced with the decision whether or not to reenlist, a worn envelope, obviously forwarded and reforwarded through military channels, had finally reached him, calling him home.

The dark spot on the horizon had become a rectangular shape, something boxlike and alien on the tufted hilltop covered with side oats grama grass. Out of habit, Dake nearly held up his hand to summon a scout forward until, with a solitary pang, he remembered he was entirely alone. After three days on the trail he still hadn't become fully accustomed to keeping company with only himself. It was a curious state after being in command of ranks of men for so long. He shoved his hat down tight and kicked his horse, a spirited bay named General Sherman, into a canter.

Within a few hundred yards he realized the rectangle was actually the underbelly of a wagon tipped on its side. He was nearly upon it when he recognized household goods strewn on the ground and realized the dark shapes lying not far away were bodies that had been left like broken dolls on the bloodstained dry grass.

His blood ran cold. Dake palmed the handle of his gun. It slipped out of the holster, a whisper of metal against leather.

There was no sign of a team of horses. Whoever attacked the travelers had either stolen the animals or driven them away. As Dake dismounted, his gaze flicked over the body of a man, a handsome, light-skinned Negro lying deathly still, facedown in the grass, his neck twisted at a ghastly angle. Dake had seen enough of the carnage of war to know the man was beyond help. Blood stained the back of the traveler's coat, the homespun wool was punctured with bullet holes.

Spying a woman's crumpled form, he hurried to her side. He knelt beside the Negress who appeared a few years older than the man. One look at the blood that oozed from the bodice of her gown and he knew that anything he did to help would be of little use to her now. Gently, so as not to cause her any further pain, he touched her shoulder. Her skin was already cool. He lifted her wrist as he pressed his other hand against the artery in her neck. Nothing.

Dake leaned back against his heels, sick at heart. The end of the war had not stopped the hatred and senseless bloodshed, merely driven it underground. Briefly, as he stared down at the woman's lifeless form, he wondered where these prairie pilgrims had been headed, what dreams had spurred them on? What hopes had sustained them through slavery and then newfound freedom—freedom that carried them to this brutal end on the Kansas plain?

He stiffened when a low, pitiful moan suddenly issued from somewhere near the upturned wagon bed. The sound sent a chill along his spine. Dake stood, shoved his hat back on his forehead, and walked around the wreckage. There, on the ground amid a ripped bag of flour, scattered rice, and other discarded goods, lay another woman, this one fair and blond. Her face was covered in dust and perspiration. She gasped in pain as her hands twisted in the folds of her bloody skirts. He knelt beside her, brushed the tangled hair back off of her face, and whispered, "Ma'am?"

"Thank God," she murmured with her eyes closed. "My baby. Save my baby."

Dake's glance shot around the area of the shattered wagon searching for any sign of a child but there was none. There was nothing beyond the wreckage save acres of open land and a backdrop of wide blue sky. He tried to think of a way to forestall telling her that her child was missing.

"Ma'am—"

She grabbed his wrist. The blood on her hands smeared his flesh like a brand. "No time. Hurry. The baby."

He stared down at once elegant silk skirts. They were not only worn and faded, but blood-soaked. He watched the large, dark stain spread, a blossoming flower of death.

Baby.

He glanced once at the woman's face, at the golden lashes resting upon sunburned cheeks. The burn garishly highlighted the sickly pallor beneath it. She licked her cracked lips with her tongue and moaned again, clutching at her skirt.

Dake wasted no time. He holstered his gun and jerked her skirt up to her waist. Swallowing, he forced himself not to recoil at the sight between the woman's legs. An infant lay in its afterbirth, soaked in the lifeblood of its mother.

"My baby—" She struggled to raise her head but fell back. Her eyes were open. They were a deep, rich brown.

Dake reached out and lifted the fully formed boy from the ground. Rather than leave the infant in the dirt, Dake laid the still babe on his mother's stomach. The woman raised her hand to touch it, felt the slick skin coated by blood and mucus, and let her hand fall away. Born and raised on a plantation where life, death, and procreation were the sidelines of slavery, Dake knew enough about birthings to know what to do.

Ripping a length of narrow lace trim off of the woman's petticoat, he quickly twisted it around the umbilical cord and tied it off. The knife in his boot slid out without protest and sliced through the fleshy cord. He put the blade on the ground, wiped the mucus out of the baby's mouth with his finger, and hefted the boy up by his ankles, gave him a sharp slap on the bottom. Dake smiled when rewarded with a lusty, angry cry.

"Thank you . . ." The woman's voice was so weak now he could barely make out her words.

In a glance he saw that she was still hemorrhaging. A sinking, gut-searing instinct told him there was nothing more he could do for her. As the baby continued to howl, he searched the strewn contents of the wagon for a blanket and found a pile of bedding. Quickly, he ripped a sheet into a workable, ragged square and twisted it around the baby. Nestling the little boy in the crook of his arm, Dake returned to the mother's side and knelt down again. He knew he didn't have long to find out all he needed to know.

"Ma'am, what's your name?"

She licked her dry lips. "Anna. Anna Clayton."

Even though he was forced to bend close to hear the words she whispered against his ear, he recognized a soft, cultured Southern accent, much like his own. "Miss Clayton, can you tell me where you're from? Where's your family?"

"Gadsden."

Alabama. And not all that far from his home in Decatur. "Your husband?" Dake pressed.

She drew a deep, shuddering breath. Her fingertips scratched helplessly at the dry earth beneath them. "Dead."

Dake had expected as much. When he'd seen no sign of her husband he quickly determined the young widow, accompanied by her two servants, had been intent on homesteading in Kansas. By the looks of her, there wasn't much time left.

"Who did this?" He wanted to know. The other bodies had grown cold by the time he had reached them. No telling how long the woman had labored over the birth. The perpetrators of the crime had time to be long gone.

There was no answer except a long, shuddering sigh before the once lovely girl, barely old enough to be a mother, slipped into death. The child in his arms squirmed and tried to nuzzle closer to Dake's chest. He held the boy out and away from his buckskin jacket.

Damn. What now?

Dake sat back on his heels and tipped his hat back on his head as he surveyed the scene. The sun rode low in the sky. He wished he could dig graves and say a few words to bid them peace and farewell, but it was late afternoon and there was no time to bury the bodies before dusk.

He didn't intend to camp out in the open either, not with three bodies bound to draw the timber wolves out of the trees. Gently, Dake laid the baby on a bed quilt he found in the rubble and walked back to its mother. He pulled the woman's lifeless body next to the edge of the sideboard of the wagon and crossed her arms over her breasts.

The glint of sunlight on gold caught his eye and he carefully examined a rolled gold bracelet on her wrist. Distinctly engraved with a unique star and crescent design, he knew the piece would be easily identifiable to her relations, so he pressed the clasp and slid the bracelet from Anna Clayton's wrist. He pocketed the piece of jewelry and then went to retrieve the other two bodies.

When he had the servants laid out beside their mistress, he reached up, grabbed the sideboard, and rocked the heavy wagon until it began to tip over. He jumped back, felt the ground shudder slightly as the heavy wood hit the ground, creating a vault that would protect the dead from wolves and other carnivores—at least for a time. He quickly dismissed the thought of the grisly discovery the next traveler who happened along the river would find beneath the overturned wagon.

Dake found the infant asleep amid the bedding. He picked him up again, realizing the little boy weighed less than a minute. He was dwarfed by Dake's big hands. The babe looked much like any other newborn with its damp, slightly curled tuft of tawny hair, nondescript nose, and round face. The infant looked more like a shrunken, wizened-up old man than a newborn. Dake grabbed up the faded quilt and walked over to General Sherman, who waited, ground-tethered, nearby. Dake debated for a moment over how to carry the baby, then decided buttoning it inside his buckskin jacket would free his hands. He tore off a length of sheet and tightly swaddled the baby with another layer of cloth to protect the inside of his jacket.

Once again, he lay the babe on the quilt on the ground while he unbuttoned his coat. Next, he bundled the child inside and was able to close his jacket most of the way, although the buttons were strained. He deftly rolled the quilt and tied it on the back of his saddle atop his own bedroll.

With one hand on the precious cargo inside his jacket, Dake mounted up. He pulled the brim of his hat down, readjusted the reins, and turned his horse southeastward again. With a glance at the late-afternoon sun, he tried to assure himself he was bound to reach a homesteader's cabin, if not a settlement, before dark. Somewhere, he reckoned, somewhere in this expanse of land and sky, he'd find someone willing to help him care for Anna Clayton's orphaned child on the way to Alabama, even if he had to pay them.

The infant inside his jacket protested the motion of the horse with nothing more than a small, catlike mew, before he snuggled down next to Dake's heart.

Chapter One

Nothing but a series of seldom-used wagon tracks marred the high prairie swell that surrounded the James homestead. With summer's crop of corn harvested long since, dried-brown and broken stalks stood in skeletal relief against the setting sun. Beyond the cornfields, a stand of timber hugged a low ridge, while fronting the acre of forest stood a lone black walnut tree. Beneath the deepening shade of its ancient twisted limbs, the observant traveler could discern four wooden crosses. Three weathered, one new.

Kansas, this land so haunting in its very loveliness, gave in abundance; a garden of wildflowers every summer, larkspur, sweet William, prairie roses, and Japan lilies, beds of wild onion; moonlight bright enough to plow by; coal for the gathering. But not all the land gave was good. Tornadoes swept out of the sky without notice, wind and rain often drove themselves through wooden walls or sent swollen rivers and streams over their banks.

Set into the hillside beyond the walnut tree, a weathered, shingle-roofed dugout was nearly invisible. To the naked eye the place looked deserted. Inside, Cara Calvinia James hummed softly to herself as she finished decorating the pine tabletop with the only matching place setting she owned. Stepping back to admire her handiwork, she studied it a

9

moment before she adjusted the dried larkspur in the cream pitcher and pulled it closer to her dinner plate.

"There. Pretty festive, if I have to say so myself," she mumbled aloud. She picked up the thread of a song she'd been humming and sang a chorus of "Beautiful Dreamer." With a quick spin that sent her mended, calf-length skirt swirling, she lifted her arms in imitation of a waltz with an invisible partner. Her toes brushed the hard-packed dirt floor as Cara twirled barefoot around the table that stood in the center of the one-room dugout.

She danced across the room to the doorway where a red Indian blanket, its edges frayed where it caught on the rough wooden door frame, swayed in the breeze. Pushing it aside and ducking beneath, Cara stepped out to see how her birthday supper was coming along. She pushed her wild mane of curly blond hair out of her face and glanced westward. With her hand shading her eyes, she stared into the red ball low on the horizon and admired the fiery glow of sunset that stained the sky with brilliant streaks of pink and orange.

In the center of the clearing before the house, a spot she used as her outdoor kitchen in summer, a fire burned low under a blackened pot that held a range hen she'd set to boil. No hoecakes for her tonight. This was her birthday, and like her Nanny James often said, "Happiness is a habit you have to cultivate."

Just because there wasn't anyone around to wish her salutations, Cara reckoned if she couldn't hold her own festivities for her twentieth birthday, then the world had indeed become a sorry place.

Cara reached down for the long-handled spoon resting on a crate not far from the fire. She shoved it into the pot to lift the hen and test its doneness. It was almost time to add the carrots and onions.

The vegetables were bagged in gunnysacks, stacked against

one wall of the house with the rest of her meager possessions. The only things she'd yet to pack for her journey out of Kansas was the collection of handmade dolls now lining a plank shelf set on wooden pins that bordered the room. Nearly twenty dolls in all. She'd made them herself out of scraps of material—bits and pieces of clothing so worn they could no longer be used. Some had faces of nuts and dried apples; others were made entirely of rags. One of her favorites had a head and body formed of a bedpost.

Before she started making them, she'd never seen dolls with calico faces, but somehow, after she had sewn on their button eyes and the touches of ragged lace and shredded rag hair, she thought them endearing, if not downright beautiful.

Cara pulled four carrots out of a sack and then reached deep into another for a fat onion. Intent on using the dented dishpan sitting outside on a rough wooden bench, she thanked the Lord once more for the abundant harvest of vegetables this summer. It was a far piece to California, that much she knew. She was assured she wouldn't starve before she found a place to settle down and look for work.

No matter what the future might bring, Cara vowed as she picked through the vegetables that she wasn't about to let herself be forever bound to this lonely scrap of land five miles from her nearest neighbor. This place had been part of her father's dream, not her own.

Everett James had always been a dreamer. But by the time Cara was ten she had stopped believing that her father's dreams would ever come true. Their emigration to Kansas, his "big opportunity" sponsored by an Eastern abolitionists' group, was supposed to have been their eventual ticket to California, but they never got there. The dream ended when he was murdered by pro-slavery advocates who had infiltrated Kansas from Missouri. Though she was still a child at the time, she was forced to do her share in the fields alongside her granny, her mother, and her older brother, Willie. Not only had they nearly starved to death that first winter, but they lived in constant fear of roaming bands of border ruffians intent on driving out settlers who would vote to make Kansas a free state.

One by one, the others were taken by the land. Her mother died of typhoid three years ago. Nanny James followed shortly after. And Willie, her serious, ever responsible big brother, had passed on a month ago when he fell from a borrowed hay rake and broke his neck.

She missed them all; her father and his dreams, her mother's easy smile, Nanny's intuitive wisdom. But she took Willie's loss the hardest, for he had been her constant companion and closest friend.

Feeling isolated and alone, Cara stared off across the land and blinked back tears. Her nearest neighbors lived a half day's walk away. A boisterous family of ten, the Dicksons had come to bury Willie after she walked over to ask them for their help.

Hooter Dickson, the second eldest son, had up and asked her to marry him on the spot. Cara took one look at the near toothless, thin-haired Hooter and refused. Without feeling the slightest bit offended, Hooter promised to help her put out her corn in the spring, but she felt no compulsion to stay to endure the loneliness and fight the elements alone. Instead of wallowing in her sadness, she had decided to take destiny by the reins and that was exactly what she intended to do come morning.

Vegetables in hand, she sat down on the bench and took up her paring knife, set to peel the carrots before she dunked them into the somewhat clean water in the dishpan. Intent on her work, she heard the sound of hoofbeats before she saw the lone rider materializing out of the west, headed straight toward her door.

Set against the low rise, the dugout was not easy to find even when a body was looking for it, but the smoke from her outdoor kitchen must have given it away.

Excitement, curiosity, and caution bubbled up like an emotional stew inside her as Cara set the carrot and knife aside, shoved her blond hair back off her face again, and shielded her eyes with her arm. It was a man all right. A big one from the looks of him outlined against the setting sun.

She darted inside, picked up the loaded pistol she kept on a stool beside the door, and then stepped back out. Since the war there had been so many displaced drifters on the land that Willie had always warned her that it was wise to take care before inviting a stranger in. Standing with the gun concealed in the folds of her faded yellow skirt, she was ready to face the man on the huge bay.

He rode straight up to the dugout. Cara watched him dismount and wondered if he'd been wounded for he moved as gingerly as a man twice his age and kept one hand on his potbellied stomach. Beneath the brim of his low-crowned black hat, his sun-darkened features were ruggedly handsome. His nose was unbroken. Deep creases bracketed his lips. His finely tapered brows were straight, not arched.

She met his eyes and in one glance Cara knew she had never seen eyes of such a deep, clear green. They appeared fathomless, yet there were shadows lurking in their depths. There was no comparing him to anyone she'd ever met. Hooter Dickson didn't hold a candle to him. This stranger was incredibly handsome.

She forced herself to break the hold of his steady speculative gaze. She looked down at his dusty boots, flicked her sight up to the holster strapped to his thigh.

Her hand tightened on the pistol. Cara stepped forward. "How do, mister?"

Dake Reed shifted the bundle hidden by his jacket, unwilling to wake the infant sheltered against his shirtfront because it had been mewling pitifully off and on since he had ridden away from the wagon. He glanced around the hard-packed dirt yard before the dugout. A broken wheel, bits of wire, a bottomless cane chair with a missing leg, assorted piles of scrap wood, bones, antlers, weeds, and pieces of wooden crates littered the ground. His gaze paused on the rag that covered the doorway. It probably hid any number of odd inhabitants if the look of the wild-haired blonde standing barefoot in the dirt was any indication.

He studied the blonde from beneath the brim of his hat. Of medium height, she was so slight that her faded yellow dress hung on her shoulders; the bust and waistline came nowhere near embracing her slender frame, but he could see the rise of her firm breasts along the dipping neckline. Since the dress was two sizes too wide and a foot too short, her lower calves and ankles showed beneath her skirt. Her feet were streaked brown with the dry prairie earth. She stared up at him with sky-blue eyes that barely shone through a tangle of curls that kept falling forward into her face. As he watched, she shoved her hair back for the third time. Dake was tempted to ask if she'd ever thought of tying it back and found himself dismissing a sudden vision of having the pleasure of brushing it for her.

She had a wide mouth. Next to her eyes, her full, pouting lips would tempt a saint to taste them. Physically, she didn't appear to be out of her late teens, but there was nothing young about the wariness in her eyes as she stared up at him.

Dake had to force himself to recall what he was about to say to her. Finally, he stared over her head at the dugout. There was no sign of anyone else about. He looked down at her again.

"I need your help," he said without preamble, praying there might be a soft spot in her heart for children.

She peered up at him curiously. "Johnny Reb, huh?"

There was no denying his drawl. He had given up trying to

lose it. "I'm originally from Alabama, ma'am. Union Army, though."

He watched her slowly arch a brow and stare up at him speculatively as if weighing the truth of his words. She didn't relax her stance at all. "What is it you need?"

He patted the mound beneath his jacket. "I—"

She cut him off. "Are you wounded?"

He blinked. "Why?"

"Because you stepped off that horse like an old-timer and you've been holding your stomach ever since."

He looked down at his hand where it rested on the front of his buckskin jacket. "Mind if we go inside?"

"I do, sir. I don't know you from Adam."

Dake nodded. So be it. He began to unbutton his jacket, slowly and carefully, keeping one hand on the infant tucked inside. When he looked up again, he saw amazement in the girl's eyes.

"I'll be battered and fried," she whispered, stepping forward. In a hushed tone she asked, "What have you got there?"

"A baby."

"Well, I can see that." She reached out with her finger and brushed the tawny down on the baby's head. Magnetically, a thin curl looped around her finger. "Boy or girl?"

"Boy."

"Yours?"

"No. Definitely not mine," he assured her.

"Where'd you get it?"

"I was just following the Neosho and came upon three people who'd been ambushed, homesteaders from the looks of them. The woman had just given birth. She had two servants with her, both dead. She told me her name and where she was from and then she died. I've been looking for a place to stop for two hours now. Yours is the first place I came to." She was staring at the baby so hard he wondered if she had taken in all he had said. He added as an afterthought, "I'm Dake Reed. Until last week I was a captain in the army, stationed at Fort Dodge."

Dake stared down at the girl's blond curls and watched her smile at the baby as he pulled it all the way out of his jacket and cradled it in his arms. The sheets he'd swaddled the baby in were stained with its mother's blood and the mucus it had been born in. Dake frowned at the damp spot on the front of his shirt and thought of the price he'd paid for the beautifully tanned buckskin.

The girl stepped back a pace and crossed her arms. It was then he noticed the pistol in her right hand. "I'm Cara. Cara Calvinia James."

She didn't move, nor did she make an offer to take the baby from him. In fact, she was studying him in a measuring way, as if making up her mind whether or not to believe him at all. Finally, she nodded toward the dugout. "Bring him in."

They were both forced to duck beneath what barely passed as a blanket to enter the low doorway. Dake bent nearly double. Once through, he straightened in the darkened interior. The place smelled of must and onions. The back wall had been cut into the low hillside. Most of the dwelling was nothing but raw earth. As he crossed to the table, he noticed the room was incredibly bare of any amenities and nearly dark as a cave.

Muted light filtered through oiled paper at the two small windows in the front wall. The table, three mismatched chairs, and a sagging rope bed against one wall were the only pieces of furniture in the sparse room. Surely Cara Calvinia James didn't live here alone?

"You can put him down over here." Gun in hand, Cara pointed to the table and watched the big man awkwardly holding the baby in the crook of his arm. She watched him take note of the single place setting at one end of the rickety table.

He looked up slowly, regarding her intently. She lifted her

chin a notch and stared back. Her hand tightened on the gun butt. It was hard to imagine that anyone who had stopped to aid a dying woman and carry a newborn to safety might harm her, but as she had told him earlier, she didn't know him from Adam and baby or no, until she thought she could trust him, she wasn't about to take her eyes or her gun off him.

The baby cried out and quickly forced their thoughts back to the problem at hand.

"Do you have a cow?" he asked.

"A *caow*?" His voice was deep, his drawl so slow that she repeated the word in order to discern what he meant. Then with a shake of her head, she informed him, "I did. Just sold her along with the pigs. Got a good price, too. Twenty dollars."

"Damn," he mumbled.

Offended by what she thought was a slight, Cara said softly, "I thought it was good money."

Dake shook his head as he lay the infant on the table. "I mean, I'm sorry you sold her. This little boy needs milk. I don't know how long he can go without eating."

"I've still got a goat that gives milk," she volunteered.

He reached down to unwrap the naked child. "Do you think that would work?"

Cara Calvinia James shrugged. "I don't see why not." The baby was a mess, his skin blotchy with dried blood. "Do you think you should wash him off or something?" She was frowning down at the stump of the baby's umbilical cord and the stained blanket beneath it.

"He might catch cold." Dake shook his head. He had learned enough growing up on a plantation to help deliver a baby, but the details of child care were out of his realm. "You think washing him so soon will hurt him?"

"I don't mean for you to drown him. Just wipe him off here and there. And he needs a diaper, I know that much."

Dake Reed looked hopeful. "Do you have any?"

"Nope." She flushed almost immediately. "But I've got some clean rags I keep . . . for emergencies."

"Maybe you can tend to that while I go out and milk your goat?"

"*Me* tend to him? I don't know anything about tending a brand-new baby." The thought of him leaving her alone to tidy up the slippery bundle on the table filled her with dread. What if she dropped the wriggly little thing?

She looked away from the baby and glanced up. The man's nearness startled her. She had been alone so long that to suddenly have this Dake Reed towering over her, his green eyes thoughtful as he stared back, made her catch her breath. She moved back a step. Who was he *really*? she wondered. He appeared both clean and sober, not to mention handsome, but the deadliest snakes often came in the prettiest skins. Here he stood asking her to care for a baby he had pulled out of his coat and she didn't know enough about babies to fill a thimble. The only children she had ever been around were some of the Dickson brood and she had never been there for any stretch of time.

She caught herself watching him stare and stepped back again. "Mr. Reed, I have no idea how to handle him. It seems to me, you've been doing just fine. Besides, you go after Miss Lucy yourself and you're liable to wind up with a rupture where you don't want one."

"Who's Miss Lucy?"

Cara sighed. "My goat. She's probably down by the creek and I don't expect she'll let you milk her, let alone bring her back. What if I go milk her while *you* tend to the baby?"

Before Dake Reed could protest, Cara made her way to the door. She paused on the threshold and then glanced back at Reed.

"You wouldn't be thinking of riding off and leaving that baby here with me once I step out to get Lucy, would you?"

He shook his head with a smile. "No, Miss James, I wouldn't. After all, I made a promise to his dying mother that I'd see him safely back to Alabama and I intend to do just that."

"Well, then fine. I'll go."

"Oh, Miss James—"

She turned around again, one hand on the door frame. The blanket lifted with the breeze. So did the hem of her skirt. She watched his eyes drop to her hemline and then trail back up to her face.

"Yes?"

"You're liable to get tired hauling that gun around with you. I swear to you that I'm an honorable man. You have nothing to fear from me."

Cara felt her heartbeat quicken and the color in her cheeks rise. The baby in the center of the table was now sucking on its hand, its sleepy, ink-blue eyes blinked up at the tall man trustingly. She felt the weight of the gun in her hand and made the decision, for good or ill, to take Dake Reed at his word.

As she lay the gun on the three-legged stool near the door, she said to him, "There's a pot out in the yard you can use to heat some water." With that, she ducked beneath the blanket and left him on his own.

It was almost dusk when Cara started back to the dugout carrying a quarter bucket of goat's milk. The creek was not more than a few minutes' walk, but sometimes Lucy tended to wander farther than was convenient. Still, like a well-wound clock, Miss Lucy always showed up in time for milking.

When she was close enough to make out the outline of the hillside, Cara's mouth began to water at the scent of boiling poultry and cursed her forgetfulness once again. For the life of her she couldn't figure out why keeping track of time was so important when one set out to cook anything. Now her greatly anticipated birthday meal had probably boiled itself off the bone and not only were the vegetables *not* in the pot, but for hospitality's sake she would have to invite Dake Reed to sit down and share what little she had.

For that matter, she knew she couldn't just send him on his way once darkness fell, not with the baby to look after. It just wouldn't be right. Besides, it was prairie tradition to share food and lodging with passing strangers. Visitors were few and far between and the appearance of travelers usually initiated a celebration. She could remember every occasion when the family gathered around the table listening long into the night as weary pilgrims related bits of news of far-off places.

Yes indeed, it was the right thing to do, and she knew it, but no one had stopped by since Cara had been all alone. She hoped to get a sense of what type of man Dake Reed might be before she came right out and asked him to stay the night.

As she rounded the front of the house she found him standing in the yard in the halo of lamplight that eked out of the windows. She paused for a moment to watch him before he noticed her. It looked as if he'd lit every lamp in the place. He had pushed back the blanket that covered the door and was pacing back and forth creating a moving silhouette of a man with a child cradled high against his shoulder. She saw his hand move as he patted the baby gently on the back and knew in that moment that he would be true to his word and do her no harm.

"I found her," Cara called out, only to be met with a curt shushing sound. She swung the bucket as she walked over to Reed and looked up at him. "What's the matter?" she whispered.

He whispered back, "He's been crying and fussing since you left. He's just now quieted down."

"Did you get a diaper on him?"

It was a moment before he answered. "I did, but don't ask me how. He's as slippery as an eel." She watched his shoulders dip as he sighed and added irritably, "I'm so hungry what patience I had is gone."

As she watched him carefully shift the baby to his other shoulder, she felt her heart melt. "I knew it," Cara mumbled, thinking of the small range hen in the cook pot. Her conscience demanded she ask him to supper even though she had thought to celebrate her landmark birthday alone. "Mr. Reed, I know this situation is as awkward for you as it is for me—"

"Probably more so," he mumbled as he adjusted the infant to his other shoulder and tucked in the quilt when one small, pink foot thrust itself out from beneath the blanket.

"—but it just isn't right to turn a man and a helpless little baby out into the night, so if you can see fit to feed him, I'll get the supper on." She started to move past him and then stopped, "I planned to leave at first light, though, so I hope we can both go about our business then."

The look of relief that crossed his face made her happy she had extended the invitation. Cara decided then and there not to worry about what she would do about spending the entire evening with him in the small confines of the cabin. She would deal with the sleeping arrangements when dinner was over with.

"How much do you think I should give him?" Dake Reed glanced down at her breasts, as if he were gauging the amount of nourishment a woman's breasts might hold. Cara felt her face flame and lowered her gaze. Her breasts were well developed and firm, in spite of the fact that she'd grown so thin of late.

Embarrassed and more than thankful for the encroaching darkness, she turned away and said, "Feed him until he's not hungry anymore." Cara avoided meeting his eyes again. She stared at the bundle on his shoulder instead. The baby was dwarfed beneath Dake Reed's strong, tanned hand. "You don't think we could accidentally give him too much, do you?"

"Hell, I don't know."

She heard the immediate frustration in his tone and remembered he said he was hungry—and he was no doubt disappointed that she knew as little as he about caring for a child.

Taking mercy on him, Cara smiled and forced a cheerful tone. "If it wasn't so late I could take your horse and ride over to the Dicksons' and see if Mrs. Dickson has a bottle with a rubber nipple she could spare. But I guess feeding him any way we can is better than nothing. Maybe you should just try little bits at a time to see how he takes to it?"

"Who are the Dicksons?"

He sounded so hopeful that she hated to have to inform him, "The family that settled northeast of here, but it's too late and too dark to ride over with a baby now." She continued to carry on a line of amiable chatter as they moved toward the dugout. "They offered to buy my land when they came to help me bury Willie," she added.

"Your husband?"

Cara turned to face him and hated the pity she recognized in his eyes. His expression dredged up the sadness again, the intense loneliness she had battled for the past weeks. Cara started to speak and found she had to clear her throat before she could say the words aloud. "My brother. He died a couple weeks back."

"I'm sorry," he said softly. He sounded as if he actually meant the words that a stranger would utter just to be polite.

Sorrow tightened her throat again. Instead of commenting, she merely led the way into the dugout. He had, indeed, lit all the oil lamps at once, an extravagance she never allowed herself, not when she wasn't certain when she could afford more fuel. But since tonight was hopefully the last in the dugout—and her birthday to boot—Cara didn't complain as she set the bucket of milk on the table.

She watched Dake Reed as he entered, curious to find out

everything she could about him, but determined to hold back her questions because he seemed so concerned with seeing to the child. Trying to lighten the mood, she asked, "Have you thought of a way to feed him?"

"Maybe we could spoon it into him."

Cara leaned against the table and folded her arms. "I don't think so. He might choke if he goes at it too fast. Could we make a"—she felt her cheeks grow hot again and refused to meet Reed's eyes—"a teat? I have some muslin."

He pulled out a chair and shrugged as he lowered himself slowly so as not to disturb the sleeping baby. "Try it. You could dip it in the milk and give him a little bit at a time."

Cara paused where she stood near a barrel stuffed with clothes, yarn, and fabric. It was full of items she had hoped to use to make more dolls when she reached California. Cara shook her head. "You mean *you* could give him some a little bit at a time."

He sighed. "Fine. While *you* put the dinner on the table." Then, in a low tone she was still well able to hear, he added, "If there's anything left of that chicken out there."

Dake watched Cara Calvinia James's pert little bottom twitch as she bent over to dig deep into a barrel of fabric scraps, yarn, and bits of yellowed lace. In that position, her raggedy dress was so short that from where he sat he could see her calves nearly up to her knees. He'd never seen a decent woman in anything like it. He also wondered at her lack of modesty. Didn't she know any better than to flash her legs at a grown man?

As he watched her toss piece after piece over her shoulder while she sought out muslin, he found himself speculating on her immediate situation and decided that Cara Calvinia James had definitely been in the midst of moving out.

The evidence was everywhere. Foodstuffs in burlap lined the front wall. Behind them stood a somewhat orderly line of crates and barrels, very few if they held all her worldly possessions, as he guessed they did. There were a few household goods still in evidence, a set of mismatched chipped plates and cups, a few pieces of cutlery, pots that were blackened from cooking over the open fire, a broom made of twigs. He'd seen better in the slave quarters at Riverglen.

There was no sign that anyone else lived here. Dake found himself wondering how long she had been on her own. Perhaps, he thought, it was the intense isolation that had led her to make the whimsical dolls that lined the only shelf in the room.

Dake had nearly jumped out of his skin when he earlier discovered the odd assortment of faces that stared down at him with sightless eyes. At first it seemed eerie, but when he walked nearer and took a better look at the dolls he couldn't help but smile. Either Cara James was color-blind or she found nothing strange about dolls with floral, blue, green, or chartreuse faces—not to mention the others made of walnuts, something dried and shrunken, and wood. Each rag doll had a slightly different, button-eyed expression. On the others she had painted whimsical expressions.

"Found it," she said, drawing his attention once again as she waved the muslin over her head. She hurried to another small box and found some scissors and thread, hastily cut the material into squares and piled them one on the other. Then she drew the wad into a nipple shape and tied off the length. "I hope this works."

"Me, too," Dake said with another sigh. Not for the first time did he think he had made a promise that would prove more than he could handle. He was surprised when Cara reached out for the baby, but gladly handed the infant over to her.

"No need to look so glum, Mr. Reed. As my grandma, Nanny James, used to say, 'Few delight in a sorrowful man.' Now, let's see about getting some milk down this little boy."

While Dake stood by, Cara dipped the muslin teat in the goat's milk until it soaked up a goodly amount, then she rubbed it against the baby's lips. The child pushed it back with his tongue, swallowed what little liquid was left there, smacked his lips, and then began to fuss. Cara tried again. This time the hungry infant pulled desperately on the muslin, nearly sucking it dry before Cara could get it away and dip it into the milk again.

Dake leaned over her shoulder and watched in amazement. "He likes it."

She looked back at him and laughed. "He's eating like a little shoat."

No matter how much she might protest feeding the baby, the girl held the child against her with a natural ease. When she peered over her shoulder and smiled up at him, Dake was taken by the radiance of her smile. It shone through her dirt-smudged face and tousled curls, both sensual and innocent at the same time. He could almost taste her lower lip and feel his teeth nipping it gently. He felt his mouth go dry.

For the first time since he'd laid eyes on her, Dake realized that this girl was not merely pretty, but in the right setting and with a little grooming, she would be downright beautiful. He felt himself quicken and was reminded of just how long he'd been without a woman. He straightened abruptly and forced himself to step back, unwilling to spook the girl since she trusted him enough to lay down her weapon.

"I'll try to feed him if you want to get supper on." He reached out and took the baby, then sat down in the chair she vacated. It took more than one try before he learned how much milk the muslin could hold and soon there was milk running down the baby's chin and neck and splattered on his own lap, but the infant was slurping peacefully as Cara made her way out the door.

By the time the baby had been fed, swaddled in more of

Cara's precious fabric, and put to sleep in the center of the grass-stuffed ticking on the bed, Cara called Dake to supper. His stomach rumbled in response and his mouth watered at the smell of succulent chicken.

"It's not much," she apologized, "just range hen that's cooked to soup and some day-old hoecake, but it'll fill that hole in your stomach. There's coffee, too, of a sort. It's been scarce since the war so I mix what I have with dried carrots to make it go further."

Confused, she watched him when he moved to stand beside her, one hand on her chair. When he pulled it out for her with a slight bow, she looked down at the chair and back up at him. Finally comprehension dawned.

Cara sat. Dake hid a smile.

Without a word she dished up the hen. The flesh fell from the bones and floated in the broth that puddled on his plate. Dake chose a piece of hoecake from a pie tin in the center of the table. The bottom crust was as black as the pots and pans. He dipped it into the hen broth and took a bite. The bread tasted scorched and the broth was greasy. Cooking, obviously, was not one of her talents, but he was too hungry to care.

They ate in silence, each intent upon the meal, both eating as if it had been days since their last bite instead of merely hours. She paused between bites, her lips glossy from the hen grease, her blue eyes curious. "Where were you headed, Mr. Reed, before you found the baby and his ma?"

"Alabama." He toyed with a leg bone as he thought of all the word conjured up for him and wondered what he would find when he finally reached Decatur.

"And you say you fought for the Union?"

He nodded.

She set down a bone and proceeded to lick her fingers. He couldn't seem to look away from the tip of her moist pink tongue as it flicked in and out. "You have family there?"

She watched the shadows in his eyes deepen. He frowned slightly. "Mama died of yellow fever a few years before the war. I recently learned Daddy died two years ago. My brother is back at our plantation, Riverglen."

She scooted closer to the edge of her chair, staring down at her plate as she chose another portion of hen. "Your family must have been rich if you lived in a house with a name."

She peered at him through lowered lashes, wishing she could take the comment back. It was none of her business how much money he had. She could almost hear her own mama admonishing her for her bad manners.

Dake shrugged. "I guess you could say we had money before the war. At least, we had as much as anyone else in our place in the South. Most of what we had was tied up in slaves."

He had paused a moment before he said the word "slaves," as if loath to admit it. He took a sip of coffee. She watched him carefully when he didn't know she did so. Without him admitting it, she could sense he had come from money. His clothes were clean as travel would allow, his hair and fingernails neatly trimmed. He carried himself proudly with an inborn confidence that couldn't be denied. She wondered what he had looked like before the war years had added the shadows to his eyes and etched lines about the corners of them. Had a smile come more easily to his lips back then?

As she reached for another piece of corn bread, Cara caught sight of her own uneven nails and vowed she'd try to scrub them a little cleaner when she washed up tonight. "Did your family lose their home during the war?"

He shook his head. "No, but I guess there's not much left. At least that's what I hear from a close friend of the family. Every male adult slave who could work the fields was worth a thousand dollars. Multiply that times the number of slaves a man owned and you'll find that's where most of the plantation owner's wealth was invested. When the slaves were freed, the planters had to stand by and watch their investments simply walk away."

"But if you fought on the side that took everything away from your family, how do they feel about having you home again?"

He picked up his coffee cup and drained it, then set it down as carefully as if it were fashioned out of the finest bone china. "My brother doesn't know I'm on my way back. One of the neighbors sent for me. She told me Burke is on the verge of losing Riverglen to the tax collector. I'm going home to see what I can do to help."

Cara broke off a piece of corn bread and ate it. "Speaking of neighbors, first thing in the morning, I'm heading off to my neighbors' place to see if they'll put up the money for the homestead like they offered a couple of weeks back. You'll probably be wanting to head out early so—"

He was watching her carefully, his brow furrowed in thought. "What are your plans after you sell the place?" Uncomfortable with the speculative look in his eyes, Cara squirmed on the chair and set it creaking. "I have plans, Mr. Reed, plans I've been dwelling on for a long, long time."

"Which are?"

"*Big* changes. Up to now, life has dished out nothing but bones for my family, bones as bare as the ones on that plate of yours. Now that I'm alone, and this being my twentieth birthday, I don't have a reason in the world not to go after what I want." Cara crossed her arms and leaned back in her chair.

Her age surprised him. In the oversize gown, with her tousled curls, she looked no older than seventeen. He picked up a leg bone, chewed the meat off it, cracked it open, and sucked out the marrow before he set the pieces down on his plate. Dake dipped a piece of hoecake in the golden broth on his plate and took another bite.

"I'm set on heading to California as soon as this place is sold," she announced.

His meal suddenly forgotten, he was staring at her intently now. "Why California?"

Her eyes took on an almost fanatical glow. "It's warm for one thing. And sunny. And there are miles and miles of sand beaches along the ocean. I've never seen the ocean, have you?"

He shook his head.

"I want to open my own shop there," she said proudly.

"What kind of shop?" He wondered what on earth she intended. From the looks of her, she wasn't a seamstress, nor was she a cook.

"I'm a doll maker."

"Ah. And you think there's lots of call for that?"

"I hope so. I figure in a city like San Francisco, folks are too busy to make their own dolls and would buy ready-mades for their children. I've already got a good supply built up."

Dake glanced around the bare-walled, one-room earth and wood shack. It was now or never. "If you would consider postponing your departure, I can pay you handsomely to accompany me to Gadsden and care for the baby along the way, Miss James."

Cara was speechless. She blinked twice. As her shock lessened, she finally assured him, "There's not enough money in the world, Mr. Reed. How can I start a new life in California if I have to worry about someone else's baby first?"

While she had been talking, he had sucked the meat off of every last bone on his plate. He pointed to the little that was left of her supper. "You going to eat that?" She shook her head. He shoved the empty plate aside and pulled hers up before him. "If you go with me, you'd have a bigger stake for your move. Besides, it shouldn't take us too long to get to Alabama."

"What do you mean, *us*?"

Dreams can't come true if you oversleep.

Nanny James

Chapter Two

"Miss James, do you think you could lower your voice? You'll wake the baby."

"Sorry." She took a deep breath. "But in my position I guess I have the right to get a little excited. Here I was, minding my own business, when a man and a baby drop in unexpected and now you ask me to go all the way to Alabama, which is the exact opposite of the direction I'm headed." More than a little disturbed by the notion, she pressed a hand against her brow.

Dake admitted, "I don't know what else I can do, Miss James."

"You can take him to Alabama without me, Mr. Reed. You never know what you can do until you try. I know one thing for certain," she told him, "the South is no place to be right now. Not since the war. The way I hear it from the neighbors, supplies are short and no one's safe on the roads. There are still troops stationed all over."

As isolated as she was, Dake was surprised that she had any knowledge of the situation in the South, but her account matched all that he had heard. Since his second plate of food was gone, he stood up and walked over to the bed where she'd tossed the dish towel. Wiping the grease off his hands and face, he carefully folded the towel and laid it back on the dry sink. "Do you have any more coffee?"

As she collected the coffeepot, he looked at the odd

31

assortment of dolls around the room and wondered what city folks would think of them. "How did you get started?" He walked over and sat down at the table once more.

"Living out here, there wasn't anyone for me to play with besides Willie, so Nanny James made me lots of dolls. When I was old enough, she taught me how to make my own and it's been a hobby ever since."

Cara was soon at his side, refilling his cup. That done, she put the pot down and without a word wandered out into the dark. He watched her go, forcing himself to give her a few moments alone. Dake guessed he would get nowhere by trying to badger her into agreeing to accompany him on the journey south. Having the baby and a nursemaid along would slow his progress, but he would go far slower if he had to stop and care for the child every step of the way. Time was of the essence. As he stared down into the pitiful mixture of carrots and coffee he pondered the desperate tone of Wilhelmina Blakely's letter when it had finally reached him at Fort Dodge a month ago.

He had known even before he opened the letter that the missive most likely bore bad tidings. Honest to the point of outright bluntness, Minna pleaded with him to return to the plantation outside Decatur. Her brief but poignant words haunted him still.

Come back, Dake. Come home. If you ever loved your brother, if you still care at all about Riverglen, you'll come back as soon as you can. I'm sorry to have to tell you that your daddy died two years ago. The house has been spared, so Riverglen is not in Yankee hands, but Burke has lost everything else and has no way to pay the back taxes. He is too stubborn to ask for help. He hasn't been the same since the war.

Please, Dake. Come home.

Dake could almost hear the words spoken in her sweet Southern drawl and knew what it had cost her to beg. He would never forget Minna as he had last seen her, standing on the veranda at Riverglen, looking like an expensive china doll with her hair in perfect chestnut ringlets and bows, a pastel silk gown with matching slippers his mother had given her, forcing a bright smile as she told him good-bye. Minna had been a part of his life since childhood and if it hadn't been for the fact that she had always loved his older brother, she might now be his.

His mother had adored Minna. She was the only child of bookish merchants who had been happy to let Theodora Reed become the girl's patron and give her everything they could not afford. From the time it was evident that Minna and Burke had taken a shine to one another, Dake's mother had treated the girl as if she were the future mistress of Riverglen.

Dake had wrestled with the decision of whether or not to return through a week of sleepless nights. There was no question in his heart about his love for his brother, just as there had been no question in his mind when it came to choosing sides before the war. Not only had he been certain, then as now, that the Union should stand undivided, but he sincerely believed that the institution of slavery had to be abolished.

Now he wondered if he had the courage to go back and see the land he once loved in ruins. How could he return a victor to face the older brother he always idolized while Burke undoubtedly hated him?

How long did he have before his brother lost Riverglen to the tax men? Minna hadn't mentioned a deadline, but her tone made it evident that he needed to hurry. If he left alone with the baby, speed would be impossible. He would have to stop again and again, on and on until he found someone willing to care for the Clayton child on the road to Gadsden. More than likely, if Cara James knew conditions in the South were bad, so did everyone else.

Dake stood, stretched his arms high overhead, and after a glance in the direction of the bed where the baby still slept soundly, he left the dugout.

Miss Lucy came up to him and butted his leg as soon as he stepped over the threshold into the cool night air. He ignored the goat and it soon gave up and wandered over to Cara, who sat on the bench against the front of the dugout contemplating the banner of stars overhead. If she refused to go, he could always offer to buy the goat, he decided. After all, the girl wouldn't need it where she was going, but then he'd have a baby *and* a goat on his hands, a notion that didn't even bear contemplating another moment.

He walked over to the bench and sat a polite distance from Cara James. Crossing his ankles, he stretched out, his back against the rough shingles of the dugout wall, his thumbs hooked in his pockets. Dake sneaked a glance at Cara who sat forward, her hands grasping the edge of the bench. Her bare toes made circles in the dirt.

"I've been thinking," she began.

He didn't dare say a word.

She took a slow look around the farmyard. "Seems to me I could always use a bigger stake for my doll shop." She glanced at him sideways. "You *do* have money?"

He wasn't surprised by her question, not when most of the country was still in upheaval. "I've saved most of my pay for seven years. I'll pay you handsomely, if that's what you're concerned about."

"If I do this, it won't just be for the money. It'll be because I want to help that little boy in there. But . . . I don't know—"

"You'll be fully compensated. If you really are the business-woman you think you are, you'll take me up on my offer."

"I'll need to sleep on it."

He could almost see her mind at work. "Fine." He thought

the subject closed and certainly didn't wish to push her into a flat-out refusal.

"When would we leave?" she asked into the darkness.

He fought down the urge to grab her and do a jig around the yard but knew he didn't dare show his relief yet. "As soon as you're ready. What all do you still have to do?"

"I have to go over to the Dicksons'. It'll take most of the morning if I walk—"

"You can take my horse."

". . . and it depends on whether they have the cash on hand to pay me for the homestead."

"Anything else?"

"I need something to pack my dolls in. I'm out of boxes."

"Maybe I could build a crate while you ride over to the neighbors' house."

She turned to him. "Could you?"

He nodded.

They both jumped to their feet when the baby began to cry. Dake looked at Cara. Cara looked at the door. "Do you suppose he's hungry again already?"

Shoving a hand through his hair, Dake admitted, "Hell, I have no idea." He reminded himself to watch his tongue, something he never had to do around the troops.

With weary resignation lacing her tone, Cara started toward the lamplight. "Well, I guess we won't know until we go see."

Dake followed, careful not to let her see him smile.

Seated on the plank floor near the foot of the bed, Dake ran a hand over the coarse, dark stubble that covered the lower half of his face. Exhausted beyond measure, he leaned back against the earthen wall, unmindful of the bits of grass and damp soil that scratched the back of his head. From beneath half-lowered lids, he sneaked a glance at Cara James.

She lay crosswise on her bed, her bare feet dangling over the edge. As he watched, she drew one leg up and he was treated to a glimpse of a shapely calf. The girl's arm was carelessly bent across her face to shield her eyes from the light of encroaching dawn.

Neither of them had gotten more than an hour of sleep, not with the persistent wails that had come from the tiny bundle of boy now sleeping blissfully not an arm's length from Cara.

When there seemed to be nothing either of them could do to comfort the fretful baby, when he had finally threatened to take the Clayton child outside and leave it for the timber wolves, Cara had snatched the infant away from him and fed it again. Once the baby was full and dry, but still whimpering, she snuggled it close to her heart and began to pace the floor, singing in soft, melodic tones.

Two hours later, when she had exhausted her repertoire of sentimental ballads, "Weeping Sad and Lonely," "All Quiet Along the Potomac," and perhaps the one Dake hated most, "The Vacant Chair," she was in full agreement with Dake's plan to abandon the baby on the prairie. He took over the pacing, minus the singing, and soon little Clayton had finally worn himself out and had fallen asleep.

While the evening was still young, Dake had intended to spread his bedroll before the fire in the yard. The idea died sometime during the night. Now, with sleep weighing so heavily on him that he couldn't feel his arms or legs, he gave up all thought of the propriety of sleeping outside and continued to doze propped against the wall.

He closed his eyes and let his mind wander in a state of half sleep, half wakefulness and thought of home, of Decatur, of the last time he'd seen his brother, Burke.

Six long, war-riddled years ago.

"Get out, then, and don't look back."
Dake stared, hard and long at the older brother he was the

spitting image of, the man who, as a boy, had taught him to swim, hunt, and climb trees. The one who had always been there to pick him up whenever he fell. Burke was stronger, more aggressive, always protective and proud of his little brother. But on that April day in '61 when Dake left to join the Union Army the bond between them had been severed, suddenly and irrevocably.

They had been arguing all morning, cutting each other with words as sharp as sabers since the moment Burke found Dake packing, intent on going to Kentucky, to enlist in the Union Army.

Passing along the hallway, Burke swung around and leaned indolently against the door frame, arms crossed over his chest to watch Dake pack. Dake's valet, or "daily give," Elijah, hovered in the background, watchful and silent.

"You can go, Elijah. I'm almost finished anyway," Dake said.

The youth who'd served Dake for the past two years stopped arranging the items in Dake's valise. He paused, his demeanor solemn, and in a low voice bid his master farewell. "You take care, Marse Dake," he said. "The Lord will watch over you."

"Thank you, Elijah."

Dake ignored Burke who stepped aside to let Elijah exit the room. He carefully folded a spare shirt atop the razor, strop, mug, and soap in the bottom of his bag and then crossed to the low, bird's-eye maple dresser to collect the money he kept in the corner of the top drawer beside the stack of neatly folded shirts he would leave behind. Earlier, he had told Elijah to have them.

"You really going to let that little argument we had at dinner last night drive you off?" Burke started slowly, his drawl thick as hot grits as he referred to their political argument over Alabama's recent secession from the Union. "You really runnin', little brother?"

"No, I'm fighting. I'm just heading north to do it," Dake told him flat-out. If he'd shot Burke dead blank in the chest his brother couldn't have looked any more surprised. Or wounded.

"Surely you can't be serious."

Dake shoved his money into his pockets and then picked up the Horologe watch that once belonged to his maternal grandfather. It had been his legacy from their mother, Theodora, when she died. As he slipped the watch into his vest pocket and expertly swagged the chain across to the opposite side, he shook his head and met Burke's stare straight on.

"I'm not kiddin' at all. I've never been more serious about anything in my life. Not when I know what this will mean to Daddy, to you—and how it will affect the rest of my life." He nodded in Burke's direction and snapped the top of his satchel closed.

A Nergo child of no more than twelve paused in the hallway bearing a pitcher of fresh water. Hesitant, he made no move to enter. When Dake looked his way, the boy asked, "You need water, Marse Dake?"

"No thank you, Jeb."

The child turned and continued down the hall, his hands carefully wrapped around the heavy pitcher handle, intent on his duty.

Hands clenched at his sides, looking as if he might physically force Dake to stay if he had to, his brother took a step into the room. Eye to eye, the two were almost identical; the same size, the same build—broad-shouldered, narrow at the hips—possessed of the same dark hair and green eyes. Fate had decreed Burke the oldest, the one to run Riverglen and inherit all that privileged responsibility entailed. Both brothers had learned the inner workings of the plantation, about the finances, and how to farm the rich Tennessee River bottomland. They knew the value of the labor force they owned, the cotton gin, the mill by the river, which acres to cultivate and which should lie fallow.

But while Burke had concentrated solely on Riverglen, a virtual world of its own, their father had groomed Dake to a life in politics. Educated in Montgomery, he'd accompanied his father, Hollis Reed, to more sessions of the Alabama legislature than he cared to count. "You'll be a senator one day, son." His father had been promising that to Dake since he had been old enough to walk. "You'll make us all proud."

Dake made an attempt to leave the room. The sadness in his brother's eyes stopped him momentarily.

"Think this over, Dake. Don't walk out of here hotheaded and make a mistake that you'll pay for for the rest of your life."

"I have thought it over. More than you'll ever know, but I don't see as how there's any other choice." He memorized his brother's features, hair, eyes, jaw. They might have been twins, they were so alike.

"This'll kill Daddy," Burke warned, successfully blocking his way.

"I doubt it. It'll take a lot more than this to kill that old man." It hurt too much to think about his father, not when fighting for the Union might mean he would never see him again. Dake shook his head, hoping his exit wouldn't lead to a fistfight.

"You still see us losin' the war to the damn Yankees?"

He knew it was a waste of breath to try to talk sense to Burke, but Dake knew it was his last chance to explain. "The South is going to lose more than the war. This secession will destroy everything we have before it's over."

"Are you so damn sure?"

"If this goes on too long the South will be bled dry. All the industry is in the North. If it comes to a standoff, they'll starve you out. You should have listened to me before when I warned you of this. Hell, Alabama wouldn't even be seceding if it wasn't for the power and vote in Montgomery being in the hands of the planters. The majority of this county is against it."

Burke finally raised his voice in anger. "I'm tired of your high-blown traitorous talk and your plan for sellin' off our people and settin' them free. Where are they supposed to go? And if they do go, is the Union going to pay us recompense for our losses? Hell, no."

His voice low, direct, unruffled, Dake tried one more time. Even as he spoke he knew he was wasting his breath. "Everything we own depends on the fortune we have tied up in those slaves. The same goes for every other slave-holding planter in the South. When the Yankees win, and they will, the slaves will be set free and you'll be left holding a lot of worthless paper. If you and Daddy had done what I suggested and started selling off or even freeing some of the older hands years ago, if you'd begun to *hire* labor and invested the capital instead, then this place would be solvent when the war is over."

Burke refused to back down. "You think I plan to sit by and let the Union take our people and land away? You think anybody else around here is gonna be content to do that? If so, guess again, *brother*."

The irony of it all was that Dake had hated the notion of owning slaves since he'd been old enough to realize what that meant, and now, the war offered him a chance to do something about abolishing the system, something more than preaching what his own family considered a form of blasphemy. But his choice might cause him a separation from his family as permanent as death.

"It's too late for any more talkin', Burke. Tell Daddy good-bye for me." Dake moved toward the door again, sidesteppping his brother, careful not to make contact as he brushed by. The pain would be far too great.

Burke put out his hand, grabbed Dake's forearm, and stopped him with his touch. "And if we should meet face-to-face on the battlefield?"

Their eyes met. Gazes locked. "You'll do what you have to do, just as you've always done," Dake told him. "And so will I."

Clutching his valise a bit too tightly for a man who was at ease with the decision to walk away from his life, Dake stepped out into the hallway.

One of the housemaids became suddenly intent on polishing a nonexistent spot on the glossy finish of a side table in the hall. Her huge, dark eyes flashed as she watched him stride by. Dake recognized her as a girl named Francie, one of the many slaves who'd been born and raised at Riverglen. She was part of the silent, well-trained army of house slaves like Elijah that his mother had personally selected to serve the family. Adept at moving through the house, the corps was ever present, observing without being observed, speaking only when spoken to. Francie and the others like her kept the place running smoothly.

Dake often wondered what they really thought, this staff of people who were so integral a part of their lives, people who moved among them and yet remained separated from them by lines as permanently drawn as the line between North and South. Lines of color. Lines of blood.

Dake heard his brother's booted footsteps pounding the carpet runner as he hurried down the stairs behind him. "Are you too big a coward to stay and tell Daddy you've gone over to the Yankees? He'll be home in a few days."

In a few days it would be too late. His father was in Montgomery, as usual, and Dake wouldn't wait for Hollis Reed's return. Not when he knew the man would do everything in his power to persuade him to change his mind. He wouldn't put it past his father to have him locked in chains to keep him at home.

"Think what you want," Dake called out over his shoulder as he reached out for the front doorknob.

His brother's parting words echoed down the stairwell. The

echo reverberated over and over in Dake's heart. "Get out, then, and don't come back."

"Get up."

Cara stood over Dake Reed and nudged him awake with her toe and then watched as his gaze trailed up the length of her skirt until their eyes met. "Time to get up, Reed. It's daylight."

"Are you always this cheerful in the morning?"

"Anybody who got as little sleep as I did last night would be a touch grumpy." She didn't budge until he eased away from the cold, earthen wall and stood up. He finger-combed his hair with both hands and looked around.

"Where's my hat?"

She pointed to the peg driven into the wall near the window. "Right where you left it. Are you going someplace?"

"I'm going to wash up. The inside of my mouth tastes like a platoon of mules tramped through it."

Even though she was bone-tired from the near sleepless night, Cara couldn't help but smile and shake her head at his colorful description. She turned back to the dry sink where she was mixing cornmeal mush and warned, "Don't be long. I need to leave for the neighbors'."

His footsteps were muted by the hard-packed dirt floor, but even so, the warmth that emanated from him let her know when he was standing right behind her.

"Where's the stream?" he asked softly.

Cara turned around and watched as his gaze was immediately attracted to her lips. Her grip tightened on the wooden spoon she'd pulled from the big, dented pot. Finally she managed to tell him, "It's out behind the house a few yards to the southeast."

When he'd cleared the doorway, Cara relaxed, thankful that he had not yet pressed her for a decision, wondering at the strange turn her life had suddenly taken. Until yesterday she had battled unrelenting loneliness. Now here she was fixing breakfast after having spent the night alone with a stranger as if it were the most natural thing in the world.

In a little while she would have to tell him if she would go with him and care for the baby or set out on her own. What would it be like to spend days, even weeks in this man's company? It was hard to deny he was handsome. It would be ridiculous to try to convince herself that she was immune to him.

As she stirred the mush, Cara reminded herself to be careful. Was this the way her father had sneaked into her mother's life? Into her heart? Everett James had a head full of dreams and a handsome face when her mother met him. Neither attribute put food on the table. Cara had seen her mother wither away after her father died, and having witnessed that, she promised herself never to put a man before her own dreams.

Cara lifted the big pot by the handle and carried it outside where she hung it on the turnspit over the fire. A few coals still glowed in the embers. Thankful for that at least, she stirred the coals, stacked more kindling, and when it caught fire, added lighter pieces of wood on top.

Back in the dugout, as she set bowls on the table, she noticed an envelope protruding from the pocket of the buckskin jacket Dake Reed had left hanging over the back of one of the chairs.

She glanced over her shoulder at the infant who was still sleeping soundly on the bed, then toward the blanket that hung in the open doorway. "Curiosity killed the cat," she whispered, and Nanny James always told her she had more than her share of it.

She crossed her arms and tapped her toe. It wouldn't be right to read someone's mail.

She walked to the dry sink and finished mixing the mush.

It would be stupid to even touch his letter when he might come back at any minute and catch her at it.

She gave the pot another stir and glanced over her shoulder. The baby was still sound asleep. The letter was still poking out of the pocket.

In a flash she had the envelope in her hand. Quickly she withdrew the letter inside. The handwriting was beautiful, each letter perfectly formed, curlicued, and flowery. Her eyes darted to the signature at the bottom.

Minna.

Cara scanned the page. *Come home. Your daddy died. No way to pay the taxes. Burke. He hasn't been the same since the war.* As she stood with the letter in her hand, her heart went out to Dake Reed. All he had said was, *"I'm going home to see what I can do to help."* Had he explained the situation to her, had he communicated one tenth of the desperation expressed in the letter she held in her hand, she would have been hard-pressed to deny him.

Cara glanced at the door. The terse, melancholy message made the invasion of privacy that much worse, but knowing the facts helped her to make up her mind. No matter how hostile a reception he might face, Dake Reed was the kind of man who was going home in answer to a call for help. On top of that, he was a man who was determined to keep a pledge to a dying woman and take her baby home. He deserved her help.

Cara slipped the letter back into the envelope, carefully replaced it in his coat pocket, then hurried about her tasks, impatient for him to return. The sooner they got started, the sooner Dake Reed would be home and she could finally be on her way to California.

He was back before the mush was cooked, his dark stubble still in evidence, but his eyes clearer and more alert after a dunk in the stream. It was hard to keep her gaze from straying to the mat of crisp dark hair that covered his bare chest.

"Is there someplace I can hang my shirt until it dries?"

She forced herself to keep her eyes on the mush pot. "Hang it against the front of the house. High enough so Lucy doesn't have it for breakfast."

As he walked away, she chanced a glance over her shoulder and was arrested by the sight of him as he moved across the yard. His upper body was well defined, but there was no excess bulk about him. Rock hard, his bare back and shoulders provided a splendid display of muscle. She watched while he carefully spread the shirt between two of the various pegs and nails driven into the front of the cabin.

He turned before she expected and caught her standing there in the open doorway watching his every move. Cara whipped her head around but couldn't hide the blush that stained her cheeks. She went inside and back to her tasks.

Dake Reed moved up behind her without a word. She could feel him standing over her, watching her work. She felt like squirming under his scrutiny and almost shooed him away, directing him to see about the baby when he announced, "Sometime during the night I recalled I've got some real coffee in my saddlebags."

Without waiting for her to comment, he went to collect it. He moved with an easy, confident stride. Having read the letter, she now knew why his smiles were so rare. Cara wished she could express her sympathy, but to do so would only lead to an admission of guilt.

He returned quickly and put the bag of precious coffee beans in her hand, then walked over to the bed and leaned down to study the child nearly hidden in the pile of bedding. With strong, lean fingers, Dake reached out and gently ran his hand back and forth over the baby's fine tawny curls.

Cara was hard-pressed to ignore the fact that the sight evoked a honeyed warmth deep inside her.

Dake met her gaze across the room and asked in a hushed

voice, "Hard to believe somebody so small could put up such a ruckus, isn't it?"

It was a moment before she could dismiss the suspiciously tender feeling that warmed her heart. "It sure is." She took a deep breath and added, "Mr. Reed, I've come to a decision. I'll take you up on your offer and help you take little Clayton home."

A blind man couldn't have missed the relief that crossed his face. "I'll make it worth your while, Cara." He was watching her intently once more. Too intently. "You won't regret it."

Clayton started fussing, squirming, and mewling, about to burst into the earsplitting wails of last night. As if voicing her decision had marked the beginning of her duty, Cara crossed over to the bed and gently lifted him into her arms. "The mush is probably ready and there's plenty of other food around here to hold you until I get back from the Dicksons. You think you two will be all right while I'm gone?"

"I think I can manage for a while."

"I'll hurry, but sometimes you just can't rush business matters. If I know ol' Mr. Dickson, it'll take him a while to recall where he buried the money he offered to pay me for the place. When I was a girl that's all his kids would talk about—how much money he had buried in cans around the house. Willie and I were always going to go treasure hunting—"

"I hate to interrupt, but don't you think you should get going?"

"I do. I truly do believe I should get going." She looked around, surveying the room. "I hope you can find everything you need to make the crate for the dolls," Cara looked at Dake again and frowned. For no apparent reason, there was a smile on his face. "What are you smiling at?"

"You, Cara."

"Why?"

"I don't think I've ever met anyone quite like you," he told her with a shake of his head.

Wondering if she should take the statement as a compliment or not, Cara shrugged and pushed her hair back out of her eyes. "Nanny James always said I was one of a kind."

She hoped she was successful at hiding the blush that stained her cheeks when she passed the infant to him. Cara felt the warmth of Dake's skin when their fingers met on the swaddled bundle.

"I'll be back as soon as I can." She walked to the door and he followed her outside. "Is there anything I should know about your horse?"

"His name's General Sherman and he has a mind of his own."

Four hours later, Dake stood in the middle of the yard, wondering what in the hell was keeping her.

She'd left him with a pile of folded rags to use for diapers, a pot of coffee, more goat's milk, and a slab of smoked bacon. The last he had seen of her, Cara was still barefooted, wearing the same tattered yellow gown, her ankles and shapely calves showing more leg then he thought proper as she rode northeast toward the Dickson homestead.

He paced the front yard avoiding for the hundredth time the broken chair, the splintered wheel, the scattered, empty cans. He kept the fire burning low, the coffee warm, and stifled the urge to stack the refuse in the yard into neat piles and rake the ground clean.

Where is she?

He scanned the horizon again. After squinting into the lowering sun, he berated himself for having allowed her to travel alone. With the cloud formations against the blue sky, the still-warm October weather reminded him too much of yesterday afternoon when he'd come upon Anna Clayton's wagon. He closed his eyes against the sun and willed himself not to envision Cara James, her hair a wild blond halo against the dry grass as she lay crumpled on the ground dying in her own blood.

He headed back inside. The crate was finished. He thought it the sturdiest of her various barrels and boxes that were lined up by the door—even if he had put it together from scrap wood. He had gone so far as to pack one of the dolls inside, then decided he had better let Cara do it the way she wanted. Instead of packing, he took little Clayton off to the creek where he changed the baby's diaper and washed out the dirty ones.

Dirty, wrinkled clothes were something he couldn't abide. A soldier would be reprimanded for looking so unkempt. One reason army life had always suited him so well was that it was regimented, predictable, and orderly—demands he'd adapted to easily and so rose quickly through the ranks until he'd made captain early in the war. He looked down at his wrinkled shirtfront, at the puckered material of his sleeves, and thought about rifling through Cara's belongings in search of a flat iron. Dake glanced over at the baby who was sleeping peacefully for the moment and headed toward Cara's crates and barrels.

One contained the fabric pieces she used for the dolls, many of which she'd already sacrificed for diapers. Near the top of the second crate were two folded day dresses. He pulled out the first, a much mended pastel blue cotton with a torn lace ruffle at the elbow-length sleeves. Another of pale peach wool was in as miserable a condition as the first.

The house slaves at Riverglen wore better. The duty of clothing them had naturally fallen to the mistress of the plantation. His mother had toiled long hours over various sized patterns and cloth, overseeing and very often stitching together the many pieces needed to outfit the hundred twenty slaves who inhabited the quarters. Not only did his mother issue clothes, but shoes and daily household stores as well. When she died, their head housekeeper had taken over the many tasks. More than once he'd heard her comment that she didn't know how Miz Reed had managed it all.

Dake looked down at the worn material of the unadorned dresses he held clenched in his hands and then at the few thin muslin undergarments piled beneath them. The simple act of holding Cara James's pitiful clothing suddenly struck him as too intimate an invasion of her privacy. A flash of wild blond ringlets and sun-tinted cheeks flashed in his mind. Dake felt his loins quicken and tried to deny it with a shake of his head. The current of emotion surprised him.

There was nothing about Cara James that usually attracted him to a woman. He favored short, buxom brunettes as a rule and he'd never been the type to fall for anything in skirts just to fulfill his physical needs. He was as particular in his choice of women as he was in his own clothes, meals, and surroundings. He valued order, not chaos—which was one reason he felt compelled to join the Union. War was the ultimate disruption of lives, and certain of its outcome, he felt it his duty to do everything he could to speed the war to its conclusion.

He knew war had changed him, that much was inevitable. A position in Southern politics was out of the question now. He refused to return the conquering hero. Reenlistment was an option. Army life had been regimented and orderly. He had taken to it like a duck to water and advanced quickly through the ranks.

Nothing about Cara Calvinia James or the way she lived was orderly.

Or, evidently, punctual.

Besides, this was no time to nurture tender feelings for anyone, let alone the slip of a girl whose only connection to him was the care and feeding of the orphan sleeping on the bed across the room.

Hoofbeats and the rumble of a wagon alerted him to an

approaching rider. Dake shoved the gowns back into the crate, pulled on the lid, and then headed for the door, forgetting to button up his shirt. Dake knew if he lived to be one hundred he would never forget the sight that met his eyes when he stepped out of the dugout.

Cara Calvinia James sat on the high-sprung seat of a wagon that looked like a rolling box with a front and back seat and very little room between. General Sherman had been harnessed between rod shafts, tossing his head in anger, pulling with an uneven gait as Cara wrestled the reins and fought him every step of the way.

"I bought a wagon!" she called out as the high rolling box swayed and thundered into the yard.

For a moment Dake thought he would have to jump aboard to stop the careening vehicle, but Cara came up out of the seat, leaned back, and used all her weight to pull the reins back and stop the General's final show of defiance.

Crossing the yard at a trot, Dake stopped beside the wagon and waited for Cara to tie up the reins. Minimal handiwork with her hairbrush that morning had been destroyed by the wind, but he begrudgingly had to admit to himself that Cara James glowed with a natural, radiant loveliness her ragged clothes and sun-stained cheeks could not hide. The ever-present breeze rippled her thin dress against her thighs. He found his gaze lingering there before it slid up to her breasts. When he looked up, he found her watching him intently with wide blue eyes.

"What took you so long?" The words came out sharper than he intended. He reached up to help her down.

She leaned down and put her hands on his shoulders when he grasped her waist. Dake lifted her, but took his time setting her on the ground. She made no attempt to move away from his touch. He felt his blood rise, his manhood throb.

His question went unanswered while Cara tried to concentrate on the words, but it was difficult with the blood rushing in her ears and her heart pounding louder than the prairie winds in a storm. She was shocked at the inexplicable feeling that standing so close to him had ignited. For a brief moment, she stood stock-still, trying to reason it out.

Standing this close to Hooter Dickson had never caused such a riotous heat to pulse through her. She could feel her cheeks burning so intensely she almost reached up to touch them. There was a catch in her breath she couldn't hide.

Cara tried to concentrate on his greeting. No hello. No—did you sell the place? Not even—did you have a good time? He sounded almost angry, but he didn't move away. Instead, he seemed compelled to remain mere inches from her. Cara had to tip her head up to meet his eyes as he towered over her.

"Things took longer than I thought." She dropped her eyes and immediately regretted it. He had yet to button his shirt.

She snapped her gaze back up and met the all too disturbing eyes outlined by a dark, heavy fringe of lashes that any woman would envy. Setting her sights on his mouth instead, she noticed he had shaved. His skin was tanned from hours outside, smooth yet possessed of a masculine hardness beneath. It tempted her to reach up and run her fingers across his jaw. Crinkles radiated from the corner of his eyes, yet she had rarely seen him smile.

He was still waiting for further explanation, so she went on. "You can't hurry a visit. Mrs. Dickson had me set a spell and eat, then there was a real fuss over me selling out. Then I asked her about taking care of babies and she told me a bit about it, almost more than I could hold on to all at once. Then Hooter wanted me to walk out with him and I was hard put to talk him out of insisting I marry him."

"Who's Hooter?"

"Hooter Dickson. Second eldest."

"He asked you to marry him?"

He seemed so surprised that anyone would offer that she drew herself up straight and assured him, "He did."

"But you said no?"

"I did."

"Why?"

"Do you think I should have said yes?"

"No. No, it's just that another woman in your position might be tempted to—"

"You think having some man to take care of me is all I need? I don't care if I have to live by myself until I'm a hundred years old, Mr. Reed, but I intend to do it in California where the weather is warm and the living is easy. Besides, Hooter Dickson has sweaty hands, half a head of teeth, and he's not only a fool, he's a damned farmer. I don't cotton to either."

Dake laughed outright, surprising her. When he had calmed down he asked, "So you sold the place?"

She grinned, feeling like a cat in the cream. "I did. Got a fair price, too. One dollar fifty an acre. And I even talked them into selling me this wagon. I got to thinking about it this morning on my way over and I didn't know how we were going to manage with the baby and all my boxes and only one horse and a goat and the busted-up buckboard in the field."

Dake began buttoning up his shirtfront and ramming it into the waistband of his trousers. An inch of hem stuck out around the top of his pants. "I was hoping you would store them here until you could send for them or passed close by on your way west. Do you really think we can fit all those boxes of yours into a jump-seat wagon, not to mention the baby and that goat?"

As if the animal understood, Lucy danced over to them and began to tug on Dake's shirt hem with her teeth. He swatted at the shaggy bearded goat and was rewarded with a butt to the thigh.

"It'll all fit," Cara assured him.

"I hope you didn't pay too much for that . . . wagon."

Cara took immediate offense to his comment. "You don't have to worry about it, Mr. Reed. This wagon's mine and I intend to keep it and there's no way I'm leaving my things behind. If I go, it all goes."

"We'll only need the wagon until we get to the Mississippi. From there we'll be taking a steamboat down to Memphis and a train into Decatur, if there's one up and running yet."

Disappointed, some of the joy of her new purchase left her. "Oh. Well, I didn't know that was your plan." She looked over his shoulder, toward the house.

As if he knew that he had embarrassed her, Dake said, "The wagon wasn't such a bad idea, I guess." He began to stride around the deteriorating wagon with his hands in his back pockets, inspecting the wheels, the brakes, the weathered side walls of the box. "It'll do just fine. When we get to the river, you'll get back every cent you paid for it."

She brightened again immediately. "Oh, I almost forgot." She reached for a small bundle beneath the seat. "Mrs. Dickson gave me an India rubber nipple and a bottle to use for the baby. She told me when to feed him and how to burp him and said in a while he could eat oatmeal mush if it was watery enough."

"You trust her?"

"She's got eight kids still living."

"Are they all as attractive as Hooter?"

She changed the subject. "How's Clayton?"

"Fine. I took him with me to the creek and washed him, laid him on the quilt and let him sleep in the shade. He quits complaining so much after he eats."

"His stomach's probably getting used to the goat's milk. You're supposed to pat his back until he burps."

"How was I supposed to know that?" He sounded defensive.

"Well, now you do. What are you being so testy about, Mr. Reed? Hungry again?"

Dake sighed and rested one foot on the spoke of a wheel. "I'm not used to waiting around like this, Cara. I'm not used to playing nursemaid and I'm not used to getting—"

He paused so abruptly that she thought she had missed the rest of his sentence. "Used to getting what?"

As he turned away, heading back toward the dugout, she heard him grudgingly admit, "Worried. I'm not used to having to worry about someone."

She hurried along behind him. "You were worried about *me*?" She could have sworn he was blushing, but Dake went on as if she hadn't asked.

"How long do you think it will take you to pack up?" He wanted to know.

"Not long."

"That's what you said about going to the Dicksons'," he reminded her.

"But this time I've got you right here to see that I don't dawdle."

*You never really know somebody
until you have to live with them.*
Nanny James

Chapter Three

After a week on the road, Dake felt like a gypsy driving a
damn caravan.

He shifted the reins and General Sherman balked just as he
had every time a command was issued. Obviously his horse
was just as put out as he was by the battered little wagon the
Dickson family had sold Cara. At one time the vehicle had
been painted a gay yellow, but exposed too long to the
elements, the paint had chipped and peeled until now the
wagon looked like a faded sunflower rolling along between
acres of blue sky and dried grass. He was surprised the word
"MILK" hadn't been painted on the side.

Cara and little Clayton occupied the front seat with him. The
wagon bed and seat behind them were covered floor to roof with
the boxes and barrels that contained Cara's possessions. He had
complained loud and long as he loaded them. She had insisted
there wasn't all that much and that he should be happy that her
entire life could be packed into six boxes and two barrels.

Before they had left the James homestead behind, Dake
realized that he would have to call upon every ounce of
discipline he possessed while they journeyed to Alabama. The
afternoon of their departure, it had taken Cara a while to speak
her good-byes over the graves beneath the huge walnut tree. He
had tried not to begrudge her the time because he knew what
it was like to leave one's world behind forever. Still, he was a

man used to routine. His life in the army had been built upon punctuality and discipline. He had planned to leave as soon as he could pack the wagon, that was until Cara announced she still had to "pack a few last minute things."

Cara James moved to the march of her own drumbeat—which seemed to beat slowly. She had delayed their departure by three hours. Each time he had asked about loading one of the boxes, she had informed him she had "one more little thing to put in." He hadn't lost his composure until she had laughed at his demand that she hurry. He could still recall the way she planted her hands on her hips, shook her head and said, "Calm down, Mr. Reed. We don't really have to be any place at a certain time tonight, anyway, do we? So why should we worry about time?"

"That's exactly your problem, Miss James," he had said.

"My problem?"

She had looked so amazed to hear that she had a problem at all that Dake tried to put it as carefully as he could.

"You have no concept of time." He then reached into his watch pocket and pulled a timepiece etched with delicate scrollwork out of his Levi's. With one hand on the reins, he pressed the spring on the watch and the lid popped open.

"Time, Miss James, keeps everything in order. If you were more aware of time, you wouldn't have wasted all morning at the Dicksons'. We would have been on the road by now."

He had wanted to point out that if she could keep time, she wouldn't be forever burning food. That with a little punctuality in her life, she would have enough hours in the day to get all her chores done and the place might have been livable. He wanted to warn her that if she truly meant to establish a thriving business, she would have to become more aware of time.

Those were the things he would have said had he not paused in the midst of his lecture to notice her staring up at him with her big blue eyes as she smiled all too sunny a smile, and he realized instantly that she was only nodding and listening to humor him.

The rest of the week had passed without incident. Even Miss Lucy seemed to be cooperating as she trailed along behind the wagon, forcing Dake to keep the General at a slow trot. If Clay hadn't been dependent on the goat's milk, Dake would have helped the ill-tempered animal chew through the rope and escape without notice. Not only did the goat slow their progress, but she insisted on trying to knock Dake over every time he went near the back of the wagon.

He cast a sidelong glance at Cara and watched her unconsciously lift the child in her arms each time the wagon bounced over a rut in the road. She held Clay for hours without complaint, turning her attention instead on the surrounding countryside, commenting on the wild onion beds and melon patches they passed. She speculated on how the fruit had no doubt sprung from seeds of the melons that passing Indians had stolen from her garden.

Dake believed her when she said she hadn't been farther than a few miles from the dugout in years. Everything was new and exciting to her. No one could feign the cheerful enthusiasm which she had shown thus far.

He glanced over at her and watched as she shifted Clay to her shoulder, peering around the wide brim of the poke bonnet she donned the day they left the dugout. Dake could see the hat had done little to keep the sun from tinting the end of her pert nose.

"How far are we from Poplar Bluff? Think we'll make it tonight?" she asked.

"If we don't see it within a few minutes of sundown, we'll have to camp again." He could tell she was disappointed but unwilling to show it. Her resilience amazed him. After a week on the trail, he knew why she had thrived where the rest of her family could not. Nothing seemed to get the girl down, not chilly nights sleeping on the hard ground beneath the wagon, hours of jolting and rocking over rutted trails, nor the weight of the child in her arms.

As much as he wanted to hurry homeward, he felt they could all use a good night's sleep in real beds and the comforts of a stop in town. Their halts along the way had been few and far between. Most times they merely rested for an hour or two during a visit at an isolated farm. The women homesteaders were always more than eager to entertain visitors. Along with a warm welcome, the pioneer women shared child-raising hints, cooed over Clay, and always sent them off with baked goods or produce, whichever they could spare.

Most of the settlers they encountered had little, but insisted on sharing in exchange for company. In turn, Cara gave dolls to the children they met and watched to see which of them quickly became the favorite. Oftentimes she asked for ideas and even played dolls with them for a while.

She prepared the wild game or fish, milked the goat, fed the baby, washed out diapers and even volunteered to keep watch so that he could steal a few hours' sleep. And she did it all without complaint. Dake tried to think of any other woman he had ever known who would have had the stamina to accomplish all Cara did and still be able to smile. He slowly came to admit that he admired her spunk.

The sound of her voice interrupted his thoughts. "What's that, do you suppose?"

He squinted to see what lay on the horizon. Often the woods appeared as a mirage as they traveled from wood to wood toward the prairie's end. "Could be Poplar Bluff. We'll know in a bit."

Dake flicked the reins, urging General Sherman on. He felt as embarrassed as the well-bred gelding must have been to be seen rigged up to such a contraption. "It'll be good to sleep in a real bed again."

Cara glanced sharply at him.

Dake felt her watching him intently but kept his eyes on the trail.

There was no denying the awkwardness between them

brought on by the intimacies of everyday life on the trail. By firelight, they had feasted on quail and trout. By daylight they shared the enjoyment of a whippoorwill's song and exchanged somewhat amiable conversation. By night Cara slept with little Clay on a pallet beneath the wagon while Dake kept watch over them, tended the fire, and bedded down with his Starr .44 on his hip and his Springfield rifle close beside him.

But now, as the civilization loomed before them, they fell silent. Finally Cara asked, "Can we stay long enough for me to shop? There are a few things I need before we go on."

Dake thought of the boxes crowded into the back of the wagon. "We've got time, but not a lot of room."

"I need to buy a dress and a new coat." Then, as an afterthought, "I probably won't need the coat in California."

He glanced over at the thin woolen shawl she wore over her shoulders. "Did you decide to let go of a little of that homestead profit?" He didn't know where she carried her money, but he guessed it was somewhere on her person.

She shrugged. "My clothes aren't much to speak of, I guess," she told him, brushing at the skirt of the peach dress that had replaced the yellow rag she had worn the day he met her. Again, like the first, this one hit her just above the ankles. As yet she'd refused to wear shoes, even though the weather had turned chilly. When he had warned her about snakes, she'd insisted she'd lived ten years with them under the floorboards of the dugout and she hadn't been bitten yet.

Not wishing to call attention to her outfit's shortcomings, he told her, "That one's a nice color."

"It's faded. Besides, I've never had a new dress of my own. Just my mother's cut down."

They rode in silence again until the buildings that lined the main street of Poplar Bluff grew recognizable. Cara shifted again, the hard wagon seat a constant irritation.

She wondered what it would be like to linger long enough to

walk the streets of a real town, to see more than ten people who weren't Dicksons in one place. To savor the sights and sounds and smells of civilization. Her childhood in the East was but a dim memory. Oswego, the closest settlement to the homestead, was little more than a few boards tossed together, buildings that had appeared worn by wind and sun before they were a week old. She could hardly wait to see what a real town was like.

As if he could sense her anticipation, Clay began to squirm and fuss. Cara jiggled him up and down in her arms and whispered softly to him, telling him about the approaching town and the sights they would see. She glanced over at Dake. His attention was devoted to the road, but she could tell his thoughts were far away.

She had never known a man to think so hard or keep silent for so long. In all the time they had been traveling, he spoke little and shared nothing about himself. She wondered if he was always so introspective or just silently speculating on what kind of a reception he would receive in Alabama. Not once did he mention his brother or the woman named Minna who had appealed to him to come home.

Before they rode into Poplar Bluff, Cara insisted they stop so that she could unpack her shoes. Dake waited, shifting from foot to foot, jostling Clay up and down as he tried to keep the fussy baby from protesting too loudly.

"Did you find them?" Dake glanced over at Cara and found her tossing items right and left as she rummaged for her shoes.

Her voice was muffled. "One. I thought I had them both."

He watched for a moment, intrigued by the idea that the girl *thought* she had both shoes.

"Found it!" She held the prize aloft and then blew at a wayward strand of curls that caught in her eyelashes. "It'll just be a minute now." Gathering up other pieces of her clothing, she wadded them up and shoved them back into the crate.

Dake winced.

Then, without bothering to put on any stockings, she sat on the edge of the wagon, hiked up her skirts as if showing him a good length of leg didn't matter in the least, and began to slip on her shoe.

For modesty's sake, Dake looked away, but slowly, surreptitiously—modesty be damned—he looked again. Her legs were firm, shapely, tempting.

"Damn!" he muttered under his breath and turned around. Did she think he was a monk? After a week of intimate travel accommodations, he couldn't help but notice everything Cara James did. More to the point, he noticed every move of her tantalizing little body.

Clay's halfhearted cries turned into wails as Dake watched Cara struggle with her shoes. Finally, driven by impatience and the fact that he didn't know how long he could take watching her teeter there on the edge of the wagon with her skirt nearly up to her thighs, he marched over and stood beside her.

"Here," he said, offering her Clay. "Give me your shoe."

She handed over the shoe in exchange for the baby.

Once Dake's arms were free, he reached up and jerked the hem of her skirt down as far as it would go. "Hold out your foot."

She lifted her leg and he grasped her ankle intending to shove on her shoe and be done with it. Her skin was surprisingly smooth beneath his palm. His fingertips brushed her ankle bone and slowly slid down to her arch. She made no move to pull her foot out of his grasp.

He looked up and met her eyes. She was staring down at him, her lips slightly parted. The baby, as if aware of the electric charge between them, had stopped crying.

He cleared his throat. "Don't you want to put on stockings?"

She licked her lips. "I don't have any."

"Oh."

"You're squeezing my foot."

He eased up and looked down, forcing himself to concentrate on slipping her shoe on. She had already unlaced it, which should have made his task easier, but by the time he pressed it over her toes, slid it up past her arch and slapped the heel in place, he realized he was rock hard.

This time he didn't dare meet her eyes. Dake kept his gaze on her foot and raised his hand. "Give me the other one."

The second shoe didn't go on any easier than the first. Finally, the task finished, he decided she could damn well lace up her own shoes. Still, he wasn't composed enough to step away from the wagon just yet.

"I'll take Clay. You can lace them up."

She handed him the baby. He let the edge of the quilt fall over the front of his pants.

Cara stepped down off the wagon. He nearly jumped out of his skin when she touched his sleeve.

"Are you all right?"

He cleared his throat again. "Sure. Why?"

"You look funny is all. Are you feeling weak?"

Stepping away from her, he looked down at Clay and mumbled, "I wish." He dared a glance and found her watching him with deep concern. "I'm all right."

"What do you think?" She drew her skirt back and stared down at her shoes, extending her right foot and prettily pointing the toe of her shoe this way and that. "I love them, but I hate wearing them. That's why they still look so new. They pinch my feet something awful. Willie bought them for me when he went into town last spring."

They were the ugliest shoes Dake had ever laid eyes on. He knew Minna would not be buried in them, but he wasn't about to tell Cara how unfeminine they were. Heavy and black, they were fit for an old woman or a spinster, not someone as young and full of life as Cara James. The fact that she was thrilled with the hideous shoes said much about her isolated experience on the prairie. Dake tucked the information in the back of his mind.

"Are you ready now?" He thought perhaps she would like to wash her face or comb her hair before they went into town. Instead, she merely nodded, her excitement more than evident in the glowing smile shaded by her deep brimmed sunbonnet.

"Let's go."

Dake held Clay while Cara boarded the wagon again and then carefully handed the baby up to her. He climbed aboard and took up the reins again. In less than half an hour they reached the outskirts of Poplar Bluff on the fringe of the Ozark highlands just above the Black River.

Main Street followed a ridge that was part of the bluff that gave the place its name. Dake guided the wagon down the street, out of habit studying the layout of the place as well as the people on the street. The town showed signs of abandonment, a boarded-up building here, a broken window there. Signs of guerrilla warfare that had nearly devastated sections of Missouri during the war were evident in the scarcity of people moving about the near-deserted town.

Cara intently took in everything at once. She cheerfully smiled and nodded in greeting at a man and his wife who passed them going the opposite direction in a buckboard wagon. A storefront caught her attention, nothing fancy by anyone's standards, but it was enough to turn her head as they passed. Two buildings down, three men stumbled out of the front of a ramshackle saloon. Bearded, dressed in various pieces of the familiar gray wool of Confederate uniforms, the trio's surly attitude put Dake instantly on the alert.

Displaced rebels with nowhere to go and nothing to do but cause trouble, the men were typical of the former enlisted men of both sides he'd dealt with at Fort Dodge. Seeing them, he couldn't help but wonder how deep the bitterness of loss ran in his brother. When one of the men took a hearty swig from a bottle of whiskey, backhanded his lips and then leered over at Cara, Dake snapped the reins and the wagon sped along Main Street.

He pulled up in front of a small hotel that stood on the square in the center of town. A hand-lettered sign that advertised clean beds, hot food, and rooms at two dollars and twenty-five cents hung outside the false-fronted, two-story wood structure. Dake tied the rig and helped Cara climb down. She pushed her sunbonnet back and let it hang by the ties around her neck while she tried to take in everything at once. They moved to the crooked boardwalk before the hotel where she glanced up at him, her expression doubtful.

"What's it cost to stay in a fancy place like this? It looks expensive."

From her point of view, it most likely did. Dake scanned the front of the shabby hotel and then looked down at his boots. They probably cost more than Cara James's father had made in a lifetime. He met her worried gaze. "I can afford it, Miss James. Now, are you coming?"

She didn't move. Instead, Cara shifted Clay to her shoulder. "I'll pay my own way."

"Consider this part of our travel expenses. Since I'm paying you to care for this child, I insist. You wouldn't be incurring the cost if you weren't working for me so don't worry about it."

Hurt registered in her eyes almost immediately. "That's all right, Mr. Reed. For a minute there I forgot I was only hired help." She stepped around him and led the way into the lobby.

Dake reached out to stop her before she could reach the door. "I'm sorry, Cara."

She turned her watery eyes to him and whispered, "I guess I'm tired, is all."

He stared down at her at a loss. She was so proud, so young and still so innocent in many ways. He was used to being in command. Issuing orders was second nature to him. The war had hardened his heart and honed his discipline. Dake reminded himself to go gently in the way he dealt with Cara from now on.

"Let's go in," he said softly.

She turned and headed for the door without a word.

The clerk behind the desk didn't look much older than seventeen. His hair was slicked down with rose-scented oil, his sleeves decorated with black garters. He ran his finger around the inside of his collar and cleared his throat when they entered the lobby.

"Welcome." The young man's voice cracked on the word. "Welcome to the Birds' Nest Hotel."

Dake looked around. There was a small dining area off the reception area, nothing fancy, but it was clean. A matronly woman with her hair parted down the middle and drawn severely into a bun at the nape of her neck bustled among the four empty tables crowded together in the dining alcove. She glanced up at them and smiled. She was curious enough to ignore the task of setting the cutlery out for the evening meal and watch them register.

"We have a nice room with a view of the street that you and your wife might like, mister," the boy volunteered.

Cara blushed scarlet.

Dake did nothing to change the youth's perception of their relationship. "We need two rooms, not one."

"Two rooms. Of course. We have two rooms with views. One looks west over the wide open spaces."

Cara nudged Dake while he was in the process of signing the register. When he didn't respond, she elbowed him again.

"What?" he said irritably, staring down at his smeared signature.

"I want the one that looks over the street," she whispered. "I've seen enough of wide-open spaces."

"Fine." Then, to the clerk he said, "We'll go on up and see the rooms before I bring in some of our things. Is there a livery nearby?"

"End of the street. Right side." The young man, who had spent more than a few minutes staring at Cara, handed Dake the keys. Stifling an urge to tell the clerk to keep his eyes in his head where they belonged, Dake stepped back and waited for Cara to walk toward the stairs in the corner. As she moved past him, Dake stepped up beside her and slipped his arm over her shoulders.

Cara stiffened beneath his touch.

Dake was as surprised as she by his move, but when he looked back at the young clerk, the boy was no longer studying Cara, but Dake's smeared signature in the logbook.

Their rooms were at the top of the stairs. Dake slipped the key into the lock of the first and let the door swing wide. Clutching Clay against her shoulder, Cara stepped inside.

"It's perfect," she sighed.

"It'll do." As the sign outside had promised, the bed was clean. So were the thin, faded blue curtains hanging at the windows. A rag rug and washstand completed the furnishings. He imagined his own room would look much the same. Cara laid Clay on the bed and then remained standing awkwardly in the center of the room. Dake glanced at the bed, the washstand, the window.

"I'm going to the livery to stable the General and Miss Lucy. When I get back, we'll go down to dinner."

He was almost out the door when he paused on the threshold. "Before I go, is there anything you need out of the wagon?"

Cara tapped her toe against the rag rug. "You know the small barrel just behind the front seat?"

He nodded. Of course he knew every crate and barrel intimately after jostling them back and forth, packing and unpacking morning and night.

"Well, my hairbrush is inside, near the top. And some"— she colored again and hesitated—"some small folded under-things. And you can bring up a stack of clean rags for diapers for Clay." He started to go. "Oh, and some canned milk and the bottle. I forgot it."

"All right." He started out again, then grabbed the door

frame. Poking his head around it he added offhandedly, "You might want to wash up before dinner." Then, because he knew it would be typical of her to lose track of time, he pulled out his watch, checked the time, and laid the open timepiece on the chest of drawers.

"I'll be back in about thirty minutes. No more, no less."

She crossed her arms. Her mouth formed a distinct pout. "I'll keep that in mind."

Before she had a chance to tell him what she thought of him giving her orders like a general, he closed the door. Cara refused to let Dake Reed get under her skin. Not when she was so anxious to enjoy herself. Dismissing him, she held out her arms and spun full circle, squelching the urge to dance around the room. It was a day of firsts; her first day in a town of any real size, her first stay in a real hotel—one with two stories no less—her first meal in a restaurant.

Not even Dake's suggestion that she wash could stifle her happiness just now. Recalling his admonition about time, she untied her hat and tossed it on the bed, then hurried over to the water pitcher on the washstand. Lifting the heavy vessel, she admired the hand-painted lilies of the valley on the side before she poured tepid water into the wide matching bowl. She rolled up her sleeves, soaped her hands, and began to work on the trail dust that stained her hands, face, and arms. She used a damp towel to mop off her neck and followed the square-cut neckline of her peach gown. By the time she was finished, the towel and the water were both stained brown.

While Clay slept peacefully for a change, she glanced over at the window to be certain no one could see her. There were no other two-story buildings nearby, so she raised her skirt and reached for the calico money bag she had fastened to the inside of her waistband. Carefully unpinning it, she walked over to the bed, opened the drawstrings, and spread the money over the coverlet. Tomorrow, before they left town, she was going to insist Dake allow her some time to shop. She counted out the cash she had received for the sale of the homestead, determined to spend every last penny carefully.

Cara took out enough to pay for dinner and the room, then slid the rest back into the bag and repinned it. Once it was hidden in the folds of her skirt, she felt easy again.

She walked over to the head of the bed, which stood near the window, and sat down gingerly so she wouldn't awaken Clay. A wagon rolled down Main Street and she watched it pass. There was nothing, she decided, better than a room with a good view. When she got to California, she would insist on a place overlooking the ocean.

"Are you sure there's no place I can buy a ready-made gown?"

Dake stood in the dry goods store staring at the few bolts of material on display. The stack of calicos and tartan plaids did him little good. The storekeeper merely stared as if Dake were asking for the moon.

Finally, the old man scratched his bald head. He looked Dake up and down, at the unworn leather of his boots, at his shirt, wrinkled but obviously new, at his expensive Stetson. "Where you been, mister? This place was nearly deserted during the war. Since the surrender, we're lucky to have anything in stock. There was a dressmaker in town, but when her husband was killed, she pulled out. Went to live with a widowed sister."

The war. What would have been considered everyday supplies at Fort Dodge—coffee, sugar, an Indian blanket for Clay—were still unavailable to the public. He had money to spend but there was little to buy.

"Got tobacco," the storekeep volunteered hopefully.

Neither chewing nor smoking was Dake's vice. He thanked the man and walked out.

The idea to buy Cara a dress had come to him out of necessity. After their discussion over expenses, he didn't know how the girl would react to such a personal gift, but if he was to spend twenty-four hours a day in her company, he wanted her covered from neck to ankle. Her peach gown was not only faded but fit far tighter than the yellow. Her ankles were exposed, her high, firm breasts, which proved to be surprisingly lush, were all too noticeably wedged into the too tight, square cut neckline. Seeing her in the peach gown without her shawl, he realized she was not as slight as he had first thought. The gown she wore when he met her must have been two sizes too large.

He almost groaned aloud when he remembered how he lost control at the sight of her long limbs and shapely thighs. Dake liked to think of himself as well-disciplined, but Cara James obviously had no notion of what showing off her legs did to a man.

He was no preacher. There was only so much a red-blooded man could ignore. The more he covered her up, the better it would be for both of them.

He found her waiting anxiously for him when he reached the hotel, so anxious that she nearly pulled the doorknob out of his hand after he knocked. The first thing he noticed was her clean face. He noticed too that the front of her gown was far more revealing than he remembered.

She blocked his entrance demanding, "Where have you been?" She held up the watch. "You're ten minutes late. After all that talk about time, I began to think you might have gotten yourself into trouble."

He shifted the articles she had requested from one arm to the other, sidestepped her, and walked toward the bed. Clay was awake. Dake set down the stack of diaper material and her brush with the missing bristles. He carefully set the bottle on top of the diapers before he answered. A can of milk rolled off the pile of cloths.

Dake reached out and took the watch from her and pocketed it without an excuse for his tardiness. "Are you ready to go down to supper?"

Cara reached out and picked up the hairbrush. "How much will it cost, do you think?"

Dake sat on the edge of the bed and played with Clay's toes to keep his mind off the front of her gown. "What did you say?"

She sighed. "The supper. How much will it cost, do you think?"

Dake shrugged. "I have no idea."

The brush tangled in Cara's curls, causing her to wince. She struggled to free the bristles. "Maybe you should find out. A fool and his money are soon parted, you know, and I don't intend to be parted with all of mine at once."

He stood up and moved to the rescue by taking the brush from her hands. He turned her away from him and pulled her within reach. Slowly, carefully, he tugged the entangled strands out of the boar bristles until she was free. The blond tendrils crackled with life and wrapped themselves around his hand. Unwillingly, he admitted he liked the feel of her silky hair as it brushed across his skin. The strands were drawn to his hand as if his flesh were a magnet.

"I'm paying for your supper, Miss James."

"I can take care of myself."

He knew she was probably counting on every penny of the homestead money to establish herself when their journey was through. He knew, too, that she had her pride. He had already hurt her when he all but called her a servant.

More gently he told her, "I didn't expect you to pay for expenses that come up while you're caring for Clay." She was still standing with her back to him. He grasped her shoulders and turned her around, forcing her to look up at him. Her eyes, so like the color of the Kansas sky, had the ability to hold him captive with their intensity. Shaken by her effect on him, Dake handed her the brush, balled his hands into fists, and hastily stepped away.

She watched him move, swept by an unbidden excitement that shook her to her toes. She was startled by the liquid warmth that had begun to melt inside her in an unthinkable place. Dake Reed's nearness definitely had a strange, undefinable power over her. Some mysterious force made her long to reach out and touch his dark hair, to press her cheek alongside his, to want to seek the shelter of his embrace. She tried to shake off the unbidden thoughts as Dake bent over Clay and began to untie the baby's bulky diaper.

Cara made a great show of carefully replacing her brush alongside the washbasin. Then she folded the towels she had tossed on the floor and busily straightened the items on the bed. Staying in motion did little to take her mind off of Dake Reed.

As she waited for him to finish diapering the baby she decided that she would have to keep a close watch on herself from now on. He was, as he so had bluntly reminded her, only her employer. Since this strange physical reaction to him didn't seem to be working in reverse, to allow it to continue or, worse yet, if he should notice the profound effect he had on her, it would jeopardize their already tenuous relationship.

She was a woman with a plan and Dake Reed had no part in it.

As Cara watched Dake deftly lift Clay to his shoulder, she tried to imagine him taking the baby all the way to Alabama without her help. For the sake of little Clayton, she told herself, she must stifle her body's curious reaction to Dake Reed.

For the time being, all she could do was follow Nanny James's sound advice, *"Foot firm and faith fast, stand still till the storm's past."*

Now, if her body would only listen to reason.

If you want a place in the sun, you have to expect some blisters.
Nanny James

Chapter Four

"You say this woman wants to sell her clothes?" Cara shook her head, unwilling to believe her stroke of good luck. As she sat awaiting Dake in the small, unadorned dining room of the Birds' Nest Hotel, she had taken up a conversation with the middle-aged owner they had first seen when they registered. Mrs. Cleo Hardesty had assured her there was no longer a dressmaker in Poplar Bluff, but there was a widow who was looking to sell some of her things.

The innkeeper pulled out a chair and joined Cara. "Has to sell 'em is more like it. Poor thing came to town with her husband and two children, a boy and a girl, all of 'em sick. Had the shakes, fever, watery bowels. They weren't here three nights and the husband died, then the little boy. Saddest thing I ever saw. She's stayin' down to the minister's house now, sellin' most of her things to make the money to pay her way back to New Hampshire."

Cara couldn't help but sympathize with the unknown widow who had lost everything. She had nursed her mother during an illness that sounded very much the same. "How awful for her."

"We've all been through some terrible times here lately," Mrs. Hardesty added. "Where are you and your husband headed?"

"Oh, he's not my husband."

Mrs. Hardesty frowned. She glanced at the baby nestled against Cara's breasts.

Realizing her mistake, Cara quickly added, "And this isn't my baby."

"No?"

She tried smiling. The salt-and-pepper-haired Mrs. Hardesty remained seated across from her, but was now staring at her as if she'd just sprouted horns. "Dake—Mr. Reed, that is, found the baby and his mama minutes after the birth. Before she died, the woman asked him to take the baby back to Alabama, and since Mr. Reed was on his way south, he swore he would. He hired me to care for little Clay along the way."

Disbelief was all too evident on the woman's face.

"We have separate rooms," Cara quickly added.

"People with children often rent two rooms."

Trying hard to keep her temper in check, Cara responded, "Well, I can assure you, one is for me, Mrs. Hardesty."

An uneasy silence gaped between them. Cara colored profusely, but refused to drop her gaze. There was no reason for her to feel shame, even when Mrs. Hardesty's telling glance made her remember the way Dake's nearness excited her. She wished he would hurry so that he could help extricate her from the situation.

Finally, the older woman cleared her throat. "Mr. Reed's a fine-lookin' man," she said.

Cara shifted Clay in her arms and refused to comment.

With a sniff, the hotel proprietress tried again. "Looks like he fared well enough despite the war."

"That's because he was a Union officer until a few days ago."

Mrs. Hardesty immediately pushed away from the table and stood up. She reached out to straighten already straight cutlery.

Cara glanced over her shoulder, relieved to see Dake striding toward the dining room. His confident stride and the way he smiled at her the minute their eyes met were reassuring. She bestowed upon him a wide smile of relief. He nodded to Mrs. Hardesty as Cara introduced them and pulled out a chair beside hers.

"Mrs. Hardesty and her son, Bobby, have only owned the hotel for a few months," Cara said, trying to keep up a line of banter while the woman eyed Dake with as much enthusiasm as if he were a grease spot on her new tablecloth.

Mrs. Hardesty leaned forward. The musky scent of perspiration mingling with a heavy dousing of toilet water issued from her calico gown.

"I was just about to tell Miss James here that she hadn't ought to go around announcing to folks which side of the fence you were on during the war, especially not in certain parts of Missouri."

Dake glanced over at Cara. She concentrated on wrapping Clay's feet in his blanket. When she looked up, she noticed Dake was no longer smiling.

"No, ma'am. I'm sure she shouldn't do any such thing," he agreed, his smile gone.

Cara gave him a swift kick under the table.

Dake didn't even flinch. Instead, he smoothly changed the subject. "Perhaps we should hear what you're serving for dinner?"

Mrs. Hardesty wasted no time telling them about the pork chops, mashed potatoes, gravy, biscuits, and green beans she'd be serving them "right shortly." Dake assured her he was looking forward to it before the proprietress walked off toward the kitchen.

When the woman disappeared behind a swinging door, Cara shifted Clay to her shoulder and met Dake's eyes for the first time since he sat down.

"I'm sorry," she began slowly, "I wasn't thinking when I told her you're just out of the Union Army."

"Where we're headed, I think it would be a good idea if you didn't mention it at all. You saw those drifters on the street today, the ones still wearing bits and pieces of rebel uniforms. They'd like nothing better than to stir up a little trouble for anyone who fought on what they considered the wrong side. Most of them have nothing left to lose."

She knew he wasn't afraid for himself. She would bet the farm if she still had one that he was the kind of man who had never been afraid of anything in his life. "Missouri was a Union state," she reminded him.

"Right, but not everyone here was elated about that."

When the kitchen door swung open Mrs. Hardesty bustled out with two aromatic plates full of food.

"I'd like to get an early start tomorrow morning. At least by seven," he told Cara as he pulled his plate closer and lifted a fork. The pork chops were done to perfection, the green beans glistened with melted butter, the biscuits were golden brown.

Cara doubted that she would ever be able to turn out such a perfect meal. Looking down at her own plate made her mouth water with anticipation. She offered a silent prayer of thanks. The food looked far more palatable than anything she had prepared on the trail.

He broke apart a flaky roll. "*Can* you be ready on time?"

Time again. "I'll be ready," she promised.

The heels of Cara's sturdy black shoes rang out with every sure step she took along the deserted boardwalk. She shifted the heavy bundle in her arms, a load composed of two secondhand dresses and a contentedly sleeping little Clayton, and looked around with interest at the buildings along Main Street. None of the inhabited shops and stores were open yet, but as she passed the dry goods store, someone inside raised the shade on the front door. Cara smiled at the face that stared back from the darkened interior and then picked up her pace.

She would love to stop, but it wouldn't do to make Dake wait, not when he had made a point to tell her exactly when he wanted to leave.

She guessed it was nearly seven, but it was hard to tell since the sun had decided not to make a strong appearance, choosing instead to hide beneath an overcast sky. She closed the front of the heavy woolen coat she had just acquired, thankful she was able to persuade its former owner to sell it along with the gowns that were, luckily, quite a close fit. Hurrying so she would have time to change out of her old peach dress before they left town, Cara carefully negotiated the step at the end of the boardwalk and headed toward the last block of stores before the hotel.

Concentrating on keeping a firm grip on the gowns and juggling Clay at the same time, she didn't see the two men who stepped out of the alleyway between the buildings until they blocked her path. When she did notice them she smiled, a reflexive gesture that was second nature to her.

Her smile didn't last long when she recognized them as two of the same three men she'd seen stumble out of the saloon on her way into town yesterday. A swift perusal set the hair standing on the back of her neck.

"Where you goin' in such a hurry, little lady?" The tallest of the three moved closer, so close that she could smell the stale odor of liquor on his breath.

Cara glanced across the street. There was not a soul in sight. Knowing full well she couldn't escape them on foot, not with Clay and the gowns in her arms, Cara tried to bluff her way out. She raised her chin. "I'm on my way to the hotel. Now, if you gentlemen will excuse me—"

A third man joined them. This one definitely lost the tooth count. He elbowed the man who had first spoken to her. "Hear that, Connie? She called us gent'men. Ain't heard that one in a coon's age."

"'Cause you ain't never been one."

Cara quickly shifted her gaze to the man who spoke and then looked away. He was heavier than the other two—his bulk intimidating. Something in his brown eyes menaced, as if he were sizing her up for some reason.

None of them moved to let her pass. She glanced into the shadowed alleyway on her left and clutched Clayton tight. He squirmed but didn't cry out.

"Where's your man?" The one they called Connie leaned over her again, stepped toward her, forcing her to step back. She felt the tooth-gapped one move in behind her.

"At the hotel." Sensing she'd made a mistake by her admission, she quickly added, "He's meeting me in front in a minute or two."

As if he knew the lie for what it was, Connie smiled.

Cara shifted her bundle again.

"Looks like the lady's carrying too heavy a load," he told the others. The big man stepped forward.

Cara tightened her grip on Clay and the gowns. "Let me pass."

"You look nervous, little gal," Connie said, stepping forward again.

Backing up until she was against the wall of the building, Cara tried to keep her expression from showing the fear that vibrated through her.

Connie nodded in her direction. "Help the lady out, Ritter."

The hulking man in a tattered Confederate fatigue coat reached out to take the bundle from her.

"Stop it," she demanded, trying to push past them.

Ritter reached for the gowns with the baby hidden in them. Cara twisted, trying to keep his dirty hands away from Clay. When she opened her mouth to scream, Connie moved in on her as well. Her shout was swallowed by his wide palm.

Ritter wrestled the bundle from her, his eyes going wide with surprise as one dress fell to the ground and Clay started crying. "It's a damn kid," he said, staring down as if Clay were an apparition.

The thin young man missing half a head of teeth glanced around with a wary expression and lisped, "Let's go, Connie. She's not worth it."

"Run, then, liverbelly. She looks *damn* worth it to me."

Cara continued to fight against her captor's hold. She kicked out, connected with his shin, and thanked Willie again for her heavy black shoes when she heard the man groan. She tried to keep an eye on the one they called Ritter as he uncomfortably held the screaming baby.

"Shut that kid up," Connie demanded harshly as he began to pull Cara farther down the alleyway.

"How?"

"However you have to."

Cara dug her heels into the ground. His greater strength overpowered her. Within seconds they were well hidden between the buildings, his hand still pressed against her mouth so hard she could feel her teeth cutting into her lips. Her senses heightened. She heard Clay crying, but his cries became muffled. As Connie slammed her up against one wall, she tried to turn away and scraped her cheek on the rough wooden wall covered with flaking whitewash.

As an overwhelming scent of whiskey mingled with heavy perspiration assailed her, she screamed again and again against his hand. She twisted, turned, and finally brought her knee up, hoping to strike a blow and gain her freedom. She missed.

The man called Connie laughed aloud, a vicious, triumphant laugh.

"Saw you ride into town yesterday with your fancy man," he said, rubbing his rough beard across her cheek as his hand fumbled inside her coat. He swiftly found the too tight neckline of her peach gown. "He looks like a rich, carpetbaggin' Yankee to me."

Cara shook her head and fought his hold. What had happened to Clay? Was that soft mewling sound his muffled cry, or had he stopped? Would the hulking, devious-eyed man be so cruel as to kill an infant in cold blood?

The sound of her bodice tearing all the way to her waist shocked her so that for a minute she stood stock-still, unwilling to believe any of this was actually happening to her. She glanced over Connie's shoulder and caught a glimpse of Ritter guarding the end of the alley. Was Clay still in his arms? The third man, his face split by a nervous, gaping leer, was standing behind Connie's right shoulder, staring down at her exposed breasts.

"I changed my mind," his voice cracked hoarsely. "Hurry up so's I can get at her, too."

When Connie lowered his head, she felt his rough beard scrape the tender, vulnerable skin of her breast. Cara glanced up at the scrap of sky exposed between the two buildings and prayed for deliverance. When his sweaty fingers reached up beneath her skirt and ripped her thin, worn pantalets open, something snapped inside her. Cara began to buck and fight for all she was worth.

Dake knocked on the door of Cara's hotel room a third time and then tried the knob. It turned easily. He stepped into a small room that was identical to his own except that his was scrupulously neat. Cara's room was divided by a line of diapers drying on a rope she'd tied from the window to the washstand. The dresser drawer she'd obviously used as Clay's bed was left on the floor beside her own.

He shook his head. The scene included everything but Cara and Clay. Pleased to think his talk about promptness had some impact on her, Dake figured she had already gone down for breakfast in the dining room. Unwilling to leave her alone with the none-too-cordial Mrs. Hardesty for very long, he hurried after her and left the upheaval behind him.

The smell of bacon drifted up the stairwell. When he reached the dining room, hat in hand, he found Mrs. Hardesty fussing over the breakfast table, but Cara and Clay were nowhere in sight.

"Have you seen Miss James this mornin', ma'am?"

The skeptical look she gave him let Dake know that she thought he was only attempting to show her he hadn't seen Cara since last night. Then, shaking out her apron, she admitted, "Last night I told her about a widow lady over to the minister's house who's trying to sell some of her clothes. I 'spect that's where she went."

"Did you see her leave?"

"No, sir, I didn't. She asked me directions last night before dinner. If you're going after her, it's down the street three blocks and then to the right."

Dake nodded, thanked the woman, and slipped on his hat as he left the dining room. Poplar Bluff, it seemed, was a town that didn't open its doors before eight. Half a block down, he noticed the shaded figure of a man hunched against a wall between two buildings. Even though the man's battered hat was pulled low, Dake recognized him as one of the three unkempt vagrants he'd seen on the street yesterday. He reached down, instinct forcing him to touch the cool, smooth handle of his Starr .44. He pulled his hat low and shifted inside his jacket. His steps never faltered.

Up ahead, the man lingering in the opening of the alleyway disappeared. Something was going on. Not one to skirt a confrontation, let alone ignore anything suspicious, Dake picked up his pace.

When a scream electrified the air around him, his blood ran

cold. Seven years of war experience took over. He palmed his gun and in a split second it slipped from its holster.

Noise of a struggle issued from the alley followed by a shout. "Let her go, the Yank's coming!"

Guarding his back, Dake pressed up against the front of the building that bordered the alley. Gun raised and cocked, he peered around the corner and ducked back when the sharp report of a pistol rang out. A bullet ricocheted off the wall beside his head. Wood splinters exploded.

Assessing what he'd seen in the single, momentary flash while he'd peered into the alley, he knew there were at least three men. Somewhere in their midst, a woman fought for freedom. The heaviest of them made a perfect target. Dake figured he could aim and hit the hulking, bearlike shape without harming the woman. If he winged one of the others in the process, so be it. He took a deep breath, dove toward the center of the alley, began fanning his gun, and rolled.

By the time he reached the safety of the other side, three more shots had reverberated in the alley, all of them his. He heard yelling, a man's stifled curse, and then the sounds of boots pounding against the hard clay soil. He chanced another glance around the corner and saw two of the three men disappear behind the buildings. His target lay stretched out a few feet from the center of the alley.

Dake took off after them at a dead run.

Halfway down the alley, he caught a glimpse of tangled, golden hair of the woman curled in upon herself against the wall. The need to chase the assailants was replaced by a far more immediate one. He holstered his gun and hunkered down before her.

"Cara?" Dake's hands that never once shook on the battlefield trembled as he reached for her.

With eyes wide and frightened, she slapped his hands away.

Her head shook back and forth, back and forth as she whispered, "Stop it. Stop it. Don't!"

"Cara, it's me."

She shoved him violently, with more force than he ever thought she could muster, and started to push herself to a standing position using the wall for leverage.

He grabbed her shoulders, tried to force her to look past her hysteria and see him. She started screaming.

He slapped her far harder than he intended. She collapsed like a broken kite and leaned into him, her sobs so gut-wrenching that he sank into the dirt beside her and pulled her onto his lap. She was shaking so hard he could barely hold her. He pushed her hair back off her face and grasped her chin between his fingers. Dake forced her to look up at him.

Two men appeared in the street-side opening of the alley. Dake instantly recognized one as the storekeep. They rushed up to him, pausing in their tracks as they took in the sight of Cara clinging to him, her face hidden against his shoulder, and the dead man sprawled not far away.

"What happened?"

"I think that's fairly obvious, don't you?" He laid his hand over Cara's face, sheltering her from their curious inspection. A small crowd was gathering at the end of the alley. "There were three in all. Two of them ran that way." He nodded toward the opposite end of the alley.

"I'll get the sheriff," the storekeeper volunteered. He was soon hustling back the way he'd come, his apron strings flapping behind him.

"You killed him, mister," the second man told Dake unnecessarily.

Dake watched the man as he walked around the body, gave it a nudge with his toe, then straightened. Cara suddenly stiffened in his arms and, unmindful of the fact that her dress was torn from neckline to waist, pushed herself away from him. Her fingers tightened on his wrists. "Where's Clay?"

"Sweet Jesus," the startled onlooker gasped, his eyes riveted on Cara's breasts.

Dake gently pulled the edges of Cara's coat together. Deep-seated hatred rose like bile when he glimpsed the purpling bruises and tooth marks that stained her ivory flesh.

"Where is Clay?" she demanded, driven by panic. She pushed her hair out of her eyes and tried to climb off his lap. "They took Clay."

Dake shook his head. "They didn't have him. I saw them run off."

Frantic now, her eyes wide, all of her fear channeled into concern for the baby. "Where *is* he?"

The sound of her words echoed in the narrow wood canyon formed by the buildings on either side. At the end of the alley, Mrs. Hardesty pushed herself through the crowd and rushed toward the pile of clothing against the wall. Surprised that a woman of such bulk could move so swiftly, Dake held his breath until she turned to them with a wavering smile and bent to scoop up Clay. "Here he is, the sweet thing. Don't fret, Miss James."

There was no animosity in her voice or her expression as the woman brought the baby to Dake and Cara. She gave Cara a quick once-over, then lowered her voice to a whisper and suggested to Dake, "Let's get her back to the hotel."

Dake cradled her in his arms and stood up.

"I can walk," Cara whispered.

"No."

"Please."

"No." He pulled the coat tight and glanced around to see if there was anything else she had dropped in the alley. He spied a gown balled up a few feet away. Mrs. Hardesty followed his gaze and added, "I'll get it. You two go on back."

The small knot of townsfolk parted like the Red Sea to let them pass. When two men started to whisper, Dake pinned them with a hard look and they quickly fell silent.

Shifting Cara higher against his chest, he didn't look back as he stepped up on the boardwalk and made his way back to the Birds' Nest Hotel.

Cara sat, shaken, on the edge of the bed where Dake had deposited her just seconds before. Clutching her newly obtained coat, she stared back at him defiantly while Mrs. Hardesty hovered over Clay in the background.

"Yes," Cara repeated emphatically, "I'm certain they didn't rape me."

"You're sure, then?"

Her voice broke, though she was determined not to cry anymore. "Damn it, Dake Reed, I said I was sure. I'm the one that ought to know." Her tone dropped to a near whisper. "But if you hadn't come along—"

His hand moved and she thought for a moment he was going to reach out for her again. Instead, his fingers brushed against the inlaid ivory handle of his gun. He fingered it with a thoughtful look in his eyes.

Mrs. Hardesty put Clay in the middle of the bed and then touched Dake on the sleeve. "The sheriff's here, Mr. Reed. Why don't you run along now and talk to him and I'll help Miss James here get cleaned up?"

Dake looked to Cara for assurance. She nodded, and without another word to either woman, he quit the room. Cara let her shoulders droop as soon as his tall frame disappeared behind the closed door.

Mrs. Hardesty, her salt and pepper hair still firmly in place, fluttered over Cara like a mother hen. "Now, you get out of that dress, young lady. I've got Bobby bringing up some hot water and fresh towels. You'll feel better in no time."

Cara started to slip off the heavy wool coat, but when she noticed that one of the carved buttons was missing, the entire incident in the alley came rushing back at her with such force that she couldn't stop a rush of tears. As one slowly tracked down her cheek, she batted at it with the back of her hand.

The older woman put a hand on her shoulder. "Did you lie to him, honey?" Cleo Hardesty asked softly.

Cara looked up, blinking away tears. She suspected the woman would like nothing better than firsthand knowledge that she had, indeed, been raped.

"No, I didn't lie," she whispered. "Truly, except for a few aches, I'm fine."

"Then you need to get cleaned up and dressed and go out among the living with your head held high or you'll have the whole town saying you were."

Never one to hide her feelings, Cara asked, "Why are you being so nice to me?"

Mrs. Hardesty seemed taken aback. "Whatever makes you ask that?"

Cara stood up and shrugged out of her coat, fighting to keep her torn dress draped across her breasts with one hand. "For one thing, I know you don't believe Dake and I aren't lovers. Besides, you didn't think too highly of him being a Union soldier."

The woman looked back at her for a long moment before she admitted, "That may be, missy, but what happened to you out there this morning has a way of puttin' us women all on the same side, now, don't it?"

A swift knock interrupted and Cara turned her back to the door. She heard the woman's son bring in a bucket of warm water and some towels and then the door closed softly behind him. With Mrs. Hardesty's help she washed and dressed, careful to avoid looking at the wounds her assailant had inflicted upon her tender flesh. Every muscle in her body ached. She washed her face, tended to her split lip and bruised cheeks, and then tried to make some semblance of style out of her hair. After a few minutes she gave up and decided to tie it back with a length of black ribbon Cleo Hardesty donated to the cause.

The new dress, of navy serge, fit much better than any dress she had ever owned, but the thrill of wearing it had vanished in the wake of the memories the gown would now and forever carry. When Cara stared at her reflection in the mirror, she realized the navy was too deep and strong a hue for someone of her light complexion. The color emphasized her pale cheeks, making her appear little more than a ghost of the suntanned prairie miss she'd been just a few days ago. The navy-blue was mirrored by the bruises on her face and neck. She turned away from the mirror, unable to stomach more.

Contenting herself with the soft whisper of the hem of the gown that brushed against the ankles of her boots, a new and welcome sensation after wearing too-short dresses for so long, Cara walked back to the bed and bent to give Clayton all her attention. She reached out and picked up the cooing babe, smiled down at him as she rocked him gently in her arms and stole comfort from the familiar warmth and feel of him.

"He's a sweet child," Mrs. Hardesty said, peering over Cara's shoulder. "Poor little urchin."

Cara watched the baby as he waved one hand in the vicinity of his mouth until he made contact and began to suck on his fist. She ran her finger over his cheek and watched him stare back at her with his wide brown eyes. "He's a good baby. He's had to be, though, since neither Dake nor I really know what we're doing most of the time."

"Nobody does when it's their first."

Cara sighed. There was no use arguing with a woman she'd never see again in her life.

Dake's voice saved her from having to.

"Cara?" he called from outside the door. "Are you dressed?"

She bid him enter as Mrs. Hardesty collected the wet towels and her ruined dress, straightened the coverlet, and then bustled out. Cara felt Dake's concerned stare from across the room. She looked up and found him standing uncertainly in the doorway.

"Come in."

He closed the door and crossed the room until he stood beside her. "How's Clay?" he asked.

"He seems fine." Those damn tears again. She blinked furiously and looked up at him. "We're so lucky. They could have killed him."

If she hadn't learned to read his moods after two weeks of travel, she might have missed the imperceptible narrowing of his eyes, the taut line of his lips, the slight flare of his nostrils when he said, "We were lucky. But you can rest assured luck's run out for the men who did this to you."

Something in his tone frightened her. She had never seen him like this before. Impatient, perturbed, grouchy—yes. But never wearing this cool facade that barely masked seething anger.

"What do you mean?"

He stepped away. Paced to the window. Stared out at the street with his back to her. "The sheriff is rounding up a posse of men to go after them. The men who attacked you were drifters. He had warned them about causing trouble, but until today he didn't have any reason to run them out of town. Now, he's got cause to put them behind bars."

"I'll feel safer on the trail if I know for certain they can't follow us."

He was back at her side before she finished the thought. "No one's ever going to hurt you again while you're in my care."

Finding his green-eyed gaze all too intent, she broke contact. "I know."

"Don't bother packing up. We won't be leaving just yet."

She met the intensity of his stare again. "Why not?"

"I'm riding out with the sheriff."

Her breath caught and held. She shook herself before she could speak. Memory flashed through her senses, visions of a toothless smile, fetid, liquor-tainted breath, the invasion of a stranger's rough beard against her breast. Those same men were capable of killing.

Her eyes narrowed as she considered Dake riding out against them. "No."

He crossed in front of her, moving toward the door. Her gaze drifted across his broad shoulders, down the seam of his buckskin jacket, to the gun belt at his waist and the weapon holstered there. He shifted his weight from one foot to the other before he turned back to face her again. The set look on his face warned her it would do no good to argue, still, she had to try.

"Please, Dake. Don't. Let's just leave."

"I can't ride out of here knowing what those men almost did to you, what they might do to someone else if they aren't caught. Don't ask me not to go."

"What if you get killed?" She pursued him, pacing across the room, jostling the dozing baby. Clay whimpered. "What am I supposed to do then? You promised this boy's mama you'd take him home."

He gave her a hard, long look that let her know exactly what he thought of her lack of confidence in his ability to survive. "Then you'll just have to do it for me. My saddlebag is hidden beneath the mattress in the room next door. Use the money to get Clay home. There's also a bracelet that belonged to Anna Clayton that'll help prove who he is." His eyes held hers for another brief second, then his gaze dropped to the child in her arms.

His hand hit the knob. The door jerked open.

"Dake Reed, don't you dare go with that posse!"

He was careful not to slam the door behind him.

*You can sit on an egg, but that
don't mean it's ever gonna hatch.*
Nanny James

Chapter Five

It was the longest day of her life.

The walls of the small hotel room began to close in on her less than an hour after Dake rode out of town with the posse. Cara had watched them go, nine men intent on finding the two who had attacked her in the alley that morning. They rode in a thunder of hooves and a cloud of dust, the very air about them charged with vengeance. They left behind a tense anticipation that settled over the town and Cara in particular.

Main Street was nearly deserted the rest of the day. From her window, she stared out at the sandy bluffs, watching for some sign of the posse's return. While she waited for Dake, more than anxious to leave Poplar Bluff behind, Cara decided she would ask Mrs. Hardesty to watch Clay while she went to the livery stable to see about Miss Lucy. While she was there, she intended to open the crate of dolls stored in the wagon and give one to the daughter of the widow who sold her the clothing. Despite her own trouble, Cara couldn't forget the sorrow in the widow's daughter's eyes. She hoped a new doll would lighten the little girl's load of sad memories.

She planned to give a second doll to Mrs. Hardesty. It was little enough thanks, even though she couldn't really imagine what the grown woman would do with it, but the whimsical dolls were all she had to give.

She got as far as the door. When it came to actually turning

91

the knob and leaving the safety of the room, to stepping out on the street and facing anyone as she walked to the livery stable, Cara froze. Tremors shook her. Chills the likes of which she'd never experienced, even in sickness, racked her slender frame. What if Connie and his cohort had somehow doubled back? What if they were out there somewhere waiting for her?

She crossed her arms over her breasts and stood clammy with fear in the center of the room. What condemnation might she face as she walked among the townsfolk of Poplar Bluff?

Fear paralyzed her. Cara put Clay back on the bed and slipped off her coat. She sat down beside the baby where she could see the wide blue sky and changing October leaves on the trees that lined the bluff. Her view of Main Street was unimpeded. It was as good a place as any to wait.

Dake stood at the bottom of the shadowed staircase. He pulled off his hat and ran a hand through his hair. Despite the chill of the October evening, his forehead was wet with sweat where his hatband had pressed against it. As his hand touched the stair rail, Cleo Hardesty left the empty dining room and crossed the small reception foyer toward him.

She managed a smile. "I'm glad to see you're back. Miss James ain't been down all day. Asked for milk for the baby, but nothing for herself."

Dake sighed. Cara's inaction added to the worry he'd harbored all day. The hotel keeper waited expectantly. He told her what she wanted to know. "We got them."

"Sheriff got 'em locked up, then?"

"One. The other's dead." He spoke softly, but his words echoed in the empty stairwell. Dake glanced upward, afraid Cara might overhear. He wanted to tell her face-to-face.

"Dead?"

He didn't have the energy or the patience to stand and give the woman all the details. Not tonight. Not with Cara waiting upstairs. "If you can't get the information from the sheriff, I'll tell you all about it tomorrow. Right now, I'd like to go upstairs and see about Cara. Has she eaten?"

"No. Turned down dinner. Said she'd wait for you. If you'd like, I'll warm up some chicken and fried potatoes for you both."

Dake nodded, trying to ignore the rumble in his stomach and the smell of fried chicken that permeated the lower floor of the building. He pictured golden fried, juicy pieces of chicken and puffy biscuits slathered with white gravy. Glancing upstairs, he was all the more determined to talk to Cara and then bring her down for dinner. "Thank you, ma'am. If you'll excuse me now?"

"Run along. And see that she comes down to eat, you hear?"

"I will." He took the stairs two at a time, then paused at the top to unbutton his jacket before he knocked on Cara's door. "Cara?"

He heard nothing for a moment, then soft footfalls behind the door. Sensing her presence just on the other side, he leaned against it and spoke in a low tone, "Cara, it's me. Let me in."

"Dake?"

"Yes."

The door opened, a crack at first, then wider as she identified him. The dim light in the hallway played across her face as she stared up at him from inside the darkened room.

"May I come in?"

She moved back to let him pass. He could tell by the soft slap of her feet against the wood floorboards that she was barefoot.

"Why's it so dark in here?"

"I'm sorry," she said quietly, "I fell asleep. I think there are some matches by the lamp on the washstand."

As he moved across the room to light the lamp, Dake said, "No need to be sorry." He fumbled with the matches, lit the lamp, and replaced the chimney. The smell of lamp oil stung the air. Cara closed the door and leaned back against it. Waiting.

Her eyes were shadowed. He stared at her, wondering at the change, then realized it was her aura of innocence that she had lost. Her full lips were slightly swollen, her clear complexion marred by bruises that would take days to fade. He could tell she needed to hear the posse had succeeded in running down her assailants. Dake refused to make her wait any longer.

"It didn't take long to track them down."

Cara smoothed the front of the navy wool gown that made her appear even paler. Her fingers toyed with the gathers at the waist. "No?"

"Their trail was easy to follow. They stopped off at a ranch and stole two fresh horses, then took off toward the hills. One of the sheriff's men knew the hill country like the back of his hand. Figured on finding them in a cave he knew of near the river, and sure enough, there they were."

"So, they're in jail now?" Her hands continued to twist the wool serge.

Dake moved across the room until he stood before her. He took her hands in his to still them. Her fingers were as cold as ice. Pressing her palms together, he warmed them between his own. "One of them gave up immediately. Came running out waving his hat."

Her eyes were wide, hollow caverns of blue. "Which one?" she whispered.

"The young one. Near toothless, thin. A spineless follower. Came from the hills around here. The men who recognized him said he wasn't quite right in the head even before the war. Did whatever anyone told him to. He's in jail."

Cara swallowed visibly. Her hands were still cold, as if her body rejected his warmth. "The other?"

Dake sighed. Riding back into town leading a horse with the

man's body tied across it had given him little satisfaction. The killing seemed to Dake to be nothing but an extension of the war. One of many ravaged souls displaced by the war, the man shouldn't have had to die, even though his crime against Cara had been unpardonable. How long would it be before men trained to kill were able to put aside the skills they honed over five long bloody years?

"He refused to surrender. Started firing on us without warning as soon as his friend was in the clear. Wounded one of the sheriff's men. They were set to wait him out as long as it took. Finally, I managed to convince the sheriff to let me try to go around behind the cave and come up on him unaware."

"*You* killed him?"

"I had to. At the end it was him or me."

He thought she would be upset at the notion, that she might even turn away from him in disgust. Instead, her reaction shocked him.

"Good." Tilting her head back so that she might face him fully, she said, "I don't mean I'm glad he's dead. I'm just thankful it wasn't you."

He squeezed her hands. "How are you doing, really?"

"I hate feeling afraid." She looked down at their hands and made no attempt to break the bond between them. "The bruises will heal—but will the fear ever go away? I haven't left this room all day even though I tried, more than once, but I couldn't bring myself to open that door and walk outside knowing that he might be out there somewhere. That he might come after me again, put his hands on me—"

He hated to hear the words because of the pictures they conjured. Dake let go of her hands and pulled her up against him, half expecting her to push away. Instead, she stayed and even seemed to welcome his comforting embrace. She pressed her cheek against his shirtfront and kept talking as if putting her thoughts into words helped somehow.

"I've never been afraid for myself before. Not ever. Even when I was alone on the prairie. I never gave a thought to anyone ever . . . hurting me. But today, all I thought of was what might happen if I went out alone." She pulled her hands away from his hold and wrapped her arms protectively around her waist. "Am I going to feel like this forever? Will I be looking over my shoulder for the rest of my life because of what those men did?"

He tightened his hold. Although he was aware of her supple body leaning against him, there was no carnality in his touch, no burning need to possess her, merely an overwhelming urge to keep her safe from harm. "You're safe now. Every day things will get better."

It was a moment before she responded. "I know that," she whispered. "I know."

They stood locked together in a silent embrace until Dake's senses became attuned to her as a woman and not merely a companion in need of comfort. He slowly released her. Because she did trust him, he didn't want to frighten her, and if he didn't step back now it wouldn't be long before she realized what holding her close was doing to him. His body was reminding him, with aching clarity, that he was a man, not a saint.

He turned around and walked over to the bed where Clay lay wide awake, waving his arms and legs with vigor. Dake noticed, not for the first time, how fast the little boy was growing. The baby's curls had thickened, his dark eyes curious.

Dake couldn't help but smile down at the contented infant. "He's getting bigger," he said aloud. Cara moved to stand at his shoulder, her arms crossed at her waist as she looked down at Clay.

"He sure is." She reached out and traced the nearly imperceptible outline of brow above one of Clay's eyes.

"Mrs. Hardesty's fixin' us some supper. You think we should leave Clay here, or will he cry?"

Cara glanced at the door, then up at him. "I'm not hungry."

Dake gave her what he felt was his most commanding look. "You will eat."

"I will not."

He shifted, realizing immediately that he'd taken the wrong approach with her again. "I'd like you to join me at dinner, Miss James. You have to leave this room sometime; besides, I'm starving. And you know how I get when I'm hungry."

He could see a smile playing at the corners of her ravaged mouth. He longed to chase the lingering shadows from her eyes.

Finally, she agreed. "All right. If you insist."

"I do."

"I think Clay will go back to sleep. We can hear him if he cries, in any case. Just let me put him in the drawer so that he doesn't roll off the bed."

"Does he move that much?" Dake was amazed.

Cara shrugged. "I don't think he will yet, but I don't want to take any chances."

He waited while she carefully picked up the baby and put him in the drawer she'd padded with the faded quilt he'd found with the baby. That done, Cara paused beside the washstand.

"I should brush my hair," she said, her hand going immediately to a stray lock.

Dake reached out and tucked it behind her ear. "You look beautiful."

She was as surprised as he by the statement. Cara ducked her head to hide the bruises he pretended to ignore.

Dake picked his hat up off the bed. "Shall we go?"

"Hurry up so's I can get at her, too."

The voice echoing in the dream was just as threatening as

reality. The threat jolted Cara's subconscious into wakefulness. Shivering with fear, even as she realized her nightgown was clinging to her sweat-sheened skin, she untangled herself from the bedclothes and scooted back until she was leaning against the headboard. She glanced around the dark room, wondering whether or not she had cried out. The night shadows loomed large and gathered about, giving life to her fear.

She had fallen asleep with the lamp burning, but the flame had long since sputtered out. She could hear Clay breathing evenly in the makeshift crib on the floor near her bed. He would awaken soon enough, demanding to be fed. Too frightened to go back to sleep, Cara pulled the covers up beneath her chin, determined to wait out the night and keep her nightmares at bay.

There was a quick knock at the door, followed by the sound of a key turning in the lock. Forcing herself to stay calm, she waited until the glow of lamplight filtered into the room ahead of Dake. Half-dressed and half-asleep, he shuffled into the room and set the lamp on the washstand.

"Are you all right?" He shoved his hair back with splayed fingers as he stood across the room, staring down at her.

Far from all right, Cara nodded anyway, still clutching the blankets beneath her chin.

"I was awake and heard you cry out," he explained.

She shook her head, fighting the urge to hide her face in her hands. "I'm so embarrassed. I suppose I woke everyone."

"Not really. If I'd been sleeping, I probably wouldn't have even heard you." Dake didn't want to frighten her any more than she already had been, but earlier, she had assured him she trusted him. He moved close to the bed, slowly, hoping that he wasn't about to end that trust.

Once more, Cara was mesmerized by the strength that emanated from him. He was nothing like her brother, Willie, whom she'd seen shirtless on plenty of occasions. Where her brother was whipcord lean and lanky, Dake was all well-defined muscle. The planes of his broad, muscular chest were darkened by an expanse of tight hair that tapered down between the washboard ripple of his midriff to a thin trail that disappeared into his unbuttoned waistband.

"I guess Nanny James didn't have a saying for something like this," he said.

"Not that I remember right now."

She forced herself to look up and meet his concerned, green-eyed stare. "I'm sorry I bothered you. I'll be right as rain in a while."

"Don't be sorry. You're still hurting."

The tenderness of his words and the truth behind them brought unbidden tears to her eyes. She looked away. "When will it stop?"

His steps swallowed the space between them until he was standing beside the bed. With a glance at the baby sleeping soundly in the drawer on the floor, he carefully sidestepped it and sat down on the edge of Cara's bed. It was a cool night, the room unheated, but even though he hadn't taken the time to grab his shirt after he'd shrugged into his denims, Dake was impervious to the chill. Not while his blood was running hot in his veins.

The edge of the bed dipped with his weight. She fidgeted with the covers. He reached out and wiped the tears from her cheek.

"Maybe you need a better memory, something to replace your nightmares." He wanted to kiss her if she would let him. There was too much between them now, too many long hours on the trail over the past two weeks, too many times he'd fought to keep himself from touching her, from holding her, from tasting the sweetness he was sure her lips had to offer. He watched her, staring into the midnight-blue depths of her eyes, gauging her acquiescence, aching to kiss her, unwilling to take advantage of her vulnerability.

Cara stared back at him, seeking the solace of his touch, knowing the strength and comfort it gave. She waited, her fear behind her now that he had come into the room.

He shifted and edged closer.

She let go of her death grip on the blankets.

Dake leaned toward her, bracing himself with one hand on the bed beside her hips. Cara waited, watching him closely. She licked her lips. He pressed closer still.

She didn't pull back.

It was all the encouragement he needed. Without touching her with his hands, Dake leaned down and lightly brushed her lips with his own. Fully aware of her bruises, he didn't want to cause her more pain. Gently, slowly, he traced the seam of her lips with his tongue and lightly kissed them.

Cara watched, eyes wide with wonder and hope as Dake kissed her. When he drew back, she found herself staring into his eyes.

"Better?" he whispered softly.

"A little." She was afraid she felt so much better that she was on the verge of asking for more.

As if reading her thoughts he asked, "May I kiss you again?"

She nodded.

His mouth gently took hers. His tongue tasted, dipped, plumbed farther into the moist warmth. He had been right. There was no way she could even compare the nurturing tenderness of this exchange with what had happened to her in the alley.

She was the first to pull away, reminding herself that they had been thrown together by the whim of fate. Dake was, after all, her employer. Certainly, after everything that had transpired, he was her friend, but definitely not her lover, not yet. She was not about to fool herself into believing any such thing.

The one and only reason their paths had crossed was lying sound asleep in the drawer beside her bed.

Still and all, his tenderness had such a healing quality to it that she wondered if another kiss might not banish her fear forever? When he straightened, she was afraid he was going to leave her alone in the darkness.

"It wouldn't do to get in the habit," she warned him. "Not with me going on to California and all."

He was slow to answer. "No. I guess not."

She looked into his eyes and asked, "Will you stay with me?"

He thought for a moment he had imagined her request. "What?"

"Will you stay here with me until morning?"

Dake swallowed. Was she asking him to *sleep* with her, or merely sleep with her? He knew at this point he could easily grant either request. But on the morrow, faced with the light of day and his own uncertain future, what could he really promise her? "Cara, I—"

"I mean, stay with no more kissing."

"No, of course not."

"Just stay until dawn. Just in case I have another nightmare."

He stood up, walked to the washstand, and turned down the lamp wick. When the room was dark again, he returned to the opposite side of the bed and then slipped beneath the bedspread, careful to keep a barrier of blankets between them.

Chapter Six

It was long past dawn when Cara rolled over and opened her eyes. She stretched languorously before she snapped to full consciousness.

Dake was gone. She glanced down at Clay's improvised crib and found the baby missing, too. Her bare feet hit the cold floor as she slid out of bed. Tossing her nightgown over her head, she found her underthings, pulled them on, and then wriggled into her navy serge. Within minutes she had slipped on her gown, shoved her hair back out of her eyes, and gingerly washed her face. A glance in the small mirror over the washstand confirmed the fact that her bruises were just as visible today as the night before.

After taking a deep breath, she left the room in search of Dake. The narrow hallway was thankfully deserted when she tapped at the door of his room. What she didn't need this morning was Mrs. Hardesty catching her outside his door.

"It's open." His voice was hushed, barely audible.

Cara turned the knob and stepped inside.

Dake lay fully dressed, stretched out sideways across the bed. The baby was snuggled beside him so that Dake could hold the near-empty bottle of milk for Clay to suckle. When Dake looked up and cautioned her to shush with a finger to his lips, she couldn't help but notice how exhausted he looked.

Stepping closer, she told him bluntly, "You look awful."

103

He was inspecting her just as closely. "I can't say as you look any better than I do. I didn't get much sleep."

She colored immediately. As he continued to watch her intently, she wondered whether she should thank him for watching over her in the night or merely ignore what was, in the light of day, an embarrassing situation. Cara glanced around the room while she decided. There was nothing out of place. His buckskin jacket hung on the back of the only chair in the room, his saddlebags were lying filled and closed on the chair seat. The sight of the worn leather bags reminded her of his advice to use the money inside should anything happen to him. Anna Clayton's bracelet, the link to the baby's past, was in there, too. Dake's wide-brimmed black hat sat atop them. There was no other sign that anyone occupied the room. Though he and Clay were using the bed, it was neatly tucked and made up beneath them.

"Are you all packed?" he asked.

Cara thought of the state of her room. It looked like she'd stirred it with a stick. "Almost," she lied, feeling more than awkward facing him after last night. She could feel him watching her closely.

Dake pulled the nipple out of Clay's rosebud mouth. "He's asleep," he told her. "Go finish up, we'll get some breakfast downstairs and then go."

Realizing she was becoming used to the tone of command he so naturally assumed, Cara nodded in agreement, as anxious to leave the room as she was to leave Poplar Bluff behind. She turned away.

"Cara?"

She paused in the doorway. "Yes?" Did he know how attractive he was to her?

"If you're not up to leaving yet—"

Forcing a smile, she winced when the cut on her lip pulled.

She told him truthfully, "I'm almost ready. We should be on our way."

Dake watched her quit the room and stared at the door long after she closed it behind her. Seeing her in broad daylight did little to ease the growing need her nearness evoked. He'd left her when the night went from black to gray, before dawn. He had just about drifted off to sleep in the wee hours of the morning when Clay had begun to fuss. Still not ready to face those deep blue eyes across from him on a pillow in the bright light of day, he'd taken Clay into his room, thinking she would appreciate a few more minutes of sleep.

Leaving her had been harder than he expected. He had never spent the night with a woman before. Made love—yes. He had paid for women warm and willing enough to help him forget the war for an hour or two. But last night was the first time he'd ever slept with a woman and he found it a disturbing experience. He'd spent the night sharing Cara's warmth, trying not to move and disturb her, fighting an overwhelming urge to pull her close and hold her tight.

Tenderness was not something he was in the habit of dispensing. Enlisted men weren't to be coddled, though God knew most of the young recruits needed it.

Last night, intimately sharing Cara's bed, he fought to ignore the sound of her breathing and the clean scent of soap that clung to her skin and hair. He had tried to center his thoughts instead on what he would face back in Decatur where he would certainly have more than his attraction to Cara James or Anna Clayton's son's welfare to think about. He tried to concentrate on Minna, Burke, and Riverglen, but nothing could take his mind off of the woman beside him last night, especially when her hand would accidentally brush his arm, or when, lost in sleep, she turned toward him and her silken, wayward hair came close enough to tease his cheek.

Dake ran his hand over his eyes, blaming the pounding

headache behind them on lack of sleep. It was time to get up, pack up the wagon once more, and be off. He figured they had sixty miles to go before they reached New Madrid, on the Mississippi, where they would board a steamboat for Memphis. If they could get one. Shipping on the river had been virtually destroyed by the war. He hoped they wouldn't encounter too much difficulty finding passage. It would be a delight to say good-bye to the last of their gypsy life in the wagon.

The baby beside him wriggled and opened his eyes. Dake looked down into the child's trusting eyes and wondered who, if anyone, they would find to care for him at Anna Clayton's former home. He reached down and teased Clay's hand until the tiny fist reflexively wrapped as far around his finger as it could. Dake smiled. "Don't worry, little man," he whispered to the babe. "We'll have you home safe and sound soon enough."

The formalities of "Miss James" and "Mr. Reed" were left behind in Poplar Bluff. Their relationship altered by circumstance, Cara took to using Dake's given name, just as he did hers. Dake suggested since there was little more than three days' travel to New Madrid and plenty of homesteads along the way where they could buy milk, that they would make far better time if they sold the goat. Knowing that parting with Miss Lucy was an eventuality, Cara tried not to cry when they left the goat behind with Mrs. Hardesty, who promised to take good care of the cantankerous old thing. Cara made good on her plan to give a rag doll to the innkeeper and one to the unfortunate widow's daughter, choosing ones she thought suitable for each. It was many a mile before she forgot the look on the child's face as she waved Cara and Dake a hearty good-bye, clutching a button-eyed, calico-faced rag doll in her arms.

Without Miss Lucy trailing behind them, they made better time, but the whole while Cara watched Dake carefully, worried about the intense frown that marred his strong features. He seemed more than merely tired. Finally, when heavy clouds in the late-afternoon sky threatened rain, she asked him what was wrong.

"I have a headache I can't shake," he told her.

Immediately, Cara reached out and felt his forehead. He tried to shrug off her hand, but she was insistent. "You feel warm."

One of his dark brows arched as he stared down at her. "Thank you, Nurse James."

Ignoring him, she looked around, wondering where and when they might find shelter for the night before the storm hit. "What should we do?"

"Do you have enough milk left for Clay?"

She thought of the crock of milk wrapped in layers of towels that Mrs. Hardesty had sent with them. "Enough for tonight, I think. We'll need fresh tomorrow."

He appeared instantly relieved. "Then if you don't mind, let's push on a few more miles. If we don't see a farm or a town ahead, we can always take the boxes and put them under the wagon and sleep on the seats."

Although she had long ago grown used to living in the dugout, was used to rain and mud shifting through the earth and ruining everything in the house, accustomed to damp bedding and soggy ticking, she couldn't think of anything more uncomfortable than a night spent sleeping on the hard wooden seats of the little wagon. Besides, if Dake was running a fever, a night out in the weather might very well kill him.

"Let's go on. There has to be something close by."

On the edge of her seat, straining to see in the waning light, Cara watched for some sign of life. It was an hour before she spied the silhouette of a cabin to the south of the road. She pointed it out to Dake, who turned General Sherman in that direction.

By the time they reached the wood-shingled cabin with the remnants of a barn near a grove of sycamores, Dake was shivering harder and trying to hide it.

"Wait here," Cara said, carefully tucking Clay into his blanket and setting the child on the floor of the wagon near Dake's feet. She hurried toward the dwelling, pulling her new coat tight about her shoulders. The wind had picked up, drowning out all sign of their approach, but she was quite certain the place was deserted. Anyone as accustomed to living out on the land alone as she was knew how important it was to have a lamp burning in the window to light the way for weary travelers such as themselves.

When she knocked at the door of the cabin, it swung inward and tilted, half off the hinges. Cara stepped inside the musty interior. She squealed when something scurried across her foot. Unable to see much in the darkness, she did locate an empty bed frame in the corner. There was no sign that the place had been inhabited recently.

As she stepped outside to get Dake, she felt the wind on her face and with it came a peppering of cold raindrops. "The place is empty," she said, taking Clay from Dake, who was sheltering him on his lap. "We can stay the night here."

Dake agreed and took General Sherman to what was left of the barn. In a few minutes he had the horse unhitched and rubbed down. Cara dug through their supplies for a lamp, set out a cold dinner of biscuits and ham, and fixed up a pallet for herself and one for Dake on the floor.

Dake added little to the conversation, which only confirmed to her that he was feeling worse. Assuring her that he was merely tired, he apologized and went to bed as soon as he finished eating. She made certain he had most of the blankets, but sometime during the night she could hear his teeth chattering.

"Dake?"

He didn't answer, so she climbed out of her bed and hurried to kneel beside him. "Are you all right?" She reached out and touched his shoulder and found him racked with shivers. Grabbing up her own blankets, she pulled him to a sitting position, sat behind him, and wrapped him in the thick wool. Dake leaned back against her, offering no protest when she wrapped her arms around him and held him against her. He let his head fall back against her collarbone.

"Get my gun," he said through his chattering teeth.

"It's all right. I can see it from here." He was burning up with fever. She could feel it through his clothes and the thick blankets.

"Promised to protect you."

"You just think about getting over this."

"Get the gun."

She did it to calm him, stretched out and picked up the gun and put it on the floor beside her.

"Never sick."

Cara smoothed his hair back off his forehead. "Shh."

"I have to go home."

"I know," she told him. "You'll get there."

"I don't know . . ."

"Of course you'll get home," she said. "Don't talk like that."

He shook his head, indicating she had misunderstood him. "I don't know what to expect when I get there. My brother told me never to come back if I fought for the Union. Minna sent for me, not Burke."

Minna. Finally.

"Who's Minna?" Cara knew that if his sickness hadn't made him so vulnerable he would never have shared his worry with her.

"Minna is Burke's."

She rolled her eyes, thankful that he couldn't see the look on her face. "Burke's what?"

"Minna always loved Burke."

She didn't know any more than she had before. "Do you think Minna will welcome you back?"

"To help Burke. To save Riverglen. Maybe I can't do it. Maybe I'm crazy to think I can make it work. Maybe no one can."

"Of course you can," she said, although she had no idea what he was talking about.

"How do you know that?"

"Well, because you're . . . punctual."

He laughed at that and was taken by a fit of shaking once more.

"And you're strong. And you have convictions. And you like babies." She lay her cheek upon the top of his head as his trembling had subsided. He seemed over the worst of the chills and able to sleep. Cara didn't move, but kept him wrapped in her arms.

Cara woke up first and discovered that sometime during the night she had stretched out beside Dake and fallen asleep. She crawled out of the makeshift bed, thankful to be able to slip out before he awakened. Slipping his gun back into the holster, she smiled. It felt good to have someone worry about protecting her for a change.

There was no stove in the small room. It was raining so hard she had to forgo building a cookfire outside so she made do with the rest of the foodstuffs she had purchased from Mrs. Hardesty.

Finally, after Clay was fed and changed, her worry had begun to mount. She crossed the room and knelt down beside Dake. His forehead was hot to the touch. This time he didn't try to pull away. Instead, he kept his eyes closed but let her know he was awake when he admitted, "I don't feel so good."

"You're burning up again, that's why."

He tried to sit up, decided against it, then pulled the blankets tighter. "I'll be all right in a minute," he said, but shortly thereafter, he began to shiver so hard his teeth clacked. "Where's my jacket?"

"It's all right. It's over by the door."

She knew full well he could suffer from "the shakes," as most folks called his ailment, for days or even weeks. If it didn't kill him. She'd seen her mother and brother through the affliction more than once, somehow impervious to the disease herself. Unwilling to accept his illness as anything more than passing, Cara became determined to have Dake on his feet again as soon as possible. She smoothed his hair back off his feverish forehead.

He tried to smile. "Everything hurts. My teeth hurt."

"I know," she assured him. "But you'll be right as rain in no time."

He opened one eye. "You really think so? I feel like I'm about to die."

Cara closed her eyes for a split second, quickly wished away his words, then said, "Right as rain."

He closed his eyes. "I haven't been sick in six years."

"Probably took some bad water."

"How come *you* feel all right?"

She sat down beside him on the dusty floorboards. "Nothing ever makes me sick. My family used to wonder at it. I just figured with all them lying around moaning and groaning, somebody had to fetch the water and keep them fed and that somebody was me."

He took her hand. "Nothing gets you down for long, does it, Miss Cara James?"

His palm was hot, his skin dry. She guessed that accounted for the heat that his touch radiated up her arm. "Heaven suits our trials to our strengths." She pulled her hand away. "How about some breakfast?"

He shook his head. "I can't eat."

"Water then." She didn't know what else she could do for him except wait and see if his fever broke of its own accord.

By afternoon he claimed to be better. Once on his feet again, he insisted they press on, if only to shorten the distance to New Madrid. "Besides," he argued with her, "Clay needs milk."

Cara assured him Mrs. Hardesty had given her a small sack of oats with the advice that she could make a thin oatmeal gruel for the baby that would suffice, but he wouldn't hear of it. Despite her arguments, he had them packed up and on the way in less than an hour. They pushed on despite his recurring chills, fever, and cramping bowels. Cara silently prayed he had a passing influenza and not dysentery.

After one particularly rough stop, he came shuffling back from a sheltering grove of trees. As he slowly pulled himself back up onto the wagon seat and picked up the reins, Cara put her hand on his arm.

"Please stop, Dake. One day more or less won't hurt."

"You drive." He handed her the reins. "I don't intend to leave you stranded in the middle of nowhere with a sick man and a baby to tend. New Madrid can't be far off."

She bundled Clay up and nestled him in back with a wall of boxes for protection and headed toward the river town while Dake slumped on the wagon seat and slept fitfully.

They reached the outskirts of town just before dusk. Dake stirred and shoved himself up to a sitting position. "Head for the river."

Her arms ached from wrestling the reins for two hours. Thankful that they were about to stop soon, Cara slapped the reins against General Sherman's rump and followed the main streets set at right angles to the river. Destruction from heavy artillery fire was still in evidence along the streets. Where sides of brick and mortar buildings had been blown away, the hollowed-out shells were still in disrepair and abandoned. The open windows in the vacant remains were like the sightless eyes of skeletal dead men. "It's worse than Poplar Bluff," Cara said aloud with a shake of her head. While her family had waged their own private war with the prairie, much of the nation had faced the constant terror and upheaval in their very midst.

Dake roused himself, sat upright, and straightened his hat as he surveyed the damage. "There's an island just offshore that the Confederates fortified. General Pope laid siege to the town, then shelled it. The rebels left the island and the Federals took control of the river again."

A wagon wheel hit a pothole in the road and Cara slid almost on top of his lap. Reacting as if she'd hit hot coals, she all but jumped back to her place. Dake reached out to steady her hands on the reins and then took them from her. Relieved, she gave them up but immediately upon doing so reached up to feel his forehead again. "You'll live. You feel cooler," she announced.

He flashed a quick smile in her direction.

Don't be looking at me that way, Dake Reed.

When her cheeks flushed with color, she looked away, concentrating on the conglomeration of shacks that lined the river. Beyond them, riding the water at the end of a crooked gangplank, was a steamboat. There were three decks visible, the top one open to the elements. In front of the pilothouse on the upper deck, two lofty stacks with flaring crowns spewed columns of woodsmoke into the gathering twilight. High atop the stacks the lights from the signal lanterns showed red and green.

The wide, sandy banks of the Mississippi held more water between them than Cara had seen in years. The closer they got to the river, the more she thought she could actually feel the power of the water, smell the rich silt that moved along in the muddy water. She could hardly wait to climb aboard the river craft and experience the feel of moving over the water as it coursed downstream.

"Before we find a place to stay the night, let's see when the boat leaves." He pulled up at the end of the gangplank and started to wrap the reins around the brake.

Cara took in the dark circles beneath his eyes and his wan complexion. She knew full well that the fever could come and go for days, lending a false sense of recovery and then striking down the strongest of men. She laid a hand on his sleeve. "Wait here. I'll go find out."

We must look a sight, she thought as she crossed the soft earth toward the small building at the end of the ramp. Her lip was still cut, her face bruised. Dake looked like an old shirt that had been washed on a rock and left out to fade in the sun. With the silly box wagon, the barrels and boxes and Clay hidden among them, she was certain anyone who cared to wonder probably though them the oddest sort of vagabonds.

The wood-sided building was deserted, but as she came out of the open doorway, she was met by a man coming along the gangway. Cara lifted the hem of her navy wool dress and hurried over to him.

"Excuse me," she said, finding herself warily studying the heavyset man as she spoke and once more hating the fact that her experience in Poplar Bluff had made her so suspicious. "When does the boat leave?"

The portly man who looked to be about fifty, rocked back on his heels, reached up to scratch the bald pate beneath his hat, then cleared his throat. "Ten minutes."

"And when does the next one come by?"

He let out a sharp bark of a laugh that came from the depths of his ample belly. "The next one? This is the first one's been by in weeks. Not all that many left on the river since the war wiped 'em out." He glanced over her shoulder at Dake and the wagon a few yards away and scratched his head again. "You plannin' on goin' downriver by boat, you best be on this one or it could be a month or more before you leave."

"Are you the captain?"

He barked a laugh again. "No way in hell."

"Can you tell him to wait?"

He pulled a dented watch out of his pocket, flipped it open, squinted at the time in the weak light that was left, and said, "You got ten minutes, lady."

She picked up her skirt again and ran back to the wagon.

Out of breath, she leaned against the front wheel and tipped her head up to look at Dake. "It's leaving in ten minutes and if we want to get downriver we have to be on it."

She watched him close his eyes for a second as if marshaling the energy he would need to get them all aboard. "Do you have to do that?"

Confused, she frowned. "Do what?"

"Lift up your skirt like that when you run. Or do you want everyone to see your ankles all the time?"

Color flared across her cheeks and she looked back in the direction of the gangplank. The heavy man was gone. It was nearly dusk, low-lying fog was gathering like spun sugar around the base of the trees across the river. In the half-light their riotous fall colors were tamed and muted. There was no one else around.

Defiantly she cocked her chin. "We can stand here and argue about me showing my ankles, which I can certainly do if I want to, or we can see about getting on that boat. Which will it be, *Captain* Reed?"

She couldn't tell if he was fighting a smile or perhaps grimacing in discomfort. At any rate, he ignored the challenge in her tone. "Let's go."

Cara walked beside the wagon as he pulled up as close to the shack at the end of the gangway as possible. He tied off the brake and then started to climb down. When he put out a hand to brace himself, Cara reached up to steady him until he had his feet on solid ground.

Dake was obviously embarrassed when Cara had to help him down out of the wagon. He was openly appalled when he had to lean on her as they made their way across the damp ground to the building.

"You're weak as a kitten," she told him.

"Thank you so much for pointing that out," he mumbled, forcing himself upright to stand away from her. She stayed close to his side as the man she'd talked to came out of the shack that served as ticket booth and office for the steamboats that pulled into New Madrid.

"So, you folks goin' tonight?"

"We are," Dake told him. "We'll need two staterooms and I'm taking aboard the wagon and horse."

"And I'm Abe Lincoln's ghost." Shifting his girth as he pulled up his pants by the belt loops, the man shook his head. "The boat's loaded to the gills. Got one stateroom left. The wagon's no problem. Still room left on the main deck for cargo. Got room for singles in the men's cabin, ladies' cabin is full up."

Dake turned to Cara. "You and Clay can have the room. I'll sleep in the men's cabin," he told her, referring to the section where male passengers unwilling to pay for a stateroom could bunk together.

"You need a good night's sleep so you can get your strength back. I'll stay in the wagon with Clay."

Dake shook his head, his jaw tensed as he set to argue with her. "You're not staying in the wagon alone on the cargo deck."

She glanced at the steamboat. So many lamps had been lit in the cabins. So many golden lights blinked from the windows that the boat had taken on a magical appearance.

"Argue on board," the clerk warned, "or you'll be watching the boat leave without you. It's three cents a mile if you want a stateroom."

Dake pulled out a roll of money and peeled off the amount

required for a private stateroom and their cargo. He mustered the strength to climb back up onto the wagon box to drive up the gangplank while Cara walked at General Sherman's head and held on to the bit to guide the skittish horse up the ramp. Just as they reached the main deck and a crewman helped unharness General Sherman and pull the wagon into line beside various other loaded conveyances, Clay set up a howl.

By the time Cara got both Dake and Clay to the stateroom, walked back to the lower deck to collect their immediate things, and was back in the stateroom on the upper deck, she was feeling as exhausted as Dake looked.

He leaned against the door while she lay the baby on the bed and began to take off his diaper. She spoke without looking back at him. "I'll just change the baby and feed him and then go to the ladies' cabin. I know I can find a place to sleep in there somewhere. This shouldn't take but a minute—"

"Cara."

"What?" She glanced over her shoulder and then turned back to her task. An expert after almost three weeks of changing and diapering the baby, she laid a clean cloth over Clay's tiny penis, having learned the hard way that there was no telling when he might decide to let go.

"You're staying here."

She slid a clean cloth beneath the baby and then pulled it up between his legs. "No, I'm not. You are. If there's one thing you don't need, it's sleeping in a crowd of strangers as sick as you've been."

The diaper fastened, she hefted the baby up to her shoulder and turned to face Dake squarely. "Now, I'll be off. I can feed him in the cabin. I'll bring you something as soon as he's settled."

Dake stepped away from the wall. Soft lamplight played off the walls and cast the sharp lines of his features in relief. His eyes were dark as the deep moss along a streambed. He reached out and smoothed a stray curl back behind her ear. "I'm too tired to argue with you. You're staying here and that's that."

When she started to protest again, he nodded in the direction of the wide bunk. "That bed's as big as the one we shared in Poplar Bluff. I might have been sick last night, but I wasn't out of my mind. I seem to recall we had no problem sharing the blankets then. I think we can manage to make it through another night."

She took a deep breath to steady the nerves that had begun to flutter somewhere in the pit of her stomach and kept her eyes from straying to the bed.

"I don't think . . . It wouldn't be . . ."

"It's not proper?"

She nodded. Dake dropped his hand and stepped around her. He took off his hat and hung it on a towel hook on the opposite wall, then sank down on the side of the bed and stretched out, fully clothed. Without taking his eyes off her, he crossed his booted feet at the ankles. He stacked his hands beneath his head and closed his eyes. "Cara," he told her with his eyes closed, his lazy drawl slower and more pronounced than ever, "I'm dead tired, but if you're gonna insist I fret all night while you're out there trying to find room in the ladies' cabin, then so be it. I'll blame you when the shakes come back and there's no one here to help. And if you think I have the strength to do anything that would put your chastity in jeopardy, well, thank you for the compliment, darlin', but I'm plum tuckered out."

Cara hid a smile behind a light kiss she planted in Clay's soft curls. She watched as the big man on the edge of the bed slowly relaxed. There indeed was more than enough room for her in the wide bed. It looked firm but comfortable. The rocking motion of the vessel as it slowly pulled away from the bank lulled her into a sense of weightlessness. It would be so nice to get a good night's sleep without having to make conversation and explanations to her fellow travelers, to stretch out beside him as they drifted down the river and lose herself in sleep.

She turned and put her hand on the doorknob.

His voice stopped her cold. "Where are you going?"

"I thought I'd just go outside for a while . . . until you're asleep."

"Alone?"

She turned around. His eyes were still closed. She was tempted to cover him up, to mother him much as she did Clay. Instead, she said softly, "With Clay. I'll be back."

Her hand was on the knob again.

"Cara?"

"What, Dake?"

He could barely mumble. "Where are you going? I don't want to worry."

She didn't see how a man could worry while he was dead to the world, but she still assured him. "Just outside the door for a little air. I'll be right back."

Cara found an empty bench just outside the cabin and chose a spot that wasn't directly beneath a halo of light from the square-sided deck lantern. She sat down and stared out at the river. The rhythmic splash of the paddle wheel and the barely audible sound of water rushing against the side of the boat as it moved swiftly downriver lulled her. Lamplight from the deck lanterns cast a glow on the water, lighting the cups and ripples of it like so many floating jewels. New smells, mud and mildew, river moss and reeds were all new to her. After so long on the open dry land of the Kansas prairie, the sights and sounds of the open water were as refreshing as the cool night air on her face.

She shifted the child to her other arm and let the night seep into her bones. Clay snuggled closer, and reflexively her arms tightened around him. A month ago she would never have imagined herself caring for a newborn. Now, incredibly, it seemed the most natural thing in the world. At times it was almost possible to imagine the three of them as a family. Almost. Until she forced herself to remember that Dake Reed was really no more than a handsome stranger who had ridden into her yard and her life and would have left again if she hadn't agreed to care for Clay.

In the miles they'd traveled along the trail it had been all too easy to sink into the routine and sameness of the days, to find herself sharing conversation as well as silence with Dake Reed as together they shortened the miles to Alabama. He'd told her little of himself or his home. He talked some of the war. Mostly he had listened or pretended to as she talked about her life in Kansas, about her Nanny James, about the land and weather. Last night, he had opened up to her even more.

Unaware of how or when it actually came about, despite her vow to herself, she found herself warming to Dake's quick, infrequent smiles, waiting for the touch of his hand as he helped her in and out of the wagon. She even relished their arguments. Cara tried to imagine what her journey would have been like if she had been on her own as she originally planned. Try as she might, all she could think of was the way it had been over the past weeks with Dake Reed beside her.

"Be careful, Cara Calvinia James," she whispered to herself as the river carried them swiftly toward Memphis. "You best guard your heart. Keep thinking of California, girl. Think of that wide blue ocean that will make this river seem like a bog."

A boatman called out the river depths and startled her into silence. Cara stood and carried Clay back to the door of the cabin. The room had grown chilly when she slipped inside and found Dake sound asleep. He didn't stir when she once again lined a drawer with Clay's quilt and lay him inside. Nor did Dake awaken when she turned down the lamp and then sat on her side of the bed to take off her shoes. She covered him with an extra blanket and then slipped beneath the bedclothes fully dressed, determined to stay as close to the edge of the bed as possible.

He turned toward her, but slept on. She was tempted to smooth his hair off his forehead, went so far as to reach out her hand, but then drew it back.

In sleep, he reached out to her, lay his hand on her arm, and left it there, as if reassuring himself she lay beside him. Cara frowned up at the ceiling, but didn't move, didn't breathe for a second, until she was certain he was really asleep.

She frowned up at the ceiling and whispered, "Don't fall in love with me, Dake Reed, 'cause I've got plans of my own." Somehow though, as she lay beside him enveloped in the satin darkness, being lulled into complacency by the lapping sound of the paddle wheel churning through the water, California seemed a universe away.

> *Heaven suits our trials to our strengths.*
>
> H. Moore

Chapter Seven

Everything was the same and yet nothing was the same, nor would it ever be again.

The Tennessee River still swept silently past Decatur. The air was alive with the rich smell of the fertile earth, the sky still as blue, the breeze off the river tickled the pine boughs and loosed the full leaves of oak and walnut, hickory and cedar.

As he stood near the old cemetery beside the railroad and stared around at the aftermath of the destruction, Dake wanted to weep. Instead, he cursed under his breath. Thankful to have left Cara and Clay behind while he ventured onto the once familiar streets alone, he glanced over his shoulder at the Polk Hotel where they had just registered. It was one of only three homes left standing in town.

Yawning gaps lined the streets where buildings once stood. The once bustling riverfront was deserted. The Tennessee River Bridge, a marvel of wood and iron, had been rebuilt. So had the railroad depot. The Union flag flew beside that of the company commander high above Burleson House, a stately colonial home that had stood for over forty years. Commandeered by the Federals, the historic home had thus been saved.

The once busy streets were nearly deserted except for small knots of men, Negroes in some places, whites in others, who clustered together to watch the occasional passerby. Strolling almost too casually in pairs were uniformed Federal soldiers of both races, assigned to keep the peace among a people who had rebelled and lost the right to govern themselves.

Dake marshaled his emotion, steeled himself—as he had been forced to do so many times during the war years—to act, not think of the consequences of those actions, to hold to the belief that the ultimate end would be for the greatest good. Now, standing in the cemetery, he stared down at the few headstones that had not been destroyed by shelling. They were silent and timeworn. He ran his hand over the low stone wall, felt the cool surface of the moss-covered stone. What might they have thought, those first settlers of Decatur who were buried here, if they had witnessed the conflict that ripped the country asunder? Did they know what had transpired, or were they truly in a better place where human drama was no longer of any concern?

He forced himself to move, to walk the avenues he had so often walked, pathways he never thought to tread again. He continued along Lafayette Street, past another survivor, the old house owned by steamboat captain James Todd. He wasn't halfway to the end of the block when the sound of hoofbeats alerted him to a rider approaching from behind. In a glance he saw the rider was a civilian, a rare sight since only the military had horses of any worth. Every mule, horse, cow, and other domestic animal had been conscripted by both armies as they marched through Alabama.

The rider was lean, his features shadowed by the wide brim of his low-crowned hat. There was something familiar in the way the man sat his horse that made Dake pause to watch his approach.

Although not much else about the man was recognizable, there was no mistaking the deep blue of Shelby Gilmore's eyes. Dake stepped closer to the man's horse and waited. Gilmore chose not to dismount. Instead, he casually leaned an elbow on his knee and merely stared down at Dake with a sullen twist to his lips. His woolen jacket was misshapen from long use and almost threadbare at the elbows. Deep lines marred the man's once-carefree countenance. Shelby Gilmore could be no more than twenty-five, yet he appeared a score of years older. Born and bred a planter's son, he was well educated, as were most Alabamans who did not have to till the soil. Before the war, he had led as privileged a life as money could buy.

He did not smile now as he continued to stare down at Dake.

"Here's a sight I never thought to see again in my life," Gilmore finally said in an emotionless drawl that was as slow as molasses pours in cold weather. "I knew you'd turned coat, Reed, but I never expected you'd be so low as to come back with the other scalawags and carpetbaggers to see our noses ground into the dirt."

"I don't have to defend myself to you or anyone else, Gilmore."

Shelby Gilmore looked over the ruins of what had once been a thriving river town. "No, I suppose you don't."

There was something about the rigid set of the man's shoulders, something in the still defiant look in his eyes that made Dake add, "I came because Minna sent for me."

There was no need to explain who he meant. In a town as close-knit as Decatur before the war, he and Shelby had all attended the same social gatherings, the parties, soirees, the cotillions. Minna was closer to Shelby Gilmore's age than Dake's. Gilmore's attention immediately cut back to Dake at the mention of her name. His posture stiffened defiantly.

"Minna? As far as I'm concerned, you don't have the right to speak her name. If you cared one whit for Minna Blakely you'd never have gone over to the North. Course, what she's suffered ain't any worse than what any other *loyal* Confederate has had to deal with."

"Is she all right?"

"She's right enough. Right as anyone would be who saw

their parents burned alive practically right before her eyes. She lost everything she owned and was forced to survive on your father's charity. Then her fiancé came back from the war a cripple."

"Fiancé?"

Shelby's expression registered doubt and then a certain cool smugness. He was obviously happy to be the one to break the news to Dake. "She's living out at Riverglen. Been engaged to your brother since he was home on leave about midway through the war. It was one of the few times Decatur was still in Confederate hands."

Minna's engagement to Burke came as no surprise, it had been expected since childhood. It was Gilmore's blunt disclosure that his brother had come home somehow crippled that stunned him.

While Dake was still reeling from the news, the former Confederate added, "If it wasn't for Minna, Burke would have lost Riverglen by now. She was there alone when the Treasury men came through taking over everything that belonged to us 'rebels.' Your daddy took her in right after the Blakely place burned, but he took ill and died a few months later. When the Federals came through again in '64, they wanted to confiscate Riverglen, but she stood up to them. Since you were fightin' with the Yankees, Minna was able to convince the Treasury agents not to lay claim to the place. Took them a while, as I understand it, to find out for sure that you were Union, but once things got straightened out, your place remained pretty much untouched except for things that could be toted off."

Dake bit the inside of his lip. "You say Minna's still there?"

Shelby nodded. "So's your brother." He looked thoughtful for a moment, then said, "If I were you, Reed, I'd take some advice. Go right back to hell or wherever it was you came from. Your brother doesn't want to see you now or ever. You know how much it shamed him to think it was Minna who saved his home for him? Minna *and* the fact that you'd gone over to the Union? If it hadn't been for that, Riverglen would have been lost and Burke would have been out of a home."

His eyes burned with the fire of a zealot's. "You don't know what it's like to feel shame, do you, Dake? See those Negroes in blue uniform on the corner up there? Some of them were mine once. Bought and paid for. Hell, some of 'em might have even been yours. Know why they're stationed here? To shame us. The Federals enlisted them just to lord it over us."

Dake glanced down the street, determined to stop Shelby's heated tirade before it became explosive. "You said my brother had been wounded—"

"Wounded ain't the word for it."

Dake steeled himself. He nodded for Shelby to go on.

"Lost both legs. One at the knee, one at the hip."

Despite the fact that he could feel the other man watching him closely, Dake closed his eyes for the briefest of seconds, stunned by the news. His mind refused to accept the fact that his once dynamic brother had been maimed and would remain crippled for the rest of his life, but he'd seen it happen to far too many men already to allow him to disbelieve it now.

"I'm telling you, Reed. Get out. Go back up north where you belong."

Dake couldn't ignore the outright challenge in Shelby Gilmore's eyes. "This was my home. I'm not going anywhere."

Two Federal soldiers crossed the street, headed toward them. Gilmore gazed at them scornfully over his shoulder before he turned back to Dake. "Here comes two of your kind, Reed. Can't see as there's any reason for me to stay and breathe in the smell of a whole passel of Yankees." Without a word or gesture of farewell, Shelby Gilmore kicked his horse and cantered down the street.

The Union men, one a corporal, walked directly up to Dake, who stifled the urge to salute and merely nodded, then held out his hand in introduction. "I'm Dake Reed, formerly a Union captain assigned to Ford Dodge, Kansas. I mustered out nearly a month ago."

Dake's introduction was met with the same skepticism and doubt he'd faced throughout the war years. Over and over again, his Southern drawl had continually cast him in a suspicious light with his northern comrades. He waited as the young corporal sized him up and then still appeared doubtful. "What are you doing here in Decatur?"

"I'm from Riverglen, a plantation down the river."

"Doubt if it's still there," the young man admitted impersonally.

"The gentleman that just rode away assured me that it is."

The enlisted man beside the corporal shifted uneasily and let his gaze drift back to the direction Shelby Gilmore had just taken.

"That 'gentleman,'" the corporal began, "is suspected of being heavily involved with a group of vigilantes that started up across the border a couple years back. Call themselves the Ku Klux. They're hell-bent to right all the wrongs they think we've done to them and their neighbors." The sandy-haired youth casually rested his hand on his gun butt, whether intentionally or not, Dake couldn't be certain. Still the threat wasn't to be denied. "They ride around in white hoods to conceal their identities and scare the hell out of the Negroes. Think it'll keep 'em in line now that they're free to come and go as they please. If the hoods and talk of ghosts don't work, there are always lynchings and burnings to fall back on."

He looked Dake over carefully once more. "If you are what you say you are, Mr. Reed, then more power to you if you really do intend to stay on around here. There's more than a few rebs who don't take kindly to what they call Tories and scalawags. They'll always think of you as a traitor. But if you're lyin', if you're here as part of the Ku Klux to stir up trouble—"

"Look, Corporal, I'm exactly who I say I am. If you don't believe me, have your commanding officer send off a telegram to Washington for verification."

"I just might do that. Where are you staying?"

Pushed too far by the offensive tone of the man's voice, Dake fired back, "Do I have to answer that?"

"You do if you mean to start off by being cooperative."

A good head taller and probably five years older than the man, Dake gave him a cool stare. "I'll either be at the Polk Hotel or at Riverglen, eight miles west of here."

"A word of advice, Mr. Reed."

Dake waited, noncommittal.

"If you're who you say you are—watch your back."

Cara was fuming. Not merely simmering, not boiling, but fuming mad at Dake because once again she somehow found herself waiting for him in a hotel room while she wondered where he was and exactly when he intended to return. Ever since the first night of their trip downriver, he had carefully distanced himself from her. This morning he seemed eager when he left Clay and her in the room with little more than a curt "I'll be back soon." She was tempted to tell him that she, too, would like to stretch her legs and see what Decatur was like, but the obvious tension in his stance and his preoccupied manner put her off. So had his studied coolness toward her.

To keep her hands occupied, she had begun fashioning a doll with a walnut head. Sitting on the edge of the bed, she looked over the materials she had on hand. Turning a walnut over and over in her hand, she tried to imagine a tiny face painted upon it, the eyes positioned just above the pointed end that would provide a tiny nose. It wouldn't take very long, nor would she need more than a few scraps to create a doll with a cloth-wrapped body.

She chose a colorful scrap of calico print, creamy yellow for a poke bonnet, and decided on a fashionable lady, the likes of which she had seen on the streets in Memphis. Scissors in hand, she started her task and kept her hands busy, but she couldn't keep her mind off of Dake. The closer they came to Decatur, the more he had turned inward, all but ignoring her. At first, Cara had reminded herself that was exactly what she wanted. It was best that there would be no emotional ties, no heart-wrenching good-byes, no giving in to her growing attraction to him. The nearer they got to Alabama, the more preoccupied he had become. She couldn't fault him for that. They often encountered the still-raw emotion between the citizens who had so recently been opponents in the bloody war. He'd been continually reminded that his own homecoming would be less than welcome anywhere.

What had hurt her was the abrupt commanding tone he had begun to use when he spoke to her. As they left the riverboat in Memphis, he had given her the curt order to remain at the railroad station while he went off for a good two hours on some undisclosed mission before they boarded the train.

Clay started to fuss, so she put down the scraps she'd begun to cut into the shape of a tiny dress and glanced out the window at the desolate view of what must have been a quiet, prosperous town before the war. As she picked Clay up, she was given a sense of satisfaction when she felt the baby's firm little body in her hands. Clayton had thrived in her care. Just as she had done so many times over the past weeks, she smiled down at him and began to whisper nonsense words, teasing his cheek with a whisper-light touch of her fingertip to make him smile.

Over the past month his features had taken shape and become less nondescript. No longer was he merely a newborn who resembled a wizened old man more than a child. His eyes had widened and the color had changed from a deep midnight-blue to a warmer tone of brown. There was more of the tawny hair that gently curled around her finger. Blessed with a good disposition, he smiled more often than not. In fact, she was certain he was the best behaved child anyone would ever want, also the handsomest, not to mention the sweetest.

She quickly changed his diaper, a task that had become as regular as breathing. Cara couldn't help but smile whenever she recalled that first awkward attempt and the twisted bundle of material she and Dake had succeeded diapering him in. As she lifted the baby to her shoulder again and walked back to the window at the front of the neatly appointed room, her hold on him tightened reflexively. Now that they had reached Alabama, it wouldn't be long before they delivered him to his kinfolk. Dake told her he planned to get out to his former home and see what he could do to help his brother before he made any plans to accompany her and Clay to Gadsden. What were the Claytons like? She hoped to God they were loving, caring people who would cherish Clay as a family should cherish any child.

Over and over she had tried to imagine the scene that would unfold when she gave the baby over to his grandmother and grandfather, aunts and uncles. They would exclaim and weep over Anna Clayton's death. Cara hoped their sorrow would be tempered by the gift of the child their daughter had left behind. They would hold Clay reverently, pass him from hand to hand, and make promises about his future.

She hugged Clay tighter, smoothed her palm along the rounded bottom swaddled in fabric, kissed the curls over the soft spot atop his head. It was the hope of her storybook ending for the baby that eased the ache that squeezed her heart when she thought about giving him over to his relations.

Movement on the street caught her eye. Cara stepped out onto the wide balcony shared by the upper rooms and watched as Dake, in a black shirt, his precious buckskin jacket, and dark hat and pants, walked up the street toward the hotel. With his strong gait, sure determination, and striking smile, he was a man who would make any woman proud. She knew he was anxious to get home, to see Minna and his brother. Would he take her to Riverglen immediately or leave her here? What would he feel for this mysterious Minna when he saw her again?

She couldn't help but wonder about the woman who had called him home. He had told her Minna was Burke's but what feelings did Dake harbor for her? What was she like?

When Dake disappeared beneath the portico directly below her window, Cara tried to quiet her mounting anticipation. Try as she might, she was obviously having less success than he at quieting the riot of emotion that threatened to engulf her whenever they were together. She glanced down at the child in her arms, kissed him so gently on the forehead that he didn't even stir, and then placed him within a boundary of pillows in the middle of the bed.

She hurried across the gleaming oak floorboards to the washstand near the door and glanced in the mirror above it. The dark ribbon in her hair kept her wayward curls out of her face. The dove-gray, secondhand gown she wore did little to enliven her complexion, but it was very warm and covered her ankles. How was the young widow, the former owner of the gown? How had her little daughter fared?

How many widows sat alone in parlors across the land waiting for the sound of footsteps they would never hear again? During her journey she realized just how much life on the prairie had sheltered her from the worst of the war. How easy it had been to dismiss the upheaval, destruction, and death that seemed so far away. As she stepped off the train and faced the wreckage here in Decatur, she could clearly imagine the terror such wanton destruction must have ignited, not to mention the loathing of the vanquished for the victors.

A swift knock at the door caused her to swing away from the mirror. She forced herself to slow her steps as she hurried to answer the summons. Cara took a deep breath and opened the door.

Hat in hand, Dake nodded absently and moved past her into the room. He glanced over at Clay. Then, turning his back to Cara, he walked to the balcony door. As if gathering his thoughts, he stood tapping his hat against his thigh as he stared across the veranda. Cara clasped her hands at her waist and waited. Finally, he faced her.

Unable to read the thoughts behind his fathomless green eyes, she wished he would smile.

"I've got to go out to Riverglen sooner than later, so I thought I'd best leave now," he said.

"And leave me here, I suppose?" She hadn't meant to sound so shrewish, but it was too late to take back her question.

"Yes."

"You walked off in Memphis for two hours without a by-your-leave. When will you be back this time?"

He paused, stared down at his hat, and then back up at her again. "I don't know."

"And I'm supposed to just sit here with Clay and wait?"

He crossed the room, grabbed her face between his strong hands. "That's right. That's what you're being paid for, isn't it? To look after Clay?"

If he had slapped her she would have felt the same hurt. Cara turned away to hide the quick tears that stung her eyes and stiffened. Her crying days were over. She batted at the moisture with the back of her hand. She felt him touch her shoulders and tried to step away. His hands tightened as he turned her, forcing her to look up into his eyes—eyes shadowed with doubt and pain.

"I'm sorry, Cara."

The warmth of his touch seeped through the fabric of her gown. It reminded her of the nights they had shared in the riverboat cabin, the long dark hours when she found herself comforted by his nearness, times when it had been all too easy to let herself imagine she and Dake and Clay as more than three wanderers on different paths.

For the first time since he rode into her yard she saw a look of uncertainty on his face. "Look, Cara, I don't know what kind of a situation I'll be walking into at Riverglen or else I would happily take you with me."

His admission made her feel the need to apologize. She knew she should step out of his reach, to break the contact of his hands on her shoulders, to keep herself moving and busy. Dake Reed was, after all, only her employer. The money he would pay her at the end of Clay's journey to Gadsden would provide the stake she needed to start her own dream.

She couldn't compel herself to move, but she did speak. "I'm sorry I'm acting like such a fishwife." Then she shrugged and admitted, "I get worried, is all. Those with nothing to worry about, worry about nothing."

He gave her a half smile. "I haven't heard any of Nanny James's wisdom in a long while now."

Was it her imagination, or had he lowered his head so that his lips were closer? If he kissed her now, would it be as sweet as the time he'd requested it in Poplar Bluff?

Dake watched her blue eyes widen as he drew her nearer, warning himself not to kiss her, but unable to let go and pull back all the same. As he looked down at her, he realized that having Cara with him made the distress of the morning somewhat easier to bear. When he found her looking fresh and radiant despite the pristine gray gown and the black ribbon that restrained her abundant curls, he wished for a moment that he could pack up both her and Clay and move on to another place and time where he didn't have to face his brother, his neighbors, or what had happened because of the war.

He pulled her closer, a bit surprised when she allowed it, and lowered his head until his lips met hers. He'd assumed, naively enough, that a brief kiss, a mere touch of their lips, would be enough to sustain him. He was certain that was all she would allow. But once their lips met, he was compelled by an undeniable urge to pull her up close, to hold her hard against his length, and with his own palm cupping the back of her head, slash his mouth against hers.

The past weeks of pent-up emotion exploded. Cara clung to him. Her arms locked around his neck as she went up on tiptoe, straining for more, reveling in the sensations his kiss evoked.

He urged her to open her lips to him, his tongue teasing the seam of her mouth and then her teeth. The excitement that mounted as he explored her with his tongue was a pleasant surprise. Tentatively she let herself follow his lead, tasted and explored on her own, met his tongue thrust for thrust until she moaned low in her throat and her breath came in quick pants.

They clung together there in the center of the room as sunlight flooded through the window, streaked the polished oak floor, and gilded Cara's curls. He let his hands roam her back, felt her warm and alive beneath the inexpensive wool, drew his palm around and cupped her breast with a feather-light touch before he sighed against her lips and ended the kiss.

They drew apart, breathing fast and shallow. As realization of what had just passed between them dawned, Cara blushed. He lay his hand along her cheek and smiled down into her eyes.

"I didn't expect to walk in here and do that," he said.

She frowned and blinked twice, searching for the correct response. "I certainly didn't plan it, either. It's like my lips just ran away without me."

He laughed, looking more at ease than she had seen him all morning.

"Don't think this changes anything, Dake Reed," she said, denying the way her pulse was still racing.

He held her at arm's length. "I'm sorry I've been less than enjoyable for the past few days, but I didn't know what to expect when we reached Alabama. Now it seems I should have expected the worst."

"Your brother?" Shaken by his kiss, she moved away, still savoring the taste of him, the feel of his mouth as it moved over hers. Trying to act as casual about it as he, she wanted to lift her hand to her lips and trace them, to see if somehow she had been altered by the experience. Instead, she walked as calmly as she could to the washstand and once there reached out and held on to the top edge to ground herself. Her earlier words to him had been an out and out lie. The power of that kiss had changed everything. Unable to concentrate, all she wanted was for him to kiss her again. And kiss her hard.

"Burke's been gravely wounded. Crippled."

The word "wounded" penetrated her heated thoughts. It sobered her as much as being doused by a pail of water. She heard him walk to the window again and turned to watch him. His face was averted, his shoulders rigid. Quickly she crossed the room to stand beside him and offer her support without touching. She was afraid of any physical connection. Afraid of herself.

"You should leave right away." Quickly she added, "I'm sorry, too, for the things I said a few minutes ago. But I've been wondering . . ." She glanced over at the child asleep on the bed. Her own concern had yet to be voiced and she couldn't hold it back any longer. "Do you think the Claytons will take care of Clay?"

He looked toward the bed and then back at her, quiet for a moment as he studied her closely. Slowly, Dake nodded. "I'm sure of it. Who couldn't love him?"

She looked up at him. *Who couldn't love you, Dake Reed? Is*

*this love that I feel for you? Is it love that makes my heart
dance when you hold me in your arms?*

"Are you all right, Cara?"

"What?" She started, looked away from him, and frowned.
"Of course," she lied. How could she be all right when her
hands itched to touch him, her arms ached to hold him again.
And her lips—she found them another problem altogether.
Tempted to embrace him, she balled her hands into fists and
held them at her sides. *California. California. California.* She
chanted the word over and over in her mind. The dream that
had given her such comfort, that had seen her through endless
months on the prairie, now seemed empty, void of meaning.

He was at the door now, watching her. What would happen
when he returned? Would his visit home change him unalter-
ably?

"There's a box on the bed in my room." He dug into his
pocket and drew out the key. He set it on the washstand. "It's
for you."

She crossed the room, looked at the key, and back up at him.
"What—?"

"Something I picked up in Memphis is all." He reached out
and touched her shoulder. "I don't know when I'll be back."

"I'll be here," she promised as he stepped out the door.
When it closed behind him she felt more frustrated than she
ever had in her life. "Right now, there's no place else I'd rather
be."

> *A man in debt is caught in a net.*
> Ben Franklin,
> *Poor Richard's Almanac*

Chapter Eight

Even the welcome the familiar sights and sounds along the road to Riverglen afforded him could not keep his mind from straying back to Polk House and Cara. Dake had no clue as to what possessed him to further complicate their lives by kissing her again. Maybe it was because he had been certain she would resist. He was inwardly shocked when she didn't protest, but he was too far lost in sensation and need to stop. As always, she reminded him immediately thereafter that their relationship was only temporary, that she was moving on in search of a dream, as well she should, but now more than ever he found it hard to imagine Cara separated from him by half a continent.

In the past few weeks, even though it was not her intention to do so, even though she herself had warned him against it, she had captivated him with her shining eyes and teasing smile. She had become part of his life during the journey back into the unfamiliar world he once called home.

He headed up a back road and forced himself to concentrate not on Cara, but on the confrontation that surely lay ahead. He'd nearly reached the old slave quarters, the double row of cabins not far from the main house. The two-room dwellings stood at attention across from each other, ramshackle remnants of another way of life. There was movement around some of the cabins and as he drew nearer he could make out one or two inhabitants who'd stepped out into the dirt lane to stare curiously as he approached.

One man in a doorway separated himself from the darkness of the interior that framed him and began running down the lane toward Dake's horse. Within seconds Dake recognized Elijah, his former valet, hailed him with a wave, and kicked his horse into a canter.

"Marse Dake!" Elijah shouted as he waved a top hat around over his head in greeting. "Marse Dake! I sure do believe the Lord has answered my prayers," he said as he ran up beside General Sherman and took the reins.

Dake dismounted, reached out and grabbed Elijah to him and pounded him on the back. Both men laughed with an underlying soberness in their voices. Dake was the first to speak after they had separated. "I didn't expect to see you here," he said.

"No, suh." Elijah shoved his hat back on his head and gave the high crown a tap to anchor it tight. "I 'spects you didn't. I left when Freedom come. Went off down the road with a whole gang of singin', shoutin' folks followin' the Federals and yellin' 'bout how the Freedom done come at last."

"But you came back."

Elijah looked off toward the northeast, the exuberance of his greeting diminished as he stared across the fields. "We all ran off like spoilt children, shoutin' 'bout Freedom without knowin' the hardship that was to come. We was free all right. Free to starve on the road or sit 'round on street corners. Least ways when we was slaves we had food and clothes and a roof over our heads. Some folks sayin' we was 'sposed to be gettin' forty acres and a mule from the Freedom, but all we got so far been an empty belly. Ain't no white folks left with 'nough money to pay us, so mos' folks is workin' for food and a place to live."

"You know about the Freedman's Bureau?" Dake asked. "I saw them passing out food to the hungry in Decatur."

Elijah sniffed. "The Bureau's all well and good, but what little food they give only go so far. A man can't sleep in the woods and eat squirrel pie forever. They's feedin' the whites, too, you know. Ain't nobody in the South got nothin' now." He shook his head sorrowfully. "Nobody."

Dake tapped his reins against his thigh and turned to look across the lane where a glimpse of the main house could be seen through the trees. "How's my brother? How are things up at the house?"

The question elicited another shake of Elijah's head. His eyes were dark, the shadows beneath them deep. He was only twenty, but looked at least fifteen years older, thin as a split rail fence, all angles and joints beneath the ragged clothes. Dake recognized Elijah's jacket as one he had once discarded.

"Not good, Marse Dake, not good at all. Miss Minna come on the place jest after you left 'cause her mammy and pappy died. Then the ol' marse, he up and died real sudden, too." He frowned for a moment and looked about to add more but didn't.

"And my brother?"

"Marse Burke be here but he's hurtin' real bad. Course, that's all's I 'spect he could do now that—" He stopped abruptly and stared at Dake. "You know 'bout Marse Burke yet?"

Dake nodded, saving Elijah from having to be the bearer of bad tidings. "I heard in town, earlier."

"He's sore beaten, Marse Dake. Don't do nothin' but sit in his chair by the window and stare out cross the fields hour 'pon hour. He's mighty bad, mighty bad in the head. Miss Minna, she'd like to keep it all from fallin' to ruin, but I 'spects it's too late." He half smiled. "Least ways I did till I seen you ridin' up just now like an angel of the Lord to save us all."

Looking out at the deserted fields, then closer, toward the abandoned vegetables patches gone to weed beside the many uninhabited cabins, Dake felt as if a heavy, sodden cloak had been draped across his shoulders. Had he been a fool to ever imagine he could salvage Riverglen? Even if his brother gave him permission to try, where would he find all the capital he needed to invest in an economy where hand-to-mouth living had become status quo for both black and white?

"Is my brother able to pay you, Elijah?"

"No, suh. But what food Miss Minna gets, she give us some now and again for helpin' out. And she let us live in our old cabins. The few of us that's still here been doin' some vegetable gardenin' this summer so there's plenty for a time. Miss Minna, she and the house girl learnin' how to put the food up in jars for the winter months, but I 'spect it's gonna be hard as the last few years."

The row was a ghost town without the usual passel of children running barefoot up and down the lane and the people too old to work watching out for them. Dake and Elijah began to walk side by side along the deserted byway, Dake pausing now and again to greet the few Negroes who had stayed on or had a taste for life on the road and then returned to Riverglen. At the end of the row he paused, Elijah having been the only one to walk all the way with him.

"I'm going up to the house now," Dake said. "I wish I could tell you not to worry, but I don't know how my brother will react to seeing me again. If there's anything at all I can do, I'll sure as hell try, Elijah."

"I know it, Marse Dake. I'm jest glad to see you home in one piece."

Dake smiled. "At least I am that." He decided to walk the rest of the way to the main house and didn't remount.

As he bid Elijah good-bye, the former slave stopped him to add, "I hope you don't mind, Marse Dake, but when the Federals wanted to sign us up to vote I had to have two names to make my mark. I got no idea what my granddaddy's African name was, so's I took yours. I'm Elijah Reed now."

"I consider it an honor." Dake held out his hand. Elijah stared down at it for a moment, hesitated, wiped his own palm on his hip, and then shook hands with Dake.

"Good luck up at the house, Marse Dake."

Dake knew he'd need it.

Cara slipped quietly into Dake's room at Polk House, overwhelming curiosity urging her on. He told her there was a box for her on the bed, a box the contents of which he'd mysteriously avoided mentioning. Something he'd picked up in Memphis, he said.

She walked as quietly as she could, unwilling to alert her hostess to the fact that she had entered Dake's room. The landlady had watched them both suspiciously ever since they registered and Cara found it easier to stay in her room and avoid prying eyes. When they registered, the woman almost refused to rent them rooms until Dake reminded her that as a former Union officer he could make things very unpleasant for her. Cara couldn't help but notice the sorrow in his voice when he was forced to issue his demand. Cara knew it would do their already tenuous residence here no good if she were found in his room—even if she was alone.

His room was as tidy as she had come to expect. Although they had just moved in, every piece of his clothing had already been folded and put away. His saddlebags were stashed out of sight. She tiptoed over to the bed with its neat, crewel-embroidered counterpane, astounded by the size of the box he had left there for her. Before she saw it, she suspected it was some unusual doll he might have come across in Memphis. It was not overly heavy when she lifted it, nor did it rattle when shook. Cradling the box in her arms, she hurried out of the room and closed the door behind her without a sound. As she moved along the hallway, she juggled the package in one arm as she slipped the key to Dake's room into the deep pocket of her dove-gray dress.

She hurried into her own room, closed the door behind her, and rushed to the bed, excited as a child at Christmas.

"Let's see what this is, Clay." She slipped the twine over the corner of the box and tossed it aside. The lid came off easily to reveal a layer of brown tissue paper. She snatched it aside. Few gifts had been given to her in her life, too few surprises during the long, humdrum routine of life on the prairie. No money for store-bought things or time to learn how to tarry over wrapped gifts.

Beneath the sheet of tissue lay a carefully folded garment. A gown, she suspected, as she reached out to touch it. Azure blue silk quilting slid richly beneath her fingertips as she lifted the gown from the box. Once unfolded to full length, its standing collar and jaunty bow that tied at the neck were visible. She felt the black velvet collar, straightened the bow, shook out the gown, and held it before her. It looked to be a perfect fit.

She waltzed about the room for a second, bowing right and left to invisible partners, smiled charmingly at the faded chintz wallpaper until she returned to the bed and looked back down at the box. There was a pile of underthings that made her blush, deep blue stockings, a fancy chemisette with a muslin bow, ruffled, knee-length drawers, and a pair of black silk slippers she thought looked entirely useless.

Beneath the undergarments lay another gown, this one of bright wool plaid. Cara pulled it out, studied the richness of the red and black plaid and the long full skirt with box pleats at the waist. A red silk scarf lay beneath it. When she pulled the scarf from the box, a print that had been torn out of Godey's Ladies Book drifted to the floor. Cara picked it up and studied the picture. Obviously the gown was an exact replica of the one featured and was shown with the silk scarf thrown over one shoulder for a rakish Scottish look. Black stockings lay folded at the bottom.

Stunned by Dake's generosity, Cara sat on the edge of the bed and studied the heap of clothing. The dresses were finer than anything she had ever seen. She had thought her recently acquired secondhand clothes fit for a queen, but these— There was no one in the South with anything so fine. Cara wondered if he had kissed her that morning because he felt she owed him as much for such luxurious gifts. Is this what being a kept woman was all about? True, he had paid for her room and board, the riverboat passage and train fare all the way from Kansas, but she had offered to do so for herself. Gowns were not part of the bargain. The extravagance of his gift puzzled her.

The gowns, though, beckoned to be worn. She locked the door and quickly began unbuttoning the dove-gray dress she'd purchased from the widow in Poplar Bluff. When Dake returned, she intended to ask him what exactly his generosity meant. But she might as well be wearing the blue gown he'd bought her when she asked.

White oak and maple lined the lane that led to the big house at Riverglen. The leaves were stained with color, their brilliant display a last grasp at life before they withered and crisped. The road curved enough that he couldn't see the front door, but he did catch a sign of movement, a flash of heather through the shadows. As he neared, he recognized Minna moving swiftly and gracefully toward him with the hem of her skirt held in one hand. Still every inch a lady, she saw him, waved, and dropped her hem as she waited beneath the trees for his approach. From a distance, she appeared unchanged since the day he'd ridden off to war. Her hair was still a rich, shining chestnut-brown. He could see the whiteness of her smile.

He waved and when she returned the salute he felt some of

his pent-up apprehension slip away. The space between them lessened. Twigs snapped and leaves scattered beneath General Sherman's hooves. Dake stopped a few feet from her.

"Minna." He said her name on a sigh and bent to kiss her cheek.

"Welcome home, Dake." Her voice was still soft as a mourning dove's coo. There was a dimple in her cheek although her smile was not as bright as it had once been. On close inspection he could see that her dress was made of a coarse homespun fabric, nothing like the silks and satins she had always worn. The heather dye was uneven, the buttons down the bodice mismatched. Some, he could see, were nothing more than layers of pasteboard pressed together. Without meaning to, he let his eyes drop to her feet. Her shoes were brogans, crude cloth uppers attached to wooden soles, the same footwear provided the slaves.

"Not a very pretty picture, am I?" she said in a voice he had to strain to hear.

"You'd look beautiful in a pickle barrel, Minna Blakely, and you know it." He tried to joke, but his heart weighed heavy seeing her like this. He looked past her, over her shoulder at the house beyond. There was an old black sway-backed horse tethered to the hitching post near the veranda. "I received your letter and left Kansas shortly after. I hope you weren't expecting an answer."

She brushed a wisp of hair back off her cheek and shook her head. "This is better. Besides, Shelby was by today and told me he'd seen you in Decatur. I've been watchin' out the window since he left, hopin' to catch you before—" She stopped, hesitant to proceed.

He came to her aid. "Before Burke saw me?"

Her smile fled. "Shelby said he told you about Burke. I wish he hadn't. I wish he'd have let me—"

"Is it bad, Minna?"

Her eyes misted. She looked down at her hands as she held them clenched before her. "He won't let me close to him, Dake. He won't let anyone break through the barriers he's erected."

When her shoulders drooped, he slipped his arm around them and pulled her close. She sobbed in silence, her face hidden in her hands as she leaned against him for support. Finally, she wiped her eyes on the handkerchief he'd offered and the dimple appeared in her cheek as she strained to smile once more.

"I'm so sorry. I just don't know what came over me, breakin' down like that. Most days I can take it, but I guess seein' you and knowin' you still cared enough about us, about Riverglen—"

He gave her one quick squeeze before he let her go. Minna had been Burke's girl since they were boys in short pants. She might have been the most desirable female in the country, but she had always been Burke's, then and now. As she invited him to follow her to the house, he moved alongside and fell into step with her shorter stride. Watching her now, he realized that although she was painfully thin and her struggle with Burke and the deprivations of war were evident in the shadows beneath her eyes, he found he felt none of the old stirrings that once plagued him.

"Shelby told me how you saved Riverglen from the tax men. I owe you my thanks," he told her as they walked through leaves that crackled beneath their feet. The dry, dusty smell of fall rode the air.

She stared up at the old house with a faraway look in her eye. "You know I've always considered this place my home. After Daddy Reed died I wasn't about to see it turned over to the damn Yankees." She quickly looked up at him from beneath lowered lashes. Her cheeks were flushed with a hint of pink. "I suppose I should ask you to forgive me for that, but I'll never be able to think of you as one of them, not to my dyin' day."

"Forgiven. Besides, the war's over now."

She paused. Her hand touched his sleeve gently enough to keep him from moving forward. "Is it, Dake? Is it over? Sometimes I think that even though the fightin' has stopped the hunger and the lack will never end."

"I'm going to try to do everything I can, Minna. I promise you that."

"And what about Burke?"

"He's the one who stayed, the rightful heir to Riverglen. He'll have the last say. He may throw me off the place, you know." Dake hoped his words were speculation and not fact. By the worry in her eyes he could see he was closer to the truth than he would like to be.

"He doesn't even know I sent for you, so please don't tell him, Dake. He'd never forgive me if he thought I doubted his ability to make Riverglen everything it once was."

She seemed so frail, so helpless, like an ill-treated puppy that could do little more than wait for the next blow. He wanted to wrap her in cotton, to keep her safe from any more trials. Oddly enough, he noticed he had no desire to do more than that, no desire to kiss her, to hold her, to steal her from his big brother. He'd savored infinite sweetness and the promise of passion in Cara's kiss that morning. It was a sensation he wasn't about to forget or exchange for another.

This was no time to think of Cara, he reminded himself as they reached the wide veranda. He gave the old nag, Sweet Pea, a sideways glance and hitched General Sherman beside her to the post out front, half expecting a passel of children to run out to greet them and beg to take his horse around to the stables for a piece of hard candy. He thought of Clay, a sudden, unbidden memory of the feel of holding the infant in his arms. How long would it be before he found his way clear to accompany Cara to Gadsden? It wouldn't do either him or Cara any good to postpone the inevitable.

"There aren't any children here." He spoke his thought aloud.

Minna turned, her hand on the doorknob. "No," she said with a shake of her head, the old smile in her eyes had been replaced by the reflection of harsh reality. "There are no children here anymore. Most everyone ran off when emancipation came."

"I saw Elijah in the quarters."

Her lips tightened. "Still just as shiftless as ever, more so now that there's no overseer. He and two or three others only came crawlin' back here beggin' for a place to stay because they couldn't make their way on their own."

Doing what? Dake wanted to ask, but held his tongue. Minna had been born and bred to a life that depended on slavery. He couldn't expect her to change her way of thinking overnight.

"Before we go in, there's one more thing I'd like to know, Minna."

Frowning now, she gazed at him intently. "What's that?"

"When did Daddy die? Elijah said it was sudden." He hoped his father hadn't suffered, hoped he hadn't languished over his own defection.

Minna's glance flitted over his shoulder in the direction of the slave quarters, then she looked back up at Dake. "Daddy Reed died in '64, but it wasn't sudden. It's just like Elijah to remember it all wrong. He had some wastin' sickness that was enough to tear your heart out. I tried to tend him as best I could. It was right after I'd just lost my own dear mama and papa in the fire." She turned away again and lifted her skirt hem to blot her eyes. "Burke came home a few weeks after Daddy Reed was buried and that's when he proposed. Naturally, he wanted me to stay on here at Riverglen, and thank the Lord I did. I was here to tell the tax men you were fightin' for the Union so they wouldn't take the place."

She turned the knob before Dake could comment and stepped over the threshold. Dake followed her inside.

What struck him immediately was the cavernous emptiness of the place. Imported Oriental carpets, antique furnishings, crystal lamps, vases, oil paintings, window coverings—almost everything had been carted off by scavengers. Minna didn't comment on the loss as she led him across the foyer toward the wide spiral staircase that led to the second floor.

Nail holes marred the stairs where the carpet runner had once been tacked down. His booted feet hit the bare wood; the sound rang hollow in the stairwell.

"Burke's moved into your old room," she told him as they moved along the entry hall. "The view is better. I'm in the master suite 'cause Burke insisted on it, but of course, now that you're back, I'll take a room down the hall."

Half listening, Dake realized with relief that his brother couldn't have seen him on the way up the lane since it wasn't visible from the river side of the house. Still, he wondered if the element of surprise might not be too much for Burke if he was ailing.

"Maybe you should go in first and tell him I'm here," he suggested.

She took his hand. "We'll go in together, just the way we used to face up to all the times he dared us to do one crazy thing or another, shall we?"

Dake took a deep breath, certain he'd rather jump off the Tennessee River Bridge than walk into his old room and face his brother. Minna ushered him in and gave his hand a firm squeeze.

It was a moment before Dake was certain that the skeletal figure slumped in the chair before the window actually was his brother. Once wide, proud shoulders were bowed. The lower half of his face was covered with a salt and pepper beard; his thinning hair was streaked with gray. Like a man decades older, Burke Reed sat in profile to the door, a knitted shawl half draped across his shoulders. What was left of the lower half of his body was not visible.

Dake took a step and halted, his heart in his throat. He would rather face a company of armed cavalry men on foot than walk across the room and face his brother, but it was too late to turn back now. Minna smiled encouragement and nodded.

When Dake moved forward, Burke turned and caught sight of him. The slumped shoulders straightened in a gesture so defiant yet so helpless it broke Dake's heart.

"Get out," Burke Reed commanded, his voice choked and gravelly.

Dake advanced. "It'll take more than that to get me to leave. I've been a month gettin' here, big brother," Dake said, easily slipping back into the slow Southern drawl that had set him apart from the men he commanded.

Burke braced his hands on the arm of the chair and turned on Minna. "You did this. You conspired to bring him here."

She nodded when Dake was about to deny it. "I did. Because it's about time someone stood up to you, Burke Reed. It's time you got yourself out of this room and started to put your house in order."

"*Your* house, you mean," he shot back. "You've got everything just the way you want it, haven't you, Minna? And now you've got the brother you deserve, too. The victor. Johnny's come marching home again, is that it? All hail the conquering hero."

"That's enough, Burke," Dake stepped in. "You can take your anger out on me, but not Minna. Not when she's stood beside you all this time."

"In case you haven't noticed, little brother," Burke sneered the once-cherished nickname, "I'm not standing at all."

Dake allowed himself a glance at his brother's legs. His left remained from the hip to the knee. Where his right leg should have begun, there was nothing. His pant legs had been carefully folded beneath him. Dake swallowed, glanced at the portrait of his father on the dresser and then back at Burke.

"The brother I remember wouldn't let anything stop him."

"The brother you remember would be better off dead."

Minna cried out and ran to Burke's side. She threw her arms around his shoulder, met his resistance when he tried to push her away. She wasn't easily put off. "Don't say that, Burke. Not if you love me."

"I don't."

"You're lyin', darlin', and you know it."

Embarrassed by the blunt exchange, Dake stepped into the fray. "I thought you were engaged."

"We are," Minna assured him.

"We sure as hell aren't," his brother said at the same time.

Burke outshouted her. "I told her when I was finally released from the hospital and sent home that I wouldn't have her."

Dake knew his brother was masking his pain with anger. It would be just like Burke to give up the woman he loved because he deemed himself unworthy. "Seems to me a lady ought to be the one to make the decision to break an engagement," Dake told him.

"Seems to me," Burke said, the forgotten shawl slipping off his shoulders, "you should turn around and butt out."

The show of strength that had returned to his brother's voice during the exchange almost had Dake smiling. Any doubt he had harbored as to the wiseness of his return vanished. His brother's anger was the catalyst needed to bring him out of his depressed state.

"You ready to put the land back into production, Burke?" Dake asked, ignoring Minna's disheartened expression.

"With what? We've no hands to work the fields, no money

for cotton seed, no money to pay the hands if we had 'em, and the taxes are due."

"I've got money saved."

"Yankee money. Money you earned killin' us off. Money that paid for the loss of my legs, my manhood."

Minna sobbed aloud. Dake shot her an angry glare. Burke demanded with a shout that she leave the room. "And take him with you," he yelled.

She drew herself up and, lifting the edge of her hand-dyed skirt, swept from the room.

"If you want me out of here, you'll damn well have to throw me out yourself," Dake warned.

"I don't want you here. You're not welcome."

"Stop yelling, Burke. They can hear you clear to Decatur. This is my home and I'm not leavin'."

"You haven't had a home since you turned Yankee."

"If Daddy were alive I believe he'd differ with you on that, big brother."

"Well, he ain't alive and that makes this place mine. You aren't welcome."

Dake sat down on the edge of the bed that had once been his. It felt peculiar to be in the familiar surroundings again knowing his brother did indeed have the right to throw him out if he so chose. Dake couldn't believe in his heart that Burke would really go that far. His brother remained silent, obviously stewing over the situation.

The room smelled of medicine, laudanum, and stale urine. He walked to the window and threw it open. A rush of tangy fall air swept in, lifting a remnant of yellowed lace curtain, ruffling the pages of a book that lay open on a small bedside table.

"I'm willing to do anything to help," Dake started again. "Anything you say."

"Then *get out*," Burke roared.

"I'm beginning to think you mean it."

"I never want to see your face again. You're dead to me, Dake. Dead and buried like the past. Mama, Daddy, Riverglen. The Confederacy. All dead and buried."

Dake walked away from the window and back to the bed. He sank down to the edge so as not to tower over Burke who sat watching him suspiciously. Dake leaned forward. In the low tone of command that had so often moved men into battle he said, "I've come back because you need me. I'll come back every day from now on until I've convinced you I'm not taking no for an answer. Do you know why?"

He didn't wait for a response he knew damn well wasn't coming. "Because if it was me in that chair needing you, I know nothin' on earth could keep you from comin' home to me, Burke. Nothin'. You think about that."

He stood up and walked across the room. Behind him, the man trapped in the chair remained silent. Minna was waiting outside in the hallway, her hand balled into a fist she held pressed against her lips. As soon as the door closed behind Dake they stood together in the silence of the empty hall and listened as Burke shouted, "Don't bother coming back! I'd rather see you in hell first."

You can go home again, but you might not want to stay there.

Nanny James

Chapter Nine

Dake stared at the door, wanting to go back to his brother, knowing now was not the time. He'd meant what he said. He'd be back again tomorrow and the next day and the next until Burke listened. For now, he would give his brother time to get used to the idea.

Minna touched his sleeve, reminding him she was still beside him. "Would you like some coffee?"

"No," he said, feeling the walls closing in around him. "If you don't mind, Minna, I'd like to get out, see the land."

They were moving toward the stairs. She led the way. "I'll come with you—"

"Thanks, but I think I need to be alone."

They reached the bottom of the wide staircase and she paused on the last step. Her face was surprisingly calm, her manner composed. She showed little sign of the stress the emotional scene upstairs must have caused her. She was used to dealing with this new Burke and he was not. Dake moved by her, his footsteps ringing hollow on the marble tile in the foyer. Her position on the stairs forced him to look up at her. She was thoughtful, her china-blue eyes studied him closely. "You can put your things in the master bedroom," she told him. "I'll move out."

"I left my belongings at Polk House," he said. Something inside told him not to burden her with the news that there would be two extra guests coming home with him. Tomorrow would be soon enough to let her know he had not come to Decatur alone. Tomorrow he'd be moving Cara and Clay into Riverglen.

"Polk House?" Obviously affronted, her anger surfaced immediately. "Why, whatever for? This is your home, Dake, just as much as it is Burke's."

"I wasn't sure how I'd be received, Minna. Now that I've seen him, I'm glad I didn't wait to come. I'll be back tomorrow and try again, but for now, it's late and I'd like to ride out and take stock of what there is to work with before I head back to town."

"I see."

She looked so upset he almost agreed to stay, but he needed to ride across the land and get back to Cara. "Don't take on so. I'll be back tomorrow first thing."

A young serving girl came in from the back of the house and stood waiting silently to be noticed. Dake didn't recognize her, but he smiled, trying to remember if she had been on the plantation when he left or if she was a recent arrival. The girl didn't move, just stared curiously at him. Minna gave Dake a last concerted look before she turned to acknowledge the servant's presence. "Well, Patsy, what is it?"

"Dinner is gonna be white beans and ham hock, Miss Minna, if that all right with you?"

Minna Blakely sighed. "I suppose it has to be. Don't set an extra plate. Mr. Reed won't be staying after all."

"No, ma'am." The nervous teen gave a half bow, half curtsy and quickly left them alone again.

Minna sighed. "Our old cook was stolen by the Hammonds, if you can believe it. They offered to pay her twice as much as anyone else around here is paying the help, and they give her room and board. She up and left after twenty years at Riverglen."

"That's what free labor is all about, Minna. It'll take a few years, but I hope to get this place back in shape enough to where we can afford to pay well, too."

"*Years?* I suppose we'll have to make do for quite a while."

He realized what a strain his arrival would have been had he come without funds. Dake made a mental note to collect as much in the way of provisions as he could lay his hands on before he returned. Things were outrageously priced, but they could be had. Minna walked him to the door. They heard the sound of Burke's voice shouting at her from upstairs.

"Minna? Can you hear me, Minna? Is that bastard gone?"

Dake closed his eyes for a split second. The words tore into him with the pain of a saber. "I've got to go—"

She grabbed his hand. "You really will be back, won't you, Dake? You won't let him scare you off?"

He held her hand between both of his. "I love him, Minna. He's my brother. Everything will be all right. You'll see."

She smiled for the first time since they had entered Burke's room earlier. "I know it will. Everything will be fine now that you're here." Her smile failed to reach her eyes.

Elijah was waiting for him, hat in hand, when he stepped out onto the veranda. A lifetime of servitude could not be replaced by a few years of freedom. He bobbed his head in deference to Dake's former status as master and appealed to him, "Can I speak to you again, Marse Dake?"

Dake put his own hat back on, carefully centering it on his head. "Surely. What is it, Elijah?"

Elijah glanced up at the house as if reluctant to begin. Dake took the cue and walked off the veranda. He stopped at the hitching post where he began to untie General Sherman. "I'm sorry things didn't go too well 'tween you and Marse Burke," Elijah began.

"Heard it all, huh?"

"I's 'spects they heard him a shoutin' clear to kingdom come. I hopes you won't be givin' up, tho'."

"Not likely."

"Them's sweet words to my ears." Elijah glanced over his shoulder and watched the house for a moment before he said, "Marse Dake, I think there might be a way you can come up with the money fo' the back taxes on this here place."

Dake could see the man was as worried about the fate of Riverglen as the rest of them. No matter what the circumstances, the plantation had been and still was the only home Elijah had known since the day he was born in the slave quarters.

Hoping to put his mind at ease, Dake said, "I have the money for the back taxes, Elijah, and if I can just get Burke to agree, I'm going to try to get this place back on its feet. It'll take some doing, some trust and a lot of hard work, but I know it can be as profitable as ever. I'll need your help."

"I sure appreciate you havin' faith in me, Marse Dake. I surely do. But what I got to tell you still needs to be said."

Dake started down the lane, leading his horse slowly away from the house.

Elijah fell into step beside him. "'Fore he took sick, I was workin' as your daddy's daily keep. I heard him talkin' about how he was plannin' to hide somethin' away to keep from payin' the tithe to the Confederacy. They was collectin' bales and bales of cotton 'fore the war ended. He say he could see you been right in your thinkin' and that the South wasn't never gonna win. Givin' everything over to the Confederacy would be a waste and he wasn't gonna do it."

Dake knew of the Cotton or Produce Loan that had been subscribed to by most loyal Confederates. Thousands of bales of cotton had been destroyed by Federal raiders near the end of the war and many thousands more had been burned by

Confederate authorities to keep them from falling into Union hands.

"Cotton sellin' for near on four hundred dollars a bale now, Marse Dake."

The price of cotton had risen like a river on a rampage after the war. If indeed there was any hidden at Riverglen, it was worth a small fortune. With the army providing for his needs, Dake had saved most of his income over the past seven years. It was a nest egg, but not enough to get Riverglen up and running again. A windfall of hidden cotton, a cache of any kind, would help pay the laborers he would need to put the fields back into production. Because he had remained loyal to the Union, if he found cotton or anything else his father might have hidden, he would be allowed to keep it.

"Did you hear him say where he may have hidden it? Did you or anyone else know or help?"

"He might have had ol' Jim and his work crew help him. I think he trusted ol' Jim."

"Do you think we could find him?"

"Now that's a problem, Marse Dake. Ol' Jim's been dead almost as long as your daddy."

Dake sat at the edge of what was left of Riverglen's old riverboat landing that fronted the Tennessee River. Moonlight tarried on the water, played hide and seek between the lapping waves created by the night breeze. Many times in the past he, Burke, and Minna ran along the river's edge near this very spot, hiding in the cattails, fishing from the bank, jumping off the landing. When anyone needed a ride into town they would light a signal fire and wait on the old bench beneath the oaks at the landing, most often dressed for a visit to town. When a passing riverboat pilot saw the smoke from the fire he would pull up to the landing and take on the waiting passengers. Slaves sent to town with passes, family members, neighbors—

all used the old dock that had been built long before the foundation for the grand house was laid.

He had spent the last few hours riding over nearly every inch of uncultivated field, had seen the burned-out shell of the building where the cotton gin had been housed, walked through the wood and stone grist mill that was still standing. While he had no idea where his father might have stashed the cotton tithe, he wished Daddy Reed might send him some sign.

Although thinking about his father inspired no clues that evening, Dake's mother seemed to be with him as he combed the land they both loved. As he rode through the gathering dusk and watched the moon come up over the river, he recalled so many things she had told him.

"I didn't want to move here, son," she'd said once long ago. He could almost feel her walking beside him, moving with the swift, flowing grace of a tall comely woman who was sure of herself and her place in the world. *"Your daddy bought this land when there wasn't anything around but a few farms here and there and not a neighbor within a day's ride. Decatur was little more than a hamlet then. But I came to love Riverglen, Dake, just as your daddy did."*

Not quite forty-six when she died, her hair had still been as black as midnight, her eyes the same emerald as his and Burke's, but far more luminescent. "Sometimes I wish you'd been the oldest, Dake. You have a real love for the land and the people." She never said "our people" as some of the planters did when referring to their slaves. Theodora Reed had never fully accepted the fact that her husband bought and sold human beings with as little thought as when he sold bales of cotton. But as much as she abhorred the fact, she did little to convince him otherwise. It was not her place to do so. As wife and mother, she felt her role was to stand beside her husband through thick and thin, to go along with his wishes whether she agreed or disagreed. She saw that the slaves were fed and clothed, ministered to them when they became ill, carefully brought their babies into the world and ushered the elders out with a decent burial.

Dake reached down and dislodged a splintered notch of wood and threw it into the river. He watched it bob along with the current until it disappeared. There wasn't a doubt in his mind that Cara Calvinia James would have handled things differently than his mother. There was no way in God's creation she would ever go along meekly with anything she disagreed with, whether her husband decreed it or no. He stretched, reached behind him to work the kink out of his neck, and then pushed himself up to a full standing position.

General Sherman stood in the tall grass behind him, quietly munching on the rich yellow stalks that summer had left behind. It was time to ride back to Decatur. Past time. As it was he'd be getting there well past midnight. As he lifted the reins, Dake was certain of two things; it would be a long uphill battle to bring Riverglen back to its former glory, and he was anxious as hell to hold Cara James in his arms again.

It might have been that his thoughts were so far away, or that with the homecoming he had let down his vigilance, but for whatever reason, he didn't hear whoever it was that moved through the dew-wet grass behind him until it was too late. General started and shook his head. Dake soothed the big horse, spoke to him gently, and was about to turn around when something struck him from behind and the world went black.

A sound outside the door woke Cara from a fitful nap. She wouldn't call it a night's sleep, not when she had only stretched out fully clothed in an attempt to wait up for Dake to return. She promised herself she was not about to fall asleep and let him get away with leaving her alone for so long, not when he had promised to return as soon as possible. There was a little matter of the gifts he had given her, and the kiss—well, she wasn't about to bring that up, but she was curious to see if he might.

The rustling sounded again. Someone was trying to open the door. She bolted to her feet and quickly ran across the room as quietly as she could manage. With her ear against the wooden door panel, she listened to the scraping against the keyhole.

"Go away or I'll scream," she whispered.

"Cara? Open the door, I need you."

She recognized his voice immediately. "Get away from my door, Dake Reed. I don't care how much you say you need me. You promised to be back early and now it's nearly dawn."

She heard a heavy thud against the door followed by a muffled groan. He was breathing so heavily she could hear it through the door.

"Cara, open the door."

"No."

"I need—"

"I don't care what you need." She fought to keep her voice down to a whisper so as not to rouse the landlady or the other guests.

"—help."

Silence followed the appeal. She strained to hear more, but he wasn't talking. *Help?*

"Dake?"

There was no answer from the hallway.

Cara turned the key on her side of the door and slowly opened it. Dake had obviously slid to the floor, for as she opened the door, he slumped in after it.

Without a word she stuck her head out into the hallway, and looked right and left. Wall sconces flickered in the long, dimly lit passage. She reached beneath his arms and tried to pull him into her room, but his greater weight kept her from making much progress. Gathering her new silk skirt in her hands, she wadded it up so that she could hunker down in front of his listing form. Kneeling between his legs, she grasped his face between her hands and tried to get him to wake up. "Dake?" She rasped in the loudest whisper she dared. Was he drunk? "Dake Reed, wake up. You're scaring the stuffing out of me."

She was about to slap him awake when she noticed that although his eyes were closed, he was smiling. "Stuffing?"

Cara leaned closer, trying to see what was ailing him. "Can you move?"

"I'm not sure I want to. I haven't had a beautiful woman between my legs in a long while."

She was holding his face between her palms and immediately let go. His head flopped back and hit the floor. "Ouch!"

"Shh!" Cara warned as she scrambled out from between his legs. "You'll wake the dead."

"I feel like I am dead. Can you help me up?"

"That's what I was trying to do, if you must know." She grabbed his elbow and waited until he got his legs under him. As she stood, she tried to pull him up with her. Dake finally had control of himself enough to make it to his feet and allow her to slip beneath his arm and help him into the room.

Cara closed and locked the door behind her, then guided him to the bedside. Clay was still sound asleep, surrounded by a nest of pillows. She helped Dake sit gingerly on the bed.

"What happened?"

"Someone hit me from behind while I was alone at the river landing. Knocked me out cold. Took my gun. My hat's missing. When I came to, I managed to get on my horse and get back, but after the trip up the stairs I'm feeling woozy again."

"Why didn't you go back to the house? How far away were you?"

"I was closer to town. After what happened this afternoon, I didn't want to upset Minna or Burke again. My head didn't hurt so bad until I'd gotten almost all the way back here."

"Lean forward and let me see." She pressed his head down

toward his knees and gently felt the swelling in the back. Her fingers came away sticky with blood. "You've been bleeding," she informed him calmly as she moved over to the washbasin and a pitcher of fresh water. Quickly splashing a liberal amount of water out, she dabbed a towel into the basin, wrung out most of the water, and then returned to his side. He opened his eyes when she reached out for him and pressed the cold towel against his wound.

"I don't think it's too deep at all. There's hardly any blood on your jacket."

"Blood on my jacket?" He struggled forward.

"Sit down, Dake," she ordered.

"But . . . it'll stain." He stood up and tried to pull off his buckskin. Cara took it and tossed it toward a chair. It hit the floor.

She held the towel in place as they sat side by side on the bed. "Aside from this lump on your head, I take it things didn't go very well?"

"You might say they went very poorly given the way I feel right now. My brother wouldn't have anything to do with me."

"Could he have had someone do this to you?"

"I don't like to think so. I met a man named Shelby Gilmore in town today. He went to Riverglen directly afterward. He isn't hiding his resentment over the war and I am a turncoat, a Tory, a scalawag, a—"

"That's enough, Dake."

"You're right. Let's talk about something else." He reached up and took over holding the towel against his head. For the first time since she'd helped him into the room he looked her over carefully.

Without meaning to, Cara blushed.

"You look just as beautiful in that gown as I knew you would."

She smoothed the delicious silk fabric with her fingertips.

"Why'd you do it, Dake? Why'd you buy me such extravagant gowns?"

"You deserve them. You've taken excellent care of Clay and even me on more than one occasion. Every girl needs a new dress now and then."

"Now and then? I've never had anything so fine in all my life and you know it."

He was watching her so intently she wanted to bolt out of range, but she held her ground and forced herself to relax. It was too late to do anything about the way the dress fit her figure like a second skin. The fitted bodice hugged her in all the right places, showed off her trim waist and the flare of her breasts and hips. His eyes took on a warm glow. Half of her hoped it was because of the way she looked to him tonight; the other half hoped it was brought on by the wallop he took on the head.

"You look lovely, Cara."

She couldn't take her eyes off his lips.

"I do?"

"You most definitely do."

He was leaning closer now. Their eyes locked. Cara licked her lips, expecting him to kiss her again, but not quite knowing for certain. She did know she intended to let him.

She didn't know he was going to pass out.

Cara was roused from a sound sleep by voices downstairs. When she came fully awake, she realized how bright it was in the room. Dake was stretched out beside her on her bed where she'd left him after he passed out on her. "This sleeping together is getting to be a bad habit," she whispered as she reached across Dake and carefully pulled on the watch chain showing at the top of his pocket. Slowly, carefully so as not to disturb him, she drew the watch from the pocket and snapped it open. It was seven o'clock.

The noise downstairs moved into the upper hallway. Clay, asleep in a well-padded drawer, began to fuss, but Dake hadn't stirred. Still fully dressed, Cara climbed out of bed and tried to shake the wrinkles out of her gown. When someone started pounding on the door, she grabbed up Clay, who was more than damp around the bottom, wrapped an extra blanket around him so as not to spoil her silk quilting, and then made a hurried stop before the mirror where she determined there was nothing to be done with the rat's nest of curls about her head.

She expected to open the door and find a furious landlady standing there ready to rail at her for allowing Dake to spend the night in her room. Instead, she found herself with her nose nearly pressed against the star pinned to the front of a tall, stern-faced man's chest. She looked up. He frowned down at her. She couldn't help but notice he had the thickest mutton-chops she'd ever seen on anyone.

"Sorry to disturb you, ma'am," he said as he rolled and unrolled his hat brim in his beefy hand. He looked her over thoroughly, her hair, her rumpled gown, the child she clutched to her shoulder. "I'm trying to find Dake Reed and the landlady said since he wasn't in his own room he might be in yours."

Cara could see the smug-looking woman who had registered them hovering in the hallway behind the sheriff.

"He's here, but he's—" she said, starting to tell the man Dake had arrived injured and had been too ill to move when the sheriff sidestepped her and pushed his way into the room.

"Get up, Reed. You're wanted for arrest."

Speechless, Cara glanced at the bed. Dake was trying to rouse himself enough sit up. "Dake?"

He shook his head as if to clear it, looked around the room, disoriented. His eyes found hers and he smiled, then focused on the bearlike figure standing in the center of the room. "Bill Jensen? *You're* the sheriff?"

"I am and I'm sorry to tell you, but you're under arrest, Dake. You'll have to come with me."

"What for?" Cara glanced out the door and saw that the biddy in the hall had moved closer. She tried to ignore the woman's dour expression and concentrated on the lawman. "What's this all about?"

"Sorry, ma'am, but for his own good, I'm takin' him in for the murder of his brother, Burke Reed."

She thought the man must be mad. *"What?" His own good? His brother's murder?*

Dake tried to shake off his grogginess. "What are you talking about?"

"Your brother's dead," the man said bluntly. "Right now, there's no better suspect than you."

"Oh, Dake," Cara cried out as she moved to stand beside him. He acted as if she weren't there, his expression one of disbelief and shock.

"My brother was just fine when I left him at Riverglen late yesterday afternoon. Are you telling me someone's killed him?"

"Shot through the heart."

Dake blanched. He put his hand to his forehead, shoved a shock of hair back, and then stared hard at the sheriff, trying to make sense of all the man was saying. "Suicide?"

"No gun left behind."

"You saw him?"

The man shook his head. "Miss Minna came in with one of the colored boys to fetch me. She was pretty hysterical, but I sat Elijah down and had a long talk with him."

"Dake, you can't let him—"

Dake cut Cara off with a wave of his hand. "If you take me in you know I'll be tried and convicted without a trial. I don't stand a chance in this town."

"You'll get a Union judge. Nobody with Southern sympathies is holding office anymore."

"And you?"

"Since I argued against pulling out of the Union, I'm looked upon as loyal enough. Federals appointed me after the war."

"Why would I kill Burke?"

The man strolled over to Cara, chucked Clay under the chin. As if he sensed the tension in the room, the baby started to cry. Bill Jensen walked back to the center of the room and rolled forward onto the balls of his feet and back again. "You rode out to Riverglen, had an argument with Burke that was loud enough for everyone on the place to hear. He shouted for you to get out. Called you a bastard. You rode off to make it look like you were leavin', then doubled back and waited until it was almost dawn. Then you killed him."

"I did not."

"Elijah saw someone he thought was you moving around outside the house. Someone crouched low in the bushes. Recognized your hat."

Cara glanced around the room. Dake's hat was nowhere to be seen. She remembered when she found him in the hallway, he hadn't been wearing it.

"It was stolen," Cara announced.

"Mighty convenient, I'd say." Jensen continued to rock forward and back, obviously in no hurry to cart Dake off.

Cara tried desperately to think of a way to keep him from doing so. She was about to speak when the door burst open and a woman with shining chestnut hair and the bluest eyes Cara had ever seen rushed into the room.

"Oh, God, Dake." The lovely figure in homespun raced to Dake and grabbed his hand.

Jensen stepped forward and tried to take her arm. "Miss Minna, I told you to wait downstairs. You shouldn't have to go through this."

She shook him off.

"Minna, is it true? Is Burke dead?" Dake asked.

Cara watched in heartsick fascination as Dake put his arm around the woman's shoulders and tenderly held her close.

So this was Minna Blakely. In an instant Cara knew Minna was everything she would never be—petite, refined, cultured. Despite her lack of finery, there was no doubt but what she was a lady through and through. It was apparent in the way she held her shoulders, the confident way she had swept into the room, disobeying the sheriff's orders. Dake was treating her like she was one of Cara's most prized dolls.

Minna took a long, shuddering breath and leaned against Dake's side. "Burke is dead. Someone killed him about two hours before dawn."

The sheriff hitched up his belt again. "Miss Minna, after talking to you and Elijah, I have more'n enough reason to believe Dake here is the prime suspect."

Minna Blakely was very obviously taken aback when her gaze swept the room and it fell on Cara and Clay. Cara nodded acknowledgment, not knowing what else to do.

Distracted only a second or two, she turned back to Bill Jensen and asked, "Did I hear you right? You're blamin' the murder on *Dake*?"

"Elijah gave me enough reason to want to hold him under arrest."

"Elijah?" Minna blinked twice as if the motion would sweep away the man's words. "He hasn't enough sense to come in out of the rain in a deluge, Bill Jensen, and you know it. Speakin' of suspects, why don't you question Elijah a little longer. I'm not surprised we haven't all been killed in our beds with all these darkies runnin' loose." She reached out to Dake and brushed his hair back off his forehead. "Now stop all this nonsense and let me get Dake back to Riverglen. Burke is dead and we need time to mourn him." She took Dake's arm as if she intended to sweep him out of the room right under the other man's nose.

The sheriff stepped out to block her way to the door. "Elijah saw someone creepin' around the outside of the big house wearin' a hat just like Reed wears about the time your fiancé was murdered."

"I lost my hat earlier in the evening when someone ambushed me," Dake said.

Startled, Minna turned anxious eyes on Dake. "Ambushed?"

Clay fussed louder. Cara jiggled him against her shoulder. Dake looked in her direction, frowned, then turned his attention back to the sheriff.

"Look, Sheriff. My brother's dead. I don't care what kind of half-assed notion you have that I did it, I'll give you my word that I'll be at Riverglen with no intention of leaving there. If you want to continue this investigation, and I use the term lightly, then by all means ride out there with us right now."

Jensen went back to rolling his hat brim while he paused to consider. He then pointed his hat at Dake. "If I take you at your word and let you walk out of here, the whole town will come down around my ears. You're considered a traitor, Reed. If I let you go, everyone will be thinkin' you got off because of me and your soldier friends stationed here."

Cara watched Minna Blakely carefully. After her initial glance at Cara, she had studiously avoided looking at her at all. Now, while Dake squared off with the big man with mutton-chop sideburns, Minna stepped up and took the sheriff's arm to get his attention.

"I have to tell you the truth, Bill. There's no way Dake could have killed Burke last night," Minna said softly.

Bill Jensen was immediately attentive. So was Dake. Cara took a step forward so that she could hear.

Minna straightened her spine and then demurely flicked an imaginary fleck of dirt from her sleeve. As if her next statement pained her, she cleared her throat.

"I know he couldn't have done it because he spent the night with me."

*If you want something, you'd best
put your shoes on and go after it
yourself.*

Nanny James

Chapter Ten

At a loss for words, Sheriff Jensen appeared uncomfortable for the first time. "Now, Miss Minna," he began in a fatherly fashion, "I know how close to the Reed family you've always been, but that doesn't mean you have to lie for Reed, here."

Cara strained to hear Minna when she insisted firmly but softly, "I am *not* lyin', Sheriff."

The room closed in on Cara. Minna Blakely was very convincing. Clay fussed at her shoulder, tugging at her hair and thrusting his legs up and down in protest of her lack of attention to him. The sun was full up now, its rays spread out upon the rose-patterned hook rug the sheriff's dusty boots were planted on. Aside from Clay's whining, there wasn't another sound in the room. Three spectators now hovered in the doorway, the innkeeper and two others, one fully dressed man, one old biddy clutching a plaid flannel wrapper close.

Cara waited for Dake to deny Minna's words.

Dake said nothing at all.

Cara had expected him to tell them all loud and clear that he had not been with his brother's fiancée all night, that he had merely ridden across his land, been knocked unconscious, and then come back to her. She waited, but he said absolutely nothing. When she met his eyes she couldn't read the expression in them. He had closed in on himself.

"Ma'am?" Cara realized the sheriff was speaking to her. She

173

shushed Clay, shifted him to the opposite shoulder, and began to jiggle him up and down.

"Yes, sir?"

"Ma'am, you're travelin' with this man?"

She nodded. "He hired me—"

The landlady gasped. Cara went on as if she hadn't heard and finished her statement. "He hired me to take care of this child until we could return him to his family in Gadsden. I'm a doll maker from Kansas, headed for California."

The sheriff looked skeptical. His gaze took in her fancy gown, one of such a fine quality that no self-respecting Southern woman would have been seen in since the war. His eyes lit on her tousled hair. Cara steeled herself, determined not to flinch or blush. Let them think what they liked. She didn't know them, nor did she intend to lay eyes on any of them after she left Clay at Gadsden. And Dake—at the moment she didn't care if she ever saw Dake Reed again.

"'Pears to me you're movin' in the wrong direction."

Cara's glance touched Dake and moved on. "I needed the money." Perhaps he had some reason for buying into Minna's lie. In that case, she didn't intend to hurt him by arguing with the sheriff.

"Cara—" Dake finally spoke.

She ignored him. "What else would you like to know, Sheriff?"

Jensen's gaze slid to Dake and back to Cara. "Was Reed here last night?"

Cara looked to Dake for some crack in the facade of calm resignation he showed. There was none. She opted for the truth. "No, he wasn't. He arrived shortly before dawn. The back of his head was bleeding. He told me someone hit him from behind and took his hat and his gun. He wasn't certain how long he'd been unconscious."

"So." Jensen began to pace the small confines of the room

like a player in a melodrama as he ticked off the facts as he knew them. "Reed visited Riverglen in the late afternoon where he and his brother argued. He didn't come back here all night. Miss Minna claims he was with her. He told you someone knocked him unconscious and stole his hat and gun. He or someone wearing that hat killed Burke Reed with a gunshot through the heart." He walked over to the windowsill, rested his hip against it, and crossed his legs at the ankles. "If I don't take him in, folks 'round here will raise holy hell shoutin' about injustice. The Federals stationed here would like nothin' better than to put someone even more loyal to them in my job. I'm walkin' a fine line here.

"Looks as if I don't have a choice. Much as I'd like to believe you, Miss Minna, I just can't take a chance. I'm takin' you in, Reed. At least for the time bein' while I follow up on the story about someone stealin' your hat and posin' as you to kill your brother. Trouble is, Burke Reed didn't have any enemies as far as I know. You're the more likely target."

Minna hadn't left Dake's side through the sheriff's dissertation. Cara wondered if she would have a chance to speak to Dake alone before the sheriff carted him off to jail. What was she to do now? She knew in her heart he wasn't guilty of killing his brother, but she wasn't at all certain as to whether or not he had slept with Minna Blakely. The woman had been all too convincing, not to mention willing to blacken her reputation.

Minna tried to appeal to the law officer. "Won't you reconsider, Sheriff Jensen, and let him go on back to Riverglen in my care? Perhaps he could ride along in your custody while you come out and"—she took a deep, shuddering breath—"and see if you can find any clues as to who did this terrible thing."

Jensen turned toward the door and found the small knot of curiosity seekers staring at the proceedings. "You all get a move on now, hear?" Then to Minna and Dake he said, "I suppose if I have your word you won't try and bolt on me, Reed, I'll let you 'company me out to Riverglen. You need to see your brother laid out proper and I need to survey the scene."

Dake ran his fingers through his hair, shoving it back off his forehead. Cara couldn't take her eyes off him. Finally, he deigned to look over at her. She moved aside to let Sheriff Jensen step out into the hallway. Minna glanced gravely up at Dake, gave his arm a conciliatory pat, and then moved toward the door. She paused before Cara, who felt the need to tighten her hold on Clay as Minna's quick perusal swept her from head to toe.

"I'm sorry we couldn't have met under better circumstances, Miss James. You'll have to pardon my surprise, Dake didn't mention you at all last night."

"And why should he?" Cara said without looking his way. "After all, I'm only hired help."

"I do hope you'll come out to Riverglen when things are cleared up. The accommodations are probably not what you're used to, but we'll try to see that you're comfortable." There was nothing but sincerity in her tone. "I'm sure you two have a lot to discuss before Dake leaves, so please excuse me."

Before Cara could utter another word, Minna started toward the threshold where she paused and told Dake, "I'll be waiting in the carriage. I don't think the sheriff wants you out of his sight for long."

Clay, who had been put off far too long, started to wail. Cara took him to the bed and spread out his blanket, laid him atop it, and began to change his diaper. She could feel Dake standing rock still behind her.

"Cara, I—"

"Your brother's dead, Dake. You're needed at home."

"You think I killed him." His tone was hollow, all the

animation in his voice completely gone, overshadowed by guilt and grief.

Ignoring Clay, she turned to face Dake and found him inches away. She had to tip her head up to look into his eyes. They were bleak, confused, disbelieving.

"You would never have taken his life in cold blood, I know that much," she assured him.

"Then why are you looking at me as if you've never seen me before?"

She took a deep breath. "Did you sleep with her, Dake?"

"Hell no. She's always been Burke's. I told you that."

Which isn't to say you didn't want her. Still hurt and uncertain, Cara pressed him. "She's not now."

"Look, Cara, I don't know any more about what's going on than you do, but I intend to find out. Just give me a little time to get this cleared up. There's money in my saddlebags. They're in the bottom of the armoire in my room. I'll send Elijah back to carry you out to the plantation."

She promised him nothing.

He walked over to her and reached out, ran his hand along her upper arm. "I've got to find out what happened, Cara. Who killed Burke and why before I can go with you to Gadsden."

She'd told him the truth when she said she believed he hadn't killed his brother. Why couldn't she be absolutely sure he hadn't slept with Minna Blakely?

"I'll see you soon," he said, stepping away. He picked his jacket off the floor and shrugged into it. He winced with pain.

When he was gone, Cara finished diapering Clay and picked him up. Before she did anything she would go downstairs and see about getting him fed. She didn't relish facing the innkeeper, but there was nothing to be done for it; besides, whether she decided to go on to Riverglen or not, she knew she wouldn't spend another night at Polk House.

She dressed Clay, kissed the crown of his head, and smiled

despite her worries when he stared solemnly up at her. A sharp rap at the door gave her pause. She opened it to find the landlady standing in the hallway with disapproval etched across her features.

"There's a servant at the back door wanting to talk to you." With the message delivered, she turned to go as if lingering in Cara's presence a moment too long would soil her own reputation.

The Negro man waiting for her on the back porch introduced himself as Elijah Reed from Riverglen. He explained that he'd been told by Dake to "carry" her and their belongings out to the plantation. Cara knew the time for decision making had come. She looked beyond him at the wagon with a mule hitched to it. Dake Reed had hired her to take Clay to Gadsden. Nothing more, nothing less. After four long weeks in his company, her heart was already entangled. She knew him well enough to know he would not have killed his brother, but sleeping with Minna Blakely was another matter altogether.

Quickly weighing the consequence of following Dake to Riverglen and becoming enmeshed in both the drama of his brother's death and her own growing need of him, not to mention having to deal with Minna Blakely's admission, be it true or false, Cara decided it was best to cut her ties to Dake Reed and go on to Gadsden alone, deliver Clay into his family's arms, and then head out for California.

She bid Elijah hold Clay while she returned to Dake's room. Once there, she took enough money from his saddlebags to pay for her stage-line passage to Gadsden and a few nights' lodging. While searching for the money, she found Anna Clayton's bracelet and slipped it on her wrist. It felt as heavy as a shackle.

Anything else she needed, she decided would be best taken out of the homestead money sewn into the hem of her old yellow gown. Hurrying back downstairs, she gave Elijah the bags, took Clay, and told him, "Tell Mr. Reed I've gone on. I won't be staying at Riverglen."

"But, ma'am—"

"I'm sure he'll understand." She smiled to assure him all was well, but was unable to feel the lightness of relief she should have experienced at setting out after her dream at last.

Still uncertain, Elijah finally gave up trying to cajole her into going with him and bid her farewell. He climbed up onto the wagon seat and released the brake. The harness jangled as he flicked the reins over the mule's rump. As she watched the big wheels roll in the dust, she wondered how Dake would react when Elijah returned without her.

Hadn't she told him enough times not to get attached? Hadn't she warned him that kissing shouldn't become a habit? She figured he'd be so wrapped up in his own problems that he would feel relieved when told of her decision.

Why, then, didn't she feel elated? Hadn't she listened to herself when she warned Dake not to fall in love?

The house was full of people, but unlike the soirees and cotillions held at Riverglen before the war, the gathering of friends and neighbors for Burke Reed's burial was hushed and subdued. Dressed in a black frock coat and trousers, a crisp white linen shirt closed at the throat with a string tie, Dake stood off to one side near French doors that led out to the formerly resplendent garden that had been turned into a vegetable patch to supply food since the war.

A tumbler of whiskey in his hand, he stayed out of the mainstream of callers, none of whom deigned to extend their sympathy to him. For days they had been delivering precious offerings of whatever foodstuffs they could spare. Bill Jensen was watching him from across the room. Not far away, Minna stood composed though teary-eyed and accepted the condolences of the townfolk she had known all her life.

She had dressed in widow's weeds for the occasion, her skin a pale ivory against black silk worn to near transparency in places. The color was so stark that it made the reddish highlights in her chestnut hair all the more noticeable.

They had buried Burke that morning, two days after the murder. His older brother lay beside their parents in the family burial ground in a grove of trees a mile from the house. His entire family was there now. It was a hollow feeling knowing all he had left was their home. Riverglen was his now, but somehow, without Burke here, bringing it back to its former splendor meant little to him. Was this how Cara felt when she found herself the last to survive the prairie? Was it such hollow emptiness that had driven her away?

He wished he had Miss Cara Calvinia James here right now so he could give her a piece of his mind for taking off with Clay without waiting for his escort. Despite the laying out and the funeral, despite the fact that he was still the only suspect in his brother's murder, he had spent all his spare time worrying about her being on the road alone with Clay. Hadn't she learned anything in Poplar Bluff? Would she be as vigilant as need be? Up until a month ago the girl hadn't been off the farm. Now, he supposed, she considered herself a seasoned traveler. She had the money from the homestead, a crate of dolls, and a head full of dreams.

He missed her more than he wanted to admit. He missed her during the day when the sunshine reminded him of her smile and he missed her more at night, during the quiet hours they'd come to share as intimately as any husband and wife without the benefit of lovemaking. Instinctively he knew that making love with Cara James would have been infinitely pleasurable.

Remarkable. Unforgettable.

Her kiss had told him as much.

How would she feel when she turned Clay over to his relations? Would she miss the baby they had both come to love? For his part, Dake knew he would surely miss little Clay. Hell, he missed him already.

Dake put the crystal tumbler to his lips and let the rich bourbon slide down his throat, impatient to have the house quiet so that he could go after Cara and then get down to the business of finding his brother's murderer. He watched Minna as she moved quietly and efficiently through the gathering. On the way back from town two days before she had begged him to go along with the alibi she had given him.

"Please listen, Dake." With one hand holding to the side of the buggy and the other on her hat, Minna had pleaded as he raced her buggy back to Riverglen with General Sherman hitched behind. "I'm sorry I jumped in and said what I did, especially in front of you . . . your lady companion and all, but I'd do it all again to keep you from hangin' for a murder you never committed. We have to hold to the story so that Sheriff Jensen has a valid reason to keep from takin' you into custody."

He had seen the hurt and underlying anger in his "lady companion's" eyes when he left her at Polk House and although he believed Cara when she said she knew he was innocent of killing Burke, she hadn't been as generous where the alibi of sleeping with Minna Blakely had been concerned. How could he blame her for doubting him? A month on the trail didn't exactly guarantee her infinite trust in him. Nor should it. He had agreed to stick to Minna's story because for her to recant now would only make him seem all the more guilty and Minna a fool.

"Besides," Minna had added as a final assurance, "my true friends will believe I only said what I did to keep you out of jail. They'd never for a minute believe I would be untrue to Burke."

"I suppose not," he had agreed.

Once they reached Riverglen there had been no further

discussion of her sacrifice. Now, as he eavesdropped on the conversations floating around him as if he did not exist, he found what she had said was true. More than one of her friends had approached, took her hand or gave her a pat on the shoulder, and after extending their sympathy, had assured her they knew exactly why she would tell such a horrendous lie, but couldn't for the life of them see why she did it to keep a traitor out of jail. She had simply replied, "He's Burke's brother, after all. I have to think of what Burke would have wanted."

He knocked back the last of his drink and walked out the open doors to the veranda. Three men were standing off to the side of the porch, near the hitching post, passing a flask back and forth. Knowing full well he wasn't welcome, Dake started back into the house until he recognized one of them as Shelby Gilmore. He had seen him at the gravesite, but not at the indoor gathering.

Lengthening his strides, Dake crossed the wide expanse and paused beside a Corinthian column. He leaned a shoulder against it to affect a casual attitude and looked down at Shelby and his cohorts. "I'm surprised to see you again, Shelby. Especially here."

The men beside Shelby, one portly and prematurely gray with black sideburns, the other short and barrel-chested, eyed each other and nodded briefly to Dake. They sauntered together back across the veranda and disappeared into the house.

"What's so surprisin' to you, Dake? Your brother and I were friends."

Dake opened the front of his coat and shoved his hands in the back of his waistband. It was a movement meant to show Shelby he was unarmed, if that mattered to the former rebel. "Well, I figured it had to be you who tapped me on the head down by the river the night my brother was murdered. You or one of your secret order brethren. I can't quite see you havin' a Yankee in your midst without doin' somethin' about it."

"Let me guarantee, if we wanted you out of the way, I'd do more than tap you on the head, Reed."

"That's what I figured. That's why I tend to think somebody had their signals crossed two nights ago and Burke was murdered by mistake. He was in my room, sittin' in the dark near the window. Someone in a hurry might think he was me and kill the wrong man."

Shelby smiled a slow, sleepy-eyed grin that put Dake in mind of the snake in the garden of Eden. "You aren't accusin' me of murder, are you Dake?"

"Not yet, I'm not."

"My mama can vouch for the fact I never left the house that night."

"I'll bet she does that for you a lot."

Shelby Gilmore straightened. In a voice that carried to the front door he asked, "Are you callin' my mama a liar, Dake Reed?"

Dake's voice was low, smooth as ice, and just as cold. "I'm not armed, Shelby. But then, neither was my brother." He shrugged and pushed away from the pillar. "Just wanted to give you somethin' to dwell on over the next few days while I go about searchin' out the man or men who killed Burke." He turned to rejoin Minna inside.

"I'm not afraid of you, Dake. It won't be long before vultures like you leave the South in peace and let us get back to runnin' our land and our lives the way they were meant to be run."

Dake paused and half turned to Shelby. "Those days are gone for good, Gilmore. It doesn't matter whether you and all the men you can round up spend the rest of your lives hidin' behind sheets and hoods dishing out your own brand of justice.

You lost the war. It's time to realize things will never be the same around here again.''

Without waiting for another reply, Dake continued on into the house. Minna was saying good-bye to some of the last lingering guests. She smiled and nodded to him over an old woman's shoulder. Her smile was warm and encouraging.

But it wasn't Cara's.

He had half hoped Cara had come back to see him through the funeral, but it was Minna who walked over to stand beside him, her eyes shadowed with concern.

"Everyone's gone," she told him. "I wish they had been a little more cordial to you but—"

"But given the circumstances, I'm lucky they didn't tar and feather me on the spot." He looked around, hoping to catch Patsy as she passed by with a tray. He could definitely use another drink.

"Dake, I know it's a little sudden and that you shouldn't be pressed into makin' any decisions so soon, but I wanted to ask you if it would be all right with you if I stayed on for a few days, maybe a week or two until I found other accommodations. I'm afraid since Mama and Daddy died, well, I've had nowhere else to go and now," she drew a deep, shuddering breath. "Well, now that Burke's . . . Burke's—"

Her shoulders started to shake and she buried her face in her hands. Dake put his arm around her shoulder and drew her close. "Hush, now, Minna. Don't take on so. You know you have a home here for as long as you want one. Hell, you're more entitled to this place than I am." He recalled Shelby Gilmore's words the day he met him in Decatur. "You saved the place for Burke and saved my neck from a rope. Stay as long as you like."

With tear-streaked cheeks, she looked up into his eyes and whispered, "Thank you, Dake. I'll do all I can to help you find whoever it was that did this terrible thing."

"I know you will," he assured her. Shrugging off his coat, he hooked a finger in the collar and swung it over his shoulder. "And I know you'll be able to handle things for a few days while I go down to Gadsden."

"Gadsden?" Her hand paused on the finely cut profile in the Wedgwood cameo she had pinned at her throat. One he recognized as his mother's favorite piece of jewelry. How like Theodora Reed to have passed it on to the girl who had been like a daughter to her. "Whatever are you goin' down to Gadsden for?"

He started for the staircase. She followed him across the room that was nearly stripped of furnishings. "I'm going to see about Cara James, to make sure she arrived safely and found the Claytons. There's a little matter of paying her what I owe her . . ."

"But, she didn't seem the type to need lookin' after, if you ask me. She was lucky enough to get herself hooked up with you and managed to get this far. Why, Gadsden's not sixty miles from here. Besides, the sheriff—"

Dake stopped in the foyer. "The sheriff has no way to hold me now that you've given me an airtight alibi."

The ebony-skinned serving girl with a head full of braids passed them, straining under the weight of a tray piled with empty glasses. "Watch those tumblers, Patsy," Minna cautioned. "They're all we have left of the crystal." Minna hiked up her skirt and mounted the stairs. "When will you be back, Dake?"

He reached for the tray, relieved the servant of the heavy load and started toward the kitchen at the back of the house. The startled teen trailed behind him. Over his shoulder he informed Minna, "Just as soon as I've found Cara and sent her on her way."

Even if you don't know where you're headed, it's better to be on the road of life than off.

Nanny James

Chapter Eleven

The Claytons' house was everything Cara had hoped it would be and more. For one thing, it was still standing, and it looked to be in good repair compared to many of the others she'd seen on her journey across the countryside. For another, it was larger than she could have imagined—Clay's family had obviously been wealthy and seemed to have somehow retained their wealth. She figured they would be folks who knew how to recover. There would be no worry where Clay's next mouthful might come from.

Someone was still taking infinite care with the rose garden laid out in front of the wide, welcoming veranda. There was a porch swing, a row of rockers begging to be occupied, shutters at the windows. In comparison to every other house she had seen in her life, including the hotels and boardinghouses she'd stayed in during her travels with Dake, this was a mansion, a palace, a perfect home for Clay.

She offered to pay the farmer who had driven her out to the house, but he refused with a shake of his head and a smile before he bid her farewell. It had been far easier than she had suspected to purchase her stagecoach tickets from Decatur to Gadsden. Once there, she inquired at the first boardinghouse she found. A widow down on her luck was willing to rent her a room in the newly opened establishment. Cara stored her boxes and changed into the dove-gray dress she'd purchased in

Poplar Bluff rather than overdress. From what she had seen of the women in the South, they took pride in the sacrifices they had made during the war. She didn't wish to flaunt her new gowns before them.

"This is it, Clay," she whispered, hugging him close and then turning slightly so the baby on her shoulder could raise his wobbly head and stare at the imposing white edifice where his mother had been raised. As she held him tight and walked up the brick walk that led to the veranda, Anna Clayton's bracelet pressed into the flesh at her wrist. It was an elegantly scrolled piece of gold far more costly than anything anyone in her family had ever possessed.

She found herself standing, as yet unnoticed, before a wide front door. Reaching up, she grabbed the brass door knocker and let it fall three times. As if he sensed her nervousness, Clay began to squirm. The door opened just as she was shifting him from one shoulder to the other.

"Yes, 'em?" A Negress a few inches shorter and a good ten years older than Cara with flawless, glowing skin of ebony stared up at her. She wore a plain, unadorned gown of cotton ticking and a wide red shawl tied about her shoulders.

"Are the Claytons at home?"

The woman was eyeing Clay and Cara in turn. "Miz Clayton is. Mr. Clayton been gone a year now." Then she added automatically, "Rest his soul."

"Then I'll see Mrs. Clayton, please, ma'am." Cara smiled.

The woman was obviously taken aback when Cara addressed her as ma'am. After a moment's pause, she stepped back to admit her into the house, and in a voice just loud enough for Cara to hear asked, "You ain't from around these parts, are you, miss?"

Cara smoothed Clay's curls and nervously straightened his blanket. He looked up at her with trusting, dark eyes and her heart contracted. "I'm from Kansas," she said, focusing on the servant again.

"If you want to get along with Miz Clayton, you won't let her hear you callin' me ma'am like I was somebody. My name's Inez."

"And I'm Cara. Cara Calvinia James. I'm pleased to make your acquaintance, Inez."

Inez smiled as if doing so was a habit. Her smile set her face aglow and lit her shining eyes.

There were double doors on either side of the entry hall. She led Cara to the room on the left and said, "Wait here, ma'am, and I'll tell Miz Clayton you're here."

She left Cara alone to stare in wonder about the room. There were tables meant for nothing more than holding a vase on display, chairs covered in brocade with such a high shine that Cara was tempted to reach out and touch them.

The longer she waited, staring at the gilt-edged paintings, the shining surfaces of the spindly legged tables, the rich fabrics, the more the thought came home to her that her family had been dirt poor. Even the furnishings and bric-a-brac in the hotel rooms and homes she'd stayed in thus far had surpassed anything she had ever seen before, let alone hoped to ever imagine owning. She ran her hand over the surface of a well-oiled cherrywood side table and thought of the scarred, rough-hewn plank table she had left behind. As much as she enjoyed seeing such finery, she had no burning desire to acquire anything of the sort for herself. Her one and only goal was to earn a living as a dollmaker, to set up a shop of her own and turn it into the finest in California. Perhaps in the entire West.

"Miss James? I'm Sarah Clayton." A weak voice that sounded strained from lack of use summoned her from her thoughts. Her arms tightened reflexively around Clay as Cara took a deep breath and turned toward the sound. Framed by double doors stood a petite woman of fifty years. From collar to ankle, she was outfitted in unrelieved black silk. Light brown hair streaked with gray had been pulled back into a severe twisted coil at her nape. Her eyes were the same shape as Clay's, only a much faded blue. Sorrow and bitterness fairly spilled out of them.

For a brief instant, Cara wondered if she should have sent a message first and given Mrs. Clayton prior warning regarding the nature of her visit. How would she take the news of her daughter's death? This pale woman with violent smudges beneath her eyes appeared as fragile as an eggshell. Inez hovered in the open doorway, as if waiting to receive further direction from her mistress. Cara was glad of her presence in the event Mrs. Clayton became hysterical.

Cara took a deep breath. "Mrs. Clayton, you don't know me from the man in the moon, and what I'm about to tell you isn't easy to say, but I don't believe in beating about the bush, so to speak."

Sarah Clayton's eyes narrowed. She swept Cara from head to toe, paused as her gaze flicked over Clay and dismissed him. "State your business, young woman."

Cara remembered the bracelet and, juggling Clay, unclasped it, slipped it off of her wrist, and held it out toward Sarah Clayton, intending for the woman to take it. Mrs. Clayton merely stared at the wide gold band with the stars and crescent engraved on it as if Cara held a snake in her hand.

"It was your daughter's, wasn't it?"

The woman's spine tightened as if she'd been struck from behind. Shoulders rigid, her cheeks flamed and then lost all color. "I don't have a daughter."

The icy tone reached across the room and sent a sent a shiver down Cara's spine. "But—"

The woman had ceased staring at Cara now and had turned

her attention fully on little Clay. Without moving an inch, she withdrew into herself.

"Are there other Claytons living near Gadsden? Anna Clayton specifically said she was from Gadsden."

"I *have no daughter.* Now, will you please leave this house?" Sarah Clayton's voice had grown stronger. She enunciated each word as if Cara were deaf, or simpleminded, or both.

Angry beyond thought, Cara sensed the woman was lying. The sight of the bracelet had evoked too obvious a reaction. "Anna Clayton is dead," Cara blurted out. "This is her boy. I'm trying to find her family so they can take him."

Sarah Clayton was staring at little Clay with as much venom as she had the bracelet. "Get out. Get him out of here."

Sheltering the infant in her arms, Cara glanced over Sarah Clayton's shoulder. Inez stood spellbound in the doorway as she took in the unfolding drama, her eyes growing wider by the second. One more glance at Sarah Clayton assured Cara there was no hope in argument. She took a step toward the woman, intending to walk past her and out the door.

Sarah Clayton raised both hands in self-defense. Her words brought Cara up short. "Don't bring that child near me. Get out! Do you hear me? Take him and get out."

Afraid for Clay's safety, Cara hurried past Sarah Clayton. The woman had begun to shake as hard as wheat blowing in a high wind. Still pale as a sheet, she stumbled out of the way as Cara strode out of the room.

Inez quickly let her through the front hall toward the door. Cara stepped out onto the sun-dappled porch and drew a deep, cleansing breath of fresh air. Without a word, Inez quickly closed the door behind Cara and left her standing alone with Clay in her arms staring at the faded green paint on the front door.

"Well, I'll be battered and fried," she whispered against

Clay's ear. "And I'll be damned if I ever leave you with the likes of that woman, whether she's your granny or not."

As she left the veranda, the significance of the exchange hit her fully. For some reason, Sarah Clayton had refused to acknowledge her own grandchild. As much as she had hated the thought of giving Clay up, Cara was now faced with the real possibility that she might never find any of his relations willing to take him.

Lost in thought, Cara moved down the walkway that fronted the house and began to make her way down the oak-shadowed lane that led to the road. The house wasn't far from town, not by Cara's standards, so she decided to walk back to Gadsden to the boardinghouse, figuring if she tired, she could always ask a ride of a passing traveler.

Mentally, she tried to tally what monies she had left sewn in the hem of her old gown. Dake still owed her for travel expenses and the care of Clay, but she hated the thought of having to turn tail and run back to him to collect it. Would he pay her anything now that she had tried to deliver the child and failed?

Clay began to fuss. It was past his feeding time, so Cara looked for a place to stop and use the bottle she had tucked into the deep pocket of her gown. A fallen log beside the road provided the perfect resting place. She sat down, cradled Clay in the crook of her arm, and fished inside her skirt pocket. The rubber nipple caught on the fabric before she could wrestle it out and pop it into the baby's mouth.

The slight breeze that had been blowing earlier in the day began to pick up. Dry leaves swirled and eddied about the grove where Cara stopped to rest. She watched an oak leaf stained burgundy dance along the road until motion farther up the way caught Cara's eye. She looked up, able to make out Inez hurrying along after her. The woman was perspiring, as if she had run the entire distance. When she finally reached Cara, she stood for a moment with one hand on her breast, fighting to catch her breath.

Cara patted a space beside her on the log. "Heavens, Inez. Sit a spell and catch your breath."

Inez sat and huffed, "Thank you, ma'am."

"Cara."

Inez nodded, still winded. Finally, she collected herself enough to speak. "I just wanted to tell you that you found the right Claytons but that woman ain't never gonna admit it or take that child." She looked down at the baby whose rosebud lips were eagerly pulling at the bottle of milk.

"That's what I thought. What I can't figure out is why? Did you know Anna Clayton?"

"Yes, 'em. I did. Since I was a girl." Inez braced her hands beside her on the log and began to rock back and forth, looking out across the clearing. "Anna Clayton was the most beautiful girl around these parts. Always was, but she was spoiled somethin' fierce by her folks. Anything Anna wanted, she got—till she fell in love with the wrong man."

Inez's drawl was so thick Cara had to listen carefully to understand. "She ran away?"

"That's right. She ran off, a year gone. Didn't ever let her mamma know where she went, not that the old woman would care. Day Anna left, Miz Clayton swore she was dead to her, never wanted to see her face again. Two nights later, the old man dies in his sleep. Some say there was a conjure on him, but I think more likely he up and died of a broken heart."

"Conjure?"

"A spell."

"A spell—" Cara repeated the word as if she had some idea what Inez was talking about.

Offhandedly, Inez inquired, "What are you gonna do with Anna's little boy now, poor child?"

Cara pulled the rubber nippled bottle out of the baby's mouth and expertly moved him to her shoulder for a burp. As she patted him on the back, she shrugged. "Take him with me, I guess. I'm on the way to California."

"That's a mighty long way. Over the ocean, I hear tell."

Cara smiled at Inez. "Next to the ocean. Not over it, but there's a sea of prairie between here and there. That was one place I never hoped to see again in my life."

"How'd you come by the baby?"

Cara sighed. "Roundabout, that's for certain. A Federal soldier just out of the army rode up to my door with him tucked in his jacket." She smiled at the memory that was still as clear as sunshine on a Kansas morning. "He came upon Anna Clayton's wagon after a massacre of some kind. Dake suspected it was raiders. Anyway, she'd just given birth to Clay here, that's what we've been calling him anyway, and before she died, she told Dake Reed to take the baby home to Gadsden and he made a promise to her as she died that he would." She fingered the bracelet on her arm and held it out to Inez to inspect. "He took this off her, so there'd be no doubt about who the baby was when we brought Clay home."

"It's Miz Anna's all right. Got it from her papa on her fifteenth birthday." Inez paused. "Was she alone?"

"No. She had two servants with her. They were both dead. She said her husband died, too. Poor man was spared the massacre anyway. Dake had to leave them on the prairie, not much else he could do with night coming on and the baby to see to." She glanced over and was arrested by the sight of Inez wiping at the corner of her eyes with the hem of her gingham skirt.

"I'm sorry to be so blunt about it," Cara apologized, "I didn't realize you might be close to her."

"Her and the other two, as well. They were all from this here place. Can't imagine them endin' up dead somewheres in the middle of Kansas. Sometimes I have to wonder what the Good

Lord is up to the way the world's been turned around lately."

"My granny always said God's driving the wagon and he means for us not to see what's around the next bend in the road. Between you and me though, sometimes I think he's asleep at the reins."

As intended, the comment brought a tremulous smile to Inez's lips. "If you wait, I can send a man down with a wagon to carry you back to town. It ain't fittin' you be walking back totin' that child. 'Sides, it looks about to rain."

Cara shook her head and smiled. "That's kindly of you, Inez, but I have a lot of thinking to do and if my hands are idle, I do it better on my feet. If by some miracle that woman changes her mind and wants Clay, I'll be at the Rundell boardinghouse in Gadsden for the next day or two until I can get my plans together. After that, I suppose I could send word back to you—"

Inez shook her head. "No, ma'am. I'm not likely to get the letters, besides, I can't read."

"There's a slim chance I may be in contact with Dake Reed at a place called Riverglen outside of Decatur." *A very slim chance.*

Inez stood and helped Cara to her feet. "I'll remember," Inez promised, "but don't go lookin' for Miz Clayton to change her mind."

Cara shoved the empty bottle back into her pocket. "I won't. Well, Inez," she said, holding out her hand to the other woman, "you take care."

Inez paused a second, then took Cara's hand. "You got a good heart, Miz Cara. The Lord will watch over you. That's for certain. You watch over that boy."

"I will." Cara had no choice but to turn and leave Inez standing in the road and head toward Gadsden.

Dake dismounted before a low, white picket fence that bordered the first house on the outskirts of Gadsden. Attracted by the neat letters of the freshly painted sign advertising the place as a room and board, he brushed road dust off the front of his buckskin jacket, hoping he'd have to search no farther for Cara Calvinia James. A north wind that was pushing clouds had increased considerably during the last mile of his ride. He glowered up at the sky, daring it to drop any rain before he found her.

The door was opened by a tall, slender woman who looked to be near forty. Behind her hovered a boy of about ten and a girl near the same age. They eyed him speculatively. He couldn't help but recognize the button-eyed rag doll the girl was holding in one arm. Dake introduced himself, briefly explained that he was looking for Cara James. The two children were obviously disappointed when they heard his question and soon lost interest and wandered away.

"I'm Judith Rundell. Come in, Mr. Reed," the woman invited him. "And please don't mind those two. Ever since my husband was killed in the war they've been looking for a likely candidate for husband and father."

Dake shrugged. "Sorry, ma'am."

"May I ask why you're looking for Miss James?"

Relieved that the woman hadn't denied knowing Cara, Dake felt himself relax. "I employed her to help tend an orphan I found on the prairie and a couple of days ago I . . . I ran into some family trouble and she came on to Gadsden without me." He watched the woman weigh the truth of his words.

"The Clayton child."

"That's right. Is she here?"

"She should be back anytime. In fact, I was hoping she'd return before this rain hits. She was taking the baby out to the Clayton place. It's not very far."

So, he was too late to say good-bye to little Clay. It grieved him more than he wanted to admit. If he felt this bad, how must Cara be taking the loss? A few weeks ago she might have been relieved, eager to start on her adventure to California. Now he wasn't so sure. He knew without her ever having said it that she would miss the baby more than he since so much of the care and feeding of little Clay had fallen to her.

"Did you know Anna Clayton?" Mrs. Rundell asked as she ushered him into a parlor that fronted the house.

The furnishings were plain, but polished to a high shine. Obvious care had been taken with the arrangement of every piece in the room. Crocheted doilies graced the backs of the chairs and settees.

Dake chose a wing chair close to a cozy, low-burning fire and rested his new hat on his knee. "No, ma'am. I found her just before she died."

"A sad tale indeed."

"How so, ma'am?"

Judith Rundell shook her head as if she were about to impart the darkest of secrets. She leaned forward and in a voice barely above a whisper informed him, "She ran off with a *Yankee*, let's see, about a year ago or more, as I recall. I didn't have the heart to tell Miss James about that. Seeing as she's from Kansas, it might not have offended her as much as it did folks around these parts." She looked thoughtful for a moment, then asked, "Whatever were you doing in Kansas?"

Dake deemed it wise not to mention his former status to a war widow. Instead, he said, "I was at loose ends, like most men after the war. Kansas was as good a place to be as any." Not the whole truth, but not exactly a lie, either.

There was a sound of footsteps on the porch. When Judith Rundell went to answer the door, Dake got to his feet. He recognized Cara's voice in the hallway, and for the second time in the space of an hour, relief swept through him. Cara stepped into the parlor with Clay in her arms and Judith Rundell thoughtfully left them alone. Dake was suddenly struck with the notion that he never wanted to let Cara out of his sight again. He tossed his hat on the chair and stepped toward her. Her hair was rain-soaked, the curls heavy with water droplets. She was pulling Clay's blanket off him as he moved.

As if he didn't need to explain his sudden appearance, he simply said, "You're wet."

Her eyes were ice-blue and wary. "You're out of jail."

"I was never in."

"It must be nice to have that much influence in town."

He took another step toward her. "Jensen can't hold me without proof."

"And then there's Minna Blakely's convenient alibi," she shot back. "What are you doing here?"

"Why don't you just admit you're jealous of Minna and get it over with?"

"Jealous?" She tossed Clay's blanket on the back of the settee and then thought better of it. Bundling the wet cloth in her hands, she looked about for a place to stash it, then just held on to it. "I'll have you know you are the last person in the world I'd be jealous over, Dake Reed."

"Because you don't care a fig for me."

"You're right as rain there."

He was within an arm's length of her. "And you intended to leave Alabama without telling me good-bye?"

"I did."

"I'm here to prove that would be the biggest mistake of your life."

"And how's that, Mr. Reed, when it isn't a mistake at all and you know it?"

Mindful of the infant in her arms, he grasped her by her shoulders and pulled her toward him. Just as his lips were about to touch hers, Cara's eyes widened in realization.

"I don't—"

Dake silenced her with his lips and kept up kissing her until all resistance drained from her. He traced her mouth with his tongue. Her lips opened for him. She moaned low in her throat and raised up on tiptoe, offering him more. Dake was lost in the essence of her, given over to thoughts of warm kisses, autumn leaves, and raindrops. One hand strayed to her abundant curls and he crushed a handful in his palm and drew her up close. His lips moved over hers and still she didn't move away. Hot desire pulsed through him unlike any he had known. Cara was back in his arms and he longed to take her farther than he had ever dared to go.

Clay squirmed and began to cry in protest as the two adults held him wedged between them. Dake ended the exchange and Cara, her cheeks flushed, her eyes snapping with a defiance that was sorely missing from her kiss, took a step back.

"Look what you've done," she said with a catch in her voice.

"What have I done, Cara?"

Cara lifted Clay to her shoulder and began to jiggle him up and down as she tried to calm him. "You've got me so mixed up I don't know what I'm doing anymore."

"Then admit your feelings for me. Come home with me."

"What?"

"Something's been building between us since the day I first laid eyes on you. Don't deny you feel it, too. Come to Riverglen with me."

She shook her head fiercely. He could see she was fighting herself more than his words. "No. I can't. I'm going to California. I warned you about that all along." Her eyes were suspiciously moist as she tried to turn away. "Now if you'll excuse me, I have to go up and get Clay some dry things."

She was about to bolt. Abruptly changing the subject, he took hold of her arm and asked, "Didn't you find the Claytons?"

"I did, but his granny didn't want him. I would never have left him with an old witch like that anyway."

Dake frowned down at the child even as he reached out to

smooth the boy's loose curls. "What do you mean she didn't want him?"

"It's a long story, but to make it short, it seems Anna Clayton ran off with some man and now her mother won't even admit to having a daughter. I swear, Dake, you wouldn't have believed the hate in that woman's eyes. You'd have thought poor Anna had run off with the devil himself."

"Or a Yankee."

"So that's what happened," she said softly.

"So your landlady tells me."

Cara sighed. "Can you imagine someone not wanting Clay?"

"No." Dake didn't have to think twice about his answer. With it came insight as to how he could keep Cara by his side, at least until he could convince her to face up to her feelings for him. He wasn't above using Clay as a bargaining chip if it meant having them both eventually.

"What are you going to do now?"

"*Me?* As far as I can see you mean what are *we* going to do now, Mr. Reed. You're as responsible for this baby as I am."

Dake was elated by her response. "That's right, Cara. So I suggest you come back to Riverglen with me while we sort out what's best for Clay *and* us. Maybe we can find someone who is willing to open up their home and hearts to him."

"Give him away, you mean?"

He looked as confused as he could. "What else can we do? You're on your way to California," he reminded her.

She looked as if he'd just suggested they leave the baby on the side of the road. "But—"

"Of course, it's going to take some time before I can do anything about placing Clay. I've got a couple of other things to tend to, like finding my brother's murderer, not to mention getting Riverglen on its feet."

"*Placing* Clay? You sound as if you don't care anything about him at all." She hugged the child protectively.

He fought to keep the depth of his true feelings from his expression. "I love him, Cara. But you said yourself, you're off to California and—"

"Will you *stop* saying that?"

"Are you coming home with me until we get this settled?"

Exasperated, she closed her eyes. When she opened them again, he smiled. "Well?" he pressed.

"I suppose I'll have to," she admitted. "At least until we have time to find someone suitable to adopt the baby."

"It could be a while," he warned.

"How long?"

A lifetime. Dake shrugged. "A few weeks at the most."

She looked torn. Afraid she'd change her mind, he added, "Maybe less, maybe more."

"I suppose I could make more dolls while I'm waiting around. That way I'd have a good supply when I do head west."

"Good idea."

"There's plenty enough fabric left to keep me busy."

I'll keep you busy. "If you get your things together, we can leave as soon as I rent a wagon."

She eyed him skeptically. "I'd have thought you'd be dog-tired of carting me and my boxes around, Dake Reed."

He finally felt safe enough to let go of her arm. "I'd have thought so, too, but life's full of little surprises."

Once you break an egg you might as well sweep it up and toss out the pieces.

Nanny James

Chapter Twelve

Cara knew the minute she was settled in her room at Riverglen that she had turned another bend in life's bumpy road. "I wish to goodness I knew who was driving." Thinking of her conversation with Inez about God's hands on the reins of fate, she mumbled to herself as she shook out the last of her gowns and hung it in the tall standing cupboard built against one wall.

Across the room, Clay was sleeping soundly in a mahogany cradle that had belonged to Dake and his brother. Stored in the attic, the cradle was one of the few pieces of furniture that had escaped plunder during the war. Cara had placed it against the tall windows in her room where the morning light would find it. Patting the blanket coverlet beneath Clay's chin, she straightened and then hurried downstairs to have a talk with Dake.

The sight of Minna Blakely waiting for them on the veranda when they arrived had shocked her, and from the look on the other woman's face, Minna was just as surprised. Cara had not expected to see Minna at Riverglen, nor did she know Minna was actually living under Dake's roof. Regretting her decision to accompany Dake back to Decatur, she intended to set him straight immediately and make plans to leave as soon as arrangements could be made. As to the question of Clay, she had already settled the issue in her heart.

She was taking him with her.

If it hurt to think of leaving Dake behind, if her heart was already suffering from the wound of separation, so be it. She would not live under the same roof with the woman who was telling one and all she had shared a definite relationship with her fiancé's brother. Cara descended the wide staircase, still in awe of the vastness of the house. House? She paused with one hand on the handrail and stared up the thirty-foot stairwell toward the skylight in the domed ceiling. Dake had explained that most of the furnishings and carpets were missing. Despite the loss, this was no house, it was a mansion.

The sounds of voices echoed along the hallway. She followed them until she reached a room near the end of the hall. The door was open. Minna was inside, that much was clear, for her well-modulated voice was easily recognizable with its underlying tone of authority beneath a thick coat of honey. Cara paused on the threshold and found Dake seated behind a wide desk. Minna stood beside him carefully pointing to a sheet of paper on the surface. As Cara stepped into the room, the two occupants looked up at her in unison.

Dake's eyes were warm with welcome but he looked tired. Minna smiled, but for the life of her, Cara couldn't read what emotions were at play behind the woman's eyes.

"Come on in, Cara, and sit down." Dake pointed to a straight-backed chair across the desk from him. He gave her a smile that would have melted her heart a week ago. "We'll be through here in a moment." He turned his attention to the paper again.

Minna smiled. "You may appreciate listening in, Miss James. Since you're so set on bein' a businesswoman and all." She primly smoothed her skirt and straightened the lace-edged cuffs of her black silk gown. Widow's weeds became her, the black a midnight contrast to her ivory complexion. The sight of the attractive woman leaning over Dake's shoulder only added to Cara's discomfort here.

Minna drew his attention. "As I was sayin', Dake. This is a copy of the contract that one of the local planters drew up between himself and the"—she paused as if seeking the appropriate word—"the *freedmen*. It's fairly clear, I think, and one you might want to put into practice."

Cara watched Dake as he swiftly read the contract. Her gaze fell to his hands where they rested on the desk. His fingers were long and tapered, but there was nothing gentle about them. They were tanned, still smooth but marked by time and sun. Here and there small scars from various cuts marred his skin. They were the hands of a man who'd seen his share of work. Hands that could take on the challenge of rebuilding his land as surely as they could caress her and stroke her senses to life. She squirmed in the chair and tried to concentrate on the exchange.

"It says here the landowner will provide 'nominal wages, rations, shelter, clothing, and moral oversight if the freedman pledges obedience and good and faithful service during the remainder of the year—in whatever capacity the owner may direct.'"

"That's right," Minna said, leaning closer to the document, her breast very near Dake's shoulder.

Cara crossed her arms. Her foot started tapping. Minna pointedly chose not to look up at her. As if he was oblivious to Minna's nearness, Dake was carefully studying the page.

"This is a clear intent to control labor much the same way it was under slavery," Dake pointed out a few seconds later. "The contract is careful not to state how much wage, what kind of rations, shelter, clothing, or how the moral 'oversight' will be administered."

"Who's going to take care of these people if we don't?" Minna argued. "They've been fed and clothed and ministered to like children since the first slaves were imported. Some of them are old enough to remember livin' like savages in Africa, for heaven's sake. Everyone knows they aren't capable of takin' care of themselves—"

"Nor will they ever if they aren't taught how to or given the incentive."

"You haven't been home in years, Dake. The Yankees have tried to implement their own ideas, but you have to admit we know what's best for the—freedmen. They're not about to work unless forced. Why, look at the way they lay around this place now."

Cara sensed Minna used the word "freedmen" only to placate Dake.

"I haven't been in the South since emancipation but I've read everything I can get my hands on. DeBow's *Review* reported that the freedmen near Vicksburg were working more productively this year than they ever had under slavery."

"Yankee propaganda."

He laid the contract aside. "I intend to rent shares of the land for a third of the crop, rations, livestock, and feed. For now, they can use the cabins along the row, but eventually cabins could be built on various parcels of land. Later on, workers can opt for a larger share of the crop as they begin to be able to provide for their own needs and can eventually buy parcels. In the beginning, we'll have to provide implements, of course."

Although his use of the word "we" gave her pause, Cara thought it sounded like a well thought out and constructed plan. She could see by the appalled look on Minna's face that the woman thought Dake had lost his mind.

It didn't take Minna long to respond. "Do you lay awake at night wondering how to stir up trouble, Dake Reed? There's not a planter in this area who's not going to be offended by this plan. It seems like you *want* the Ku Klux breathin' down your neck."

"As far as I know, this is still America and I damn well have the right to draw up any contract I want for the workers I hire. As far as drawing Shelby and his gang of thugs out into the open, let them come."

"Shelby?"

"You know damn well he's involved with them, Minna. I think he knows who killed Burke. Maybe he even did it himself."

"Why, I can't believe you'd blame Shelby Gilmore."

"Do you have any other ideas?"

Minna shook her head. "No." Tears misted her eyes and she hastily blinked them away. "I'm sorry I lost my temper. I'm still so upset. I just can't imagine who'd do such a hideous thing."

He reached around behind him and took her hand in a move that was spontaneous and natural. He cleared his throat. "I'm sorry, Minna. You've had so much to bear, and now Burke's gone. I promise you I'll find his killer and whoever it was will pay." He let go of her hand, turned back to the desk, and leafed through the other pages on the desk. "What's this?" He pulled out one that had obviously been folded.

Minna shrugged. "I found that with some other papers shoved in Burke's desk. I'm not sure what it means, except it mentions a deposit with Rankin, Gilmour and Company in Liverpool."

Losing all patience, Cara stood up and began to wander around the room. Listening to the exchange, she realized how little she knew about contracts and business and was overwhelmed. What legalities would owning a shop of her own entail? She ran her finger over the windowsill and moved toward the library shelves, pushing away her fear. She knew how to make dolls, that was certain, and she wasn't about to let a few sheets of paper stand in her way.

"This might account for some of Burke's depression," Dake

said, lifting the page and studying the seal at the bottom. Cara turned to see what he was talking about.

"What is it?" Minna drew closer, nearly leaning on his shoulder now. Cara paused beside a shelf of books, tempted to reach out and snatch Minna bald.

"It seems my father deposited substantial funds in a bank in Liverpool before the end of the war," Dake said, his tone preoccupied as he read. "Which means he knew the Confederacy was doomed." Half to himself he said, "This must be what Elijah had overheard Daddy talking about. He was giving allegiance to the Confederacy but hedging against failure. When Burke saw this it must have broken his heart."

Minna straightened, her anger all too apparent. "You mean to say Burke *knew* he had the money to save Riverglen and would have willfully lost it because of some insane loyalty to the cause?"

"Minna, that *insane loyalty* cost him his legs and more lives than we can count." Dake shoved everything but the bank note aside. "I'm not surprised at his decision to ignore this."

She was frowning down at the papers, hard anger apparent in her eyes. "If he hadn't died, we'd have never found this. He kept it hidden even when he knew he might have lost Riverglen. How could he, Dake? How could Burke have done it?"

The two fell silent for so long that Cara took the opportunity to speak. "I'd like to talk to you, Dake, if you can spare a minute."

Dake looked over at her and she watched his expression change from one of preoccupation to one so full of warmth and promise that it shamed Cara to think of what she was planning to tell him.

Minna's own thoughts were obviously far away. She stared at Cara as if trying to place her and then picked up her skirt, stepped around the desk, and swept past. Before she quit the room, she paused, framed in the doorway, and asked Cara, "Where's little Clayton?"

"He's asleep in the crib."

"I'll see if he's all right up there alone."

"I'm certain he is," Cara told her. "He needed a nap."

"All the same, it doesn't do to leave children on their own without lookin' in on them. I know from all the little ones I helped Dake's mama care for in the quarters. Why, he could smother or get his head caught in the bed slats or—"

"Thank you, Minna," Dake interrupted the distressing talk. "We'd appreciate that."

Once again, the saintly Minna Blakely had made Cara feel inept. She waited until the woman left the room, the sound of her footsteps echoing down the hallway before she spoke. "Dake, I—"

He stood and came around the desk. Without a word, he took her in his arms. She told herself to move away but she didn't. She told herself she wouldn't let him kiss her, but she did. Her gaze dropped from the heated want in his eyes to his lips. Like a charmed snake, she stood perfectly still, their combined breath the only sound she was aware of except for the riotous beating of her heart.

"Did I tell you how glad I am that you're here?" he whispered against her lips before he covered them with his own.

She moved closer, tasting, allowing herself to feel, savoring the deliciousness of his kiss. She slipped her arms around his neck and pressed closer, encouraged by the deep groan low in his throat. His response gave her a heady sense of power that was only heightened when his hand slipped to the small of her back and he pressed her full length against him and she felt his arousal.

The kiss deepened, an exchange of sighs and tongues and exploration that was fast careening out of control. He took a step forward, pressing her back against the library shelves. She strained upward, leaning into him, wanting more, needing more, and knowing full well she may have just turned another blind corner into unexplored territory. Her breath was coming fast and hard. Her heart beat savagely.

Cara dragged her mouth away from his and as she fought to catch her breath, she shuddered. "I can't stop you if I can't stop myself."

He nuzzled his nose against her ear. "You know you want me as much as I want you, Cara," he whispered against her ear. The act sent chills racing through her. "At least I'm willing to admit it."

"Sometimes folks want things they shouldn't have," she whispered back. "Things that are bad for a body—like too much liquor."

He slid his hands over her, let his fingers play along her throat, cupped her face between his palms. Cara closed her eyes. "I'm drunk with need of you, Cara."

She giggled, opened her eyes, and found him smiling down at her. *"Drunk with need?"*

He threw his head back and laughed aloud for the first time in days. "I just wanted to be sure you were paying attention."

The levity sobered both of them as nothing else could have. Dake kissed her again, this time a deep but swift promise of more. When he was through he stepped back, but threaded his fingers between hers, unwilling to let go of her hand.

She realized how seldom he really laughed and cursed the war, the upheaval, and the pain left in its wake. It was suddenly important that she get him away from his worries, away from all he'd faced since he'd come to Riverglen, away from the restructuring of the plantation, his brother's murder, the grief that was so very apparent in the shadows beneath his eyes.

She thought back to Poplar Bluff, to the way he had comforted her when she asked him, the way he had stayed with her when she needed him. Now he needed her. Now was not the time to tell him she intended to leave.

She tipped her head and smiled up at him. "It's stopped raining. Why don't you take some time and go for a walk with me? Show me this Riverglen you love so much."

"You just want to get me away from the house."

"You're right. This place is too crowded for my taste." She paused, remembering the baby asleep upstairs. "I almost forgot about Clay. I'll bring him along."

"Minna will watch him. Or there's Patsy."

"I wasn't thinking—"

He waved at the pile of work on the desk. "You may not be able to talk me into it again," he warned. "I do need time outside. Please go with me."

Had he argued, she might have been able to say no, but the simple entreaty appealed to her heart as nothing else might have. She knew in that instant she could deny him nothing.

"All right." She feigned a sigh. "I guess it won't do any good to make you promise to keep your hands to yourself, will it?"

"If that's really what you want."

It was her way to answer in complete honesty. "I don't know what I want anymore."

He pulled her around to face him. "I think you do. I just wonder how long it will be before you admit it to yourself." As if he could sense her confusion he added, "Change into something comfortable."

Instead of moving away, she held on to his hand and tipped her face up to receive one quick kiss before they parted. "I'll be ready in no time at all," she promised.

"Just in case I'll come up to your room in five minutes. I want to see Clay before we go."

Cara gave his hand a squeeze before she hurried off to change, her mind racing as she tried to convince herself that her abrupt about-face had more to do with getting Dake to walk away from his troubles for a while than the way his kiss had dissolved her resistance.

The old mill hadn't ground wheat in years, but that didn't keep the waterwheel from slowly revolving as the river flowed beside it and water continued to trickle from the chute onto the blades. Side by side, Dake and Cara sat against the moss-covered stone foundation of the two-story wooden building. A pool of sunshine surrounded them, a gentle breeze loosened dying leaves that floated slowly to earth. Cara reached out for one that was dappled orange and yellow. She lay it against her gray wool skirt and ran her fingertip along the still supple veins.

They had walked farther than she intended, but with every step from the house, Dake had slowly become more relaxed. She told herself that Clay was in good hands, that Minna might rub her the wrong way, but that was because of her own jealousy and nothing more. Patsy was there as well as two other girls who'd just come begging work and Minna reluctantly hired at Dake's urging.

"Feeling better?" Cara asked, putting aside the leaf.

The slight breeze ruffled the dark lock of hair that fell across his forehead. "Who's to say I felt bad?"

Her chin went up. "I am. I've spent enough time with you to know your moods."

"Are you calling me moody?" He turned to give her his whole attention.

"Oh, no. No more than most folks, I guess. But I do know you lose your temper when things don't run on time. You don't rant and rave, but I can see you holding it all in like a steam engine without a valve. And you have to admit, if things are in a mess, you get a little more than tense. I know you'd do about anything to keep that jacket clean," she told him, reaching up to smooth the seam along his shoulder. "And that you hate wrinkles in your clothes. You're always on time, never messy, and far too regimented."

"I'd say you're becoming an expert on Dake Reed, ma'am. Just what do you plan to do with all this expertise?"

"I don't think it's worth much," she said, shrugging.

"It is to me." He leaned over and picked up her hand, brought it to his lips and kissed her palm.

Cara closed her eyes and let her head drop back against the stone foundation of the old mill. He was right. She knew him too well, far too well, to claim theirs was a casual relationship.

His tongue traced across her open palm and she shivered.

"Open your eyes, Cara."

She did as he asked. He'd moved to lean over her. His dark hair fell over his forehead. His eyes bored into hers. Expectantly, she raised her chin, her lips parted slightly. She heard him groan before he captured her mouth beneath his.

The stones at her back were cool despite the sunshine. Uneven, they pressed against her shoulder blades as Dake's kiss deepened. Engrossed in the kiss, she barely noticed that slight discomfort, but Dake guessed at it. When they drew apart he suggested softly, "Lie down, Cara."

It was all too easy after that. She complied, let him help her relax against the warm, grass-covered earth beneath them. When he slipped off his buckskin jacket, she couldn't help but smile. When he took another moment to carefully fold it and lay it aside she almost giggled. Almost. But too soon afterward he turned his heated gaze her way and the sound froze in her throat.

He reached out to trace her lips with his fingertips, then brushed her heavy curls back and away from her face. "I love your hair," he told her. "It's as unconfined by pretension as you are."

Her own fingers were shaking when she lifted them to his lips to touch them. His mouth was warm, his lips softly curved into an inviting half smile. The invitation in his eyes was magic. She reached up to thread her fingers through his hair and drew him down to her until their lips met. Opening her mouth, she tasted the sweetness of his kiss until the tenor of it changed and he became the aggressor. His mouth moved over hers with insistent demand and she opened to him. A slow, demanding ache began to pulse at the juncture of her thighs.

When his hand caressed her breast, she arched against his palm and moaned again as she came alive to his touch. There would be no turning back. Not now. She was about to give herself to this man as she had given herself into his keeping during the journey east. Their first kiss on that long ago night in Poplar Bluff had been her undoing and as impossible as it seemed, somehow deep within the secret recesses of her heart and mind she had known then that inevitably they would become one.

As his hands cupped and cradled her breasts through the rich wool of her gown, Cara let go of everything but the tension building within her and the knowledge that the man pressing her down against the earth was Dake Reed. She responded to his touch like dry prairie grass set aflame by summer lightning. Reaching out to him, she grasped the front of his shirt and jerked it away from the waistband of his trousers. Her hands slipped beneath the dark cambric shirt and she sighed when her fingertips made contact with his flesh. She traced the hard surface of his abdomen, played her fingers lightly over his ribs, and heard his swift intake of breath when she touched his nipples.

His lips were at her throat, his tongue tracing a path down to the edge of her collar. The modest bodice of her gown kept him from tasting farther. His hands strayed to the back of her gown and he began to fight the row of tiny buttons there.

Cara looped her arms about his neck and lifted her upper body off the ground to allow him access to the tedious buttons.

Deftly he worked them free and without hesitation drew her gown off to her shoulders and down her arms to her waist. He mouthed her breasts through the thin muslin of her chemise, first one and then the other. She felt her nipples go hard and tense as a massive shiver quaked through her. Cara grasped Dake by the waist and held on, stunned by the overwhelming need throbbing through her.

Her hands slid around to the buttons of his waistband as he pulled down the straps of her undergarment and bared her breasts. With lips and teeth he gently nipped and suckled. Cara cried out, first in awe and then for want of more. Her legs spread wide involuntarily and her head thrashed from side to side.

"Dake," she gasped as the October sunshine poured down on them. "Oh, Dake."

His breath was warm against her damp skin, the rough maleness of his skin rasped against her as he whispered, "You like that?"

He grasped her breasts in both hands and laved the flowering nipples with his tongue until her breath came in rasping sobs. He wrenched up her skirt and slipped his knee between the V of her legs. Without thought, she followed her need and clasped it against her, riding him, writhing and pressing herself against the corded muscle of his thigh until a shower of sparks ignited somewhere deep inside her and pleasure so intense engulfed her that his name burst from her lips.

She clung to him, clasped him to her breast, and hung on for dear life as the throbbing burst and then slowly ebbed. When she finally collected herself, Cara opened her eyes to find Dake braced on his elbows above her, watching her carefully.

"It will be even better once I'm inside you, Cara love."

She didn't, couldn't believe him. Nothing could be any more exhilarating than what she had just experienced. Savage desire filled her now that she had tasted unbridled pleasure. She freed the last button on his pants and jerked open the waist, then began tugging them down past his hips.

"Again," she ordered.

"With pleasure," he said.

Feverishly, she explored him with her hands, running them over the firm flesh of his buttocks, his hips, the tops of his thighs. He came up on one knee to give her access and she found him, cupped him in her hands, and heard him groan. Filled with a heady sense of her own power, Cara wrapped her fingers around his shaft. It was ramrod-hard, velvet-tipped. She wondered at the miracle of it.

Erotic textures she had never imagined were slowly revealed as her hands explored. His inner thighs were on fire. The nest of hair at the base of his shaft was crisp and at the same time silken. He throbbed against her palm. The tip of his member became slick with a drop of moisture.

His hands were at her waist. Roughly he reached for the top of her undergarment and rent the fabric in two. He moved over her, fitting himself between her thighs, still braced to keep the full weight of him from crushing her.

Cara knew she would beg if she had to, but when she grasped him tight and rubbed the tip of his manhood against the slick, hidden opening between her thighs and heard his swift intake of breath, she knew she wouldn't have to beg at all.

"Now, Dake."

Without preamble he plunged into her, penetrating her maidenhead, tearing his way into the inner sheath that was moist and ready for him. Cara cried out, clasping him against her naked breasts, centering her concentration on the pleasure rather than the pain. He buried himself deeper and went suddenly still, his only movement the rapid rise and fall of his chest as he fought for breath.

She arched her back and drew him deeper, cradled him

against her to his hilt, savored the quivering tension that threatened to send her over the edge once again.

"Dake . . ." She gasped his name between ragged breaths. "Dake, *please.*" She didn't want to wait, couldn't physically hold back any longer. She could feel the tremors that rocked him as he tried to prolong his release. Grasping his buttocks, she thrust her hips high and felt him explode within her as he cried out her name over and over again.

He had thrust so deep, buried himself so far inside her that as his seed poured into her Cara was carried away on wave after wave of raw pleasure.

She buried her face against his neck and clung to him, unwilling to move or speak. To do so would break the spell that bound them together there at the river's edge. Slowly, she felt him relax, still holding himself above her on his elbows. His breathing slowly recovered. He kissed her earlobe, her cheek, her eyelids, and finally her lips.

A slow smile, as lazy as his drawl, spread across his face. "Marry me, Cara."

"What?" Her arms slid from around his neck and she stared back at him in amazement.

"Marry me. Be my wife. We'll raise Clay together, watch him grow into the kind of man the South needs. Hell, we can even have a passel of kids of our own to bring up with him."

"Marry me. Be my wife." She had been prepared to hear him say, "Kiss me, Cara. Let's make love again," but she never in all her born days expected him to propose flat outright.

The idea scared the very stuffing out of her.

"Well?"

She found him watching her intently, waiting for an answer. "I don't know what to say."

His open vulnerability shut down and she found herself facing the hard-edged Captain Dake Reed once more. There was no denying her blunt honesty had angered him.

"You don't still believe I slept with Minna?"

Cara thought of the woman they had left behind at River-glen. Minna was cool, collected, beautiful, but something was missing between the woman and Dake when they were together. There was no love there besides friendship.

"No." She shook her head in denial. "I know you didn't sleep with her."

He relaxed visibly. "I'm not one to hide from the truth, Cara. What just happened between us has never happened to me before with any other woman."

She blinked. "Are you trying to tell me you were a virgin, too?"

Dake kissed her again and laughed. "I'm not *that* good of a liar. What I'm trying to say is that no one has ever made me feel this way before. It's as if I've found a secret part of myself I never even knew was missing—and now that I have, I don't want to lose you."

He sat and pulled her up with him. Gently, he brushed her wayward curls away from where they clung to her damp, sweat-sheened skin. He rose to his knees and jammed his shirttail into his trousers and then buttoned them up before he reached out to help Cara button her dress.

While he knelt behind her and fastened the row of buttons, she drew off what was left of her underdrawers, balled them up, and stuffed them into her pocket.

"I owe you another pair," he said softly, near her ear.

A shredded pair of drawers was the least of her worries.

"Well?" He waited for some response.

"It was . . . incredible."

"I'm not fishing for compliments, Cara. I want an answer. Will you marry me?"

"Dake—"

"If you're going to warn me against falling in love with you again, it's too late."

It's too late for me, too. "I love you, too."

"We'll have to wait until I'm cleared of suspicion of Burke's murder. If we were to be married now, or announce our engagement, Minna's alibi would be shot to hell. I can't do that to her, not after she's tarnished her reputation to save me."

Cara got to her knees and shook grass out of her skirt. "No, I don't suppose you could do that."

"We'll tell her, of course. She'll keep the secret."

"Of course." Cara wondered how Minna would take the news. "There's only one thing."

He stood up and brushed at his pants with his hat. "Which is?"

"My doll shop in California."

"What's wrong with making dolls right here? You can sell them in Decatur, ship them to Montgomery. I don't see the problem."

Cara put her hand against the wall of the old mill and stood up. "The problem is, this isn't California. That's where I was headed until you rode into my life and—"

"Swept you off your feet." He tried to take her in his arms again.

Cara held out a hand in protest and stepped back. "I've been waiting years to get there," she said, trying to sort things out in her mind even as she voiced them aloud to him. "I hadn't counted on falling in love with you, but I have, and now there's Clay to think about, too. But don't you see, Dake, if I give up on my dream, if I don't go to California at least long enough to decide, how will I know what I really want?"

"I love you. You love me." He made a grand gesture, sweeping his arms across the grass where they had just laid and made love. "What happened here doesn't happen every day. There's something special between us, something powerful and real that means a hell of a lot more to me than the realization of a dream."

"Fine. Then you won't mind leaving Riverglen and going to California with me. We can get married there."

"What?"

"You heard me. Leave."

"I can't leave here."

"Oh?" She crossed her arms beneath her breasts as her foot began tapping out rapid beats. "And why not?"

"For one thing, the sheriff would issue an arrest warrant the minute I left the county. For another, I just can't walk off and leave this place in the mess it's in."

"Sell it."

"Sell it?"

"Dake, I feel like I'm talking to a parrot. Sell Riverglen. Give it away." She stared out at the river for a moment, gauged the fact that the sun was riding lower in the sky, and then a thought struck her that she felt was brilliant. "Deed it to Minna. She was your brother's fiancée. She obviously loves the place and she has nowhere else to go."

He was quiet for a long while. So long that she was forced to face him again. What she saw in his eyes told her she had pushed too hard. He turned cold and hard. "Obviously, you don't love me enough to change your plans, is that it?"

The question cut her to the quick. Didn't he know what California and the promise of a new beginning meant to her? Didn't he care? Now that she had admitted her love for him, he actually expected her to forget all the years she'd spent on the prairie just waiting for the opportunity to leave. She knew how the land could bleed a body dry. Could she stay with him and watch him lose his hope, his dreams?

"Obviously, you don't love me enough to go with me," she said.

More than a few feet of earth separated them now. Years of thought and planning, hours of dreams yawned deeper than a chasm between them.

She was stubborn enough not to budge an inch, and he knew it.

He was both determined and disciplined enough not to bend, and she knew it.

"I should never have come here from Gadsden," she mumbled to herself. What had happened between them this afternoon couldn't be undone, but there was no use crying over spilt milk. Any fool knew that. "Nanny James used to say once you broke an egg you might as well just sweep it up and toss out the pieces." With that, she picked up her skirt and headed off across the cotton fields, back the way they had come.

Dake shoved his hands in his pockets and watched her go, her blond curls bobbing around her head, her tempting little bottom swaying provocatively.

"What the hell is *that* supposed to mean?" he shouted.

Always watch your step or you might land in something you can't wipe off.

Nanny James

Chapter Thirteen

When Cara entered the house, she found Minna waiting for her in the foyer at the bottom of the stairs. Out of breath from running most of the way, she reached up to try to coax her unruly hair into place.

After a once-over that swept from Cara's head to toe, Minna asked. "How was your walk?"

There was nothing at all in the woman's cheerful tone to hint at her mood, but Cara sensed Minna was hiding her displeasure over their outing. No one, she decided, could be as habitually even-tempered as Minna Blakely.

"Fine," Cara said, wondering if she had the look about her of someone who'd just been deflowered. "How's Clay?" she asked, hoping to quickly change the direction of the conversation.

"He's fine. Still napping." Minna waited for Cara to respond and when she didn't, added, "Last night at dinner you mentioned your doll making and today when I was up in the attic looking for any old clothes that might be made over, I came across some old dolls and toys you might be interested in."

Cara's curiosity was instantly piqued. "Why, thank you, Minna. I'll go right up."

"Oh, by the way. Someone is waiting for you in the kitchen."

Cara frowned. "I don't know anybody from around here."

"A *Negro* woman. She said she met you the other day."

"Inez?"

Minna shrugged. "I really didn't ask. Just told her to wait for you."

"Thank you." Cara started past her to move down the hall toward the back of the house.

"Oh, Cara?"

Cara rolled her eyes heavenward before she turned back. "Yes?" she answered in her sweetest tone.

"That woman has a bundle with her that I'm sure must be her belongin's. If she's come here to beg work, you'd best ask Dake about it, but as far as I'm concerned, I believe we've already got one too many house girls about the place now. Sooner or later we're gonna have to tell these people to move on and light somewhere else."

"I'll remember that." Too concerned that she was about to learn that Sarah Clayton had changed her mind and sent Inez to collect Clay, Cara hurried toward the kitchen.

She found Inez seated at the kitchen table stringing beans and chatting amiably with Patsy. They fell silent when Cara entered the room and Inez got to her feet. There was, indeed, a bundle on the floor beside her chair, just as Minna had announced. Inez appeared more worried than glad to see her.

"Miz Cara, we've got to talk."

Cara glanced at Patsy and then said, "Come up to my room with me. I've got to look in on Clay anyway and we can talk up there."

Inez stood and hefted her bundle. They walked back through the hall in silence, Cara thankful that Minna was nowhere to be seen. When they reached the guest room on the east side of the house, Cara immediately ushered Inez in and then walked over to Clay's cradle. The baby was wide awake, waving his arms back and forth in the air and gurgling happily to himself.

For the moment, her concern over Dake fled as she lifted the little boy and cradled him to her. Across the room stood a woman who might well have come to take him away. For a heartbeat she thought of sending Inez back empty-handed, taking Clay and walking out the door, out of Dake's life, and heading off to California on her own.

But only for a heartbeat.

"There's no right way to do a wrong thing," she reminded herself, forcing a smile as she turned to Inez. "You've come a long way, Inez."

"Yes, ma'am, Miz Cara. I did. And I hope to God I don't have to go back."

Cara dared to hope. "Then Mrs. Clayton didn't send you after Clay?"

Inez shook her head. Her hair had been plaited into countless tight rows. "I left. I had to see you, had to tell you the truth about that child before any more time passed. I was hopin' to find work here, if I could. If not"—she shrugged, resigned—"then I'll move on until I find some. But I'm not goin' back to Clayton Hall."

"You know something about little Clay?"

The door to the guest room was closed tight, but Inez still looked over her shoulder to be certain, then lowered her voice. "There anyplace we can go where you'll be sure nobody's listenin' to what I have to say?"

Cara glanced at the door and then the windows. "I don't think anyone will come in."

"Miz Cara, I worked in a house like this all my life. The walls got ears, you know."

Dake was still outside somewhere. Cara was surprised he hadn't come to search her out already. She heard him calling her across the fields as she ran toward the house, but she ignored him, unwilling to take up the same argument again. Unwilling to run into him, especially given the nature of Inez's news, she tried to think of somewhere they could go to be alone.

"The attic," she decided aloud. Turning to the black woman she said, "Minna told me there are some old dolls up in the attic. Let's go have a look." When Inez started after her, Cara suggested, "Leave your things here. We'll go find Dake later and ask him about work." Knowing full well she couldn't avoid Dake much longer, Cara decided pleading Inez's cause would afford her an opportunity to talk to him.

Cara cradled Clay in her arms as they walked down the hall until they reached the narrow doorway to the attic at the end of it. She tried the door and found it unlocked, glanced down the hall, and then led the way up the steep, narrow stairs.

Years of accumulated dust swirled beneath the hems of their skirts. Cara sneezed before they reached the top of the stairway. Inez moved along behind her, both of them with a hand on the wall for balance. The stairway was barely wider than shoulder width. Weak light from a window above filtered through dust motes to show the way.

"What a mess," Cara declared when she reached the top. Books with brittle leather bindings, a broken brass lamp base, and a rusted iron headboard were only some of the castaway pieces in the attic. Moving carefully through the memorabilia of times past that were strewn across the length and breadth of the gabled roofed room, Cara found an open trunk, gingerly grabbed the edge of the lid, and let it drop. "We can sit here."

"I'll stand, Miz Cara, if you don't mind."

"It's your choice, Inez. Now, what is it you know about Clay?" Cara glanced down at the baby on her lap and then looked up at Inez again.

Catching the waistband of her gingham skirt in her hands, Inez began to twist and untwist it as she spoke. "I know who that child's daddy is."

"Well, so do I," Cara commented. "And technically, since I'm a Yankee myself, I don't see any great crime in that, do you?"

"A *Yankee*?"

"There's no sense in looking so appalled, Inez. That's what we heard from Mrs. Rundell at the boardinghouse in Gadsden. Anna Clayton ran off with a Yankee."

Shaking her head in denial, Inez took a deep breath. "That baby's daddy wasn't no Yankee. Miz Anna ran off with a slave her daddy freed before the war—a high-yellow boy name of Price."

High yellow? Cara's mind raced ahead. "Price—"

Inez shoved a broken picture frame out of the way with her foot and sat on the floor. Perspiration shone on her forehead and upper lip. She blotted at it with her skirt hem, eyes wide and fearful. Barely whispering, she continued. "Price was a house slave. Best-lookin' boy you'd ever seen." She glanced at Clay. "That baby got his looks. Price was brought up with the best of everything old Mr. Clayton could allow. Even learned the boy to read and write and do the figurin' for him sometime. Price came up alongside Miz Anna until they was old enough to cause worry 'bout what could happen between 'em. But by then it was already too late. Miz Anna wouldn't hear of marryin' anyone but Price. Course, she didn't tell nobody that, just kept turnin' down one beau after another. Finally, they run off. Didn't tell nobody, just disappeared together."

"Sarah Clayton *knew* they'd gotten married?"

Inez nodded. "The day they left, old Miz Clayton put on a black dress and wouldn't mention that girl's name again. Made the old man suffer so much he took to his bed and died of the shock of it. A few months later, a letter come from Miz Anna to her folks. Miz Sarah threw it away, but 'fore it got burned with the trash I had it read to me."

Absently, Cara patted Clay's back as he grasped the narrow band of lace at her collar. A sudden thought fell into place. "Then the man who died beside the wagon in Kansas was Price?"

A tear slowly trickled down Inez's unlined cheek. "Had to be. They were movin' on to Kansas, meetin' up with some other folks they met in Memphis. It's against the law for black and white to marry here, Miz Cara, so they kept movin'. Trouble is, there wasn't no place they were welcome. It didn't matter how light-skinned Price was, there wasn't anyplace they was wanted."

Cara lay Clay across her knees and smoothed out his curls. "Clay doesn't look like he has any black blood."

"No, ma'am. He surely don't, but that can be a blessin' and a curse. No tellin' what he'll look like when he's grown. That's why I had to come and tell you the truth. Now you know, I'm willin' to take the boy if you don't want him anymore. I feel obliged, seein' as how Price's mama was my sister."

Cara wondered how many more surprises were in store for her this afternoon. Inez was watching the boy closely. "So, you're his aunt?"

Inez nodded, watching the baby closely with barely concealed love in her eyes.

"Would you like to hold him?" Cara picked up Clay and gently handed him over.

Cara smoothed her skirt over her knees and then wrapped her arms around them as she watched Inez smile down at Clay and chuck him under the chin in an attempt to get him to smile. Her heart felt as heavy as lead in her chest. "You said, if I don't want Clay that you'd take him. Does that mean you don't want him yourself?"

Inez's response was instantaneous. "I'd keep him in a minute, Miz Cara, if I thought I could feed him and raise him up proper, but I don't even know where my next meal is comin' from and I sure can't take him back to Clayton Hall."

Cara watched Clay stare up at Inez before his gaze moved to the light from the window. When he found her watching him, he smiled and waved his hands up and down. "I'm not giving him away, Inez. Not for anything in the world."

"You sure, Miz Cara? Maybe you ought to think about it for a spell."

Cara shook her head. "I don't need to think about it at all. I think the Good Lord meant for me to have him—why, when I think of the roundabout way He brought us together, I figure it's just meant to be."

"What about your man? How's he gonna feel when he knows the truth about—"

"Shh. What's that?" Cara headed toward the door to the stairs. "I heard something."

Inez was silent, watchful. She cuddled Clay close and shushed him as Cara jerked the door open and called softly down the stairs. "Who's there?"

Silence. They heard the soft ticking sound of a bird as it ran lightly across the roof overhead. Cara wove her way back through discarded pieces of broken furniture, a bottomless cane chair, a pillow ravaged by roof rats. Reaching the trunk again, she sat down. "Did you hear anything?"

"No, ma'am."

"I don't mind telling you I don't like this place much," Cara confided with a shiver. "Dake's brother was murdered here not a week ago."

Inez's eyes grew wide and watchful. She peered into every corner of the room and whispered a hushed "Lord save us. Up here?"

"No, he was in Dake's old room. But let's not talk about that now. What I have to decide is exactly how much of this tale I should tell Dake."

"That your man?"

Cara smiled. "He's nobody's man but his own. Stubborn as a cross-eyed mule, ornery as an old bear." *Exciting, delicious, tempting as all get out.* "I guess you could say I'm still deciding exactly what he is to me. He asked me to marry him today."

"You mind me statin' my mind, Miz Cara?"

"Not at all."

Clay started to fuss. Inez handed him back. "Your man might have been a Yankee soldier and all, like Patsy told me, but he's still Alabama born and bred. You want to keep Clay, then you best be keepin' the secret about his bloodline."

"But Dake loves Clay as much as I do. He's had him since the minute he was born."

"I'm tellin' you straight, that man will think different when he learns the boy's an octoroon. He might want to do right by the child and raise him up, but he won't ever be callin' him his son. Why, Clay's own granddaddy never even claimed Price was *his* son. Why should your man be any different."

"Price's father was white?"

"That's right. And his mama was my half sister, like I told you. She was always too good-lookin' for her own good. Tall and thin, her daddy was white, too. She had the look of an African queen about her. Always held her head up, proudlike. Wasn't no way Marse Clayton wouldn't have noticed her. He bought us together, but it was Janella he took a shine to."

"*Marse* Clayton." Cara repeated, trying to untangle the players in the drama of little Clay's heritage. "Wait a minute." She got to her feet and stood over Inez who had to crane her neck to stare up at her. "You're saying *Master* Clayton? You don't mean Anna's father—"

Inez nodded. A woeful expression dimmed the light in her eyes. "Miz Anna done run off with her own half brother."

"Oh, my God."

"Where did you say you found this, Elijah?"

Dake stood in the shadow of the barn, staring down at his own black hat, the one he'd lost the night of Burke's murder.

"In the barn, Marse Dake. Saw it sticking out from under the straw in the back corner. I found it when I was movin' Miz Cara's crates out of that buggy you rented in Gadsden."

Brushing bits of straw and dust off the crown of his hat, Dake turned it over and over in his hand as if close inspection might lead to some answers. "I wonder why whoever stole it didn't destroy it?"

"What if they was plannin' to use it again?"

Dake frowned. "It would have to be someone who felt confident about moving around the place. Shelby would be noticed outright."

"Not in the dark, Marse Dake. Not if he was sneakin' around. You sure it was him that killed Marse Burke?"

"I don't have any clear idea as to who might have done it, but he saw me in town that first day, hightailed it out here to tell Minna, and he just happens to be in league with the Ku Klux." He looked down the lane, past the row of cabins that made up the quarters, and studied the open fields beyond. "I knew coming home would have repercussions, but I never would have come back if I had known it would cost my brother his life."

"What you gonna do now?"

Dake turned back to Elijah. "I need to draw him out. And to do that, I need your help."

Fear was Elijah's first reaction to Dake's request. Fear that showed crystal-clear in the man's dark eyes. He looked at the ground, back up at Dake, and then toward the house. "I'll be honest with you. It depend on what I have to do."

"On your way back from returning the wagon to Gadsden I want you to talk to any freedmen who want work. Tell them I'm willing to provide housing, rations, tools, everything they need to put out a crop. They'll work for one third of the profit on the share of land they rent."

"Some of the planters 'round here not gonna like that. Most got folks workin' for they keep and not much else."

"Which is nothing more than another form of slavery. I'm almost *hoping* the other planters won't like it, Elijah."

"You sure you want this much trouble, Marse Dake?"

He thought of the men who died beside him in battle, of the war-torn cities and towns and the families who would never again embrace fathers and sons. "The ironic thing about freedom is that it's far from free, Elijah."

"Yes, sir. You right about that." Preparing to depart, Elijah straightened his baggy wool jacket, the one that had once been Dake's. "Folks gonna be glad to hear their families are welcome to come along. Lots of folks marryin' up all legal like now and findin' their kin that was sold away. Just after the Freedom come, I walked all the way to Montgomery lookin' for my mama. That's the last place I can remember bein' with her 'fore old Marse Reed bought me. Couldn't find her, though." He shook his head, his expression one of sad resignation. "Probably passed over." He straightened his top hat and made one last request.

"You best write me a note, Marse Dake, so's I can be on my way."

"You don't need a pass to travel anymore, Elijah."

The former valet persisted. "No, I reckon that's what the law say now, but most folks still feel safer with a pass tucked away in their pocket. Still some out there who'll stop a body and ask 'em where they goin' and what business they be on. If you don't mind, Marse Dake, I'd just as soon be carryin' a letter from you explainin' what I'm doin' with this rig from Gadsden. Ain't hardly nobody left with a fine outfit like this."

The hired man's precaution reminded Dake just how slow some things changed. With the stolen hat in hand, Dake started for the house. "Come with me, Elijah, and I'll write that letter for you."

*   *   *

"Anna Clayton ran off and married her own *half brother*?" It was almost impossible for Cara to give credence to Inez's intricately woven tale, but the look on the other woman's face was so distressed and Sarah Clayton's reaction to Clay had been so venomous that she couldn't help but believe.

"The poor child didn't know Price was her half brother," Inez said.

"But—"

"That's the way it was, Miz Cara. You bein' from the North, you have no idea about such things. If the marse took a shine to one of the girls he owned, he lay with 'em and like as not, sooner or later they'd have the man's child."

Cara walked back to the trunk and sat down. "Surely everyone knew. Sarah Clayton must have known. You said the boy, Price, had been born there, was educated, that he worked in the house, and even did the accounts. He looked—what'd you say?—high yellow? Where did Mrs. Clayton *think* he'd come from?"

"Now that's the strange part. Miz Clayton could probably list you every mulatto child sired by her neighbors' husbands, but when it come to looking under her own bed, she turned a blind eye—till Miz Anna ran off with Price. She blamed old marse until he had a stroke. Never got out of the bed till he died."

Clay began to fuss. Cara knew it was getting close to time to feed him. Still, she persisted in questioning Inez. The child's future depended on knowing the entire story. "What was the word you used? Octoroon?"

"That's right. But the law says it only takes one drop of black blood to make you black."

The sound of loud footsteps filtered up the stairwell from the hall below. They both froze where they were.

"Cara?"

Dake's shout carried clearly through the house.

Her heart skipped a beat. "What'll I do?"

"*Don't* tell him, Miz Cara," Inez begged. "Not if you want to keep that baby."

Cara knew in her heart she couldn't deceive Dake. She wanted to believe that Clay's heritage wouldn't matter to him in the least, but how could she truly guarantee how he would react? "Now's not the time," she whispered to Inez. "But I certainly intend to tell him."

Not today. She couldn't tell him about Clay today, not after what happened at the mill and certainly not after their argument after his proposal.

"If he refuses to acknowledge Clay, I won't have any choice, will I? Clay and I will head to California."

"Cara!" Dake shouted again from below stairs. "Where in the hell are you?"

She handed Clay to Inez as she stood. "Take him down to the kitchen while I talk to Dake, will you, Inez? Have Patsy fill his bottle with milk and give him as much as he wants." She glanced at the door to the stairwell. "I have no idea how long this will take."

Dake started down the hall, intent on going back downstairs to find Cara when he heard her voice coming from the attic stairwell. In two long strides he was back at the end of the hall where he jerked open the door and squinted to see up into the darkened interior of the narrow stairway. He could barely make out Cara who was followed by an unfamiliar woman carrying Clay.

"Didn't you hear me calling?" His words echoed in the stairwell.

"Well, of course I did. Bellowing was more like it. I was ignoring you."

"Damn it, Cara. I can't understand why you're acting like this."

The gap between them narrowed as she made her way carefully down the steep stairs. As his eyes adjusted to the light, Dake's gaze swept up the steps and caught sight of some small round objects two steps away from Cara's feet.

"Wait—" He began a warning just as she moved onto the littered step.

With little more than a squeal of surprise, Cara's feet shot out from under her. Before he could move forward to stop her momentum, she fell back, hit her head on the step behind her, and then came sliding down amid a hail of walnuts.

Watching his own footing, Dake vaulted up the bottom two steps and grabbed her before she rolled all the way to the bottom, but when he caught her up in her arms and cradled her there, she was unconscious.

"Cara?" He grasped her face and gently shook her head from side to side. "Cara, sweet, wake up."

Glancing up at the woman with the baby in her arms frozen on the stairwell, he warned, "Don't move. Just sit down where you are until I sweep the steps clear. Do you hear?"

Clay started crying, frightened by Dake's harsh tone echoing in the stairwell. The woman sat down. With Cara braced in one arm, Dake used the other to sweep the walnuts off the steps. "Come down carefully," he told the woman as he started down the hall toward Cara's room. "Watch your step. When you get down, go find Miss Minna."

He hoped the woman knew who Minna was but spared no more thought to the question as he carried Cara down the hall. Her face was as white as the mended linens on the bed when he stretched her across it. Grabbing up her hands, he began to chafe at her wrists, all the time speaking softly.

"Cara? Can you hear me? Wake up, Cara." He smoothed her hair back off her face, bent to swiftly kiss her, then carefully felt along her limbs to see if anything felt broken. There were no visible signs of injury, but still she lay unresponsive.

He hurried to the door, down the hall, and called Minna's name down the staircase. She called back and he listened to the rapid staccato of her footsteps as she ran through the house. Confident she was on her way up, he hurried back to Cara's side. Kneeling beside the bed, he took hold of her hand again and held on tight.

"Oh, my God, Dake. What happened?" Minna paused in the doorway, one hand at her throat as she stared at the girl lying on the bed.

"She slipped on some damn walnuts on her way down the attic stairs. What in the hell was she doing up there and who was that woman?"

Minna walked immediately to the pitcher of water on a side table and poured some into a chipped washbowl. She reached for a washcloth and wet it, then hurried to the bedside. With great care, she pressed the compress against Cara's forehead. "I told her there were some old toys up there, I'd seen them when I went up to get the cradle for Clay. I have no idea why she took that woman up with her."

"Who is she?"

Minna shrugged. "I just asked that myself when I found her in the kitchen asking for Clay's bottle. She's from Clayton Hall, someone Cara met in Gadsden. I'm not sure what she was doing here, exactly." She laid a hand alongside Cara's throat, feeling her pulse. "Oh, Dake, what are we going to do? Poor Cara."

"She'll be fine. She has to be." He held tight to her hand, unwilling to take his eyes off Cara for a second, as if his will were her lifeline. "She's made of strong stuff. She's never sick. She told me that herself."

Minna stood and walked over to the window. She pushed

aside the lace curtain and stared down into the yard below. "I'll send Elijah into town for the doctor."

"He just left for Gadsden to return the rented wagon."

Moving to his side, Minna volunteered, "I'll sit with her while you go after him, then."

Dake shook his head. "I'm not leaving her. You go down and tell Patsy to run down to the quarters and get one of the other men. Have him saddle up my horse and ride into town."

"You think that's wise, Dake, things being the way they are?"

"I'm not leaving. If you don't trust one of the men with my horse, then you should go yourself."

Obviously stung, she stiffened and walked to the door. "Then that's what I'll do. Yours is the best piece of horseflesh in this county right now and I know once you're thinkin' clearly, you'll know why none of these people should be trusted with it. Excuse me, I'll go change into somethin' I can ride in."

Dake stood and followed her to the door. "I'm sorry—"

Minna paused in the hallway. Behind her, the walls sported discolored outlines where paintings once hung. "I understand. You're just distraught. I didn't realize how much she means to you."

"She means the world to me, Minna. Surely after your own loss, you understand why I'm not willing to give up one minute by her side."

Minna clasped her hands together at her waist. For a moment she said nothing, merely watched him intently. She frowned as if trying to comprehend what he'd just said and then her dark eyes misted. "Of course. You get on back in there, Dake. I'll ride into town."

Muddied waters seldom clear.
Nanny James

Chapter Fourteen

Kerosene lamps fouled the air as they worked to dispel the encroaching darkness of evening. The only sound in Cara's room was the soft rustle of the bedclothes as Dr. Julius Hinton carefully examined the still-unconscious girl. The doctor's bag gaped open on the floor beside him as he bent over her. Of average height, the man wore small, wire-rimmed glasses that balanced precariously on the tip of his nose. More often than not, he peered over rather than through them.

Behind the doctor, Dake sat on the edge of the window seat, arms on his knees, forehead propped in his hands. Minna hovered beside him, looking composed even after her ride to Decatur to fetch the doctor. Still dressed in a much worn burgundy riding ensemble, she had somehow found time to touch up her hair and smooth it back into a neat, refined chignon.

"Can I bring you some tea?" she whispered to Dake as they kept their vigil. "You really should—"

"No." His gaze shot back to Cara after he cut Minna off.

After a few more moments of silence, Dake drew his watch out of his pocket, flicked the silver case open, and watched the minute hand slowly tick off the time. *"Time, Miss James, keeps everything in order."* How pompous he must have sounded issuing that declaration. He snapped the engraved case closed and shoved the timepiece back into his watch pocket.

239

How like her, he thought, to keep him on edge this long, to make him wait for her to recover consciousness. Right now he didn't care if she was never on time for anything again. All he wanted was for her to sit up, spout one of her granny's proverbs, and to see the love for him shining in her eyes.

Dr. Hinton pulled the covers up to Cara's chin and straightened.

Dake stood up. "Well?"

The doctor shrugged. He slipped the stethoscope from around his neck, folded it, and carefully placed it in his bag. "It appears nothing is broken. You'll just have to wait until she wakes up to see if she's suffered any permanent damage."

Dake reached out and grabbed the man by the lapels of his misshapen, baggy coat. "I knew that much before you walked in here."

"Dake, please." Minna laid her hand gently on his arm. "The good doctor is doing all he can."

Dake fought to rein in his fear and anger. He let go of the man's coat and stepped back, grudgingly apologetic. "Sorry," he mumbled. Dismissing the doctor, he returned to Cara's bedside.

Behind him, he heard Minna usher the man out of the room and send him to the kitchen for some supper. The next thing he knew, Dake felt her hand on his shoulder.

"I'll sit with her for a while," Minna offered. "You must be starvin' by now."

"I'm fine. I'm not leaving her."

"Very well. But you have to eat. I'll have Patsy prepare a tray." She walked to the door with a purposeful set to her shoulders.

Gently enfolding Cara's hand in his, Dake carefully lowered himself to the edge of the bed.

"Dake, that woman is still here, the one from Clayton Hall. Right now she's tending to the baby, but since we don't know who or what she wants here, I think you should talk to her. I can't seem to get anything out of her. Perhaps if you—"

"Send her up here," he said, hoping the diversion would momentarily ease the pain that had a stranglehold on his heart. "Have her bring Clay."

There was nothing he could do but sit in silence beside Cara and wait for some change in her condition. Within moments of sending Minna off, the Negress holding Clay hesitated outside the open door.

"Come in," Dake said, releasing Cara's hand. He reached out for Clay and the woman handed the baby over to him. Dake nuzzled his nose against Clay's cheek and fought back a bittersweet memory of Cara's astonishment when he had pulled the newborn from his coat at the cabin.

The woman smoothed a white apron made of a flour sack over her skirt, waiting awkwardly for Dake to speak or dismiss her from the room. After he settled Clay on his shoulder and adjusted the baby's blanket, he remembered her. "I'm Dake Reed," he said softly, unwilling to leave the room to carry on the conversation.

"I'm Inez. From Clayton Hall. I didn't take no last name yet, sir. I met Miz Cara the other day when she came to give Miz Anna's baby over to his grandmama. I like Miz Cara, so I thought I'd come and ask her can I work here."

"What did she say?"

Inez blinked back tears, obviously frightened as she chanced to glance over at Cara. "She says we'd have to ask you."

Dake paced back to the window with Clay. "What were you doing in the attic with her?"

Tears were openly streaming down the woman's face as Dake turned to hear her reply. "Miz Cara went up lookin' for some old dolls. Took me with her. We got to talkin', then heard you callin' out and started down, that's when she fell and—"

"I know the rest." Dake frowned. "Didn't you see the walnuts on the stairs when you went up?"

"They wasn't there, Mr. Reed. Nary a one of 'em."

"You're sure?"

"Yes, sir. An' if they woulda been, I 'spect we'd have picked 'em up so as not to fall."

Preoccupied with suspicion, he barely mumbled, "I expect so."

He and Inez turned in unison as Minna walked in the door bearing a tray laden with covered dishes. She walked over to the side table and set the tray down. Turning back, she went up to Dake and took Clay from him.

"Now," Minna directed, taking charge, "you sit down and eat. It won't do any good to have you fall on your face, will it? This child needs changing." Without hesitation, she walked to the cradle and laid Clay inside. Then, efficiently locating a stack of folded cloths Cara used for diapers, she expertly began to unfasten his wet clothing.

Dake watched her for a moment, Inez's presence forgotten. "I didn't know you were so adept at handling babies, Minna."

Minna glanced over her shoulder with a smile. "Why, have you forgotten all the babies that used to be born on this place? Many's the time your mama let me help her tend to the birthin's. It's a woman's place to know what to do on a plantation the size of Riverglen. Ministering to the sick and elderly, clothin' and feedin' and supervisin'. That's somethin' it takes years to learn."

She rewrapped Clay in his blanket and had him back in her arms in no time. "There. All done, aren't we, little man?" She frowned at Dake. "Go on now. Eat."

He walked to the table and uncovered the plate to reveal a generous portion of ham and string beans, mashed potatoes and corn bread. "Looks good."

"It's food left from the tribute the neighbors brought for Burke's funeral."

The reminder soured Dake's appetite. He looked over at Cara again and refused to contemplate two such heavy losses in so short a time. She would be well. She had to be.

He sat on the only chair in the room while the women stood. Minna began to gently sway back and forth as she rocked Clay in her arms. Inez alternately watched Dake and then Minna.

After a few hasty bites Dake said, "What I can't figure out is who put those walnuts on the steps and why anyone would want to hurt Cara—unless they did it to hurt me."

"You can't blame this on Shelby Gilmore," Minna told him.

Dake shot her a hard glance. "No. I can't. That's what scares the hell out of me."

Minna turned to Inez. "Did you see anyone? You were there with her."

"No, ma'am. I didn't see nobody."

Dake took another bite of ham and swallowed it down. "Patsy's the only other person who's been in the house."

Minna spoke up. "I caught Elijah creepin' around in the front hall. He very well could have just come downstairs. I didn't think about it at the time. I sent him packin' though. He said he had to find you, Dake. Did he? Or was that just some excuse for his slippin' around inside the house?"

Dake set the tray aside. He turned to Inez. "You go on downstairs, Inez. Have Patsy show you where to put your things. I'll talk to you tomorrow."

Inez retrieved her bundle of clothes and other goods from the corner where they had been set aside. Then he turned back to Minna to answer her question. "Elijah did find me. He wanted me to know he also found my hat—the one stolen the night of the murder."

"What?" Shock registered on Minna's perfect features.

"He found my hat. The gun's still missing."

Minna began to pace the room. She was quiet, preoccupied with her thoughts. Finally she snapped her fingers. "Why, of course! He's the one who killed Burke."

Dake stood and walked back over to Cara's bedside. He reached out to touch her hair and then, needing to do something, he straightened her already straight coverlet. He remembered to lower his voice as he turned back to Minna. "I can't believe that, Minna. Elijah has been with this family for years. He'd never—"

"How do you know? He's *served* the family, but certainly can't be considered part of it. Now that those people are free they think it gives them the right to do anything they want. Why stop short of murder?"

"I can't believe that, Minna. Not of Elijah. It's my fault Burke's dead. I should have been here that night. It's me they wanted. Now even Cara's had to pay for my joining the other side during the war. It's got to stop before anyone else gets hurt. I can't risk your life, or Clay's, or any of the freedmen who've come here to work. They deserve protection."

"To think that you're too stubborn to know when you're harborin' a murderer—"

Minna's warning was cut short when Cara moaned. Dake crossed the distance to the bed in an instant and took her hand. "Cara? Cara, darlin', wake up."

A cool breeze wafted over them, chilling her skin and raising duck bumps where his tongue traced a path between her breasts. Cara arched and moaned low in her throat. It was dark, not a star in the sky there by the river's edge but she wasn't afraid because Dake was beside her. They were meant to be together, she knew that now. How could it be that this never-ending darkness made everything so brilliantly clear?

She felt languid, as if she were floating somewhere disconnected from the earth and yet was part of it still. The lush grass that grew beside the river was soft as a down featherbed. Dake's hands were warm where he touched her, his lips blazed a fiery path down the length of her. She writhed. Moaned again. Wanted more. Just as he was about to take her, to make love to her beside the river in the star-spattered darkness, he was gone.

She cried out. Disappointed. Lost without his touch.

But there was Clay. A woman who claimed to be his aunt held him just beyond Cara's reach. The baby was crying for her, for Cara, his tiny arms and hands outstretched as he squirmed and screamed his outrage, but no matter how hard she tried, she was unable to move forward to take him from Inez. His cries grew louder as his patience diminished.

"I'm coming Clay. I'll take care of you."

But she couldn't move. His pitiful cries soon hushed to whispers.

Suddenly she found herself trapped inside a place she had never even seen before. She could hear the rushing sound of the river outside the dilapidated walls but there were no doors or windows in the room. It was stifling hot. Deserted except for her—or so she thought until something crashed behind her.

A dark presence entered the room and a sensation so menacing swept through her that Cara began to tremble. "No. Leave me alone. I never hurt you. No." She shook her head from side to side, unwilling to succumb to the evil presence that stalked her.

"Please," she begged. "Please let me go. My baby needs me. Dake needs me." She tried to throw up her hand to ward off the shadow moving toward her, but she couldn't move.

Dake's voice whispered to her. He seemed very close. So close she might have reached out to him if only it were not so very dark.

"Cara? Cara, darlin', wake up."

She tried to respond. Tried to tell him she was awake. Tried to let him know she was somewhere near the river and that if she could find her way out of the darkness she would come back to him and Clay. She wanted to let him know how much she needed them both, but the rushing sound of the river had increased tenfold and the darkness was closing in.

Cara opened her eyes and found the room bathed in the soft glow of light from a single kerosene lamp. For a moment she was content to simply lie there and stare up at the ceiling, which, she noticed, was cracked, some of the plaster had even fallen. Spider-line cracks spread out from the center. She took a deep breath and tried to recollect how she got here and exactly when she went to bed. It was dark outside, that much she knew by the lack of light in the room, but her disorientation was such that she wasn't quite certain when or how she had gotten to bed.

Somewhere in the room, someone sighed and shifted. She heard the creak of a wooden chair. When she tried to raise her head, a furious pounding started at the base of her neck and she fell back against the pillow with a groan.

Riverglen. She recalled that much. She was at Riverglen and had just argued with Dake. She smiled up at the cracked ceiling. She'd lost her virginity to him. That much she certainly remembered—and without regret. He had proposed. They had argued over dreams.

At least they didn't lack for dreams.

More than that, she could not recall. Slowly, cautiously, she tried turning her head because she feared lifting it would hurt. She met with some success. And she saw Dake.

Her heart swelled with love. She blinked back tears and smiled at the sight of the big man stretched out on an uncomfortable chair, his feet crossed at the ankles, his arms locked around the baby asleep on his chest. The reality was so unlike any image of Dake that she couldn't help but smile. His dark hair stood out in clumps around his head as if he'd run his hands through it countless times. The dark stubble of his beard shaded the lower half of his face. The front of his shirt that she could see, usually so clean and neatly pressed, was spotted. No doubt Clay's doing. The baby held a wad of cambric clutched in each tiny fist.

Overcome with the urge to slip back into sleep, she was about to close her eyes again when the baby stirred and Dake shifted. His eyes opened and immediately connected with hers. He sat up and leaned forward, straining in the dark to see clearly.

"Cara?" The word barely came out. He cleared his throat. "Cara?"

"I'm awake," she said, forcing the sound from her lips.

He was at her side immediately, Clay still asleep in his arms. He fell to his knees beside the bed and took her hand. "How do you feel?"

"Tired." He looked so ravaged that she tried to smile to reassure him that she would be fine.

"Your head?"

"Hurts. I have a terrible headache. What happened?"

"We don't need to talk about that now. It's enough that you're awake."

"Dake, if you squeeze my hand any harder you're going to break it."

He backed off the pressure but leaned down to kiss her just the same. "You scared me to death."

"You look it. Please, tell me what happened."

"You fell down the attic stairs."

She frowned, fighting to remember. Her gaze lit on the child in his arms. "Clay's all right? I didn't drop him, did I?"

"You were with Inez, the woman from Clayton Hall——"

"Oh, God." She remembered. It all came rushing in on her

with utmost clarity. They had hid in the attic while Inez spun the twisted tale of Anna and Price Clayton, of Clay's parentage.

"What is it?" Dake was instantly solicitous. "Are you hurting?"

Cara closed her eyes. Of course she was. It hurt to lie to this man who cared so much. "No. I'm fine. I just remembered, that's all. I stepped on something."

"Walnuts."

"Did you say walnuts?"

"Someone left them on the stairs between the time you went up and came back down."

She remembered hearing a sound that Inez had not heard. Why? she wondered. Why would anyone want to hurt her? The pain in the back of her head began to intensify again and she closed her eyes.

"Cara?"

There was a new element in Dake's voice. Fear. She fought to open her eyes again to reassure him. She managed to clutch his hand tight. "I'm all right. Just tired. Don't leave me."

"I won't," he promised.

He let go of her hand. The sound of his footsteps retreated across the room. She struggled to see where he was going and watched as he gently lowered Clay into the cradle. As Dake returned to her bedside, she relaxed again.

"Hold me, Dake."

The bed dipped with his weight as he lay down beside her. "I'm right here," he said. She felt him kiss her temple, her eyelids, her cheek as he once again held tight to her hand. "You'll be all right in the morning."

"I know." She wasn't certain she had spoken aloud or if she merely thought the words.

What she did know was that Dake was beside her, holding her tight. Clay was asleep in his cradle. And for tonight at least, they were all safe and sound.

* * *

The next morning Cara's bedroom door swung open without warning and Dake awoke to the sound of a startled gasp. He sat up, focused, and found Minna looking pale and tired in unrelieved black silk. Rubbing a hand through his hair, he gingerly climbed out of bed without disturbing Cara. He reached down, felt her forehead, and found her cool. She was breathing deep and evenly, lost in a sound, healing sleep instead of unconsciousness.

Minna started to speak and he shushed her with a shake of his head. Tiptoeing around the room, he picked up his boots and then stood aside as Minna exited the room first. They paused outside the door.

"I'm starved," he announced. "Has Patsy made breakfast yet?" He started toward the stairs and Minna followed.

"Hours ago."

"What's wrong with you?"

She paused halfway down the wide, curved staircase. In a whisper she told him, "The sheriff is in the kitchen waiting to see you. I hardly think it wise to be sleeping in Cara's room when the only reason you are not rottin' in the Decatur jailhouse is because I told him you were sleepin' with me not two weeks ago."

"Bill Jensen won't know where the hell I slept last night unless you tell him. Cara needed me." He didn't like having to explain his actions to anyone. He watched Minna as she looked about to argue, then changed her mind. "What does he want?"

"To talk to you."

Dake sighed. "I know that. About what?"

"Obviously somethin' important for him to come all the way out here. He wouldn't tell me anything."

"Great."

"Dake, that woman's still here."

"Inez?"

"Yes. What am I supposed to do with her?"

"Why, Minna, just last night you told me what an expert you are at dealing with the help. Send her up to Cara's room to wait until Clay wakes up and tell her to bathe and feed him."

She stopped again. This time it was obvious to him that she was fighting to control her temper. He'd never seen her so visibly upset. "You don't have to make any more rude, uncalled for remarks, Dake Reed."

"Sorry, Min. I've got a short fuse today."

"You best not smart-mouth Sheriff Jensen. And if I were you, I'd tell him all about that boy, Elijah, who by the way is back already."

He grabbed her arm as she started to walk past him, headed for the kitchen. "Don't you say a word about Elijah. Jensen would like nothing better than to hang someone for my brother's murder just to get the locals off his back. You know Elijah wouldn't stand a chance in hell if we so much as point a finger at him. There'd be a mockery of a trial and the Ku Klux would gladly show up to do the honors at the hangin'. Do you understand me?"

Her lips thinned. "Of course."

"Good." Sorry he'd taken such a high-handed tone with her, Dake was about to apologize, but they had reached the door to the kitchen and it was too late.

Bill Jensen stood up as Minna entered the room with Dake on her heels. He toasted them with a cup of coffee. "Nice to see you up, Reed. Don't look like you're quite awake yet, though."

"I had a rough night," Dake admitted as he ran his hand over his stubbled cheek.

Minna sniffed.

Dake dropped his boots, pulled a chair out away from the table and sat down. Reaching for the first boot, he noticed Patsy frying eggs at the stove. Inez stood beside her slicing corn bread. "Black coffee, please, Patsy, if you have some."

The teenager, obviously nervous with so many people crowded in the small kitchen, merely nodded and reached for the coffeepot. Minna asked Inez to follow her into the hall. The two women left and the sheriff settled back in his chair.

Dake felt the man's eyes on him, watching his every move. He took his time pulling on one boot and then the other, shifted his chair when Patsy came to serve him first coffee, then a plate of runny eggs and sliced bread. He'd be damned if he'd ask Bill Jensen what prompted his visit, not when he knew damn well it wasn't social.

Bill Jensen pulled a folded piece of newsprint out of his back pocket and threw it on the table in front of Dake. Without looking up from his plate, Dake finished an egg, broke off a piece of crust, and began to mop up the yolk with it. Finally, he glanced at the paper.

"What's this?"

"Thought you might be interested."

Dake drew the page close but let it lie on the table beside his plate as he read. *NIGHTOWL CAVE, NO. XIX, DARK MOON! BLOODY HOUR! SEVENTH MOON! K K K DIVISION XIX, CHIEF'S DECREE. I salute. Brothers are preparing! The hours are growing auspicious! Be firm, steadfast, true! Justice shall be meted out! Evil must not prevail! DUTY! SILENCE! WATCH! BY ORDER OF C.G.S., D XIX.*

He shoved the paper back at the sheriff. "Is this supposed to mean something to me?"

"It means you'd best watch your back, Reed."

"You're not the first man who's told me that. Too bad no one warned my brother."

"The Klan never hurt your brother."

"What makes you so damn sure?"

"He was one of 'em."

Dake froze. The coffee cup halted halfway to his lips. "I don't believe you."

"Why? Because he couldn't ride with 'em? He still met with them. Took part in the plans. Held one or two meetin's right here, as I recall. That curl your hair?"

"Minna knew?"

"Course she did."

Dake remembered Patsy and looked over to find the girl standing in front of the stove. Her hands gripped the iron handle on the oven door. "Why don't you run along outside, Patsy. You can clean up later. You look as if you could use some fresh air."

He could see the fright in her eyes as she gave him a thankful nod and fairly ran from the room.

"Ever wonder why none of your daddy's slaves stayed after the Freedom? Just the handful that were more starved than scared lived out in the quarters. Your brother run them off. Told 'em they were free and he didn't want them around. Couldn't stand the sight of 'em after the war and what happened to him. Some came back to beg Minna for jobs when they couldn't find work. With Burke crippled and all, she needed the help and let 'em stay. She kept 'em out of his way."

Lost in thought, Dake said aloud, "So some of those former slaves would have every right to hate him, then, wouldn't they?"

Bill Jensen nodded.

Dake still couldn't bring himself to accuse Elijah of the killing without proof. Not when he knew the consequences.

"What is it these Ku Klux boys hope to gain, Bill?" Dake leaned back in the chair, his appetite appeased for the time being, he hoped for some insight into his brother's involvement.

"It's been two years since the war ended," the tall man began. "You have no idea what things have been like here in Alabama. There's no pretense of local government. Officials loyal to the Confederacy were thrown in prison. People like me who sympathized with the North were put in office. Citizens were stripped of everything and still heavy taxes were levied. To add insult, they aren't allowed representation. You're on the winnin' side, Dake. You can't imagine the powerlessness most folks feel here in the South.

"The Klansmen think of themselves as regulators of the law. They claim the Northerners have come down here to teach the Negroes to hate all Southerners. Some of the former slaves were ill treated, I'll grant you that. Some of 'em turned insolent, wantin' to get back at all whites for what their owners did to them. Deserters from both armies turned into bush-whackers and outlaws and for months there was no real protection against any of it. So, the Klans took matters into their own hands, meting out their own form of justice."

Dake stood and paced to the stove with his coffee cup. "How can you call that justice? Riding around in the dark in disguise? Committing what amounts to murder, all in the name of justice?"

Bill Jensen shrugged. "All I'm sayin' is that they didn't kill your brother."

Dake could see there was no changing his mind. "What if it was an accident? Burke was in my old room. We look enough alike to be taken for each other."

"You say someone hit you over the head and took your gun—"

"Someone did."

"Then that someone knew the difference between you and Burke. And I'm tellin' you that *someone* wasn't part of the Klan."

Dake reached out and tapped the article on the tabletop. "Then why the warning?"

"As far as everyone's concerned around here, you're a Yankee. You're as likely to stir up as much trouble as the best of 'em."

"You're right about that, if making some changes is stirring up trouble."

Jensen nodded.

"Will you be riding with these men, Bill? Do I have to guard my back from even you?"

"I'm a lawman, Reed. Besides, they wouldn't have me. No matter how I came by it, I take my job seriously." Silence stretched taut between them.

Dake poured a cup of coffee. "I didn't kill my brother."

"I don't believe you did. But as of right now, there isn't anybody else to point the finger at."

Chapter Fifteen

Embarrassed by all the attention being showered on her, Cara lay propped against a mound of pillows piled against the headboard of the bed. As Minna Blakely entered the room, Cara found herself wishing it were Dake, for she hadn't seen him since that morning.

"Minna, really, you shouldn't trouble yourself over me like this. I'm fine. I ought to be helping out, not lying here getting spoiled."

Setting a supper tray across Cara's lap, Minna stood back to admire her handiwork. "There. Now you just relax. I won't hear about you gettin' up before you should. There's plenty there to make you feel better, that's for certain. You be sure to eat up all those green beans."

"Thank you, Minna. I will." Embarrassed that she had ever thought ill of the woman, Cara smiled and silently vowed to drop the jealous animosity she had once harbored toward her.

Minna started to go, then paused with her hand on the door frame. "Inez is tending to Clay downstairs so you can get some rest when you're finished."

"I've never had so much rest in my born days," Cara admitted with a smile. "I was thinking of getting up and dressed. Maybe getting outside for a little fresh air."

A startled expression crossed Minna's face.

"What is it?" Cara wanted to know.

255

"I didn't want to trouble you with this, not with you recovering and all . . ."

"Please, go on."

Minna walked back in and closed the door behind her. "I've been tryin' to get to Dake, to convince him to call off this foolishness tonight."

"Foolishness?"

Drawing the bentwood chair over to the bedside, Minna sat down and began to explain. "So much has been goin' on in the past couple of days that I don't know where to start. Dake's been goin' out of his mind tryin' to figure out who might have put those walnuts on the steps. Then there's that evidence against Elijah that Dake's all but ignoring."

"Elijah? The man who works for Dake?"

"Yes. Elijah found Dake's hat, the one that was stolen the night of the murder—at least he claims he found it. He was sneakin' around in the house the day you fell. I think he was the one that stole the gun and the hat and murdered Burke—"

"You do? Have you told Dake?"

"Of course I have, but he won't tell Bill Jensen, at least until he has more proof, 'cause he says they'll hang Elijah right off. In the meantime, Dake's intent on stirrin' up trouble around here, even though he doesn't think that the Ku Klux killed Burke anymore."

Thoroughly confused, Cara felt like Rip Van Winkle, awakening after years of sleep. "Why not?"

"Because the sheriff told Dake that Burke was one of the Klan."

Cara wanted to be with Dake, to hear him assure her he was being careful, that he had everything in hand. Minna's news was upsetting. She looked down at the plate, her appetite flown.

Without any encouragement, Minna went on. "Then, to make matters worse, Elijah came back from Gadsden leadin' a ragtag crew of darkies with him. It seems Dake is set to lease the land to them for shares in the crop. The quarters are overflowin' now with freeloaders. I don't know how we're supposed to feed these people."

"Dake has money. And there's that money in Liverpool that his father hid before the war ended."

Minna looked aghast. "That money should go to save Riverglen, to restore it to its former elegance, not be squandered on the likes of those—"

"But Dake needs workers to put out the crop."

Minna shook her head, as if to deny the logic of Cara's statement. "He's filled the cabins with them and don't think I don't know they'd like to take over. Why, one of them calls himself a preacher and they're holdin' a prayer meetin' tonight, right there in the meadow behind the quarters. You can bet there'll be a caterwauling like you never heard. They're liable to get all worked up and—" She shivered.

"What can it hurt? I know all this must be hard for you to accept, raised as you were, Minna, but I don't see what prayer can hurt anything, no matter who's doing it."

"I'm concerned about Dake is all. The Ku Klux is sure to get wind of this and he knows it. He's plannin' on bein' there tonight to protect the people who attend."

Cara set the tray aside. "I have to dress."

"I don't want you gettin' up too soon, Cara."

"I've laid about too long now. Dake needs me. Clay needs me, too." She thought of Inez, Clay's true aunt, and knew he was in good hands, but she missed the child sorely.

"Maybe I can talk some sense into Dake. Maybe it's too soon to try to implement his ideas. His brother is dead and the real murderer is still on the loose." Tossing the blankets aside, Cara swung her legs over the side of the bed. She stood, held onto the bedpost while the room swam before her eyes, and waited until her vision cleared. Ignoring the slight pounding at the back of her head, she walked to the wardrobe.

"I'm going to find Dake and talk to him, Minna. Where is he?"

Minna stood up and replaced the chair by the window seat. "As far as I know, he's down at the quarters helpin' those men repair the cabins. If you want me to go with you—"

Cara reached out for her hand and squeezed it gently. "No, I'll get there on my own. Thanks for everything, Minna. I'm glad you told me all this. I need to talk some sense into Dake Reed. That much is certain."

Dusk gathered as Cara made her way slowly down the oak lane toward the former slave quarters turned freedmen's cabins. The noise of hammers pounding was muted by the rich sound of voices on the crisp October air. She paused to watch a crowd of former slaves gather at a meadow where logs were being rolled into place to serve as benches for an open air church. A passel of children ran down the lane to greet her. When Cara laughed with them and asked their names, they crowded around, pleading to walk with her, wanting to know where she was from. Their natural exuberance lightened her mood and she soon found herself laughing with them and asking after Dake. They happily led her to a cabin at the far end of the row where he was working on the roof.

She paused beneath the sloped roof that covered the earthen front porch. Spying the ladder, she began to climb up and surprise him. Finally, after he finished driving in the last nail, he lay down the hammer and looked over toward the ladder he'd left leaning against the front of the house.

"Why, Captain Reed. Imagine finding you here." Cara smiled, head and shoulders above the roofline.

He scooted carefully across the wood shingles until he

reached the edge of the roof. "What are you doing? Why aren't you in bed? Don't you know you could fall and—"

"I misscd you."

Her simple statement stopped his protest. He looked around to see if anyone was watching. His hands covered hers where she clutched the ladder rails before he bent down and planted a long, slow kiss on her lips. Below them, the children burst into a chorus of giggles.

"You children get out of there, you hear?" A woman's voice was heard above the laughter. Dake waved to a stately, full-figured woman, one of the new arrivals who was headed toward the clearing where the prayer meeting was to be held.

"I missed you, too," he whispered against Cara's lips.

"Then why did you stay away all day?" She reached up, careful to maintain her balance while she draped an arm about his neck. Cara was certain she could stand on the ladder, suspended in time, as long as he was staring back with such love in his eyes.

"You were much too much temptation, Miss James, lying there helpless."

"Come home and let me tempt you some more."

Dake sobered. "I wish I could, but I have to stay here at least until the meeting breaks up."

"You're expecting trouble, aren't you?"

"Let's just say I'm hoping there won't be any, but I'm taking precautions."

"Minna told me about what's been going on around here. I came to hear your side of it."

He arched a brow, questioning what Minna told her. "My side of what?"

Cara glanced around before she lowered her voice to a whisper. "She said she's certain Elijah murdered Burke but that you don't believe it."

"I don't want to believe it. Besides, there's no motive, not to mention proof."

"Maybe he just hated Burke and wanted you to manage Riverglen. Maybe he thought he was helping you. Isn't that enough?"

Dake shook his head. "I know Elijah. He served me, personally, for years. I just don't think he's capable of it."

"War changes people."

Sadness crept into his gaze. "It does at that."

The first strains of song swelled through the trees. Cara smiled. "If you're staying at the prayer meeting, then so am I."

"I don't want you there. In fact, I'm going to get someone to walk you back to the house if you'll move your little bottom back down that ladder."

"Not until you tell me I can stay."

A steady, rhythmic hand clapping accompanied the singing. Harmonious voices called out the chorus of the spiritual. Dake let go of her hands and picked up his hammer and a bag of nails. "Move, Cara."

She knew better than to argue when he used his most commanding tone. As she began her descent, the thunderous sound of horses erupted through the trees beyond the land just before Dake shouted for her to take cover. He dropped the hammer and nails, grabbed the edge of the low roofline, and swung over, dangling a few feet from the ground before he dropped and rolled.

She felt him reach up and grab her around the thighs, bundling her skirt around her as he pulled her to safety. Lunging for the rifle he'd left propped against the front of the small cabin, he shoved her inside. She collided with a frightened little girl who appeared no older than eight or nine. The child was screaming, the sound earsplitting in the compact cabin.

"Get back and stay down!" Dake yelled at Cara as he took

off running toward the prayer meeting. It was evident by the rising swell of song that no one else had heard the riders yet.

Cara grabbed the screaming child and put her hand over the girl's mouth to stop the shrieking. "You're all right," Cara crooned. "Just stay quiet and you'll be all right."

The child's eyes showed wide with fear above Cara's hand. Cara knelt beside her and pressed the child's face against her shoulder. Kneeling on the dirt floor in the interior of the darkened cabin, she tried to decide who was quaking the hardest, the little girl or herself.

Outside, she heard the horses as they thundered by the house and looked out in time to see ghostly figures of hooded riders sweep past. Some held torches of flaming pitch aloft, the firebrands burning an indelible image on her mind. She kept her hand pressed to the back of the child's head to keep her from witnessing the frightening tableau.

A small knot of riders paused beside the row of houses. Cara was barely able to make out two of them just outside the door.

"Burn 'em down," someone shouted.

How many other cabins were occupied? How many of the new inhabitants had not gone to the prayer meeting? What of the children?

Without a thought for her own safety, Cara grabbed up the child in her arms and ran out the door. "Hold it right there!" she yelled so forcefully she arrested the man on horseback just outside the door. Moving out away from the porch, she let him see her clearly. Although she couldn't see anything through the eyes, nose, and mouth holes cut in the hood he wore above his white robe, she could tell by the way he sat the horse that he was watching her closely. The four others with him had turned at the sound of her voice.

"If you're going to burn down this house, you're going to have to do it with me standing here. But first you'll let this child go free." She tried to put the little girl on the ground, but she clung to Cara's neck with strength born of fear.

"Get away from there, woman. Our fight's not with you, but we'll make it so if you want," one of them yelled back.

"Burn her out," another commanded.

The man she'd seen first called back to him, "My fight ain't with unarmed white women."

She wanted to rail at them, to call them cowards to their faces and tell them that their fight shouldn't be with any innocent man, woman, or child, but out of fear for the girl in her arms, Cara held her tongue and prayed they would leave them alone.

Down the lane, the singing became a chorus of shouts. Gunfire popped through the trees and all she could think of was that Dake might even now be lying dead or wounded, shot down for defending the freedom he believed in so fiercely that he had broken ties with everyone he'd held dear. These hooded men on horseback might have once been his schoolmates, playmates, companions. Now, because they had been torn apart by their ideals, had fought under different flags, they were willing to end his life.

Bile rose up in her throat and she swallowed it just as she tried to swallow her fear.

Hooded riders came back, some bent low over their horses' necks, their robes billowing around them as their horses' hooves churned up the soil.

"They're armed, damn it to hell. They got two of us." A man in the foreground called to the men halted in the middle of the lane. Two of them swung their horses around and headed out before the throng. The others soon followed suit, but not before one tossed a burning torch past Cara through the open doorway of the cabin.

All of the regulators rode away with a barrage of gunfire, shouts, and curses. Cara ducked into the corner of the porch. As the night riders disappeared, she shoved the child off her and darted toward the glowing fire inside the cabin. The fire provided a wavering light as the flames licked upward toward the back wall. She pulled a near threadbare blanket off the bed and began to beat the flames back, choking on the smoke that billowed around her. Faster and faster she worked, frantic to save the humble cabin, not that in and of itself it was worth saving, but because it stood as a symbol of tonight's events. The night riders' attack had made her a part of Dake's cause more than sweet words of love ever could.

In fighting the flames, she chose to fight alongside him to make the changes he wanted implemented at Riverglen. As she struggled, she prayed he was still alive.

Just as the edge of the blanket caught fire, she realized the flames on the torch that hit the back wall were nearly diminished. She threw the blanket to the floor.

"Cara!" Dake burst in the door behind her as she began to stomp out the smoldering blanket. He grabbed her wrist and tried to sweep her into the safety of his arms. She gave the blanket one last stomp and then threw her arms around him.

With her face buried against his shirtfront she asked, "Are you all right?" Now that the threat was over, she was shaking violently.

He shoved her head back, unable to see her clearly in the darkness. "Are you?"

"Yes. But I don't know if I can stand up much longer."

The events of the past few days began to come tumbling in on her as she stood there surrounded by the lingering smoke in the cabin. Her eyes smarted with it. Tears began to stream down her cheeks.

She could feel the silent, watchful presence of the others crowded into the small cabin. "I can't breathe," she told him.

Dake scooped her up into his arms and the crowd parted as

they stepped out into the chill of the October night. Wearily, she lay her head on his shoulder.

Wiping tears away from her smarting eyes, she recognized Elijah. Gun in hand, he stepped up to Dake. "You want me to collect the guns, Marse Dake?"

Dake stared at the crowd of freedmen and women gathered around them. A few of the men held guns and rifles at the ready. Hound dogs whined, children in their mother's arms cried. Cara watched Dake gauge the fear of the crowd.

"Let the men keep them tonight, Elijah." He faced the man directly, a challenge in his eyes. "You're in charge."

"Dake—" Cara started to protest.

Dake cut her off. "You're in charge, Elijah," he repeated. There was no fear, no doubt in his eyes as he put the man suspected of having killed his brother in charge of the other freedmen. He had made a decision and Cara could see he would stand by it no matter what. "Have the men take turns on watch. Report to me if you see anything suspicious, no matter what time, day or night."

"You think they'll come back, Marse Reed?"

"Not tonight."

As Dake started to move on, a woman with a chignon tied around her head stepped up to block his way. Cara recognized the child she had sheltered earlier clutching the woman's skirt. The woman nodded at Dake, her mouth working as if she were unable to speak. Finally, as tears began to stream down her face, she took Cara's hand in her own and squeezed it.

"Thank you, missus. Thank you for savin' my baby. She tol' me what you done, how you stood up to those men and tol' them to move on. How you said if they was gonna burn down the house they was gonna have to burn you in it—"

"Please, it was nothing." Cara felt Dake shift her in his arms and draw her tight against him. She reached up to drape her arm around his neck.

The woman shook her head. "It was a miracle. Bless you, ma'am."

"Thank you," Cara whispered, more touched than she could say.

"I'm taking Miss James back up to the house," he told them all. "Elijah is in charge tonight. All of you men with guns will report to him and unless there's trouble, I'll see you at first light."

"You can put me down, Dake. I think I have my wits about me again," Cara told him as he left the small crowd behind and strode toward the house.

"Not on your life. And when we get back to the house, Cara James, you and I are going to have a little talk."

Dake didn't know whether to kiss her or strangle her. She sat on the edge of his bed looking every inch a bedraggled ragamuffin. Her blue eyes were red-rimmed, still stinging from smoke. Her hair was tangled. Her hands, arms, and face were covered in soot.

He ached to kiss her.

When he thought of how close she'd come to being injured for the second time in as many days, he wanted to lock her up where she couldn't possibly come to any more harm. Fear had such a stranglehold on him that he hadn't spoken a word to her all the way to the house, across the foyer, up the stairs.

He had marched past Minna, who naturally demanded to know what had happened, past Patsy and Inez, and into the huge room that had once been the elegantly appointed master suite. A lamp had been left burning on the floor a safe distance from the bed. He had kicked the door shut behind him and locked it against intrusion.

Besides a couple of tables, all that was left was the huge tester bed that had been his parents'. Its velvet draperies gone, the plump, cotton-filled mattress replaced by one filled with lumpy, rustling corn husks. He plunked Cara down in the middle of it, but she scrambled to the edge where she remained staring up at him.

He abruptly turned away and walked directly to a washbasin filled with tepid water. He shrugged out of his jacket and carefully draped it over the nearby doorknob. Taking up a washcloth, he wet it and walked back to the bed. Standing over Cara he demanded, "Take off your dress."

Dumbfounded, she stared down at her dove-gray gown. It was streaked with soot. Her gaze snapped back up at him. "No."

"Miss Reed, you take off your clothes. Now."

She jumped to her feet. "I'll do no such thing. I'm not someone you can order around, *Captain* Reed, no matter what you think. This isn't the army and I'm not one of your troops. Now if you'll kindly move aside—"

He threw the washcloth on the ground, reached out, and jerked her up hard against him. Her hair smelled of smoke. Crazed with fear and need, he ground his lips against hers so hard that she flinched and tried to push away. When he released her, she raised her hand to her lips and inspected the damage. Her eyes were wide, blue, and frightened.

He felt like a cad.

"I'm sorry, Cara."

"Why did you do that?"

"You scared the hell out of me out there."

"*I* didn't do anything."

"You almost got yourself killed," he reminded her.

"So did you."

He reached out slowly, so as not to frighten her this time. "This is my fight, not yours."

"Not anymore. A wife has to stand beside her husband. Through good times and bad, thick and thin, hell or high water. That's what—"

"—Nanny James told you."

Cara nodded.

He stepped closer. "Did you say *wife*?"

She concentrated on his shirtfront. "I did."

He lowered his head. His lips hovered above her tempting mouth as he asked against it, "And California?"

"Looks like I'm at the end of the trail."

They came together. He parted her lips with his tongue. The exchange was heated, his need born of the remnants of fear and thanksgiving. She clung to him, melded against him, offered herself without words as her lips moved over his, her tongue thrust in and out of his mouth.

Dake couldn't stop the low groan that escaped him any more than he could keep his swollen, turgid member from aching with need. The feel of her as she moved against him, prodding him with her hips and pelvis by imitating the motions of lovemaking, was about to drive him over the edge. He ended the kiss, afraid he might lose control, and began to lave his tongue around her ear. He trailed kisses down her neck, kissed her jaw, and cursed at the prim collar of her dove-gray gown. Its narrow lace trim came halfway up her throat.

Releasing her abruptly, he stepped back. Her breath was coming swift and hard. Her breasts rose and fell beneath the gray wool, tempting him. Dake balled his hands into fists at his sides, his need so great it was frightening in its intensity.

She looked confused, her blue eyes questioning. He tried to speak and found he had to clear his throat. "Take off your clothes."

She never broke her stare as she reached back for the top button of her gown. Releasing the buttons as far as she could, she then unfastened the waistband of the dress. Finally, having freed herself as far as possible without help, she turned her back to him and swept up her hair in one hand. Holding it aside, she waited.

He stepped toward her again, his heart pounding, blood roaring through his veins, singing in his ears. His hands shook. Reaching out, he slowly opened the rest of the buttons along her spine and as her dress opened to reveal her satiny skin beneath, he bent forward to taste it with lips and tongue.

Her head dropped back against him and she shivered. Dake opened the dress fully down the back and shoved it forward, over her shoulders and down her arms. The bodice hung limp around her waist for a second before Cara hooked her thumbs into the waistband and then shoved the gown over her hips. It pooled onto the floor around her feet.

Dake turned her around until they were standing face-to-face once more. She was wearing the new chemise he bought her in Memphis. His hands reached out and he cupped both of her breasts at once, lifted them, traced the shadow of her nipples through the silky fabric until they flowered into tempting peaks.

He lowered his head and mouthed her breast through the thin fabric. She reached out to him, ran her fingers through his hair before she cradled his head in her hands and pressed his mouth hard against her breast.

Dake grabbed her waist to steady her, his head moving back and forth as he suckled her. She moaned. The sound urged him on. Despite her protest, he lifted his head from her breast and than bent to give pleasure to the other.

"Dake—"

He kept up the exquisite torture.

"Dake . . . I need you."

With her head flung back and her eyes closed, her long blond hair teased his forearms as he held her imprisoned in his strong embrace.

"Please, Dake."

Their last encounter had been only two days ago. It seemed like a century since he'd taken her virginity. Now, she had agreed to be his wife and for a brief instant, Dake wondered if they should wait until their vows had been exchanged before he took what she was all too willing to give again. He lifted his head and gazed down into her eyes. They were glazed with passion and a need as intense as his own.

"Are you sure this is what you want?"

"Yes. Oh, Dake, yes."

His arms moved around her, cupped her beneath the back and knees, and in two strides he laid her across the bed. His voice thick with need, he bid her, "Take off the rest."

She raised herself up to an elbow and slipped the thin straps over her shoulders and down her arms. He stood beside the bed, still fully dressed, as still and silent as a statue as he watched her strip to bare flesh.

He bent and retrieved the damp cloth he had tossed aside a few minutes earlier. Placing one knee on the coverlet, he reached over her still form and pressed the cloth to her cheek. He gently swabbed her face. He closed her eyes and lightly ran the cloth over her lids, then against her lips. Her eyes opened. With a deep blue, penetrating stare that held no hint of fear, she watched him.

He moved the cloth along her slender throat and she swallowed reflexively. After trailing the moist rag between her breasts, he circled first one and then the other, each rotation narrowed the circumference until he teased the peaks.

Cara held her arms at her side, grasped the coverlet in her hands, and held on. When the wet cloth touched a nipple her hips arched up and off the bed as her heels drove into the mattress. The corn-husk filling rasped as she moved. The bed ropes creaked as Dake brought his other knee upon the mattress and straddled her waist.

His turgid sex was a hard ridge pressed against the front of his trousers. Astride her, he kept her imprisoned beneath him. She let go of the cotton covering and grabbed his hips. Her hands slipped to the front of his pants, explored the rigid length of him beneath the fabric. She ran her fingers up and down his thighs before they moved higher and she found his waistband. In a flash she had wrenched his shirttail out of his pants. Before he could act, she grasped both sides of his shirt and ripped. Buttons flew in all directions.

She laughed, but only for a moment.

Instantly sobered, intent on her mission, she opened the buttons at his fly and shoved his pants down over his hips. His swollen member, freed from the imprisonment, stood erect above her abdomen. He watched Cara as she closed her eyes, her tongue darting across her lips in an unconscious move that made his blood boil.

She found him even with her eyes closed. Held him and explored his shaft with her fingertips. He raised up on his knees. She cupped him, stroked and petted, urged him higher until she could tease him with her mouth and tongue.

On his knees above her, Dake arched back, eyes closed as she took him in her mouth and nearly drove him over the brink. "Cara—" he rasped out the sound of her name.

She whimpered, protested, but the sound stopped when he shoved first one knee and then the other between her legs. She arched to meet his thrust. He gained entrance easily, slipped into her moist, heated depths until he was sheathed to the hilt. She cried out so sharply that he was certain he had hurt her. He began to withdraw, but she cried out again and her legs wrapped around his waist, demanding, locking him against her.

Her hips began to move, to pump him with her need to reach a climax. He clasped her head between his hands and held it still as he kissed her hard and deep, plunged farther inside her with each thrust. She cried out. He swallowed her scream with his kiss. As she convulsed around him, the tremors kneaded his shaft, rocking him to his core until there was no holding back, no sustaining the erotic agony any longer.

He lunged forward into her. His head hit the walnut headboard but he didn't feel pain or annoyance. He was too lost in wave after wave of release as he poured himself into her, filled her, and in so doing became fulfilled.

Beneath him, she didn't move, but he could feel her riotous breathing begin to subside. Replete, Dake lay stretched out full length against her, inside her, his arms protectively wrapped about her.

He raised his head to look down at Cara and watched as her eyes fluttered open. If he had the power of a magician, he would capture the love reflected in her eyes and carry it with him as a talisman against evil. But he wasn't a magician, he was a mere mortal. All he could hope to do was keep her safe from harm and keep that love alive forever.

"What are you frowning about?" she asked softly, her tone one of concern.

"Am I?"

"You were. What were you thinking?"

"I was thinking about how much I love you," he said.

"Does that make you worry?"

Dake shook his head. "No. But I can't help but wonder how quickly you changed your mind about California. What happened?"

"Tonight happened. When I saw those men I realized what you're fighting and what you're trying to accomplish here at Riverglen, and I realized the difference in the things we each wanted. I never really understood until tonight. Your dream stands for something real, for a way to make the world a better place. You're fighting incredible odds to establish a new way of life for people who have had nothing, not even their own freedom, when what I wanted can be boiled down to something selfish, something that's only going to help one person. Me."

"I've seen the look on a child's face when she holds one of your dolls in her arms, Cara. Your dolls bring joy, hours of pleasure and imagination." He kissed her forehead as she rubbed her feet along his calves and shifted to a more comfortable position beneath him.

"That may well be, but tonight made me realize two things. When I heard those shots ring out in the woods and realized you could be dead, I knew right then and there that I didn't want to live without you. It made me furious to think those men could ride roughshod over private land and threaten anybody they wanted. And I knew I wanted to stay and fight beside you."

He couldn't keep the worry from his tone. "After tonight I'm not so sure I'll accomplish anything but harm. We were lucky no one was wounded or killed and after the fight we put up tonight, I'm sure the regulators will be back. They won't be able to stand the thought of armed resistance, especially if Negroes are holding the guns."

She was silent for a long while before she admitted, "Minna told me she's suspicious of Elijah. Could he have murdered Burke?"

"I haven't a clue. But I'll be damned if I'll blame Elijah just because he mysteriously shows up with my hat and was seen in the house the day you fell. Do you think I'm stupid?"

"No. But I don't know how you could have put a gun in his hand and left him in charge if you're the least bit suspicious."

"Because"—he smiled down at her—"my daddy always said if you give a guilty man enough rope, he'll hang himself."

Cara laughed aloud and wriggled her bottom against the mattress. He was still smiling down at her when she gasped with surprise, her eyes wide. She clasped him to her and involuntarily climaxed again.

Dake smoothed wisps of hair back out of her eyes as she settled back down to earth. A bright blush stained her cheeks. He couldn't hold back a chuckle. "If I knew my conversational skills were so arousin', I'd have tried using them in the bedroom long before now."

With her eyes closed, she warned him, "I wouldn't say it was your conversation I find so . . . arousing." Suddenly she opened her eyes and narrowed her lids to a threatening squint. "Let me warn you, you'd better not be testing them out on any other woman in any other bed from now on, Dake Reed."

"On my honor as a Southern gentleman, I wouldn't think of it, ma'am," he drawled. "But I have to go down and tell Minna what happened tonight, warn her to keep an eye open for trouble. I pretty much ignored her when we came in."

"I should see about Clay," Cara put in.

He rolled to his side and took her with him. She rested her head against his collarbone. He kissed her temple and silently thanked God for sending him past her cabin as he crossed the Kansas prairie.

"Inez seems to be taking good care of him. We're lucky she decided to leave the Claytons. I'm willing to hire her on if you agree."

Her answer was a long time in coming. He nudged her gently, thinking she had fallen asleep. "Cara?"

"What? I'm sorry, I was just thinking."

"I said Inez can stay," he told her again.

"Yes. You're right. That would be fine."

He slipped his arm out from beneath her and climbed out of bed. Cara sat up and covered herself as he found his pants and stepped into them. "I'm going down to talk to Minna—"

"—For five minutes," Cara warned.

He buttoned the front of his pants and then shook out his shirt and slipped it on. Closing the fabric, he shook his head as he discovered the buttons missing and the evenly spaced tears up the front. He pulled it off and tossed it aside.

"Five minutes." He assured Cara as he chose another shirt. "I'll bring back a tray of cold supper for both of us."

Clutching the sheet to her breasts, she shook back her hair and watched as Dake carefully closed the door behind him. Her bubble of happiness had burst when he mentioned Inez and she remembered the secret she guarded. It was not something she wanted between them. His love was too precious to her. She was not about to turn him against her by withholding the details of Clay's background. All she could do was trust that he loved her and the child enough to want to cherish them equally.

She would tell him as soon as possible. Definitely before they were married.

But not until things had calmed down a bit.

There's no fool like an old fool.
Except for a young one that's not
payin' attention.

Nanny James

Chapter Sixteen

Afraid to be seen leaving Dake's room the next morning, Cara opened the door of the master suite and stuck her head out into the hallway.

"Good morning, Cara." Minna was standing just behind the door, dusting the wainscot that ran the length of the hall. She paused and watched as Cara, caught in the act, stepped across the threshold.

Although her cheeks burned with embarrassment, Cara held her head high, refusing to suffer any shame. Minna, she noted, looked as fresh and lovely as ever with her brown hair neatly combed and looped back over both ears. Since Dake was already up and gone, Cara's gown was still open down the back, the buttons too tedious to manage alone. She held her shoes in one hand.

Her hair never took well to finger-combing. It stood out in a tangled riot of curls about her head. She feigned a smile. "Morning, Minna."

Instead of ignoring her and getting back to her task, Minna merely stood there, as if expecting an explanation. Cara squelched the urge to flee to her own room and waited, unwilling to give any excuses as to why she had spent the night in Dake's room.

"I wanted to be the first to congratulate you," Minna said. "Dake told me you accepted a proposal of marriage." She

275

sighed and then smiled with a faraway look in her eyes. "I remember the day Burke proposed to me. It was just before he left for the war. Of course, everyone around these parts knew we'd marry someday, but when he finally asked, I was the happiest girl in the world." Her huge brown eyes filled with tears. She pressed her fingers to her eyes and brushed a tear aside. "Things just didn't end the way we expected."

"Minna, I'm so sorry."

Shaking off her sadness, Minna smiled through her tears. One hand toyed with the exquisite cameo she always wore pinned on the high collar of her black silk mourning gown. "I'm sorry, too. I didn't mean to spoil your happiness."

Cara glanced down the hall toward her own room. She was anxious to see if Inez was there with Clay. "You didn't. Please don't worry."

Minna was staring out the window across the wide hall. "You'll be mistress of Riverglen now," she said softly.

Sympathy welled inside Cara for this lost and lonely girl who had virtually grown up at Riverglen. Feeling beneficent in her happiness, Cara assured her, "I'll need your help, you know. Why, I haven't got any notion of what it takes to oversee a household like this. I lived in a one-room cabin with my folks—even plowed the fields beside them."

Minna was listening to her again, watching her closely.

Cara shook her hair out of her eyes. "Dake's got enough to do with getting the hired hands settled in, not to mention getting the fields ready for planting in the spring. I'll be looking to you for help with everything. I don't know where to start."

Smoothing the shining, worn surface of her skirt, Minna said, "Don't worry, Cara. I'll be more than willing to help out." As an afterthought she asked, "Have you made any wedding plans?"

"Heavens no. It's too soon after Burke's death. Besides,

Dake still has to clear his name." Cara felt herself growing embarrassed again, but knew what she was about to add needed to be said. "We can't be announcing our plans while he's still using the alibi you gave him the night Burke was murdered. I hope you'll keep the news to yourself."

Minna appeared offended. "Of course, I will. Dake and I talked about that at length this mornin'."

"Then you understand."

"Perfectly. Congratulations again, Cara." With that Minna turned around and walked down the hall. The whisper of silk followed her soft footsteps.

When Cara entered the guest room she found Inez had just finished diapering Clay. A sense of welcomed relief warmed her when Inez handed the baby into her arms.

"I missed you, little man," Cara cooed in the baby's ear and was rewarded with a smile.

"Did you see that? He smiled at me."

"He surely did, Miz Cara. He missed you last night."

Cara walked around the room with Clay, swaying back and forth when he started to squirm with excess energy. "I missed him, too." She could feel Inez watching her closely. "You heard about the trouble?"

Inez nodded. "I'm glad you and Mr. Reed are all right."

"So am I, thank God." Cara kissed Clay on the crown of his head. "I've decided to marry Dake."

"Did you tell him yet?"

Cara shook her head, knowing full well what Inez was asking. "I can't yet. He's got too many worries as it is, but I'm not going to let this go unspoken between us much longer."

Inez gathered up Clay's wet diaper and straightened the bedspread. "You want me to heat some water so you can have a bath, Miz Cara?"

Cara wondered how long it would be before she became used to having servants do the chores she had always done for herself. "Please. Would you also find Dake and have him send someone up with my crate of dolls when he can? And when you come back, please bring a couple of those big reed baskets I saw in the kitchen."

Dake watched some of the men working together to erect another cabin, this one set farther back from the others on the row. After talking with them all, he weighed their desires with practicality and decided there was nothing wrong with wanting more privacy than slavery had afforded.

He had spent the day working among them and concluded that Elijah had chosen well. All of the men had families, most had already legally married the women they had been paired with during slavery. Among the twenty men and their families was a preacher, a man in his late forties, and an herbalist who claimed she was good at healing. Dake counted himself lucky to have them.

Intent upon returning to the house to see Cara, he led General Sherman down the lane. As he passed the meadow where the prayer meeting had been held the night before, he heard the children's laughter and smiled. The sound lightened his burdensome thoughts and he turned toward it without hesitation.

He expected to see the newly arrived children playing in the clearing. Instead, he was treated to the sight of Cara seated in the midst of a group of them. She'd chosen a seat on one of the logs that had served as a bench for the prayer meeting. She was wearing the bright plaid gown he'd given her. The skirt was spread over the log, a shock of red and green plaid against the brown and yellow colors of fall. In the clear autumn light of the meadow, with the sun shining down upon her golden hair, she looked like an ethereal forest princess.

Dake halted, content to stand beside the gnarled trunk of a twisted old oak and watch. He couldn't hear what Cara had just said to the children, but their joy was clearly evident as they laughed again. The younger were seated on the ground at her feet while some of the older stood beside and behind her. A girl of about twelve sat holding Clay on her lap because Cara's was occupied with a basket. As he watched, she reached into the basket and drew out one of the dolls she had so painstakingly created.

He dropped General Sherman's reins and slowly moved forward until he was close enough to sit unnoticed on a log at the back of the outdoor cathedral. For the first time in days, he let himself relax.

"This is Mr. Pickle," Cara told the group. Dake heard them giggle. One of the smaller youngsters near the back of the group turned an impromptu somersault and wriggled back to his place at Cara's feet. "He's made out of an old bedpost my brother found one day as he was riding over to visit our neighbors."

"In Kansas?" a little girl asked.

"That's right. You've really been listening."

"Me, too, I been listening," the somersaulter chimed in.

Cara nodded in agreement. "Yes, you have." Dake saw her bite her lip, her eyes wide and serious.

One of the older children tapped Cara on the shoulder. His voice was skeptical. "Where'd a bedpost come from right out in the middle of the field?"

Cara twisted to face him. "That's just what we tried to figure out. Like as not, some family had to lighten their load as their big wagon rolled across the prairie—"

"Wide as the ocean," someone in front reminded them.

"That's right. All that was left of the bed was the bedpost. Anyway, he brought it home and I thought to myself, 'Well, this is Mr. Pickle, but nobody knows it yet.' You see how the round knob at the top makes a perfectly good head? And the post is the body."

"What 'bout the arms?"

"And the legs?"

Cara opened Mr. Pickle's navy homespun jacket to reveal a cloth body. "I covered the post with cloth and stuffed it. The arms and legs are sewn onto the body." Dramatically, she paused and studied the group, looking them over carefully. "Mr. Pickle is *very* special, because of the bedpost he's made of. Why, I think Mr. Pickle is sort of a miraculous man, since he was dumped out on the prairie, miles and miles of it, and was lucky enough to be found by my brother at all."

"He's magic?"

The group sobered. Dake knew how superstitious the children were, how many of their parents still clung to some of the spiritualism of Africa passed on by their ancestors. Intuitively, Cara must have sensed their fear, for she quickly said, "Mr. Pickle is so happy to be found that he only does good magic, if he does any at all. He'll need a very special parent." She turned to one of the older boys standing behind her. "How about you?"

The group broke into gales of laughter.

"Dolls ain't for boys, Miz Cara. Everybody knows that," the confident youth told her.

Cara shook her head. "Why not?"

"They just ain't."

At that point, Dake stood up to stretch his legs. "Dolls are for anyone who has enough love to care for them," he said. The occupants of the quiet glade swiveled around to stare up at him. They watched him, curious but wary.

The love in Cara's eyes nearly took his breath away. "I'm so glad you're here," she told him.

He reached out and took Clay from the girl holding him and settled the baby on his shoulder. "Not as glad as I am to have you here." They exchanged a secret smile.

"You really think dolls is for boys, Mr. Reed?" A little boy in the front row with a yearning look in his eyes popped his thumb back in his mouth.

Dake shrugged. "Well, there are dolls and there are dolls. I had a whole regiment of toy soldiers when I was a boy, and they're like dolls." He reached out and Cara put Mr. Pickle in his hand. "And Mr. Pickle, well, I think anyone can see he's a doll that definitely might need a boy to take care of him."

The little boy asked around his thumb. "Can I do it?"

Dake looked to Cara for support. She nodded.

"I think you can, young man. But treat him good, you hear?"

"Yes, sir, Mr. Reed. I will." The little boy reached out and took the bedpost doll and set him on his lap between his knees. Up close, Dake could see that most of the children held dolls already. One by one, Cara's whole clan of rag dolls, apple-head dolls, nut-faced and corncob dolls had been adopted.

There was one little girl left, the same child Cara had so selflessly protected last night. She was seated as close to Cara's skirt as she could get. Cara glanced down and reached into her basket once more. "Ellie," she said to the silent child, "there's one left." Cara took out one of the largest dolls, the one Dake knew to be her favorite. It had round, blue button eyes on a peach face, almost a skein of yellow yarn hair, painted ruby lips, and a blue calico dress with a white apron tied about its waist. "This is Miss Cornflower. She's from Kansas, too. Would you like to have her?"

Ellie shook her head. The answer was definitely no.

Cara's gaze flashed up to Dake, a frown marring her brow. She looked back down at Ellie. "No?"

"No," Ellie said. "I want a doll like me."

"This *is* a little girl," Cara said, turning Miss Cornflower over in her hands, brushing the doll's skirt and straightening the apron. "You don't want her?"

Ellie shook her head again. "You got any dolls like *me*?"

Dake stepped closer. All heads swiveled to stare up at him again. "She can make you one, I'll bet," he assured Ellie.

"One that's black like me?"

Cara's expression reflected her instant understanding. She smiled and shoved Miss Cornflower back in the basket, then took Ellie's small dark hands between her own. "Of course I can do that. Can you wait until I have time to find the right materials and get her finished?"

Ellie glanced around the circle of children, all of them holding a doll. Brown nut heads, the rich walnut tone of Mr. Pickle's polished wooden head, rag dolls with burnt orange, burgundy, and even faded yellow calico faces. Dake could see the child weighing her choices; to wait or to choose Miss Cornflower. The little girl hesitated only a moment longer. "I can wait," she announced.

"I'll make her as soon as I can," Cara promised.

"Tell us some more stories, Miz Cara."

"Tell us about Kansas again."

"Right now, I want to have Miss Cara all to myself." Dake's announcement was met by a chorus of disappointed groans. "I think you should all take your new children home, just like Miss Cara is about to do with Clay." Some of the children stood. Others lingered, unwilling to leave her. "Run along now."

Soon the meadow was empty except for the three of them. Cara stood up and placed a hand on his shoulder. To Dake it felt right, Cara and Clay alongside him on the land where he was born. He bent down and they shared a long, lingering kiss in the sunlight. "Good morning," she whispered when they moved apart.

"Good *afternoon*, Miss James. I was surprised to find you here."

"Why?"

He handed Clay over to her and they began to walk toward

the trees where he had left General Sherman. "You didn't get much sleep last night."

She colored prettily. "You didn't either, as I recall. Too much conversing."

He laughed. With Cara beside him it was all too tempting to set aside his worries and let her innocent charm tempt him into ignoring his duties. If only life could be so pure and simple. If only everyone had half the love that he was experiencing right now. With it came a feeling of peace that anyone with all the problems he had yet to face should have been denied. They walked side by side through the fallen leaves, Cara's plaid skirt swaying around her ankles, her arms wrapped tight about Clay. He wished for a moment that he could take them both and walk away from it all, from Riverglen, from Burke's murder, from all of the responsibilities he had taken on here. His hope to reestablish Riverglen with free labor was still nothing more than a dream at this point. Was it worth putting Cara and Clay at risk?

"Dake, what's wrong?"

"Just thinking again."

"Well, if it's going to upset you that much, you should stop."

He turned and took her hand in his. "You gave away your dolls," he said, as if thinking aloud.

"Happily. Did you see the look on those faces?"

He shook his head. "I was watching you. I don't know who looked happier." He looked down at her small hand nearly hidden by his. A surge of protectiveness welled inside him. "I can't tell you how happy you've made me, Cara." Astounded at the outpouring of love he felt, his eyes smarted with a moist warmth that threatened to spill over. Looking skyward, he blinked rapidly. When he looked down into Cara's upturned face again, he saw that her own eyes were brimming with tears. "I'll thank God every day for the rest of my life that he led me to you."

She reached up and hooked her arm around his neck. Dake pulled her close, mindful of the baby she held between them. Quiet moments passed. Somewhere down the lane, two women called out to each other. General Sherman shook his head. His harness made a metallic sound in the clearing. As much as he wanted the moment to last, Dake couldn't put aside years of learned responsibility. Time moved on and life with it. He released Cara and lifted his horse's reins.

"I was looking for you earlier to tell you I'm going into town after Bill Jensen."

She didn't try to hide her concern. "Is it safe?"

"I'll be all right."

"But why go today? Why now?"

He checked General Sherman's halter and bit. Cinched his saddle strap tighter.

"Dake?"

As if he was reluctant to say, he finally told her, "Elijah's missing."

"But he delivered the dolls to me just this morning."

Dake stared off toward the house. "I know. I sent him to do the job and sent Reverend Willis with him—I figured Elijah wouldn't be able to wander around inside alone if there was someone along. The preacher came back, told me Elijah was with him until they reached the barn, and then told him to go on, that he'd catch up. That's the last anyone's seen of him."

"You think he's gone to town?"

Dake shrugged. "I don't know what to think. I thought I'd check the road, look around here some."

"You think he knows we were suspicious of him?"

"*We?*"

"Well, Minna. And me, I guess."

"I'm not sure why he's gone or where. I know I won't rest easy until I know." He kissed her quickly on the cheek. "Get on back to the house and stay there. Promise?"

She nodded and arranged Clay's blanket tighter around his bottom. "I promise. Just don't be long."

Cara leaned over the old cradle slowly lowering Clay to the husk-filled mattress. The faded quilt Dake had found with the little boy had been laundered. It was scented with strong soap. She tucked the hand-stitched blanket around his chubby little body and gave his bottom a pat. Anna Clayton's gold barrel bracelet weighed heavy on her wrist today. Cara straightened and stared down at it, traced her fingertip along the star and crescent design. She wished the story of Clay's parentage were a simple one. She wished she could ignore it forever.

"If wishes were horses," she reminded herself aloud, "then beggars would ride."

A knock broke the stillness in the guest room. She walked to the door and found Inez on the other side. She bid the woman enter.

"Miz Cara, I came to see if you need me."

Cara shook her head. "I was about to lie down and try to take a nap." Although for the most part, her head injury was behind her, she felt a headache building and decided a rest was in order. After all, it had been a hectic night.

"I'll leave you alone, then. And I'll look in on Clay in a while so he don't wake you, if you want."

Cara rubbed her forehead. "That would be fine."

Inez paused, one hand on the knob of the open door. Cara could sense that the woman didn't want to leave just yet. "Anything else, Inez?"

Inez shut the door. "You know the man Elijah?"

Cara's heart dropped to her toes. "Yes. Why?"

"I was comin' back from helpin' Patsy collect eggs out at the henhouse when I saw him walkin' away from the barn today. He was lookin' mighty scared, so we stopped to ask him what was wrong."

"And . . ."

"He said Miss Minna told him she knew he killed Marse Reed's brother and that he was gonna hang for it. She asked him where he found Marse Dake's hat and asked if he knew what happened to the gun, too. Then she said you all think it was him that put the walnuts on the attic steps."

Pressing an open palm against her heart, Cara tried to calm her mounting fear. How would Elijah react now that he knew he was suspected of murder? Would he be forced to play out his hand? Dake was out on the road somewhere alone and unsuspecting. If Elijah felt threatened, there was no telling what he'd do.

"Do you know where he went? No one's seen him since this morning."

Inez nodded yes. "I know where he said he was going. He went off to buy a conjure."

"A what?"

"A conjure. To keep him safe from Miz Minna."

Her head was really pounding now. "I don't even know what a conjure is or why Elijah would need protection from Minna."

"You best sit down, Miz Cara. You're lookin' mighty pale."

Cara sat on the edge of the bed and waited for an explanation she hoped she could understand. "Go on."

"Elijah said Miz Minna was out to kill him just the way she did old Marse Reed. He said before she came to live here that the old man was fit as a fiddle and that he wasn't never sick a day in his life. She took to fixin' all the old marse's food and little by little, the old man started wastin' clean away. Finally, he was so bad he couldn't get out the bed and Miz Minna wouldn't let any of the house servants go in his room."

"That doesn't prove anything—"

"No, but Elijah said after old Marse Reed up and died, she sold off all the folks what worked at the big house, like she didn't want anybody around who could tell the tale."

"Why did Elijah get to stay?"

"He never worked in the house since Marse Dake went off to the Union Army. He been turned into a field hand since then. When Miz Minna told him today she thinks he killed Marse Burke, he got scared. Said she's blamin' him just to get him out of the way so he can't tell the truth about the old marse. Said he wouldn't tell anyway, 'cause it wasn't none of his business. He said Miz Minna ain't no damn good.

"He told us he was goin' off to the place down the river where an old conjure woman could make him a spell that would keep Miz Minna from hurtin' him."

Cara wondered how many years it would be before she could fully understand this new world Dake had brought her to. "Make him a spell?"

"You know, probably a jar with a snake or a lizard or bones or somethin' to keep the evil away." ·

"Did you believe him?"

"Miz Cara, I don't have any reason not to. You think he's tellin' the truth? You think Miz Minna killed the old marse?"

This time Cara rubbed her forehead with both hands. "I don't know what to think anymore. Go down to the cabins and see if you can find out exactly where this conjure woman lives. If Elijah knew her, some of the others might, too."

"I'll see what I can find out. How about you, Miz Cara?"

She glanced over at the cradle. Clay had been awake quite a while. He would sleep for at least an hour. "I'm going to try to get to the bottom of this once and for all."

Her dove-gray gown was still soiled, but since her destination was uncertain, Cara changed into it, prepared to ride the old nag in the barn if she had to. Able to slip easily out of the monstrous house without calling attention to herself, she realized how simple it was for someone to move about the place unnoticed. She hurried down the lane, keeping well within the shadows of the trees so that no one would see her.

She was passing the old slave quarters when two of the children spied her and called out. They waved and ran up the lane toward her.

"Miz Cara, come see the house we made for the dolls."

"Mr. Pickle got the best place now. Course, in the night he come in and sleep with me."

"I really can't—" She glanced toward the barn and then back down at the children. "All right, I'll come see, but just for a minute."

It took longer than a minute, of course. She not only had to see the two doll houses made of twigs, bark, and fallen leaves, but she spent precious minutes complimenting each in turn and then moving the dolls in and out of their new houses. Kneeling in the leaves beside the children, she took the time to show them how to fashion pieces of doll-sized furniture from twigs and how to find the right leaves for bedding.

She could almost hear Dake chiding her for losing track of time. Finally, she was able to bid the children good-bye with a promise that she would play with them again very soon.

The barn had been built a good way from the once elegant mansion, halfway to the quarters. By the time Cara reached the peaked-roof building, she was out of breath. One of the tall double doors stood open, but it was impossible to see in the darkened interior.

She stepped inside and waited just past the threshold while her eyesight adjusted to the dim light. Sweet Pea, the old mare, whinnied. Cara turned toward the sound. Someone other than the horse was moving in the shadows.

"Elijah?" Her heart was pounding so hard she could barely speak. An overwhelming urge to run out the door nearly sent her flying down the lane, but she gathered her wits and took another step into the dark interior.

"Who's in here?"

Minna stepped out of the shadows, leading the swaybacked

mare. "Why, Cara, you startled me," she said with a relieved laugh. "I was just hitchin' up old Sweet Pea here and then I was going to look for you."

Cara's pulse slowed. She breathed a sigh of relief herself and asked, "Where are you going?"

"Didn't you see Dake?"

Puzzled, Cara frowned. "I saw him earlier. He said he was going into town to—" She paused, wondering how much Minna knew about Elijah's disappearance and the reason for it.

"—To get the sheriff. I know. But he rode up to the house not five minutes ago and said he changed his mind and that we should both follow him out in the carriage." She was backing the horse into the buggy traces.

"Oh, then, I'll just go on in and tell Inez to listen for Clay to wake up."

Minna stopped her. "I already took care of that," she said. "I told her to watch him until we get back."

Cara walked back to open the second door so that the buggy would fit through. The swaybacked mare's head drooped nearly to the ground as the two women led her outside. One huge brown eye looked over at Cara as if to beg for a respite from pulling the carriage.

"Why does he want us to meet him there?" Cara asked.

"He said something about tracking Elijah down. I think he wants some witnesses," Minna said.

"Shouldn't we get some of the men to go with us?"

Minna snorted. "How could we trust any of them?"

"But—what about a gun? Don't we need a gun? I don't think—"

"I have one." Minna climbed up into the buggy, picked up the reins and a carriage whip, and looked down at Cara who was still standing with her hand on the front wheel. "Dake needs us. Are you coming with me or not?"

Beware of a wolf in sheep's clothes. Sometimes he'll take 'em off right in front of you.

Nanny James

Chapter Seventeen

Dake, with Sheriff Bill Jensen beside him, rode up to the front of the mansion and dismounted, handing the reins to one of the older boys who rushed up to greet him.

"What's your name, son?" he asked.

The boy was tall for his age, the hems of his overalls tagged his calf a good three inches above his ankles. "Robert, sir," the boy stated clearly, although he cast a wary eye on the sheriff.

Dake finally recalled this was the preacher's son, one of the new arrivals. "Take the General to the barn for me and give him water." He reached into his pocket, took out a coin, and handed it to Robert, who stared at it for a moment before he nodded, "Yes, *sir*."

"Come on in, Bill." With a weary sigh, Dake took off his hat and wiped his brow on his shirtsleeve. His heart hadn't been on the trip into town. He wanted to turn around and head back to Riverglen most of the way. Just as he expected, he hadn't spotted Elijah on the road anywhere. Nor had anyone he'd questioned.

He took the steps to the wide veranda two at a time and reached the top just as Inez came out the front door carrying a broom, her hair hidden beneath a scarf.

She appeared surprised to see him back so soon and, like the boy, Robert, kept one eye on the sheriff. "Hello, Marse Dake."

"Hello, Inez. Miss Cara in her room?" He knew it was crazy,

that it was the middle of the day, that he shouldn't be wanting Cara as sorely as he did, but his mind had been on little else on the way back.

"No, sir. She went off in the carriage with Miss Minna."

He paused, halfway to the door. He'd been thinking of her for hours. Disappointment shortened his temper. "Where in the hell did they go?"

Inez shrugged. "I can't say exactly. But they headed that way." She pointed down the lane that led across the fields toward the river. "Miss Minna tol' me they was goin' after Elijah."

Anger quickly replaced his disappointment. Why had the two women gone off on some harebrained scheme to chase down a man who was a murder suspect? He shoved his hat back on, prepared to follow them.

"You don't remember them saying anything about where they were going?"

He couldn't help but notice Inez's sullen expression. Her dark eyes barely met his as she began to sweep and talk at the same time. "Miss Minna said she knew where Elijah was hidin' out and that she wasn't gonna wait for him to kill any more of you in your sleep."

"Damn it!"

"You believe it, Marse Dake? That Elijah kilt your brother?"

"At this point, I don't know what to believe. How long have they been gone?"

"Near on an hour."

"Let's go, Bill," he said as he stepped off the veranda again. Pausing at the bottom of the steps he turned back to her. "You see to Clay, will you?"

He heard her mumble, "Course I will," as he hurried toward the barn.

It was cool in the shadows beside the abandoned mill house. The waterwheel, long silent, had moss clinging to the bottom paddles. Cara couldn't help but glance at the place beside the wall where she and Dake first made love. It seemed weeks ago, but the time could still be counted in hours. A chill raced through her as she remembered their tryst, a chill of excitement that had little to do with the crispness of the fall air. Her blood warmed as visual images flashed through her mind.

Minna walked behind her as they crept silently toward the ramshackle building. When her eyes lingered for a moment too long on the shadowed ground beneath the stone wall, Cara tripped on an exposed maple root. She caught herself before she fell headlong.

"Watch where you're goin'," Minna warned in a whisper.

Cara threw her an annoyed glance over her shoulder. If Minna had been so concerned about her safety, why had she driven like a madwoman across the fields, snapping at the horse's flanks with the long-tailed buggy whip? After crossing miles of prairie with Dake, even Cara knew better than to whip a carriage horse anywhere but on the hocks. To whip that old nag, Sweet Pea, was a wasted effort at best. Cara was surprised the horse hadn't collapsed right there between the shafts.

"Where *am* I going?" Cara turned and demanded of her companion. "Where's Dake's horse?"

Minna's gaze quickly shot back to Cara from where it had just swept the field behind them. She stopped long enough to push an uncustomary stray lock of hair back in place. Again in a whisper, she said quickly, "Do you really think he'd be stupid enough to leave his horse out in the open? We're going into the mill because Dake has probably already got Elijah cornered."

Cara didn't budge. All the way to the mill she had questioned her own hasty agreement to accompany Minna on her wild ride. Now that they had reached the sight of Elijah's supposed hideout, there was no sign of Dake. She was certain that caution was the better part of valor. "Then why don't we hear anything? Why hasn't he brought him out? What if we're in danger?"

"Don't worry. I can take care of Elijah."

"How?" Cara wanted to know.

Minna withdrew her hand from the folds of her skirt. Cara found herself staring down at the long barrel of a pistol. "With this," Minna informed her.

Cara stared at the gun for a moment. "Where did you get that?" There was something elusively familiar about the weapon.

Minna looked momentarily confused. She stared down at the gun for a moment and then back at Cara. "I told you I had it. It was wrapped in the blanket on the floorboards."

"Do you know how to use it?" Cara seriously doubted that anyone as sweet tempered and refined as Minna Blakely knew which end to aim and which to hold on to, but from the steadiness of her grip, Cara could see she meant business.

"Of course. I learned to do what I had to do durin' the war."

Once again, Cara knew she was subtly being reminded of all she had *not* suffered during the war years. "You go in first," Cara suggested. "You're holding the gun."

With a look of impatient disdain, Minna took the lead. Cara followed her as they crept close along the side of the wall. The river ran dark and mud brown on the far side of the building. Dampness seeped into the stone foundation. When they reached the door, Minna paused beside it and then, with her toe, gave it a shove. Swinging inward by the force of its own weight, the rusty hinges on the huge wooden door creaked and groaned in protest. The sound screeched in the empty interior and carried up toward the vaulted ceiling.

Cara held her breath as they waited for some sign that Elijah had heard them, certain that although she wasn't breathing, her heartbeat was echoing a loud warning. Minna stepped inside first and stood staring up at the high ceiling where sunlight streamed through missing shingles and filtered down through the rafters. Dust motes shifted in a tireless dance.

Cara followed her inside and looked to Minna for guidance. She silently mouthed the words "What now?"

Minna reached back and gave the door a shove. Slowly, inch by inch, it closed again with a long, rusty moan. Cara stepped into the shadows whispering, "Fools rush in." Now here she was, creeping around in a rickety old building looking for trouble. They should have waited for Dake, she realized all too clearly now. It was one thing to race off headlong into danger. It was another altogether to be standing there looking it in the eye.

Minna signaled her with the gun barrel to move to the side wall where a staircase ran to the loft that covered the back of the building. Only a portion of the ledge of plank flooring was barely visible from where they stood. Cara shook her head no.

Minna motioned with the gun again.

Cara pointed back and mouthed, "You first. You have the gun."

"That's right, I do," Minna said aloud, her voice echoing in the emptiness even though she had used her melodic, conversational tone. "That's why I think we should end this charade and you should do as I ask. Now start walkin' up those stairs."

Minna slowly aimed the gun barrel at Cara's heart. Cara felt her mouth go dry. "What . . . what are you doing?"

"Me? Nothin'. Just makin' sure once and for all that I become mistress of Riverglen." She tilted her head charmingly to the side. Dimples creased her cheeks as she smiled at Cara. "I'm the only one fittin', you know. Theodora Reed trained me herself. Said since I was to be Burke's wife, she'd personally teach me everything about runnin' the house and how to take care of our people."

The door was a good five feet away. And closed. Cara

measured the distance with a quick glance to keep Minna from expecting an escape. "They aren't *your* people anymore, and Burke's dead," Cara reminded her bluntly.

Minna's smile faded. Her lips became taut, pursed. "I know that," she snapped. "As soon as I saw Dake the afternoon he came home, I knew Burke had to die."

"You had your own fiancé murdered?" Knowing how much she loved Dake, Cara couldn't conceive of such a thing.

Minna shook her head. "Of course not. I killed him myself."

Cara couldn't help it. She gasped. Not only did Minna show no sign of remorse, but she appeared more amused than troubled. With a faraway look in her eyes, she fingered the cameo at her throat with her free hand, toyed with the precious piece of jewelry that had once belonged to Dake's mother.

"Burke was a wasted, crippled shadow bent on revenge. All he cared about was the Klan, holdin' Klan meetin's and seein' to it the Yankees were terrorized. He didn't even care enough to use that money his daddy hid from the Confederacy."

"But, you loved him—"

"Damn it all! What I *love* is Riverglen. This is more my home than anyone's. Theodora Reed was more of a mother to me than my own mother ever was. She understood me, knew what I needed and wanted out of life. Right up until she died she gave me all the pretty things my parents couldn't afford. There was no pinchin' pennies here, no wearin' old hand-me-downs and reconstructed clothes—not before the war anyway. After the war started and the burnin' and lootin' began, I made certain I was here to safeguard the plantation for Burke. One night, my parents *conveniently* died in a fire that had been set"—she smiled beguilingly—"by raiders."

Cara braced herself, prepared to charge Minna if she had to make good her escape. It was as still as a tomb in the old mill as the sound of Minna's admission faded into the dense silence. Mentally, she calculated the steps it would take to rush Minna, her stare concentrating on the gun barrel. She knew now why the gun looked familiar—she'd seen it before. It was Dake's Starr .44 with the pearl-handled inlay.

The gun Minna used to kill Burke in cold blood.

"After all I've done to have Riverglen, do you actually think I would let a white trash farmhand become mistress of this place?"

Cara's blood ran cold. "You put the walnuts on the stairs."

"Of course, Cara darlin'."

"You'll never get away with this." Cara ran her damp palms down the sides of her wool skirt.

Minna smiled again. "Oh, I think I will. Especially since it won't be me that kills you, but Elijah."

"But he's not here."

"No, but it'll be my word against that darky's, and you know damn well who folks will believe. Why, look at the way everyone was willing to accept the fact that I slept with Dake his first night home."

"You didn't *sleep* with Dake."

"Oh, didn't I? You are more naive than I thought."

Be careful, Cara warned herself. Don't let her get you so riled up you can't think straight.

"It'll be like takin' candy away from that baby you brought here. I'll shoot you, leave Dake's gun behind, smear my dress with blood and tear it open. When I arrive home screamin' about how I was attacked and you, poor thing, were killed by Elijah, why, there won't be a place in this state he can run to to save his worthless black hide."

Cara took a minute step back, evenly distributing her weight on both feet.

Minna's sharp eyes didn't miss it. "Don't think of tryin' anything." A perfectly formed brow arched almost seductively. "You won't get by me. No one does."

"Is it really worth it, Minna? How many people will you kill to have Riverglen? What about Dake? What if he docsn't marry you?"

Minna shrugged. "I'll kill as many as it takes. Wild tobacco can be brewed as tea. If you give someone enough of it over time it leads to paralysis and death. I got rid of Daddy Reed that way while Burke was off fightin'." She waved the gun again. "Now move toward the stairs," Minna ordered.

"No." Cara didn't budge. Dake loved her. Clay needed her. She had too much to live for.

Minna took a step forward, closing the gap between them. The gun barrel was still aimed square at Cara's heart. At such close range, there was no escape.

Cara turned around, her mind racing. She looked up the narrow open stairs. They appeared as rotten as the rest of the place and she wondered momentarily if she would even reach the top before they gave way.

Step after slow step, she crossed to the far corner of the room and began to mount the stairs. Minna followed close behind. Cara held her breath, certain that any moment she would feel the force of the bullet as it tore through her back. Would she hear the sound or feel the shock first? Time seemed suspended. Thoughts crowded in one upon the other, flashes of questions, musings about death.

The instinct to survive was stronger than her fear. Almost instantaneously, her senses became fine-tuned. They were halfway up the stairs, halfway between the rotten plank floor of the loft and the stone floor below. She heard a whisper of silk, felt Minna move closer.

Cara took a deep breath and threw herself backward.

She crashed into Minna with the force of a dead weight and felt the other woman's feet go out from under her. Together, they tumbled down, a bundle of arms and legs, a tangle of wool and faded black silk. Fabric tore. Breath was expelled in a series of whooshes and grunts as they hit the blunt edges of the stairs, propelled toward the floor.

Everything was a blur around her, but Cara remained ever aware of the fact that Minna might still be holding the gun. As sure as God gave a goose wings, she meant to be on top when they landed at the foot of the stairs.

The tracks of the metal-rimmed buggy wheels were easy to follow down the lane. Dake leaned over General Sherman's neck, blaming himself for his own hesitation. If he'd have questioned Elijah sooner, if he'd gone after Bill Jensen earlier, Cara wouldn't have had to put herself in danger. Cara *and* Minna he reminded himself.

"They're headed for the mill," he called out over his shoulder to Bill Jensen, whose horse couldn't keep pace with the thoroughbred. That much was evident when the tracks veered off toward the river. He kicked the General in the flanks and whipped him with the reins, sure of the horse beneath him as he was of his own competence in battle. They had both been tested, more times than he liked to count.

As the mill came into view he could smell the river, the rich, fecund soil along its banks. The earth flew from beneath the General's hooves. A slight breeze dappled the water and made the pine boughs' hiss sound like whispers of warning.

There was no mistaking the sound.

Just as there was no mistaking the sound of a gunshot he heard echoing from the old mill.

Chapter Eighteen

At first there was no pain.

Cara shook herself. Minna lay beneath her, stunned, blood dripping from a gash in her forehead, but still in possession of Dake's Starr. Cara lunged forward, intent on wrestling the gun away, and felt a searing pain in her shoulder. She then made the mistake of glancing down for some sign of a wound.

Minna stirred, jerked her arm out of reach, and tried to level the gun at Cara's head. Despite the pain, ignoring the disgusting feel of warm blood seeping against her skin, Cara reached out again and this time grasped Minna's wrist in both hands. Fighting like a tiger, Minna nearly heaved her off, but Cara dug in, gouged her fingernails into the woman's skin, felt the satisfaction of raking Minna's flesh. Cara tried to pull herself to her knees but Minna kept thrashing beneath her. Tempted to let go with one hand so she could strike Minna in the face with the other, Cara was afraid to test her injured shoulder.

She shoved against Minna's strength, pushed with all her weight until Minna's gun hand lowered beside them. Behind them, the door swung open.

Cara felt Minna flinch. The gun went off again.

When the second gunshot rang out, Dake didn't hesitate in the open doorway. The sight of Cara half straddling Minna, her skirt hiked up around her thighs, her hair standing out in wild disarray, sent him tearing across the chaff-littered stone floor. Gun drawn at the ready, Bill Jensen ran beside him.

Dake reached out for Cara, but she clung tenaciously to Minna's arm and wouldn't release her hold. Minna lay silent and unmoving.

"Let go, Cara."

She shook her head, gasping for breath. "No. She's still breathing, I can feel it."

He reached over Cara, slipped his hand beneath her, and took the gun from Minna's hand. "I have the gun. You can let go."

"What in the hell is going on?" Bill Jensen moved up behind Dake and hunkered beside the two women sprawled on the floor. "Did she kill Minna?"

Dake gently lifted Cara off of Minna. The shoulder of her gown was covered with a spreading crimson stain. She looked down at it forlornly.

"She ruined my gown," Cara whispered. "I could kill her for this." She looked up at him, her eyes glazed with pain.

Dake could sense she was nearly delirious. He tucked her beneath his arm and held on tight, then tried to push her hair back off her face, touched a bruise beneath her right eye. "I can't take my eyes off you for a minute, can I?" he whispered.

She closed her eyes. "I hope not."

"Miss Minna's been shot in the thigh," Jensen said, his tone laced with concern and irritation.

Dake felt Cara struggle to sit up and lifted her gently. She opened her eyes and looked at the sheriff who knelt beside Minna, holding her hand, turning it over to inspect the bloody streaks where Cara had raked her with her nails.

"She tried to kill me," Cara told them.

As soon as the words were uttered, Minna's lashes began to flutter. Her usually rosy cheeks were pale. When she opened her eyes, her pallor only enhanced the deep hazelnut brown. A powder burn surrounded a bloody hole in her skirt. Blood stained the silk a deeper hue. Minna licked her lips, took a shuddering breath, and grabbed Dake's arm.

"Don't listen to her, Dake. She's out of her head." Her glance flicked over Cara and found Dake's eyes again. "That lyin' Yankee slut tried to kill me."

Dake didn't know what really happened, but he didn't for a minute believe Cara had tried to kill Minna. He glanced over at Bill Jensen.

The man looked like he'd rather be off skinning a skunk.

"You can thank the Lord that bullet went clean through your shoulder without breakin' no bones, Miz Cara." Inez straightened after putting the finishing touches on the bandage she'd just wrapped about Cara's wound. "Which dress you want to put on?"

"I don't care." As Inez crossed the room to the tall standing closet, Cara changed her mind. Shakily, she got to her feet, one hand on the back of the chair until the room stopped spinning. The sight of her blood-soaked gray gown did little to settle her nerves. "On second thought," she said, attempting to lighten her tone, "I think the blue one. I've only worn it for Dake once."

Inez smiled and took the gown out of the closet. Shaking it out, she ran her hand lightly over the azure quilted silk. "One of the purtyist dresses I seen since the war." She carried the dress across the room. "That man's about to come out of his skin waitin' to see you. He's sore worried, Miz Cara."

"I know he is." Cara carefully stepped into the gown, pulling it up to her waist with one hand. "Dake's having a hard time believing that someone as close to him as Minna could have murdered Burke." She wished she could take the burden from him, but didn't know how to begin.

The servant helped Cara into the gown, a complicated task because of her bound shoulder, then offered to brush out her hair. Cara let her head fall back and her eyes close as Inez gently worked the tangles out of her hair. Lulled by the smooth, even strokes, she sighed.

For a moment the brushing ended and disappointed, Cara requested, "Don't stop yet, Inez." She heard the soft swish of Inez's cotton skirt as the woman behind her moved. After a second, the brush strokes began again. The pain in her shoulder had increased, but wasn't unbearable. Finally, after a sense of calm settled over her at last, she opened her eyes and turned to thank Inez.

It was Dake she found standing behind her with her brush in his hand.

"How—"

He ran his hand down her hair. "I slipped in a few minutes ago. I missed you. Besides, I didn't like watching you take such pleasure from someone else's touch." He reached around her and set the brush on the table.

Cara smiled as his hand came to rest against the nape of her neck. "She was only brushing my hair. Besides, I wouldn't exactly call it pleasure."

"No?" He leaned down and kissed her gently without touching her. "You had your head thrown back, your eyes closed, a dreamy smile on your lips. I've only seen you look that way when I make love to you. That's the way I want to keep it." He teased her ear with this thumb.

She reached up with her uninjured arm and slipped her hand around his neck, drawing him back to her mouth for another taste. Need coursed through her. She wanted to feel him inside her, needed his touch to reassure her that they had survived, that they were as alive as their love. She whispered against his lips, "Make love to me now, Dake."

It was a long time before he lifted his lips from hers. When he did, they were unsmiling. "Bill Jensen's still downstairs.

He's finished questioning Minna and now he wants to talk to you."

"Where is she?"

"You needn't look so frightened—"

"You have no idea what she's capable of, Dake."

As he looked at her shoulder, his expression darkened. "Oh, I think I do at that. Minna's in her room. I'll help you downstairs."

"Is her door locked?"

He nodded. "I took the precaution myself as soon as Bill left the room. She was in a lot of pain. Said she was going to sleep."

A desperate fear nearly engulfed her. "Don't believe a word of it," she warned him.

"Cara, please don't worry. I'm not about to let her near you again."

"Where's Clay?"

"Inez is watching him in the kitchen."

Cara glanced over at the empty cradle. Both her men were safe. With a sigh, she stood up and let Dake take her arm, knowing it was her duty to go down and tell the sheriff what she knew. The sooner Minna was behind bars, the better. Together they left the room.

Bill Jensen looked bushed. He ran his hand over his bald forehead and then across the few strands of hair that still covered the shining crown of his head. Bags hung beneath his faded blue eyes. When Dake ushered Cara into the sparsely furnished front parlor, Jensen came to a half stand in an effort at politeness and then sank wearily back into the chair.

Cara sat down on a worn settee and carefully spread her skirt across a patch of protruding horsehair. Dake sat beside her, took her hand in his, and threaded his fingers through hers.

Jensen took a deep breath and sighed. "Now, Miss James,

you tell me, clear as you can recall, what happened here today."
He sat back and rested his foot on the opposite knee.

Cara watched the toe of his scuffed leather boot shake up
and down as he sat ready to listen to her explanation. Finding
it hard to pull her thoughts together, she noticed there was a
hole in the sole of his boot.

"Minna drove me out to the old mill and then tried to kill
me." Cara watched Bill Jensen carefully. His face was impas-
sive. She had no idea whether or not he believed her.

"Start at the very beginning," Jensen advised.

She looked to Dake for help. He squeezed her hand.

"I got up this morning and spoke to Minna in the hallway.
She seemed pleased to hear that Dake and I plan to marry."

"Marry?" Jensen's foot hit the floor. He leaned forward,
elbows on knees, and looked from one to the other of them.

Leaning forward, his forearms resting on his knees, Dake
looked Jensen hard in the eye and said, "Cara and I are going
to be married, Bill. As soon as all this is cleared up." Dake's
explanation left no room for argument.

Jensen squinted and rubbed the top of his head again as if he
expected the action to stimulate thought. He pinned Dake with
a stare. "So Minna *was* lyin' before? You never spent the night
with her?"

Dake shook his head. "No. I didn't. But she'd put her good
name on the line and since I didn't kill Burke, I went along
with her story to buy some time to find the real killer."

"Who just happens to be Minna," Cara announced matter-
of-factly. "She told me herself she killed Burke."

Both men turned to stare at her at once. She could see the
deep hurt in Dake's eyes. He believed her, yet didn't want to
believe, that much was apparent. He stood up and paced to the
doorway and stood with his back to the room, braced against
the door frame with his forearm. As he stood there brooding in
silence, Cara longed to go to him, to slip her arm around his

waist and share his sorrow. She knew he wouldn't want her pity, but it wasn't pity she offered, it was simply love.

Jensen gently reminded her the interview was not over. "Why don't you get back to your side of the story, Miss James?" he encouraged. "At this rate it's gonna take all night."

"This morning," Cara continued, "when I came in from playing with the children, I talked to Inez. She told me that Elijah had gone off to hide. It seems Minna had told Elijah she knew he killed Burke and that he was going to hang for the murder. She asked him about the hat, where he found it—"

"Dake's hat."

"That's right, Sheriff. She asked him where he found Dake's hat and asked him if he'd found the missing gun, too. Which, by the way, was the gun she tried to kill me with."

"I already identified it for him," Dake said from the doorway. He returned to Cara's side.

Jensen settled back again. "Go on, ma'am."

"I was worried when I heard Minna told Elijah she suspected him. I didn't know what he might do." She took Dake's hand. "I was afraid for Dake, that's why I went with her."

"To the old mill."

She shook her head. "Don't jump ahead, Sheriff, if you want the whole story."

Dake laughed. Jensen rubbed his face with his meaty hands.

"Inez said Elijah went off to buy something called a conjure to protect him from Minna. He thought Minna was out to get him because he was the only house slave . . . ex-slave, who suspected she had poisoned Dake's father."

"This whole thing is tangled tighter than a spider's web in a windstorm," Jensen grumbled.

Cara stiffened. Her shoulder ached, her eyes burned, and she wanted nothing more than to lie down and sleep, but even that was impossible with a madwoman housed under the same roof. "This is the bald truth, Sheriff Jensen. If you try to hide the truth, like as not it'll leap out and trip you, my nanny always said."

"Go on."

"I decided to find Elijah and question him myself. I ran into some children again and lost track of time—"

"She does that with astounding regularity," Dake explained.

"—I went to the barn to saddle Sweet Pea. I heard a noise and for a minute I thought Elijah might be hiding there. It almost uncurled my hair, I tell you. But it wasn't him. It was Minna. She was hitching Sweet Pea to the buggy." Cara turned to Dake. "That's when she told me you'd come by looking for us and that you wanted us to follow you to the mill."

"I never saw her or told her any such thing," Dake assured them both. "I was on my way to town and she knew it. She knew how long it would take me to get there and back again."

Cara nodded in agreement. "We got to the mill and went in, crept in really. I was beginning to worry when I didn't see your horse anyplace," she told Dake. He squeezed her hand, encouraging her to go on.

"Minna got tired of me balking the whole way and finally told me to start up the stairs, and admitted that she was going to kill me so she could be the rightful mistress of Riverglen. She said she realized the night Dake came home that she had to kill Burke—that he wasn't interested in saving this place as much as he was in avenging the Southern cause. She hinted at setting the fire that killed her parents and claimed she'd poisoned Dake's father, just as Elijah suspected. She had Dake's gun pointed at me. I started up the stairs and halfway up, I couldn't think of anything to do but fall back on her. We rolled down the stairs, the gun went off and hit me in the shoulder. We fought. You came in. The rest you know."

"Is that it?"

Cara nodded. "Except for the walnuts."

"Walnuts?" Sheriff Jensen shook his head in confusion.

Dake tried to help. "Someone spread walnuts on the attic steps. Cara fell. She could have been killed."

Cara nodded in agreement. "Minna told me she'd done it and had then blamed that on Elijah, too. She was going to shoot me, make it appear he'd killed me and then tried to rape her. She wanted to let him hang for both Burke's and my murder. She said with me out of the way, Dake would be hers and so would Riverglen. She said if you didn't want her"—Cara turned to Dake and blinked away stinging tears—"she was going to get rid of you, too."

"That's an interesting story, to say the least," Jensen said.

"It's the truth," Cara assured him once more.

He stood up, stretched, and walked over to the cold fireplace. "Funny thing is, Miss Minna told me virtually the same tale, except the roles were reversed. You tried to kill her and planned to blame Elijah. You killed Burke Reed so Dake would hold sole title to Riverglen."

"What?" Cara continued to be awed by the depths of Minna's twisted deviousness. "How could I have killed Burke Reed? I'd never seen him before in my life. Besides, I never left the Polk Hotel that night. I was there with Clay all night long."

"Anyone see you?"

Cara nodded. "The landlady watched me like a hawk. I could see she hated having a 'traitor' like Dake under her roof, not to mention a Yankee."

Bill Jensen sighed as if he'd just walked a mile with a bale of cotton. "I'll talk to her when I get back to town."

"You actually doubt my word?" Cara was affronted. "You actually believe that murdering—"

Dake laid a hand on her arm. "Calm down, Cara."

She shook him off. "Don't tell me to calm down. That woman is as low as a lying snake and here I sit being accused of—"

"Miz Cara?"

Cara, Dake, and Bill Jensen turned at the summons from Inez in the doorway. The woman's dark-eyed glance went from Cara to Dake, to the sheriff and back to Cara again.

"What is it, Inez?" Cara was relieved by the interruption. It would give her a chance to bring her temper under control. "Is Clay all right?"

"Yes, ma'am. He's in the kitchen with Patsy. I need to talk to you."

"Can't this wait?" Dake asked, obviously irritated by the interruption.

Inez didn't appear to be intimidated. "No, suh."

Cara gave Dake's hand a squeeze and then stood, intending to answer Inez's summons in the foyer. Bill Jensen stopped her. "I'd like you to stay right here for a while, Miss James."

Cara swung around to face him again. "I told you all I intend to tell you, Sheriff. Perhaps you'd like to lock me in my room. In fact, with that woman upstairs, I think I'd prefer it."

Jensen leaned back again and draped an arm over the back of the chair. "I'm sorry if you take offense—"

"You're damned right I do," she shot back.

"You're damned right she does," Dake said at the same time.

"Miz Cara," Inez interrupted, "Elijah done come back. He said he wants to talk to you."

Dake stood. "Send him in, Inez."

The woman twisted her apron and swallowed. "He brought a conjure woman with him."

"Hell, send 'em both in," Jensen ordered. "It's a regular circus around here anyway."

Inez disappeared, only to return within seconds with the two who were obviously waiting nearby. Elijah, his discomfort highly obvious, ducked his head in greeting to Dake and Cara, barely glanced over at the sheriff, and held tight to the brim of his hat. His clothes were rumpled and dusty. Bits of twigs and leaves were stuck in his hair. From a rope around his neck dangled a canning jar filled with what appeared to be bits and pieces of garbage, leaves, a bone, something green and wrinkled.

Beside him stood a woman Cara had not seen before. Unlike Elijah, the black woman seemed perfectly comfortable among the white occupants of the room. She was garbed in a jumble of colorful clothing, a striped skirt of green and yellow muslin, a red vest over a man's linen shirt, all of it topped by a patchwork knit shawl. Huge gold hoop earrings dangled to her shoulders, multicolored, beaded necklaces hung around her neck. She was taller than Cara, her back straight, her eyes dark and somehow knowing. She nodded at Dake.

"Eugenia," he said in greeting.

"What have you got to say for yourself, boy?" Jensen asked Elijah.

"Would you like to sit down, Elijah? Eugenia?" Dake asked, ignoring Jensen's bluntness.

The woman simply ignored the suggestion. Elijah shook his head. "No, suh, Marse Dake. We come to tell you what we know 'bout Miz Minna. Didn't know nothin' about the trouble Miz Cara was in this afternoon till a while ago."

"I tol' him about the shootings," Inez interjected.

"Go on, Elijah," Dake encouraged.

"When Miz Minna told me she was gonna have me hung for murderin' Marse Burke, I knew I had to do somethin' fast, so I went to see Eugenia here to get me a conjure made."

When Dake nodded in understanding, Cara touched his shoulder. "I'm not sure I know what he means," she said.

Elijah lifted the rope around his neck and showed her the jar. "This be a conjure. It's to keep the evil off me, the evil Miz Minna tryin' to—"

"Get on with it," Jensen groused. "What're you doing here, Eugenia?"

The commanding figure turned to the sheriff. It was a moment before she spoke, a long moment while she pinned him with an unwavering gaze. A lesser man would have squirmed, Cara decided, as she carefully studied the strange woman. If ever she needed to wither a man with a look, she hoped she remembered Eugenia's expression. Between these two it was a game of wills. Finally the woman spoke. "I worked here in the house for many years," she said in perfectly accented tones before she turned to Dake for verification.

"She was my mother's maid," Dake told them.

Eugenia went on. "Shortly after Theodora Reed died, Minna's parents died in the fire. She moved in here. Burke Reed was gone to the war. Minna took over care of the household. That's when she started to poison old Mr. Reed."

"How do you know that for a fact?" Dake asked.

"If that's true, why didn't you do anything about it?" Jensen wanted to know.

She ignored Jensen and spoke directly to Dake. "I know. I saw her give him wild tobacco for his tea. She insisted they drink a cup together twice a day. Of course, hers wasn't the same concoction." Adjusting her shawl across her shoulders, she then added, "I did nothing because I cared nothing for Hollis Reed."

Cara was shocked by the depth of hatred in her voice. As Eugenia went on, she soon understood the source of that hate.

"After the war started, Hollis Reed sold my children away from me one by one until there was none left. Begging didn't help. I ran off twice. He had me brought back and whipped both times. When I found out what Minna was doing, I didn't lift a finger to stop her. When the old man finally died, she sent all the house slaves to the fields and trained new. I ran off again, but because of the war, things were in a sorry state here, no one bothered lookin' for one runaway woman. I been livin' in a shack in the woods down by the river ever since."

"Why tell us all this now?" Jensen asked what Cara had been wondering.

Elijah spoke up. "I got scared hidin' out by the graveyard, so I come sneakin' back this evenin' to find out what's goin' on and learnt 'bout Miz Cara bein' hurt. I figured, this be the time to tell the truth 'bout Miz Minna while she laid up and can't hurt nobody, so I went back to get Engenia—"

"I heard of Burke Reed's murder," Eugenia spoke for herself. "I feared for Dake Reed's life. This woman is innocent. It's the one upstairs who is evil and must be stopped."

A sudden weakness swept over Cara. She sank back down onto the settee. Dake went to her immediately. "Are you all right?"

She tried to smile. "Just a little light-headed is all."

"Inez"—Dake turned to the woman hovering in the doorway—"get Cara some coffee, will you? Sheriff, coffee?"

"None for me. I'm gonna be up all night ponderin' on this as it is."

Inez left the room.

Still in command of the situation, Dake reached out and shook Elijah's hand. "Thank you, Elijah, for coming forward like this, and, Eugenia, thank you. I know you don't owe this family your loyalty—"

Eugenia studied Dake hard and long. Without the blink of an eye, understanding passed between them. "No, sir."

"I thank you anyway."

As stately as a queen, the woman turned to leave. She lingered for a moment in the doorway, carefully watching Cara. "Your trial is far from over," she told her. With that, she turned and left the room.

Elijah said, "I'll be goin' back to the cabin, Marse Dake, if you don't need me."

"Bill, do you need to ask him anything else?"

"Just don't leave the plantation," Jensen ordered.

"That's all for tonight, Elijah. Next time you get worried, come to me first," Dake added.

Elijah smiled with relief. "I'll remember, Marse Dake." He started for the door, but before he reached it, they heard Inez hollering in the hallway. She ran into the room screaming, careened off of Elijah, and stopped dead still with her hands clasped to her breasts.

A foreshadowing of doom swept through Cara as flashes of Minna holding Dake's gun on her in the eerie gloom of the old mill came back full force. Dake took the woman's arm and shouted over her piteous cries. "What is it, Inez? What's happened?"

"Patsy's layin' dead in the kitchen and the baby's gone."

*Most times what you're lookin' for
is right under your nose.*

Nanny James

Chapter Nineteen

Cara was trembling so hard it amazed her to discover that her legs still worked. She rushed past everyone in the room, headed for the kitchen.

Dake called out for her to wait but she ran on, driven by fear of what Minna would do to Clay. Her shoulder ached something fierce. She refused to let the pain stop her. Halfway down the hall, her knees buckled. When she was forced to lean into the wall for support, Dake's strong arms encircled her from behind and she leaned into him, giving way to her fear and loathing.

"Oh, God, Dake. She's taken Clay."

He supported her as they continued down the hall with the others crowded close behind him. She could hear Jensen's labored breathing, Elijah's prayers, and Inez's sobs as they raced along the narrow passageway to the kitchen. Expecting to find Patsy's lifeless form in the room, the colorful entourage was met by the sight of Eugenia kneeling on the floor, cradling the sobbing young servant girl in her arms. Blood streamed from a wound near Patsy's temple but she was far from dead.

Inez took one look at the resurrected Patsy and screamed again. Elijah was the first to move. He threw his hands in the air and shouted, "Praise the Lord, she come back from the dead!" He fell to his knees. Inez immediately joined him.

Jensen shoved his way into the room. "Shut up! All this caterwaulin' is enough to raise everyone in the graveyard."

"She wasn't dead," Eugenia said firmly over the din. "I need a towel, Inez." The woman's calm slowly permeated the room. Inez moved to grab a dish towel, handed it over. After folding it into a compress, Eugenia pressed it against Patsy's wound.

Dake helped Cara to a chair at the table. Pain in her shoulder forced her to sit, but didn't silence her. "Where is Clay?"

Hunkering down beside the wounded girl, Dake put a hand on her shoulder and forced her to look at him. She was shaking so hard her teeth rattled. "Patsy?"

Patsy roused herself enough to look up at him. Her black eyes grew round and startled as she took in everyone crowded around her. "Miz Minna come at me with a rollin' pin. I don't know nothin' else."

"Did she take Clay?" Cara demanded.

Patsy nodded. "I 'spose so. She's the only one who came through here and the baby's gone." She covered her face and started wailing.

"Oh, Dake, how could she have gotten out of her room?" Cara got to her feet and stood beside him, her hand on his shoulder, weaving from fatigue, pain, and fear. She warned herself not to faint.

"I locked her in her room," he assured Cara, but his face was stricken with guilt.

Eugenia spoke up again. "Minna kept a set of keys to every room in her bureau drawer when I lived here."

Dake stood. Gone was his momentary anguish. Instantly taking command of the situation he announced, "I'm going after her. Inez, Elijah, get Cara back to her room and don't leave her. Jensen, come with me. Eugenia, take Patsy back to her cabin, if you will."

Cara got to her feet and was able to reach Dake before he

was out the back door. "I'm not waiting for word. I'm going with you."

He was cold and unyielding. In complete command. His eyes were green shards of ice, his lips hard, his expression closed and unreadable. This was a side of Dake Reed she'd seen in Poplar Bluff the day he rode off with the posse. She shivered and almost pitied Minna when he found her. Almost.

"You'll do exactly as I say," he told her.

She grabbed his sleeve when he started to move away. "No."

He took her by the elbows. The sharp tone he continued to use with her cut her to the quick. "I won't lose precious time arguing with you." Moving her across the room, he handed her over to Inez. "You'll only slow us down."

Cara reached up and clutched the front of his shirt, knowing time was of the essence but unwilling to let him go before she begged, "Please, Dake, be careful."

He threw his arms around her and held her tight.

Her eyes stung with unshed tears. If anyone could save Clay, it was this man who brought the baby into the world. Finally, she loosened her grip on him, let go, and watched him turn away.

"Please, bring our baby home," she whispered.

"She can't get far wounded," Jensen reasoned as he and Dake shrugged into jackets and stepped out into the brisk night air.

With a lantern in hand, Dake paused on the edge of the wide veranda. Silence surrounded them in the darkness. The tall trees, some bare now, spread twisted limbs and branches like grasping, skeletal fingers against the starry night sky. Somewhere in the distance, an owl hooted.

"No, she can't be that far away yet," he agreed as his eyesight grew accustomed to the darkness beyond the ring of lamplight. "Not with a baby." There were miles of fields and roads to cover. The river was not far away, nor was the old mill. There were countless places for her to hide. Dark, sinister thoughts flooded the very edges of his mind and he fought them back. Minna surely wouldn't hurt a harmless child. No one was that demonic.

Not even Minna Blakely.

He told Jensen, "Saddle the horses. I'll look around the yard and see if I can pick up any sign of her at all." The command left no doubt as to who was in charge. Dake waited to see if Bill Jensen would balk. He didn't. Instead, he headed for the barn.

It was too late to blame himself for not ever suspecting Minna of Burke's death. And why would he? He'd known Minna since childhood, played in the fields and swam in the river with her, his brother beside them, accepted her as part of the family. Had there ever been any outward sign that she was capable of the heinous murders she had committed? Dake could not recall any incident that might have given him a glimpse into her now twisted mind.

"That old nag of a horse is gone," Bill Jensen called out as he led General Sherman and his own saddled mount out of the barn.

Dake looked up from where he bent over horseshoe prints in the dirt. "That's what I thought. These fresh tracks are mixed with ones the carriage wheels made earlier. They head back toward the river."

"You think she's ridin' bareback with a baby?" Jensen asked him. "I saw an extra saddle in the barn. She didn't have time to saddle up."

"Minna's one of the best horsewomen I know," Dake admitted grudgingly as he swung up into the saddle. "Still, I think she'd stick to the road." For the second time that day, he led the way toward the river. Jensen followed close behind as they raced off into the night.

Low-lying fog hugged the river. When they reached the river's edge, there was no sign of Minna, Sweet Pea, or Clay. The men reined in before they reached the deserted mill. Dake dismounted and signaled for the sheriff to follow. "Let's leave the horses. No need to announce our presence."

Bill Jensen swung out of the saddle and tied his horse to a pine bough. Dake ground-tethered General Sherman. "I'll go around the river side," Dake told him and the two split up.

The dry grass beneath his boots muffled the sound of his steps as Dake approached the old building looming in the darkness. *Cry Clay.* He willed the child to make a fuss that would help lead them to him, then immediately thought better of it. What would Minna do if forced to silence the child to save her own neck?

The trail was impossible to read. He found no sign of them and cursed the darkness. After circling the far side of the mill, he met up with Jensen outside the heavy door that stood closed.

"She'll hear the door if we open it," Dake warned, remembering the shrill sound of the rusted hinges.

"That's a chance we have to take if we're going in," Jensen whispered back.

"She could be armed. But not with this." Dake patted the Starr that had been returned to his holster. Jensen reached for the door handle. Dake put a hand on his shoulder to stop him. "You yank the door open and I'll go in first. I know the layout."

Dake drew his gun.

Jensen jerked the door open fast and hard. The hinges groaned in protest. Dake rushed in, crouched, and rolled to the far wall. No shots rang out in the emptiness. He was on his feet in an instant, headed for the stairs. While jogging three quarters of the way up, he felt one of the rotten boards give way.

"Look out!" Bill Jensen called from below. "Those stairs might not take the weight—"

The next thing Dake knew, he was hurtling toward the ground.

Cara refused to wait in her room.

Terrified for Clay's safety, furious at Minna, helpless because of her shoulder wound, she was acting sullen and uncooperative and she knew it, but there seemed to be no way to shake herself out of her temper.

Inez and Elijah had stopped trying to cheer her an hour ago and were giving her as much room as they might a skunk that was loose in the house. They wouldn't leave her alone in the parlor, but they no longer offered conversation or coffee. The hour had passed slowly while she had to content herself with alternately pacing before the window and standing on the porch staring out into the night.

She was certain she'd cried every tear she had in her, telling herself the whole time that crying wouldn't help change things. Nor would blaming herself with "if onlys." There was no one to blame for Minna's perverse act of kidnapping. Not Patsy, Inez, or herself for letting Clay out of her sight. Dake had locked Minna in her room. Land sakes, the woman was sorely wounded. Who'd have thought she would rise up to strike again?

Cara walked to the window for the umpteenth time and pressed her forehead against the cool glass. She closed her eyes and realized that despite her worry, even standing she was exhausted enough to slip off to sleep.

"Miz Cara?" Inez barely whispered behind her. "Miz Cara, let us help you up to bed—"

Her head jerked up. "No."

"Soon as Mr. Reed comes back, I'll wake you up."

"You don't understand at all, do you? I *can't* go upstairs. I can't sleep until Dake brings that baby back home." Cara put her fist to her lips to still their trembling. "If anything happens to Clay, to either of them, I don't know what I'll do."

A single tear slipped from the corner of Inez's eye and ran down her cheek like the countless others she had already cried. "I understand, Miz Cara. More than you know. Don't forget that child's special to me, too," she whispered.

Cara covered her face with her hands. "I'm so sorry, Inez. So sorry. I just don't know what I'm saying anymore."

Inez slipped her arms around Cara's shoulders and led her back to the settee. Before Cara could sit down, she heard the sound of horses entering the yard.

"Marse Dake's back," Elijah called out from the doorway.

A rush of emotion roused Cara to her feet once again. Inez grabbed her hand and together they hurried toward the door.

They watched from beneath the covered veranda as Dake and the sheriff dismounted. There was no sign of Clay. Frozen where she stood, Cara clutched Inez's hand and waited. As relieved as she was to see him back safe and sound, she was unwilling to rush forward and meet Dake, afraid of what he might say.

She waited on the edge of the veranda. Shivers ran the length of her spine with annoying regularity. They seemed to echo the beat of her heart. Dake finally reached the step just below her.

"Are you limping?" she asked. _Anything. Tell me anything but the truth if it's bad._

"A little. I fell."

She tried to read his eyes, but they were shadowed by his hat brim. The harsh lines around his mouth and the firm set of his jaw told her more. "Dake? You're scaring me."

He took her hands and held them tight. "It's not bad news, but it's not good. We couldn't find them anyplace. It's as if she simply disappeared. It's too dark to keep sight of the trail, but we'll go back out at dawn."

She shook her head, denying his words. Furious to think he

would give up so easily. "No. You'll go now. If you won't go look for them, I will. Elijah will go with me." She turned to the man standing behind her. "Won't you, Elijah?"

Dake squeezed her hands. "Cara—"

He seemed so calm, so resigned, so collected that she became more frantic with every passing second. Clay was hers now, just as he had been hers since the first day of his short life. She couldn't bear the thought of him in Minna's hands any more than she could picture him lying cold and alone, abandoned somewhere in the darkness.

"Our baby is out there in the dark someplace. He's never been away from us before and I want him back. Minna won't know how to take care of him; she won't even care what happens to him." Cara tried to pull her hands out of Dake's grasp, intent on moving past him to the horses Bill Jensen had tied to the hitching post. Clay needed her. She had to go.

Dake stepped up beside her, grabbed her around the waist, slipped an arm beneath her knees, and picked her up. She shoved against him, tried to wriggle free. Pain radiated from her injured shoulder and she gasped. "Put me down, you're hurting me."

"You're hurting yourself. Hold still." He carried her indoors.

She kicked her legs and took a swing at him with her good arm. He held her tight and ducked but didn't slow down as he headed for the stairs.

"Let me go, Dake. I have to find Clay before it's too late."

Halfway up the stairs he stopped to shift her weight in his arms. Cara pulled back. In the glow of lamplight from the top of the stairs she could see him clearly. The tracks of his own tears stained his cheeks. She watched him swallow, as if he had to work to form the words.

"I'd move heaven and earth to find that child and you know it, Cara. But there's nothing we can do till dawn."

*   *   *

She refused to sleep in her own room where she would see the empty cradle. He wasn't going to leave her alone anyway, so Dake carried her into the master bedroom and finally put her down. Inez had left a lamp burning on the bedside table. He turned away from her quickly, embarrassed by his tears, and went directly to the washbasin, shrugging off his jacket as he went, and without a thought tossed it on the end of the bed.

With a catch in her voice she said, "Now I know you're upset."

He watched her pick up the finely worked buckskin, smooth out the soft material, and untangle the fringe with her fingers before she draped it over a chair. Dake turned back to the washstand and poured some water into the china bowl decorated with a woodland scene. He splashed his face, reached for a towel, and scrubbed his skin dry.

"Come here," he said as he straightened.

Cara came to him without argument. He took her in his arms and held her as tight as he dared with her injured shoulder. How had he allowed his life to spiral so out of control? When had order and desensitization been replaced by chaos and passion?

From the very day he'd first laid eyes on Cara James.

"Dake?" Her voice was muffled by his shirtfront.

He kissed the crown of her head. "What?"

"We'll find him. I know we will," she whispered against him.

He wanted to reassure her more than anything on earth, but he had spent years being far too sensible than to give her false hope. Silence was his only answer.

He felt her sigh against him and turned her in his arms until she stood with her back to him. "Let me get you out of this gown so you can get a couple hours of sleep."

She didn't protest, but waited like a lifeless doll, arms out at her sides, while he opened the buttons down the back of her dress. He slipped it off carefully and let the blue silk fall to the floor. She stepped out of the dress and rubbed her arms against the chill in the room.

He stared at the flawless ivory skin usually hidden beneath her clothing. The thin material of the chemise he'd given her offered little protection against the cool night air. Goose bumps rose to mar the perfection. He put his hand against the small of her back. She leaned into him for support as he ushered her toward the bed. Raising the bedclothes, he held them while Cara slid beneath the covers and pulled them up to her chin. She turned away from him.

Feeling as old as Father Time, Dake sat heavily on the edge of the bed and worked his boot off over his slightly swollen ankle. In another hour he might not have gotten his boot off at all. He turned down the lamp wick until the flame went out.

Fully clothed, he slid beneath the covers and moved close to Cara, cupping her body with his. He slipped his arm beneath her waist and drew her close up against him.

He knew she wasn't asleep, but he hoped fatigue would soon overcome her torment. He wished he knew the words to say that would ease her mind, wished he could be like her granny and offer a wise proverb, a prayer, a gift of hope.

But tonight, there was nothing he could give her except the comfort of his arms.

Dake came awake aware of two things at once; his ankle was throbbing and someone was pounding on the door. It was still dark, but he felt Cara sit up beside him.

The pounding intensified. "Reed. Get up."

It was Jensen's voice. Dake got out of bed and glanced over at Cara before he went to answer the door. In the shadowed light before dawn he saw her pull the covers up to her chin. He opened the door wide enough to speak to the sheriff without exposing Cara to his view.

"One of your hired men found the old mare wandering around the quarters and brought him up to the house."

"I'll be right out." Dake closed the door and returned to the bedside. "Somebody found Sweet Pea," he told Cara.

"I heard." She scrambled out of bed and reached for her gown. "Don't leave before you help me get this on." Dress in hand, she rounded the bed and waited while he forced his injured foot into his boot with a muffled curse.

"Come here." She stood before him and he held her dress while she stepped into it, then gingerly pulled it up and held it while she worked her arms and injured shoulder into the sleeve.

"We're quite a pair."

"When Clay is home safe and sound I think we both deserve a holiday," she mumbled.

Amazed by the depth of her faith he said, "You never give up, do you?"

"I can't," she said softly. "Not when hope is all we have."

He waited while she found her shoes, knelt, and put them on her. When she was ready, he kissed her quickly, unwilling to wait any longer to resume the search for Minna and Clay. Collecting his jacket on the way out, he then opened the top drawer of his bureau and drew out another gun from beneath a folded shirt. He slipped it into the pocket of his coat. Then Dake took Cara's hand and together they left the room.

Inez was pouring coffee for Bill Jensen in the kitchen. Dake seated Cara at the table and waited for details.

"Your preacher heard something outside his door early this morning and found the nag wandering around. Seems word of the kidnapping has spread through the quarters, so he took it to Elijah who stabled the mare and woke me up."

"What does it mean, Dake?" Still sleepy-eyed, Cara reached out for the coffee Inez had readied for her.

"It means that Minna's out there somewhere on foot or she's left by way of the river or hitched a ride on the road," Jensen said.

Dake set his coffee cup down and tapped the edge of the table with both hands. "I'm startin' to wonder if she did get away on the river."

Jensen leaned forward, elbows on the table. "What do you mean?"

"Minna's devious. She might have hidden an old skiff or a raft. She could have made arrangements for someone to meet her."

"She could have," Jensen admitted.

"You mean she could be miles away by now?" Cara sat forward on the edge of her chair. "Is that what you're thinking?"

Dake nodded. "That's what I'm thinking. We always played at the landing when we were kids and tried to guess where all the boats might be headed. There was an old skiff hidden in the reeds. It's probably not much good now, but if it did float—"

"If it floats the Yankees probably confiscated it durin' the war," Jensen reminded him.

Dake downed the last of his coffee and stood up. Slipping into his jacket on the way to the door, he paused and waited for Bill Jensen to follow. "Look for any more signs of blood that we might have missed last night and head down to the main road and look for any signs that a wagon or carriage stopped there last night. See if you can pick up any of Sweet Pea's tracks near the property line. Inez, you can walk through the quarters and see if anyone has seen anything suspicious. Send Elijah back here to the house and you come back as soon as you're through. I'll head back to the river and follow it as far as I can. She may have put in downriver."

"What about me?" Cara was waiting for him to assign her a search duty and Dake knew immediately by the ice-blue challenge in her eyes that he had better come up with one.

"This is the command post. Wait here for everyone to return and we'll all keep in touch through you. When Elijah gets here, have him take some men and search the woods."

"I can—"

"*You* will stay put." The hurt that shadowed her eyes was instantly apparent. He tried to make up for it. "Cara, I need you here. I can't concentrate on finding Clay if I'm worrying about you, too."

Her gaze dropped to the table. "All right."

"Promise me."

She nodded, but didn't look up.

"Cara . . ."

"I promise," she whispered. "I'll stay put."

"Good. I know you'll keep your word." He reached into his buckskin pocket and pulled out the derringer and handed it to her. "Keep this with you and be damn careful because it's loaded."

Her eyes snapped with anger as she looked up at him again. "I forgive you for treating me like an imbecile, Dake Reed, because you're upset and I know it, but don't think you'll get away with this ever again."

Despite the graveness of the situation, Dake laughed, but knew better than to comment. He grabbed his hat off the table and said, "Let's go, Bill."

Cara watched the men leave. Inez poured her one more cup of coffee before she left on her own mission. Glancing down at the hand in her lap, Cara uncrossed her fingers. "I won't leave the house, Captain Reed," she grumbled to herself, "but I'm certainly not going to sit here like a bump on a log while that woman is out running around loose with our baby."

Pushing away from the table, she then crossed to the window

to be certain everyone was gone. Inez had disappeared down the lane. Dake was nowhere in sight. She saw Bill Jensen on horseback, carefully staring down at the ground as he rode along the lane that led out to the main thoroughfare.

She got up and wandered back through the house. Outside the kitchen the huge, near empty rooms were cold in the half-light of early morning. Cara rubbed her arms against the chill but decided to get her coat before she lit a fire in the parlor fireplace.

She walked up the staircase, still awed by the massiveness of the structure. Although the wall coverings were faded and even ripped in places, she could see how beautiful the house must have been in its glory. What portraits had graced the walls where only smudged outlines remained? Although it intrigued her, she harbored no love for the place, certainly not the obsessive need to possess it that Minna Blakely's warped mind had nurtured. Riverglen would only feel like home to her as long as Dake and Clay were there. She cared nothing for the land and the house, only that it represented Dake's dream. Their love would make it a home.

Cara hurried down the hallway to her room and steeled herself to accept the sight of the empty cradle when she opened the door. Situated on the north side of the house, the guest room was chillier than some of the others and she decided to have Elijah move the cradle into Dake's master suite. Once she had Clay in her arms again, she vowed never to let him out of her sight.

It took but a moment to take her wool coat from the clothes cupboard and slip it on. She had closed the cupboard door and stopped beside her washstand to find her hairbrush when somewhere down the hall, she heard a door latch close.

"Inez?" Cara walked to her open door and paused, listening. "Inez, I'm in here," she called out, trying to ignore the new, rapid pace her heart had begun.

Her hand went to the deep pocket of her gown and her fingertips connected with the cold metal of the gun. She cupped the weapon in her hand, not daring to look down. Scanning the empty hall, she kept close to the wall and moved on silent feet toward the door closest to hers, the only one that was closed. The room had once been Dake's, the place of his brother's murder. Cara had chosen not to enter it since her arrival.

Holding her breath, she paused outside the room and pressed her ear to the door. There was no sound inside. Slowly, carefully, she reached out for the doorknob, caressed the cold brass, and then with infinite patience, she turned the knob until the door unlatched. Once open, she gave the door a push and let it swing inward with no more force than a gentle breeze. She waited to hear someone move inside the room, waited for some reaction to the open door.

There was none.

Straightening, she took a deep breath and slipped into the room. With her back pressed against the door frame, Cara paused just inside the threshold and looked around. There was nothing in the room besides a bed topped by a mattress stripped of bedding, and an empty table by a window with the lower half boarded up.

She let out a sigh of relief and chided herself for her silliness. Cara backed out into the hall and closed the door behind her. Just as she was about to start back downstairs, her eyes caught sight of what she thought was a coin halfway down the hall and she went after it. Before she reached the find, Cara realized the circular spot on the wood was not a coin at all. Close inspection showed it to be a spattered drop of blood.

She bent down and touched the spot. Her fingertip came away wet. Cara rubbed the end of her finger with her thumb and frowned. She glanced back over her shoulder and then down at the floor again. A few feet away, there was another spatter, this one near the door to the attic.

Minna Blakely was in the house.

Cara crept down the hall toward the door that led to the attic stairs. Half expecting it to be locked, she was surprised when the knob turned easily. There was another blood spot on the bottom step. She waited at the bottom of the narrow stairwell, stared up into the gloomy light above, and listened. Again, there was no sound. If she hadn't seen the wet bloodstain, she could have convinced herself that Minna might have merely hidden during the night and then gone, but the trail of blood was fresh.

Cara clutched the gun in her hand and started to climb the stairs to the attic. Common sense told her to wait for Dake, to lock the door and keep Minna trapped inside, but she had never been one to let common sense be her guide. If Minna discovered the trap, she might very well harm Clay, or use him to gain her freedom. Cara opted for the element of surprise. Besides, this time she was armed and ready. She knew her enemy. This time she would win.

She stepped over the top step into the attic and cursed the gloom. For a few seconds she thought the place as deserted as the room downstairs, but in a heart-stopping second, she saw something move near the back of the gabled roofline. Deep within the shadows, a figure in white began to slowly drift toward her.

Cara cocked the gun and aimed. "Don't come any closer."

"Surely, you're not afraid of me?"

The voice was Minna's. The honeyed drawl and dimpled smile were hers as well. Cara stared, awestruck by the sight of Minna slowly advancing along the attic floor. She was dressed in a long, bell-shaped white gown. Rows of lace cascaded down the skirt like froth on a waterfall. The picture was as perfect as a page from Godey's except that the bride's skirt was marred by a wide bloodstain. A long lace veil was gathered on a band she wore around the crown of her head. Fingerless gloves of white lace adorned her hands. Her complexion was not much darker than the stark white gown, her cheeks pale, her lips seemed bloodred by contrast, her eyes dark pools void of reason.

Cara shook her head, trying to deny the reality of the macabre sight. "Where's Clay, Minna? Where's the baby?"

"The baby? What baby?"

You know damn well what baby! Cara wanted to scream. Instead, in the most casual, soothing tone she could muster she said, "Little Clay. The baby Dake found in Kansas. You remember, Minna, surely."

Minna dismissed the notion with a blithe wave of her hand. "Oh, that baby. Why, I don't know. It was just in the way, after all. Besides, Dake can't be bothered with a baby, not with us gettin' married today and all."

Cara took a deep breath. "Dake sent me up here to get you, Minna. He said . . . he said he can't wait to see you in your . . . your gown. He wants to see the baby, too."

Minna reached down and lifted the sides of her skirt, preening before Cara. "You like my dress?"

Cara swallowed the bile in her throat and tried to keep her hand from shaking hard enough to drop the gun. "Of course I do. It's beautiful."

"I had it made right after Burke proposed. There was still money back then, fabric and such. Nothin' like now." She fingered the lace on the hem, ignoring the bloodstain as she did. "I had to hide it, you know. Couldn't let the Yankees get it. They wanted everything. I put it under the floorboards back there, wrapped it in flour sacks, and hid it away until the weddin'." Minna swayed. Her mud-stained bare toes and the perfectly shaped arches of her feet peeked from the edge of the gown.

Cara took a step forward looking right and left for some sign of Clay but there was none.

Minna lowered herself to the old trunk in the middle of the room. Afraid to take her eyes off the demented woman, Cara took another step forward and caught her foot in an empty picture frame. The movement caused her to lunge forward. She spread her hands wide to break her fall and the pistol flew out of her hand.

You can't pluck a goose all at once.
It has to be done feather by feather.
Nanny James

Chapter Twenty

"You are incredibly stupid," Minna said as she leveled the gun at Cara.

Her shoulder wound exploded with pain and Cara nearly agreed. Instead, she held her tongue, struggled to push herself to a sitting position, and glared up at the madwoman holding the gun. "I'd rather be stupid than crazier than one of granny's quilts," Cara mumbled.

"What did you say?"

"I said you're in for a surprise."

Minna cocked her head. "Oh, and how's that?"

Cara scooted back until she could grab hold of a broken chair and lever herself up. "Dake won't be in a marrying mood if you've hurt Clay."

The bright, vacant smile on Minna's face darkened as she frowned. "He won't care. He'll be glad that brat's gone." Then, she rocked forward onto the balls of her feet and back again. "We're goin' to have babies of our own. Lots of them and live happily ever after."

"What do you mean—Clay's gone?"

Minna shrugged and began humming. Time was of the essence now. Desperate to find Clay, Cara decided to push the deranged woman into action. "You'll never get away with this. When Dake finds out you've hurt Clay, he'll never make you mistress of Riverglen."

Minna tossed her head. The veil swayed around her shoulders. "I know now we'll have to leave this old place anyway."

Cara stared at her in alarm. "After all you've done to save Riverglen, you're willing to leave now?"

"Since *you've* ruined everything, I have to, but it's still not too late to convince them that you're responsible for Burke's death."

"What about Dake? I thought you were getting married today." Cara tried to follow the twisted reasoning of a sick mind.

"Why, yes. I expect I am, as soon as Dake finds out about how I had to kill you in self-defense. He'll be so proud of me. Besides, he's goin' to love this dress so much, you see."

"Miz Cara?" Inez called from the second floor. "Miz Cara, where are you? Mistah Reed's back."

"Don't say a word," Minna warned as she took careful aim at Cara again.

"If you shoot me, she'll hear you and Dake will come running. The sheriff is here, too. They already know you killed Burke and his father."

As if the process of reasoning was painful to her, Minna frowned. "Then I'll have to be very, very quiet, won't I?" She walked forward, her bare feet moving silently across the wood until she stood over Cara. "Get up."

"Miz Cara?"

For a split second, Cara thought of knocking over an iron headboard propped beside her in the hopes that Inez would hear it and go for help, but she couldn't risk forcing Minna's hand, nor did she want to lead Inez into the same trap she'd walked into herself. She complied with Minna's request and followed her to the back of the attic where there was a nest of old blankets and a kerosene lamp. A silver match case caught the sunlight and glinted among the blankets. Cara wondered exactly how long Minna had been here. A few minutes she guessed, for the blood she'd seen downstairs had been fresh. When and where had she hidden Clay?

Waving the gun at the blankets, Minna ordered, "Sit down."

Cara sat, feeling around the blankets for Clay. They were empty. With the gun aimed at her heart, Cara didn't dare move any farther. She watched in anger as Minna bent and picked up the lamp. When the wide bell skirt flared back against her ankles, Cara noticed that Minna's left foot was covered in blood that had dripped from her wound.

Cara watched as Minna pulled off the lamp chimney and dropped it onto the blankets at her feet. Then, she liberally sprinkled the pile with the kerosene and tossed the empty lamp on top of the blankets.

"Everyone will see the smoke," Cara warned, her heart in her throat. Frantic to escape, she glanced toward the trunk in the center of the room and her heart stopped as realization dawned on her. It was the only place in the room that Minna could have hidden Clay. What if he had already run out of air? If the blankets burst into flame, if she couldn't reach the trunk in time—

Minna offered the cylinder of matches to Cara. "Light one."

"Light one yourself."

Cara thought for a moment Minna would refuse, but a look of sheer pleasure came over her. Then, as cordially as a debutante asked for her first dance she said sweetly, "Why, I'd be delighted."

Minna stepped back a good yard, juggled the gun, and lit the match. She held it at waist height for a brief second, time enough for Cara to lunge forward and grab Minna's injured leg by the ankle. Minna fought to kick her off.

Cara yanked with all her might.

"Damn it, Inez, where is she?" Dake reached the second floor and bore down on the startled maid standing in the guest room doorway.

"If I knew I wouldn't be shoutin' her name, now would I?" Obviously more concerned than angry, Inez stepped out of Cara's room with her hands planted on her hips.

Dake shoved his fingers through his hair with an exasperated sigh. The ride to the river had proved fruitless. There was no sign of a skiff, no footprints in the muddy ground along the bank. It was as if Minna Blakely had taken Clay and mysteriously vanished. Now Cara had taken it in her head to go off after them when he expressly asked her not to.

"Damn it," he cursed beneath his breath. "This is all I need."

"She's not up here," Inez told him. "I looked in all the rooms."

"Jensen's waiting downstairs. We were going to take the road toward town and look for some sign of them. Maybe she got there last night and left on the morning train."

"What should I do about Miz Cara? You want me to send Elijah out to—"

They both stared at the ceiling when something crashed into the floor overhead. Dake bolted for the attic door and threw it open so hard it bounced back against the wall. He was bounding up the narrow steps two at a time when he heard a woman scream.

His head cleared the stairwell opening and he turned in time to see Cara shove herself away from Minna Blakely, who appeared to be standing before a mound of flames. Minna backed toward the window at the end of the attic, screaming as she went. The fire followed her. Tongues of flame licked up the front of her white gown.

Tearing across the room, he ducked to avoid the low beams of the slanted roofline. Dake ran to pull Cara to safety as she scrambled backward, crablike, away from the flames. Minna continued to scream and scream as she backed along the wall, trying to escape the fire that was fast engulfing her wide-belled skirt. The attic was slowly filling with billowing smoke from the blazing blankets.

Cara backed into his legs and turned, her eyes wide and terrified. She clutched the front of his jacket and raised herself to a standing position as he reached down and pulled her to him. "Help her, Dake," she shouted over Minna's screams. "Don't let her die. I can't find Clay!"

Once he was certain Cara's gown wasn't on fire, he set her aside and rushed toward Minna. Her gloves were charred to her hands where she had tried to beat out the flames. Her eyes were rolling with a terrorized madness that was far beyond one of pain.

"Minna, stand still!" Dake yelled, trying to get close enough to throw her on the ground and roll out the fire. He watched, helpless as a tongue of fire licked the lace edged sleeve at Minna's elbows. If he didn't act now, the entire bodice would be aflame in a matter of seconds.

He lunged forward, intent on knocking Minna to the ground, but when he made his move, she screamed "No!" and swirled around, heading for the window behind her.

"Minna, stop!" Dake bellowed. "Don't!" He reached out to grab her.

The window shattered with a crash and Minna disappeared through it, her screams echoing behind her. Dake came away with nothing but a piece of blackened lace in his hand. He stepped up to the window but a gust of wind blew in, fanning the flames that threatened to engulf the room. He covered his face with the crook of his arm and ducked back beneath the smoke.

"Cara! Where are you?"

"Here!"

He heard her call out somewhere in the center of the room and yelled back, "Get out! Go downstairs and get help." He tried to stomp out the fire but it was already raging higher than his thighs. He backed away, searching for something to use to beat out the flames. Everywhere he looked there was plenty for fuel but nothing with which to smother the blaze. Finally he found a length of tattered drapes. He remembered them from his childhood, draperies now so faded and worn that even the scavengers of war deemed them unfit to steal. Dake grabbed up the fabric, shook it out, and approached the fire without hesitation. He threw what was left of the thick material over the flames and immediately began to stomp out any spark that escaped the drapery.

Finally satisfied that the fire was out, he backed through the dense smoke, coughing as he went. His eyes smarted so badly that he was very nearly blinded. He almost fell over Cara who was crouched beside an old trunk in the center of the room.

"It's locked." Tears were streaming down her face as she looked up at him from where she knelt amid the cast-off pieces of his past. "I can't open it." She was wrestling with a rusted lock, tearing at it with her fingernails.

He knelt beside her. Afraid the entire episode had unhinged her, he gently put his arm about her shoulder. "Cara, what are you doing?"

"It's Clay," she choked. "The baby's in here."

He didn't question how she knew. He gently set her aside and stared at the old lock for a moment before he stood and began searching the room for something to use to break the trunk lid open. Shouts echoed in the attic stairwell. Dake ignored them. He picked up a piece of iron curtain rod and went back to the trunk.

Jensen's voice boomed up the stairwell. "Reed?"

"Up here, Sheriff," Dake called over his shoulder. Cara was slumped on the floor, one arm draped protectively over the trunk lid. The smoke was hugging the beams at the pinnacle of the roofline. The breeze from the shattered window pushed the smoke in and up.

"Please, hurry, Dake," Cara whispered.

Dake carefully inserted the rod between the keyhole-shaped lock flap and the side of the trunk. He pounded it farther into the space with the heel of his hand and then pulled back, trying to lever the lock open.

Bill Jensen's head and shoulders appeared in the stairwell. "What in the hell happened up here? Did you know Minna's dead? I rode up in time to see her come flyin' out the window like a ball of flames, hit the veranda roof, and break her neck before she reached the ground."

"Hold this trunk, Bill," Dake instructed, still pulling on the iron lock.

Jensen hesitated. Dake glanced over at him and saw the confusion on his face. "Cara thinks Minna locked Clay in here."

The tall man knelt across the trunk from Dake. Cara moved back to give them room. Bill Jensen kept the trunk from moving while Dake tried to pry open the lock, but it wouldn't budge.

"I don't hear anything. Wouldn't he be crying?"

Dake quickly glanced over at Cara and watched her shudder. He glowered at Jensen. "Shut up and just hold it still." He pulled with all his might, leaned into the task until the lock gave, and he toppled backward into a sitting position.

Cara fell on the trunk and shoved the lid up, nearly smacking the sheriff in the nose with it. Dake got to his knees and peered over her shoulder.

"He's not there," she cried out in anguish. "Oh, God, Dake. He's not there."

Alone in the quiet glade behind the quarters, Cara sat on one of the log benches drawn up for the prayer meeting, her arms wrapped around her knees, her face pressed against the folds of her skirt. The gut-wrenching, heart-pounding anxiety over Clay and her final confrontation with Minna had receded, only to be replaced by a sense-dulling numbness that left her feeling half-alive.

Too exhausted to cry anymore, her tears had subsided to an occasional shuddering sob.

Something scrambled through the leaves to her right and she lifted her head to see who dared disturb the silent retreat. A small brown squirrel paused on hind legs and stared at her as he held his bounty of a walnut between his paws. He blinked twice and turned tail, scurrying off through the patchwork of fall leaves on the ground. She watched him until he darted up a nearby tree and disappeared between the thicker limbs overhead.

With her head tilted skyward, Cara squinted up into the overcast sky, sighed, and closed her eyes. The hushed glade with its amphitheater of logs and carpet of leaves gave her a feeling of peace. She clasped her hands in her lap and bowed her head. "Please, God," she whispered aloud in the meadow, "please take care of baby Clay wherever he is. Don't let him come to harm or be cold and alone. Please."

"Cara?"

She lifted her head, took a swipe at her tear-stained cheeks, and then pushed her hair back out of her eyes. She turned to find Dake standing close behind her.

"I didn't hear you," she said, forcing out the words from a throat that felt raw from crying.

Dake stepped over the log and sat down close beside her. He reached out for her hand and she offered it without protest. His warm fingers closed over hers. Staring down at her hand, he traced her fingers one at a time as he spoke. "We searched the house but didn't find Clay."

"I knew he wasn't there."

"I'm not giving up, Cara. As soon as I get cleaned up and have something to eat, I'm going to start searching again. I'll get the men out in squads; Bill will go into town and organize a search party. You have to believe we'll find him."

Cara leaned against him, taking courage from his strength. "I've been sitting here praying and trying to think what Minna might have done with him, but she seemed so far gone I can't even guess what she was thinking." She squeezed his hand. "What happened to her? What are you going to do?"

"Bill took over. We aren't going to have any kind of funeral gathering for her, but she'll be buried in the family cemetery in an unmarked grave."

"To my mind she doesn't even deserve that much."

"I know what you're thinking, but it's clear to me now that Minna was entirely mad at the end. I don't know when or how it happened, but the Minna I knew as a child truly loved Burke and the rest of us. Maybe it was the war and everything she had to endure. Maybe she had this in her and grew sicker as she grew up. We'll never know."

"How's Inez?"

"Still crying her eyes out. I told her it wasn't her fault, but she's inconsolable."

Cara took a deep breath and sat up. She took both of Dake's hands in her own and turned to face him squarely. "Inez isn't only blaming herself. She's upset about Clay because . . . because—" A sudden fear gripped her. What if she told Dake about Clay's heritage and he reacted to the knowledge by calling off the search? What if, after the revelation, he no longer cared what happened to Clay?

"Because what, Cara?"

She thought of the tears she'd seen him cry over Clay last night, remembered his very words. *"I'd move heaven and earth to find that child."*

He wouldn't desert Clay. She had to believe it as fiercely as she intended to cling to the hope of finding the baby alive. Once Clay was back with them, they would be a family again.

She would tell Dake the truth no matter what, for there was no way she could live a lie forever.

"Cara?"

"Inez is Clay's great-aunt."

"His great-aunt?"

She nodded. Fear began to uncoil inside her and slip like tiny tentacles around her heart. "Anna Clayton ran off with a man named Price who was born and raised on her father's plantation." She watched Dake carefully. His emerald gaze held steady as he listened intently to every word. She swallowed and went on. "Inez said Price was . . . was a mulatto—I think that's the word she used—and Price's mother was partly white, too—"

"Are you trying to tell me that Clay's father was a slave?"

"Yes," she whispered, "I am."

"And Anna Clayton ran off with him?"

"She did. They married in another state, but she didn't know he was her half brother." She hadn't meant to tell him everything at once, now she'd gone and hit him broadside in such a rambling, confused manner she didn't know how to repair the damage she'd done. Cara cursed under her breath.

Dake let go of her, propped his elbows on his knees, and lowered his head to his hands. She watched in horrified silence while he rubbed his brow and massaged his temples. The seconds lengthened into minutes as he stared down at the ground in silence. Finally, he drew a deep breath and sat up.

"How many others know about this?" He turned to her, his brow creased in thought.

"No one. Just Inez and me."

"Good."

She felt her world tilt. Would he force her to choose between them? "Then it does matter to you?"

"Of course it does. This changes everything." He reached

out to draw her close, but she pulled away. "What's the matter?"

"How can you even ask me that? I had convinced myself that even though you were raised here in the South that you were truly different. You fought to hold the Union together; you're standing up for a new way of life here at Riverglen. I prayed that your dreams for the plantation and your fight for freedom and equality wouldn't prove to be empty words when I told you the truth about Clay. Now you don't want him anymore."

She was shaking with uncontrollable anger. He reached for her again and when she tried to stand and move away from him, Dake refused to let her go. He held tight to her wrist and pulled her down beside him. His fingers clasped her so tightly she winced with pain and tried to twist out of his grasp.

"What do you mean *don't want him anymore?*"

"You said 'this changes everything.' Obviously you'll never accept him as yours now that you know he has black blood."

Dake let go of her wrist. Cara cradled her arm against her waist and rubbed it briskly. She backed away from him a step.

"Cara," his voice was low and even as he tried to calm her, "don't ever tell me what you *think* I will or won't accept, or what you *think* I believe, or what you *think* I will do."

"But—"

"Listen to me." He lifted his hat, ran his fingers through his hair, and shoved his hat on again. "Ever since the day I picked that boy up out of the dirt and shoved him in my jacket, he's been part of my life. Finding Clay led me to you. I fell in love with you, Cara. I am still in love with you. Together"—he paused and looked at the ground, forced to stop and clear his throat—"together we have come to love Clay. What I meant when I said this changes everything is that I don't see how we can stay here in Alabama as a family."

"But Riverglen is your home. You've dreamed of making this new system work for so long—"

Dake stepped forward. She didn't flinch or step back. He took her in his arms and she relaxed against him, thankful for the shelter of his arms. "After everything that's happened here, Burke's death, the Klan, Minna . . . do you really think I'd mind starting over someplace else? Somewhere Clay can grow up as our son without having to live a lie, constantly living in fear someone will find out?"

The sound of children's laughter filtered through the trees. She envisioned the families housed in the quarters, people who had no homes at all a few days ago. "What of all these people, Dake? Can you just walk away from them all?"

He pressed her close, his hand riding warm and secure at the small of her back. "For you and Clay? I'd do whatever it takes to keep you. Both of you." His hands moved to her shoulders and he held her away from him, studying her closely.

She hadn't meant to start again, but by the time he was finished, tears were slipping down her cheeks. "I was so scared," she told him. "I thought I would have to choose between you and Clay, and as much as it hurts to tell you this, Clay's so little, so utterly alone and defenseless, that no matter how much I love you, I would have had to choose him."

Dake put his arm around her and started to lead her back to the house. "The first thing we have to do is find him. Then, when things have settled down, we'll decide what to do next." He put his finger beneath her chin and tipped her face up to his. Dake lowered his head and pressed his lips to hers, gently at first, and then with a growing urgency. He slipped his tongue between her lips and kissed her deeply. It was a gentle, silent sharing. A pledge and a promise that said more than words. When their lips parted, he reached out with his thumb and wiped her tears away.

"I need to change clothes and eat. Then I'll be on my—"

Two of the youngest children from the quarters burst into the clearing. "Mistah Dake? Miz Cara?"

Cara sighed. Not even the sight of the children could lift her spirits. Dake waited for them to scramble across the meadow, watching the youngest, the little boy to whom Cara had given the bedpost doll, clamber over the logs, fighting to keep pace with the others. She shot Dake a pleading look that said, *You speak to them.* He nodded slightly and kept her tucked safely next to his heart.

"What's going on with you all? You look mighty excited," he called out.

The little girl named Ellie who had refused Miss Cornflower reached them and stood twisting one of the braids atop her head in a circle. "You 'member when you said Mr. Pickle was a magic doll?"

Cara nodded.

"She remembers," Dake volunteered.

"He done some *big* magic already."

"Yep, he sure did," agreed Mr. Pickle's diminutive owner, who glanced back in the direction from which they'd just come.

Impatient to get on with his search for Clay, Dake glanced through the trees in the direction of the house. "Well, that's real nice. I hope he keeps it up. We've got to go back to the house now, so—"

"He left us a real big doll. Just like a real baby. It's so big it don't fit in the dollhouse so we gots to make it bigger."

Preoccupied, Dake was more concerned about Cara, who had pulled away and was staring down at the children as if she'd truly become interested in what they were saying. "Well, that's real nice for you," Dake told them.

"Where is this new doll Mr. Pickle left you?" Cara had picked up her skirt and started moving across the meadow, stepping over logs, staring at the trees beyond.

The children turned and were running at her heels before

Dake realized she was actually going to see what they were talking about. "Cara, this is no time to—"

"Come on," she called out over her shoulder. "Hurry." She waited for Dake and the children to catch up before she reached down for the little boy's hand. "What's your name?" she asked as she tugged him along.

"Orion. You're hurtin' my arm!"

She let go abruptly and bent down until she was nearly nose to nose with Orion. "Take me to see this big doll."

Dake reached out to stop her. "We've got to get back."

Cara turned to him with a smile as bright as the renewed hope in her eyes. "Don't look at me like I've lost my mind, too. Did you hear what they said? They have found a *doll* that is as big as a *real* baby."

Ellie piped up. "We didn't find it. Mr. Pickle did magic and left it in the dollhouse."

Dake grabbed the girl's shoulder and turned her to face him. "Does the doll move? Does it cry?" He shot Cara a look over the child's head.

Obviously frightened of the huge man towering over her demanding an answer, Ellie began twisting her hair again and said absolutely nothing.

"Don't be afraid," Cara said, taking each of the children's little hands in her own. She started toward the woods. "We just want to see this baby."

"Doll," Orion corrected. "Found him in the dollhouse I made, but he doesn't fit so good."

When Cara reached the edge of the wooded grove, she forgot exactly where the children had built their crude doll shelters. "Show me," she told them. Orion took her hand and began to pull her through the trees. Ellie lagged behind, staring back over her shoulder at Dake who brought up the rear.

"Over there," Orion pointed. "There he is."

Cara ran to the pile of sticks and leaves and knelt down

beside them. Dake hunkered down into a squat. They immediately recognized the faded colors of Clay's quilt peeking out beneath the leaves. The bundle didn't move.

"Oh, Dake," Cara said before she balled her hands into fists that she pressed against her lips.

"Let me," he said softly. Gently brushing back the debris, he quickly uncovered the bundle.

"He was cryin' when we left," Ellie assured them.

"We covered up his face so he wouldn't get no leaves in his mouth," Orion added.

Dake pulled back the quilt. Clay's wide dark eyes blinked against the light. Dake scooped up the baby and handed him over to Cara's waiting arms. She held him close and buried her face against the quilt. Dake put his arm around them both and held on tight.

He couldn't for the life of him stop smiling.

Orion crossed his arms and stuck out his lower lip. "You broke the dollhouse, Mistah Dake."

"You can make a new one, can't you?"

"You takin' that baby doll?" Ellie asked, squinting ferociously at them both.

Cara finally looked up. She bit her lips together and blinked back tears of joy. "Do you remember the day I gave you the dolls? I had this very baby with me that day."

"It's our baby," Dake assured them when neither looked about to relinquish ownership. "Really."

Cara smiled up at him, then mustering a serious demeanor, said to the children, "We've been looking all over for him—"

"You gots to take better care of babies than that," Ellie assured them. "When you get my doll made, I ain't never gonna let her get lost."

"You can bet we're not going to let this baby get lost again, either." Dake stood and helped Cara to her feet. Clay was surprisingly well tempered for having spent the night in Minna's care and then the past few hours in the woods.

"I promise to take better care of him from now on," Cara swore before she turned to Dake. "How about you?"

His words were for the children, but the love that shone in his eyes, as well as his pledge, were for her alone. "I promise to take care of both of you forever."

Epilogue

Riverglen. April 1868.

A delicate April breeze blew in the open window, caressing the sweat-sheened lovers entwined upon the bed in the second-floor master bedroom. It was midday, a time when most farmers were busy overseeing workers or tilling the soil alongside them, watching plows churn the fertile ground of the Tennessee River Valley, preparing the land for planting.

But not Dake Reed.

At the moment he was occupied with the pleasurable task of making love to his wife. A newlywed, recently married on Christmas past, he still found it impossible to resist his wife's laughing blue eyes and quick smile. Dake knew for certain they were the talk of the house staff, but far be it from him to resist moments like this morning's, when he found Cara ready to step into a waiting bath. He had locked the door behind him, carried her to the high four-poster, and spread her naked and always welcoming body across the still rumpled sheets.

Her eyes weren't smiling back at him at the moment, though.

Just now, her long slender neck was arched, her eyes closed, her hands gripping the headboard as he knelt between her thighs and buried himself full length into her silken depths. Ragged, in-drawn breath became a cry as she clasped her legs tighter around his waist, sweetly and effectively imprisoning

349

him inside her. Dake reached out to cup her breasts where the nipples budded tight and beckoning. He teased the flowered buds between his thumb and forefinger, the action eliciting another gasp from his wife. She arched, hips and buttocks coming up off the mattress, forcing him farther inside her until he touched her womb and he nearly cried out himself.

He knew it was a matter of seconds, heartbeats really, before he would lose control and spill himself inside her. Dake slid his hands along her arms, up to her wrists, and then pried her fingers off the headboard. It was his invitation and demand that she put her arms around his shoulders and cling to him then, which she did, just as he knew she would. He let his legs slide down until the soles of his feet were pressed against the footboard. Braced against the cheerywood, he grasped Cara around the waist and thrust into her until she cried out and began to convulse around his shaft begging, "Now. Now. Oh, God, Dake, *now*."

He was beyond reason, beyond control. He thrust and thrust and pounded into her, filling her with himself and his seed, his eyes closed, his own head thrown back as he cried out hoarsely between clenched teeth the sound mingling with Cara's shuddering sighs.

When it was over, when he had nothing left to give, when she had wrung from him every ounce of seed and strength, he dropped his head and buried his face against her neck and lay there, replete, satiated, loved.

They lay in silence, listening to the sounds of birdsong common of an April morning as the breeze cooled their fevered skin and their heartbeats quickly diminished from drumbeats to steady normalcy.

"Mmmm." Cara shifted and nuzzled her cheek against his forehead.

"Mmmm hummm." He cupped her cheek in his hand and gently used his thumb to wipe away a tear he found there. "Are you all right?" He found it hard to believe his voice sounded normal to his ears. After making love to his wife he always wondered that he was not physically changed by the experience, because he felt that his very being had been irreversibly altered by the miracle of her giving.

"I'm fine," she whispered. "More than fine, I'm fit as a fiddle, right as rain, happy as a June bug in June."

He slipped his arm out from under her, leaned up on his elbow, and stared down into her shining face. She was beaming, her eyes sparkling with a satisfied glow, her skin radiant. "Then you won't mind my deserting you." He bent down and gave her a quick, noisy kiss on the lips and then a playful slap on the bottom.

"Do you have to?"

"We're leaving bright and early tomorrow, m'dear. Or have you forgotten?" He rolled over and climbed out of bed, laughing as he watched her pull a pillow over her face, effectively leaving her shapely little form fully exposed to his view.

"A headless wife. What a thought."

She mumbled from beneath the pillow. "You'd probably like it if I couldn't nag you anymore. All you want me for is my body anyway, Dake Reed."

"That's right," he teased, walking to the side of the tub that had been prepared for her bath. The once-steaming water was now lukewarm. He glanced over at Cara, found her still lying with the pillow over her face, her feet now crossed at the ankles. Bending down, he used her bathwater, soap, and washcloth to soap himself clean in a hurry, quickly dried, and threw the balled-up towel at her.

One round blue eye was exposed as she peeked around the corner of the pillow to see what had hit her. Dake was tugging on his pants. Cara groaned and sat up, shoving the pillow aside and then pushing her hair back out of her eyes. "You really are a beast."

"You weren't complaining a few minutes ago."

"I suppose the water's cold by now," she groused as she padded barefoot to the side of the tub and tested the water with her fingertips.

He smiled. "I'll have Patsy bring up another bucketful."

"No," she said quickly. "Don't you dare. I'd be too embarrassed. They'd know what we've been doing up here."

Dressed in a white cambric shirt and dark pants, he picked up his boots and sat down in a chair by the window to put them on. "Odds are they know what we did anyway."

"It'll be nice to live in a house with just ourselves," she mumbled.

Dake paused and glanced up to find her stepping over the side of the tub, grimacing at the tepid water as she lowered herself in. "When I have you all to myself, we'll never get anything done," he said.

"We'll see." She looked at him over the rim of the high brass bathtub, her eyes midnight-blue and serious. "You're sure you won't regret leaving, will you, Dake? You're really ready?"

He stared down at the boot in his hand, turning it over, looking at the sole without seeing it. Then he met her questioning gaze again. "I'm sure," he said, knowing he told the truth. For Cara, for Clay, for their future as a family, for the children of their own flesh they were sure to have, he was gladly leaving the South behind. "The things I wanted to change will eventually change, Cara—I can only hope and pray—but not in our lifetime, and not in Clay's, and they might not come at all without another fight."

"Not another war?" She grasped the side of the tub with her hands, her fingers pressing into the edge until the knuckles were white. He knew what she was thinking, she was a mother now, a wife. Should a war come, she would not remain isolated from it.

He shook his head and bent to pull on his boot. "Not a war like the last, but it'll be a struggle, a long uphill fight, and the South will be the last to fall because of slavery, because of the war and all that was gained and lost."

A knock on the door quickly put an end to their discussion. "What?" Dake yelled as Cara sank deeper into the water and began to furiously soap her right calf.

"The sheriff's here, Mistah Reed. He's waitin' on the porch."

"Thanks, Inez. Tell him I'll be right there."

Cara glanced over at him, her smile gone, her brow marred with a worried frown. "What now, do you suppose?"

Dake crossed the room, bent, and kissed the crown of her head. "Probably nothing. Don't you worry yourself at all." When she looked up at him, her eyes still shadowed, he forced a smile. "We're leaving here tomorrow, Cara, because I want to go. There won't be any looking back, either. Nothin's going to stop us, you hear? Because I love you."

"I love you, too."

He opened the door just wide enough to let himself out and as he closed it, he heard her call out, "Offer Sheriff Jensen something to drink and I'll be right down."

Dake's smile faded as he moved along the hall.

He found Jensen comfortably ensconced in an old wooden rocker on the veranda, a tall glass of cool spring water in his hand, his hat on his knees. He was watching a laughing group of the tenant farmers' children playing tag down the lane. Dake walked over to the railing that bordered the porch and sat on it directly in front of the sheriff. For a few minutes, both men remained silent as they enjoyed the sound of the children's laughter, the warble of the birds, the spring breeze that marked another new beginning.

Finally Dake asked, "What is it, Bill?"

If it was possible, Dake thought the man had aged years over the past few months. His jowls were hollow, his mouth drooping, the creases around it deeper, as were the lines about his eyes. Being an appointed sheriff with Northern sympathies in a Southern town was obviously not an enviable, nor healthy profession.

"Come to tell you good-bye, Reed. That and tell you Shelby Gilmore was killed last night."

Death was never good news. No matter what animosity lay between them since he'd been back, Dake never wished for Shelby's death. "How'd it happen?"

"Shot in the back during one of the Klan raids. I guess they rode into a campsite where a band of known thieves were hiding out and when the dust settled, his body was found hidden in the woods nearby."

Dake stared out at the newly budded oak trees. Life was too good, hope for a new beginning too great to have it ruined by another false murder charge. "You don't suspect me, do you, Bill? Shelby's left us alone since Minna died and since he didn't murder Burke, I had no call to harm him."

Jensen shook his head and set his empty glass on the porch beside the rocker. "No, I don't suspect you. There's so much infightin' started up in the Klan, I reckon it could have been one of his own brethren. There's near eight hundred men ridin' in Monroe County alone now, not all of them easy to control. There's a new element been joinin' up that are takin' things just a little too far, even for the old guard like Shelby and some of the original founders of the local dens." He sighed and looked out across the fields. "You're smart to leave, Dake. Get your family out of here and start over."

"Why don't you go west, Bill?"

The sheriff ran his hand over his lower jaw. "Got family, my mother, three sisters. None of them have any husbands left since the war. I've got to see to them all, no matter how much they don't like to admit they need me. They still aren't willing to accept the fact that I refused to go against the Union and fight with the rebel troops. There's no explaining why I didn't get into the fight at all. It's easier to let them think me a coward."

"War isn't for everyone, Bill. That's for damn sure." Even now there were nights when Dake woke up in a cold sweat, nights when he relived the death and dying of his friends and enemies on the field. No, war wasn't for everyone.

He wondered who it was for.

Both men glanced up when Cara came rushing through the front door. She was barefoot, still in the process of buttoning the top button at the nape of her neck. Her hair was damp, dripping wide wet blotches on the shoulders of a calico gown.

Dake couldn't help but smile. There were just some things that would never change. "You can calm down, darlin'. Bill's here on a social call."

Her reaction was immediate. She smiled, took the sheriff's hand, and shook it. "Then I'm *so* glad to see you, Bill. Can you stay for dinner?"

Both men laughed. Bill Jensen stood up and shoved on his hat. "No thanks, Mrs. Reed. I just came by to say good-bye and tell y'all to have a safe journey to California. When will the new owner be takin' over?"

"The Reinigs are supposed to be arriving from Ohio tonight, but all the paperwork is done. If they aren't here tomorrow morning when it's time for us to pull out, we're going anyway. The house staff will be here to let them in."

"Any of your people going with you?"

Cara walked over to Dake's side and he slipped his arm around her shoulders. As she leaned against him, he told Jensen, "Inez is going. So is Elijah."

"I think they're falling in love," Cara added in a whisper,

glancing toward the front door. "She's a few years older, but Elijah worships the ground she walks—"

Footsteps inside the house cut her off effectively. She rolled her eyes at Dake as the door opened and Inez came out with Clay in her arms and handed him to Cara. "If you don't mind, Miz Cara, I've still got a lot of things to pack up and this boy is so spoiled he won't let me put him down."

Dake watched as Cara laughed and hugged Clay tight. The baby's bright eyes shined up at him over her shoulder. When Clay recognized Dake, a wide smile broke out on his face. Now that the child was almost seven months old, he had developed features of his own. He was still a pleasant-natured infant with a button nose, a head of thickening brown-red hair, and dark brown eyes. His skin had begun to take on a hue not unlike Dake's own sun-bronzed tone. Cara loved the child to distraction and rarely let him out of her sight, entrusting him only to Dake and Inez.

When he looked over at Bill Jensen again, Dake found the man watching the baby closely. If he suspected the child's mixed heritage, he kept his questions to himself.

"I'll say good-bye, then," Jensen said, extending his hand to Dake. "Good luck to you folks."

"Thanks Bill. Good luck to you, too," Dake said. Cara added her farewell and the sheriff stepped off the veranda and walked toward his horse. Dake and Cara remained at the top of the steps, she holding Clay, both of them sheltered in the crook of her husband's arm. They watched Bill Jensen mount up, wave his hat over his head in a dramatic farewell, then ride away.

Cara smiled up at Dake, the love in her eyes all too evident. His heart swelled with pride. "Well, Mr. Reed, according to the beautiful watch you gave me for a wedding gift—which by the way I forgot to hang around my neck and left on the bureau—"

"As usual."

"—it's time I get packing if we're going to leave for California bright and early."

"See that you do that, wife." He kissed her and then let her go. "I'd like to leave at dawn."

She paused outside the door and smiled at him over her shoulder. "Of course, you would. And of course, I'll be ready." She gave him her cheekiest smile and disappeared inside. Clay rode off on her shoulder, chewing on his fist as he stared back at Dake.

Dake knew as sure as the sun would rise tomorrow that Cara would be late.

He also knew as long as she was beside him, he didn't care.